Cashing In

Cashing In

Antonia Gowar

Boston

HOUGHTON MIFFLIN COMPANY

1982

Library of Congress Cataloging in Publication Data

Gowar, Antonia.
Cashing in.

I. Title.
PS3557.O93C3   813'.54   81–23960
ISBN 0–395–32112–3   AACR2

Printed in the United States of America

V 10 9 8 7 6 5 4 3 2 1

To the team

Part One

1

JOHN ROLAND KILGOUR SAT at the smooth mahogany desk in the corner office, thumbing through the contents of a glossy orange folder. GLOBEBANK, the folder proclaimed in raised blue letters across the top. A small globe, the seas in blue and the continents in orange, followed the name.

Kilgour looked up, glancing through the open door of the office to see if anyone had arrived. He liked to know who came to work early and at exactly what time they got there. It was now eight A.M.; he was the first one in.

His secretary had left the folder for him, as he had ordered, along with a checklist of everything it was supposed to contain: A copy of the press release "GlobeBank's Automated Transfer Goes Live." A list of the publications the release had gone to— the business desks of major papers, both domestic and international; all the business and banking magazines; the press services. A fact sheet on the system, Autotran. And three pages stapled together, in Orator all-caps type, entitled "Remarks by John R. Kilgour, Executive Vice President and Sector Head, Banking Operations Sector, Global Bank Corporation" — his speech for the press conference.

Kilgour heard a movement in the outer office and saw Elaine Green pushing through the glass doors. "Morning, Elaine," he called out, his voice nonchalant.

"Morning, John." She stopped outside the door.

"Come in for a sec when you get a chance, will you?" he said, his eyes bent resolutely to the folder.

"Right there."

Light streamed through the high windows that wrapped around the big office, elegant with its smooth brown and ox-blood leather furniture. Kilgour looked across Park Avenue to other office towers, much like GlobeBank's own. The long, wide avenue seemed like a canyon between cliffs of skyscrapers. Cars moved north and south on each side of the center island. Pedestrians huddled against the cold, waited at intersections for the light to change, then scurried across on their way to work. From the twentieth floor, their movements reminded Kilgour of electric trains.

"Big day today, isn't it?" Elaine Green stood in the doorway, a lined pad in her hand. "You all set for the press conference and everything?"

"You tell me," Kilgour answered, smiling. "I took your advice about what to wear."

Elaine surveyed him. He was wearing the dark gray three-piece suit made by his London tailor. And he had remembered the light blue shirt. "It photographs better," she had told him.

"It's just right," she said.

"Is fashion advice part of the human resources director's job description?" Kilgour asked jokingly.

Elaine laughed. "Sure. It's a valid personnel function."

Kilgour suddenly felt uncomfortable. He looked through the open door again to see if anyone were there. No one.

Kilgour's beeper sounded, startling both of them in the silent office. He leaned over the desk and tapped two keys on his Ardec computer terminal. The terminal screen lit up with a message: MR KILGOUR'S LIMO AT PARK AVE ENTRANCE 0815.

"I guess I'm off," Kilgour said, placing the orange folder carefully in his attaché case as he stood up.

"Isn't it exciting, John? I mean, Autotran going live and everything."

"Yes, it *is* exciting." Kilgour snapped shut the case, grabbed his coat from the sofa, and strode past Elaine to the waiting elevator.

◊ ◊ ◊

Outside Kilgour's suite of offices, down the carpeted corridor and to the right of the specially cooled computer room, was another set of glass doors. Like the ones leading to the sector head, these had raised blue lettering and a GlobeBank logo. The lettering read: BANKING OPERATIONS SECTOR, NATIONAL SERVICES DIVISION—WEST, LISA GOULD, VICE PRESIDENT.

This corner office, only slightly smaller than Kilgour's, was furnished to Lisa Gould's own taste in a cream-colored Scandi-

4

navian look. Her desk was a long, uncluttered blond wood table at which she sat reviewing papers.

Lisa enjoyed the solitude of the office before the nine o'clock arrivals started trickling in; it was a good time to catch up on paperwork. She could think best at this time of the morning, when the only sound was the scratching of her red felt-tipped pen.

A slight woman, trim, dark-haired, she had dressed with special care this morning. She would, after all, be on the stage during the press conference, and she was aware, as always, that the image she projected would be a reflection on both herself and GlobeBank. She knew she would be described in the press as "one of the highest-ranking women executives in the financial industry." She had become used to that, but it always gave her pleasure.

So she had worn the navy wool suit with the pale blue pin-striped blouse and navy kid shoes. For jewelry, all gold: love-knot earrings — the small ones — a wire bracelet at one wrist, a slim gold chain around her neck, and the narrow wedding band on her left hand. Sedate, understated, professional.

The soft ringing of the phone annoyed her. She let it ring twice while she continued to scan the paper before her, then reached for the receiver. "Lisa Gould."

"Hello, Lisa." It was the familiar voice of John Kilgour's secretary. "Time. You are to meet John at the elevator."

"On my way," she said.

◊ ◊ ◊

It's up now, he thought, alone in the glass booth. OK. Let's say hello to London.

At 176 Wall Street, on the seventeenth floor, Sandy Lippert, a GlobeBank vice president, sat in his shirtsleeves and looked over a field of computer screens and keyboards. Before him was the large console of terminals, switches, and buttons that powered the data center he had created.

Deftly, he typed a message on the keyboard, watching it appear on the screen before him. He crossed and recrossed his legs impatiently, his lanky athlete's body never quite comfortable in the operator's chair. Although he was well into his thirties,

Lippert, with his brown hair forever falling over one eye, was always taken for a college student. The unanimous opinion in the Ladies' Room, where the secretaries and female operators chatted while they smoothed on eye makeup, was that he was "adorable," that his smile was "cute," and that he had a "terrific body." They liked the grin that lit up his irregular face, his slightly awkward manner.

"Hi there, London," Lippert said to himself as the screen lit up with Autotran's first message. I'm on-line, he thought, all set now.

He leaned back, trying to stretch against the anatomically correct design of the office chair. "Not my anatomy," he had joked with the furniture consultant who chose the equipment for Autotran. The chair was the only object in the booth that he did not feel a part of.

The rest of it, all of Autotran, was his. He had conceived it, designed it, watched over its construction and installation, chosen its name. He knew that at this morning's press conference, Autotran would be presented to the world as GlobeBank's system, and it would be John R. Kilgour who would claim success. But Sandy Lippert knew that Autotran was his.

The terminals in the booth were familiar faces to him, friendlier and more responsive than people. He loved the feel of the keyboard under his fingers, the dials within his long reach. He more than anyone could make Autotran do all it had been designed to do, and he knew that it had reserves of power and sophistication to do much more. Autotran would catapult Globe-Bank into the forefront of banking technology. And Sandy knew that was only the beginning.

Through the glass wall of the booth he could see Jessica Moser, wearing a forest green flannel jumper over a red plaid shirt and holding a clipboard. She thrust her back against one of the swinging doors to the platform area, letting in a troop of white-coated waiters pushing two long tables on wheels. Jessica pointed toward the large open space near the glass booth, waved at Sandy, and led the breakfast to its resting place.

Sandy came out to meet her. "Coffee. Great. I could use some."

"Anybody touches anything on this table, I shoot him in the kneecaps," Jessica said brightly. "This is going to look like a very elegant setup in about two minutes. Coffee in brass urns. Your porcelain cups, inscribed Global Bank Corporation and sporting a logo. Danish that is *not* from Chock Full O'Nuts. If there is one crumb on this white tablecloth, Killer Kilgour will have me hanged."

"In that case," Sandy said, smiling, "come down to my office for coffee. I need to take a look at my notes for my speech, anyway."

"Now at the eleventh hour you're first going over this?" Jessica said with mock severity.

"Now, but not for the first time. You know John. He had us go over the program at least a hundred times."

"Give me a couple of minutes," Jessica said.

The porters wheeled in the lectern and the microphones to a space at one end of the wide platform floor, near the long row of windows that looked out onto the East River, and up along it to the bridges linking Manhattan to Brooklyn and Queens. Jessica watched as the lectern was set up and wires were drawn out of a small closet on the side. She helped lift the tile on the floor that revealed a box containing sockets; the floors were hollow, false surfaces above the real floor to allow for the cables and power outlets for the computers.

When the microphone was hooked up, Jessica walked over to test it. "Testing, one, two, three. Four score and seven years ago, our fathers brought forth on this continent a brand-new automated system for processing funds transfers." She tapped the microphone head. "OK. How about the shepherd's crook? And the pointer? OK. Great. Thank you. I guess we're all set."

2

RICK SCHMIDT LAY IN BED at the St. Magnus Hotel, breathing slowly, waiting.

Two more days. The day after tomorrow, he would have to go back to California, back to what everyone believed was a charmed existence as a Fellow and M.B.A. candidate at the elite

Wolcott Foundation's Senior Management Program at Bay University. Back to Donna, the wife who had begun to bore him six months after their marriage, and to his son, Ricky, the little boy he didn't really like.

He would so much rather be here, in New York. Much as the city alarmed and repelled him, there was excitement in the air. New York also meant GlobeBank, his real home, where he had learned business and management better than any course of study could teach it, where he was a "star." GlobeBank meant action to Rick Schmidt, the power of command as he had known it in Nam, where troops snapped to attention when he spoke and carried out his orders crisply and eagerly.

Rick closed his eyes for a moment, remembering.

At work it was the same. He had brought with him a taste for command that translated easily from the battlefield to the corporation. GlobeBank had singled him out as a fast-tracker, a sure success. That was why he had been chosen, over seventeen other GlobeBank candidates — many of them at higher levels — to spend a year at the prestigious Wolcott program. It was the bank's way of grooming him for bigger and better things. To Rick, GlobeBank indicated that if he deployed his forces properly, he could look toward four stars on his cap. Maybe even before he was thirty-five.

But right now, waiting in bed, GlobeBank meant Linda.

Linda Glover was also a "star," a star whom he had helped raise in the firmament. She was one of the new breed of women M.B.A.'s who, he discovered when he stopped being threatened by them, were very much like himself: tough, ambitious, clever, demanding. Linda was the best of them; it was Linda he was waiting for.

Rick sighed, rolled over toward the bedside stand, and reached for a cigarette. Lighting it, he watched the smoke curl in the darkened room. His watch said it was nearly eight-fifteen. Yesterday afternoon, she had said she'd be here by eight. Rick stubbed out the cigarette.

It wasn't unusual for Linda to keep him waiting. She did it all the time. Deliberately, he thought, as a kind of revenge.

Within GlobeBank, he outranked her by far. She was, after all, still just the financial controller for Lisa Gould's division.

8

Just a staffie. She deferred to his power, snapping to attention in his presence and cooperating beyond what was expected of her in filling any requests from his department. But in the bedroom, he had no power over her except the pleasure she took from his body.

Around the office, everyone called him the Bomber, a reference not only to his war experience but to his size, his physical bulk, his aggressive way of moving, as if he could cut down everything in his path. He knew Linda had been surprised the first time she saw him naked, saw that his broad shoulders were bony, his chest sunken. His legs were skinny runner's legs, and he knew that his drinking had given him a paunch that no amount of jogging seemed able to reduce. He had been embarrassed to have her see him that first time.

He needn't have been. The only size that mattered to Linda was the size of his erect cock — when he could get it up. Then he could make her scream with pleasure. He was enormous, and he was fierce.

"The Bomber's a good name for you," she had said the first time they had sex. That was before she knew that he sometimes had a little problem, especially when she made him nervous. She didn't like such problems, and though she kept coming back to him, she punished him for his poor performance, arriving late, leaving early, taunting him. Like yesterday.

What was it she had said? She was across the room, near the dresser, getting dressed. It was nearly six o'clock and she had to leave. She didn't want her husband to get suspicious, she said.

"And what about me?" he had asked. "Christ, Linda. I came a long way for this. I made arrangements. I had to set up all that research for my paper. I counted on seeing you." That was dumb, he had realized. He shouldn't have given her an edge. Never give Linda Glover an edge.

"That's your problem," she had answered coolly, putting on her earrings. "But look, we can have a long time together tomorrow. There's the Autotran press conference downtown." She turned to face him. "It won't involve you."

He heard the sneer in her voice.

"It's only for Kilgour's direct reports," she went on. "Just Lippert and the heavy hitters."

9

Lippert. That prick. That turkey. Sandy Lippert had once worked for Rick. He had been Rick's boy. Now he was on top of the world, and Rick was off in California while the project he had started had become Autotran.

"Anyway," Linda said, "Lisa's going to be there, too, because the message is going out of her division. I don't know how she wheedled that one. Maybe she went down on Kilgour." She turned to face Rick, running her tongue suggestively along her lips. "But Lisa won't be back uptown till ten-thirty or so. I told her I had some errands to run. I'll come by at eight."

That's what she had said. But it was already — he looked at his watch again — eight twenty-five. He had been awake since seven, thinking about it, imagining her. He had given her a key; she could get in on her own. He would pretend to be asleep but would watch out of one eye as she undressed. He loved to watch her, loved to see her cream-colored body being revealed bit by bit. Her smooth, full breasts. The white back sloping down to the round bottom. The V of orange-yellow hair. Rick shivered, thinking about it.

Then she would come to the bed, slip in beside him, begin to caress him to wake him up. Until finally, he would roll over, and take her.

Eight-thirty. He was angry. He lit another cigarette. Desire and anger were making him nervous. It was no good when he was nervous. Linda would be angry again, and sullen. She was very big on performance — in all things.

Rick smoked his cigarette down and lit another. He was just putting it out when he heard her key in the door. Ten to nine. Rick was aware that he was trembling with fury.

"Hi," Linda said casually as she pushed into the room, her thick hair like a lion's mane above the brown coat. She did not look at him as she closed the door behind her.

3

NINETEEN REPORTERS SHOWED UP for the press conference. Lisa Gould took no small satisfaction from the fact that this coup had been engineered by someone on her staff, her communications manager, Jessica Moser. Even the *London Financial Times* had sent a representative. Lisa, a coffee cup in her hand, was chatting with him when she felt a gentle nudge at her elbow. It was Jessica. Lisa put down her coffee and followed Jessica to the lectern, taking a chair beside it that faced the crowd of reporters now adjusting themselves in their seats, opening their orange press kits to find GlobeBank pens and GlobeBank notepaper for their use.

Then Lisa saw the swinging double doors open for Ray LaRocca to enter the room. That must be the signal, she thought. John must have been waiting for Ray. Where had he been? The Far East or something. Maybe he just got off the plane. That wouldn't be unlike him. A twenty-hour trip from Manila to New York and then straight to the office in order to catch Kilgour's press conference. LaRocca was important to Autotran — and to Kilgour. Lisa knew that. He was the international guy after all; "GlobeBank's Global Reach" someone had called him. Autotran would go international soon, and LaRocca would get the credit for it.

In the meantime, here he was, a breath of Mediterranean spring in the New York winter, lean, black-haired, impeccably dressed, and sporting a new tan. Taller than most of the crowd, he picked out Kilgour and caught his eye.

Kilgour nodded slightly in return, then, smiling, moved to the lectern and hung the microphone around his neck.

"Good morning and welcome," he began. "I'm John Kilgour, executive vice president of Global Bank Corporation and the head of the Banking Operations Sector, which you people continue to call our 'back office.' "

The reporters chuckled and shifted in their chairs.

"I'm going to introduce some other people to you, and they're going to introduce Autotran, which you see around you. Today, Autotran stands for Automated Transfer. Simply put, this system handles all the functions of the funds transfer operation. All of them. In a completely automated, fully integrated fashion. On-line, in real-time. And I mean from soup to nuts. All input, all processing, advising of the customer, accounting for our records, our own MIS, management information system, and all customer service. That makes it unique among banks.

"Many of our competitors have automated the processing, or the input, or the accounting. That puts them where we were eighteen months ago. But none of them has put the whole thing together into an automated, comprehensive network.

"With Autotran, we can effect any transfer of any amount in any currency from any point on earth to any other point on earth, virtually instantly. We do it accurately, cost-effectively, and exactly as the customer ordered it.

"Sandy Lippert — Alexander Lippert, a vice president and a division head within my sector — is the real architect of Autotran." Kilgour gestured toward Sandy, who nodded awkwardly. "Sandy's got an engineering degree from M.I.T. and an M.B.A. from Wharton and a lot of experience in funds transfer right here at GlobeBank. He's put it all together in building Autotran. And he's in charge of installing Autotran in our other operations here as well as in London, to handle our European traffic right there on the spot."

Someone — Lisa wondered if it was Jessica — began to applaud, and there was a minute of lackluster clapping.

"The conceptual framework for Autotran really started, however, a number of years ago." Kilgour paused. "I wouldn't want to say how many. But at the time, I was a vice president just back from Australia and suddenly assigned to an important staff task force. And Ray LaRocca was a new hire at GlobeBank, an alumnus of the manufacturing sector and eager to source some of his ideas into the mainstream. Ray and I used to play around with ideas, and one day we were talking about the ideal way to process funds transfers if you weren't constrained by any realities at all."

There were some chuckles from the crowd.

"Autotran was really born then, and Ray has had a role in it ever since. That hasn't been easy because I've got him handling all the transactions for all our overseas operations. I'm sure I don't have to tell you people what a big job that is, how important." This time Kilgour nodded toward LaRocca, who stared straight ahead. "Ray is a senior vice president now, head of the International Services Division, the biggest and richest division we have. And we're very fortunate to have him here this morning because he's just gotten off a plane from Manila and he's about to get on a plane for Zurich."

The reporters glanced in LaRocca's direction while they applauded. LaRocca sat erect, tall, his long Roman nose accentuating his stoical alertness.

Kilgour went on. "Now BOS — Banking Operations Sector — is, as you know, organized by market segment. So that BOS is essentially a mirror image of the rest of GlobeBank. You know, I'm sure, that GlobeBank has a National Sector, an International Sector, a Multinational Sector, and a Metropolitan Sector. Each sector serves those markets, does all the banking business each of these market segments requires.

"BOS doesn't do banking business; instead, we produce the services and process the transactions that are the back end of the business. So we organize ourselves to face off to the bank's customers, to face off to our front office sectors. We've got an International Services Division — that's Ray's — and a Multinational Services Division, a Metropolitan Services Division, and two National Services Divisions — two because they're such a big market segment in terms of numbers of customers and transaction volume. The National Services West Division is perhaps the fastest-growing piece of business in GlobeBank. And that's due in no small measure to this lady here" — Kilgour turned to look at Lisa — "Lisa Gould, vice president and division head."

Lisa felt herself blush at the sound of the clapping, Jessica's fervent applause ringing out above the rest. She told herself to watch her posture.

"The transaction we're going to effect in a minute or so to inaugurate Autotran," Kilgour went on, "will be an order from one of Lisa's customers in National Services West. And it is Lisa Gould who is pressing forward to apply the Autotran formula to other kinds of financial services.

"I said a moment ago that *today* Autotran stands for Automated Transfer. In the not too distant future, I believe it will stand for Automated Transactions. I believe that all financial transactions will be effected this way before very long."

Kilgour studied the audience, pausing to let his words sink in.

"Ladies and gentlemen, I suggest that you look around you." Kilgour waved his arm toward the field of terminals. "I suggest that you watch and listen carefully. Because what you're about to see is nothing less than the bank back office of tomorrow. And I'm proud to say it's here at GlobeBank today."

Lisa herself began the applause. The workers on the floor chimed in. The reporters scribbled.

Kilgour sat down, and Ray LaRocca stepped to the lectern.

Jessica had cautioned all of them to "keep it short." LaRocca obeyed her to the letter, describing in two minutes the "conceptual framework" of Autotran.

"To the customer," LaRocca said, "how we process his transfer is of no importance. All he cares about is that it's done right, it's done fast, and that it's done exactly as he wants it. We are in the service business, and if we can't deliver on those three things, we're not running our business right." What he and Kilgour had come up with on that day years ago, what he and Sandy Lippert had worked on over the past eighteen months, was "ensuring the ideal future of funds transfers from the customer's point of view."

LaRocca's delivery was, as always, serious and straightforward. He was not a man for quips. To Jessica, he had always looked like a Renaissance portrait of an Italian nobleman. She pictured him in green velvet, one hand on his sword, his look haughty. Closing her eyes, she could almost imagine the deep voice reciting Dante. Instead, she realized with a jolt, he had just finished speaking what she referred to as "corporatese" and was sitting down.

Sandy was next. Jessica smiled at his tall gracefulness, at the honesty of his face. He began to talk about "building Autotran." "We knew what we needed — wanted," he said, "and we knew what we had in place — our current situation. What was left was to bridge the gap between the two. We decided to take a modular approach in order to spread the risk and cost, to deal in more manageable pieces. In some cases, the technology was available. In other cases, we had to develop it."

Lisa gazed out the window. Across the East River the Jehovah's Witness Watch Tower signaled the time and temperature: 9:42; 38 °. She reminded herself to tell Barry that the tailor had called to say his coat was ready. She had meant to tell him last night at dinner, but he had gotten into an involved description of his latest case, a very complex copyright litigation, and she had completely forgotten.

". . . Lisa Gould to tell you about our customer communication effort," Sandy said. It was her turn.

She delivered her piece well, as always. She was good at public speaking; she enjoyed the sense of power it gave. And, of course, she had rehearsed thoroughly with Jessica. "We knew that we didn't want to force our customers into anything. That would be entirely antithetical to the spirit of service we are committed to. Some banks may think it's OK to force a particular format, for example, down customers' throats simply to streamline their own internal processing and costs, but that's not GlobeBank's way." The reporter from *Finance Journal* was writing furiously to catch this obvious slap at Citibank.

Instead, Lisa went on, they had embarked on a program of communication to inform customers about the coming change and to assure them that it would make their lives easier, not more complicated.

Watching her, Sandy was amused at how businesslike she looked. A dark suit, he mused, just like the men. Pinstriped shirt, too. Still, she was, he felt, an attractive woman in a small, dark way.

Lisa sat down and Kilgour took over the podium. "I guess we're ready to turn the thing on. If you'll all come over here . . . There'll be time for any questions afterward."

Chairs scraped and chatter ensued as the group rose en masse and shuffled over to a terminal where Edna Repke, picked for her pretty face as well as her agility on the keyboard, was nervously waiting.

The phone rang, according to plan, at precisely ten o'clock. It was the Ensold Corporation, one of Lisa Gould's biggest customers. A technologically advanced corporation, it had requested and won the honor of initiating Autotran's first live transaction. A group of Ensold officers had struggled out of bed at five, California time, to be at the terminal at seven. In a trembling voice

Edna Repke said, "National Services West." The press crowded closer, Kilgour deferring to the *Business Week* reporter. "Yes," Edna replied, "ready." Her fingers were poised over the keyboard; the specially constructed telephone headset half-circled her head.

"Access code?" Edna asked, then entered it on the keyboard. "OK. Inside. Password authentication?"

"We have a variety of security measures at the present time," Sandy said in a low voice. "Constantly changing access codes, though the schedule for change varies. We may change daily, weekly, hourly — no one ever knows. That's part of the security mechanism, of course. What we're building in, eventually, is a voice-print mechanism."

Green numbers flickered on the screen. "You're confirmed," Edna said. "Go ahead."

She tapped the keyboard and a list headed Main Menu appeared on the screen.

"This'll let Edna choose the set of fields to fill in." Sandy's voice, as he hovered over the terminal, was just audible.

The list disappeared. Edna's fingers were working rapidly. A new list came up on the screen — lines of type.

"Remitter is Ensold?" Edna asked, her voice growing more confident as she concentrated on the screen. "Beneficiary?" She typed, filling in the spaces. "Amount?" Then: "Oh. Multiple. OK."

Sandy turned to the crowd. "They're doing a multiple transfer here, several payees, so Edna will ask to have them grouped by value date."

Edna was absorbed, her fingers translating Ensold's wishes into commands for Autotran.

"Notice the prompts in the system," Sandy said excitedly, his eyes sparkling. "It's the system that's getting her to dimension the transfer in terms of value date, prompting her to ask the right questions for each of the multiple transfers. Because we've got different amounts here, different payees and account parties. And it's the system forcing her to get these down accurately."

"Means of advising payee?" Edna asked. "Cable at your expense or deduct from transaction?"

The *Business Week* reporter was writing quickly on her Globe-Bank pad; the others watched, fascinated.

"Advise you, Ensold?" Pause. "OK."

"The system has ongoing self-edit checks," Sandy was saying. "You see, she just made a typo. Hold it a minute, Edna; hold the screen."

The reporters peered. Edna had typed Zurchi for Zurich. The screen was flickering.

"For that location field," Sandy said, "the system will balk at a misspelling. And that's an extra security check too, because the system has to recognize the address. You see how the system itself just won't let you make a mistake. And the cleaner the input, as I'm sure you know, the cleaner and faster and more accurate the output."

"OK," Edna said. "Got it."

"She'll run one more check here," Sandy said, "as standard operating procedure. Then" — as Edna hit the Return button on the keyboard — "she releases the transaction.

"Now that transaction is done; it is on-line right now. Ensold's account with us is being debited the varying amounts, and, via the Clearing House or SWIFT or whatever the appropriate interface, we're crediting the accounts of the payees at the varying banks. And also" — he was standing tall again now, not hovering, his hand resting gently on the terminal — "we're hooked to a teletype machine that is generating the cables that advise the payees of these credits. And we can get hard copies of those cables." He turned to Edna. "Edna, would you pull one off so we can show it to these folks?" Edna rose dutifully.

"And, of course," Sandy continued, gesturing with his free hand, "the system is also at this time generating the MIS we need. And it's moving the proof data to the bank's books electronically — no magnetic tape here. And I think a very dramatic thing that you've seen here" — his timing was excellent: Edna was returning with a sheaf of Telexes — "is that not a single piece of paper has been generated except for the hard copies of these cables, which we wanted only to show to you folks."

Edna ripped off chunks of Telex and handed them around.

"So the transfer — and it's a multiple transfer, I remind you, involving more than ten payees — the transfer's been done, the payees are being advised, the data is lodged in a place where it can be instantly accessed in case of inquiry, and there's no paper to get lost or mutilated or to mess the place up. And" —

he looked at his watch — "it's all taken about three minutes. Three minutes to transfer a total of two million–plus dollars."

The new age had begun. In the crowd Sandy spotted Kilgour, almost lost behind the *Times* man; LaRocca, tall and straight; Lisa, looking cool and professional next to Kilgour. The reporters were writing, looking up at him, nodding with him.

Sandy felt light-headed with the pride that seemed to rise from his toes. Autotran was live.

In the darkened room at the St. Magnus, Linda Glover took her time getting undressed. Rick Schmidt, smoldering with anger and tense with excitement, watched from the bed.

Why is she so late? Where has she been? Was she with Charley? Oh God, maybe she and Charley had made love, and that's why she was late.

Schmidt knew Charley Glover only from Linda's description but hated him just the same. He was a turkey in Rick's eyes. The only success he had ever known was marrying Linda, and he couldn't even hold her. She had wanted a husband, someone presentable who wouldn't distract her from her main interest — herself. Charley Glover filled the bill. He was good-looking and irrelevant. That was all that mattered.

At business school, where Linda and Charley met, Charley struggled to keep up, making grades that just barely kept him in school. Linda easily won high marks and the enthusiastic recommendation of the faculty.

When they came to New York looking for jobs, it was Linda who had her pick of offers; she was even able to dangle the competition before GlobeBank till they gave her "the right slot." Charley was asked to leave — asked to leave! — after the three-month probationary period as a trainee at Time Inc. Now he held a boring research job at a brokerage firm, his office an unused conference room where supplies were dumped, and he didn't seem to be doing well there, either. He kept complaining to Linda that they weren't using him to his "full potential," that his M.B.A. wasn't paying off, that the job was beneath him.

Linda humored Charley Glover, Rick realized, occasionally agreeing to have lunch with him, sometimes — but not often — going home on the same train with him. The same way she humors me, Rick suddenly thought, building me up just to let me down hard. She controls us both.

He couldn't take his eyes off her as she stepped out of her shoes, dropped her skirt, and unbuttoned her blouse. She seemed to consider her next move.

"Today's the big day," she finally said, looking at herself in the mirror to remove her jewelry. "I bet everyone's really hot and bothered down at 176. Of course," she chuckled, deep in her throat, "we're pretty hot and bothered right here, aren't we?"

She turned to face him. Her mouth was curled into a little smile; her eyelids were nearly closed over her eyes. Staring at him, she took off her bra, then bent and pulled off her panties. She stood for a moment, one hand on her hip, still smiling, still staring. Then she came toward the bed. "Are we all geared up for this?" she asked a little too brightly. He knew this mood of hers. She could turn nasty in a second and demote him. That's what it felt like.

"Oh Jesus, yes," Rick moaned, trembling, forcing himself to be still. He looked down at himself. *Oh yes.*

He lunged for her, pulling her down hard beside him. He clamped a hand over one of her breasts, found the other one with his mouth. His mouth traveled down her body while with his knee he pried open her legs.

"Not yet," she said. "Not so fast. I want to play with my nice toy first." She leaned over him and started licking his erection very delicately with the tip of her tongue. "Mm-mmm," she said. "I like this toy, and I like Ricky when he lets me play with it. And when Ricky is hard, when he's a good boy, I want him to do all sorts of things." Linda straightened up and began to chew at Rick's neck. "I want Ricky to put his pretty thing here" — she pointed between her breasts — "and here" — she rubbed her belly — "and all over me." Linda was almost whispering now, her tongue running across his ear. "And when Linda is ready, Ricky will know."

Rick glanced down at himself. He was still big. She still wanted him.

"Rub that hard cock on my stomach," she commanded. "Just my stomach." She was leaning back against the headboard. He obeyed her.

"My tits," she said. "Now my tits." He pressed each of her

breasts with his hardness, found the nipple centers and stroked. On his knees, his back arched, he traced her body with his erection, along her arms and legs, across her buttocks as she raised her legs, then thrusting, as she ordered, between her breasts.

Oh, God, he thought, I hope I . . . He couldn't wait much longer. He felt it might be going. Why did she keep him waiting?

"Now!" she cried. "Inside!"

She spread herself open with her fingers. He leaned down toward her and rammed.

His eyes were closed, and he concentrated on the sound. He always heard it when he fucked Linda: artillery shells screaming through the air. *Whoo-eee, whooo-eee,* and then the explosion. He was ramming her fast. He could do anything in this place.

"Do it, do it," she urged in his ear. "Fuck me hard. Hard! Hard!" Then, "Aaah, aaah, aaaaa-aaah."

Rick felt himself throbbing inside her. His sweat was soaking them both. Slowly the artillery barrage died away.

Linda lay still and quiet beneath him. Rick rolled off her onto his side. He looked down at himself. Doesn't matter now, he thought quickly. He was sated. He looked at Linda's face. She was too. Her face had turned pink, the way it always did when he had given her a good ride.

"Well," she said, patting his hand as it rested on her breast, "I guess Autotran's going live any minute now."

◊ ◊ ◊

It was after eleven when the last reporter left, his arms full of orange folders. His questions had been too technical for Jessica. She passed him over to Sandy, then fetched more backup material.

"And if you've got any questions," Jessica intoned as she and Sandy waited with the burdened man for the elevator, "please call. Really. Sandy and I want to be as helpful as we can."

The elevator doors closed. "One of the most successful and gruesome mornings I've ever spent at GlobeBank," Jessica pronounced. "God! My face is exhausted from all the heavy smiling."

"It really went super, Jessica." Sandy was elated. "Good turnout, good interest. I think the speeches went well, don't you?"

"Everybody did fine."

20

"Come to lunch. Frank and I are going to go off and celebrate. You come, too. You really did most of the work."

They went to Michael 2, a place Jessica disliked, though no more than she disliked most of the restaurants in the financial district. There was about them, she thought, a too-hearty air of hail-fellow-well-met camaraderie, too much blustery talk of football and deals. And they were all too cold, "geared," she liked to say, "to bankers and brokers who wear pulled-up socks, undershirts, and three-piece suits whatever the temperature outside."

Jessica had two Bloody Marys before the meal arrived and a glass of beer with her overcooked chicken Kiev. Sandy, she noticed, drank four Cutty Sarks on the rocks, ordered a beer when she did, and was about to have an after-lunch cognac when she said she really did have to go back uptown.

Sandy looked at his watch. "Jeez, yeah. We should be getting back, too. I've got a staff meeting. Jesus, Frank! What time are the guys coming?"

Frank Kozlow, Sandy's chief controller, had almost kept pace with his boss's drinking, and he appeared momentarily panicked. He looked quickly at his watch. "Relax. Not till two." It was one-fifty.

"Get the check, Frank, will you?" Sandy was getting to his feet. "Put it on your card and I'll sign the expense account on it."

◇ ◇ ◇

The five men who reported directly to Sandy Lippert sat on either side of him at the big conference table. "This morning went off real well, as I guess you all heard," he said. "Jessica Moser thinks we could get some good coverage out of it. Kilgour should like that. And also, it just went very smoothly. The system worked like a dream — the whole demo was a big win. And nobody sounded like a turkey." He smiled. "Not even me."

His staff smiled.

"Anyway, we've got a shitload of work to do, and we've got to get a planning cycle in process right away. Hi, Frank."

Kozlow, a calculator in one hand and a cup of coffee in the other, took his seat.

"The two major things on our plate," Sandy went on, "the top two priorities, are: one, the division-specific enhancements for Autotran — the conversions; and two, putting up Autotran in London. Kilgour's going to announce at the Friday morning division head meeting that each division is now formally tasked to implement Autotran division-wide. It's going to be a phased implementation, as we discussed, and it's going to go like this: LaRocca, Gould, Faber, North, O'Connor."

Sandy rapped out the names rhythmically on the table with the side of his hand.

"O'Connor's last because, obviously, the Metro is going to be the most complex and we need the most time for planning the specs. But the point is, you've got to get with these people right away and start the planning. I know LaRocca's division is pretty well along, and we've started the preliminary stuff for Gould. But the point is — yes, Marie?"

His secretary stood in the doorway, quietly signaling to him.

"It's Kathy," she whispered as he came over. "I tried to put her off, but she said she really had to talk to you and I had to interrupt the meeting."

Sandy stifled an oath and nodded. "OK. I'll take the call in just a minute. Have her hold."

4

KATHY. MOSTLY WHEN SANDY thought about her, it was because she was an intrusion, a reproachful voice at the other end of the phone, chiding him, reminding him, nagging him about payments.

Even when he was able to think of her without bitterness, she was part of the pinwheel blur that his life had been until two years ago. He couldn't say for certain what his life was now. He thought it better not to probe too deep. But his life of before seemed unreal, a spinning wheel that had gone faster and faster until one day, with a jerk, the motion had slowed enough for him to be thrown off. He lay beside it, a little broken, while the wheel went on spinning without him.

That was how he thought about it now. But at the time, when he was spinning with it, he hadn't thought about it at all. He had gone along in the roles prepared for him, dressing the part, looking the part, playing the part.

Sandy was the dutiful son of the corporate father in the solid suburb outside Cincinnati. In the neighborhood they called him the Spearmint Kid, he was so clean and bright-looking. At M.I.T. he was the conscientious engineering student. His course work was good but not brilliant. A professor told him he had "a natural technical bent."

He gave his parents a bit of a scare during his junior year. Her name was Gail Levy, and she was everything Carl and Jean Lippert thought they feared: New York, Jewish, not rich, liberal, a student of anthropology at Harvard. Sandy's letters home grew less frequent and more obscure. His sister, Kay, was dispatched from Smith to "have a talk." She spent a boozy Sunday with him, reminding him "where he came from," chiding him about the pain he might cause their parents if this "went any further." It seemed to Sandy that he was always being chided and reminded.

The Lippert family need not have worried. Gail broke it off herself. She said she didn't think they had "the fundamentals in common." Sandy went back to engineering. He felt at home there.

He went to the Wharton School of Finance and began to do very well indeed. His second-semester course in decision sciences spent the first two weeks on the case study of GlobeBank's Banking Operations Sector. How John R. Kilgour had overhauled back office processing in the giant corporation. By the time Sandy Lippert heard of it, Kilgour's back office renaissance, as he liked to call it, had been in effect for five years. GlobeBank claimed to have saved millions of dollars. And Kilgour was clearly one of the most powerful men at the world's most powerful bank. He was becoming a celebrity.

Other banks were aping GlobeBank. Wharton, Harvard, and Stanford wrote case studies about the change. The Wolcott Foundation, the prestigious executive training program run by

Bay University in California, named Kilgour Manager of the Year. Kilgour spent a week at the foundation's languid pink estate in Marin County, making speeches, going to lunches, gracing special seminars with his presence. The proceedings of a day-long roundtable there were published; the slim volume sold well at the Wharton bookstore.

To Sandy Lippert, there was an aura of heroic romance about John R. Kilgour and the changes wrought at GlobeBank. The preface to the Wolcott roundtable book contained a line that Sandy never forgot: "John R. Kilgour did more than just perceive the conceptual breakthrough that changed his bank's back office; he did more than just implement an 'industrialization' of a service organization tailored to that organization's needs. What Kilgour has done is to change the face of banking forever."

In the summer between his two years at Wharton, Sandy was accepted as an intern at GlobeBank.

It was a golden summer. GlobeBank treated its interns like young royalty: lunches with corporate brass, boat rides on chartered yachts around New York Harbor, tours, theater parties, orientation sessions. Sandy glided through the project he had been assigned, a program for an enhancement to the bank's computer system for processing international funds transfers. REDI, it was called — Ready to Enter Data Input. Sandy was to design a special flexibility for the banks from Switzerland. He did it easily and he did it well.

He met Kathy Andrews at an East Side bar on a hot July evening. He was playing darts. She was on her way to the Ladies' Room. He stopped her.

A week later, she discreetly moved in with him, into the large studio he had sublet from the sister of a Wharton classmate. There was a white fur rug on the polished parquet floor. They would close the curtains, turn the air conditioner on full blast, put a Chuck Mangione record on the Marantz, and move to the rug.

He would undress her in an almost ritual way, virtually in time to the trumpet's rhythm whining from the speakers. He took off her jewelry first — small pearl earrings, a delicate gold bangle, and a Cartier tank watch on her left wrist. He would loose the wraparound skirt, slip her top over her head, and untie the silk scarf that pulled back her blond, lightly frosted hair. Then, while she watched, he would undress quickly. She would match him at the end, pulling off her bra and panties just as he stepped out of his briefs. Cold in the chill air blasting from the air conditioner, they would fall together onto the fur rug. "Sandy, Sandy," she would whimper into his ear. And he would hear himself moan from deep in his throat.

The end of the summer was its zenith for Sandy Lippert. He was chosen to be one of the ten interns asked to make a presentation to Kilgour himself about his summer's work. He rehearsed every day for a week, drilled by his project mentor, Frank Angelo. It was a Friday when the two of them were ushered into Kilgour's office, the great corner space on the twentieth floor of Head Office on Park Avenue, all polished wood and leather feeling like silk.

As planned, Frank introduced the project while Sandy stole sidelong glances at Kilgour, his hero, in shirtsleeves. He considered the appearance of this man whom all admired and most feared. It was unexceptional. Nowhere in his face or body was there a trace of the ruthlessness that had marked his path to power or of the power that he now wielded.

Lithe, not tall, his graying hair still shot through with traces of strawberry yellow, Kilgour had a farmboy's face, which Sandy thought clashed oddly with his J. Press pinstripe. Generations back, Kilgour's Connecticut ancestors had pushed out to the Midwest for the land. These Kilgours had become farmers in Illinois, but it was only a short time before they sent their sons to Yale. Back East, the sons assumed the easy posture and cool self-assurance of the best schools, the broadest possibilities. But their faces remained midwestern, with the unobtrusiveness of good modern design. Like the machines among which he moved, Kilgour's nonreflective casing hardly hinted at the powerful and intricate network it housed.

When Frank Angelo had finished, Kilgour turned to Sandy. "Sounds interesting," he said. "Let's hear about it."

Letter perfect, that's how he had been. He knew his stuff and presented it well. He was ready for the unnerving questions Kilgour had a reputation for asking, but when the questions came, they were gentle, asked out of interest, and Sandy answered succinctly.

"Could this kind of flexibility be achieved elsewhere and let us knock more heads?" Kilgour asked. "Could we do this and still knock the heads we want to knock in a shop, still decrease our manpower?" He was talking directly to Sandy; Frank was out of the conversation. Sandy felt a rush.

"I believe so, yes," he answered.

At the end of the session, Sandy had an offer from Kilgour to work as a consultant for GlobeBank during his second year at Wharton. Frank took him to lunch, which lasted three hours. Sandy went home to the studio from lunch and napped until Kathy arrived. They got engaged that night.

5

THE PRESS CONFERENCE HAD BEEN a success, John Kilgour knew. Everything had gone smoothly, better than he had expected. Autotran was a big win, but now he felt drained. He decided to keep the afternoon easy.

He swiveled in his high-backed leather chair to face the screen of his information processing system, the Ardec.

The system, powered by one of Sandy Lippert's minicomputers, had been built to Kilgour's specifications. There was one terminal on his desk, one on his secretary's desk, and a few scattered in key areas of the bank. At the moment that was all, but by the end of six months all of Kilgour's division heads and their secretaries would have Ardecs; in a year they would be in use all through the Banking Operations Sector, and in two years throughout GlobeBank. That was the plan. Then the system would make most of what arrived in GlobeBank's In boxes obsolete. Without paper, without mail and reports, without notebooks, GlobeBank's managers would electronically write and edit, send memos, perform calculations, draw organizational charts, and file a vast array of information as little electronic beeps, to be called out like genies from this modern Aladdin's lamp whenever they were needed. And Kilgour would be GlobeBank's Aladdin.

For the moment, though, Kilgour used his Ardec mostly to post and update his daily appointments.

He pushed a button on his white telephone console, one of twelve that connected him with all his top managers, with the data center at 176 Wall, and with his wife. Now he pushed the button marked INTER, which connected him with his secretary, Barbara Finn, who sat in a glass cubicle just outside.

"Yes, John?" she responded.

"Get my calendar on the screen, will you, Barbara?"

In a moment the screen was covered by slightly wavering green letters.

By pressing a special key on the terminal, Kilgour made the cursor, a little wedge of green light, move down to 1 P.M. Then he pressed another key, and the appointments listed for the morning were erased from the screen, leaving only the afternoon's schedule.

He had an hour with Danny Faber, whose division, National Services East, had recently increased its financial forecast for the year by half a million dollars. Kilgour had wanted to go over the numbers carefully with Danny before he had to report to Toby Pruitt or Charlie Hardesty. The president and chairman — *his* bosses — for all their clubby amiability, could come down hard on him if he were not prepared. But he couldn't face Danny this afternoon. Short, stocky, bespectacled Danny Faber, the smart Jew from City College; Danny Faber wore him out. What else was there? Boy's Village. Kilgour was on their board. That could wait. And the Maxitech fellows, who were trying to win him over to their hardware. That could wait, too. That just left his three o'clock: Paul Gregson.

"Barbara?"

"Yes, John?"

"Reschedule everything this afternoon, will you, please? Except Gregson. I'll see him. And hold my calls." Gregson. My God. How long had it been? Eighteen, nineteen years? Kilgour stretched out on his leather couch and shut his eyes.

◇ ◇ ◇

Almost twenty years before, John Roland Kilgour had been a young man in dark, correct suits from Brooks Brothers with a young wife just out of Connecticut College for Women, one of many young men with similar backgrounds. With a B.A. in economics from Yale and a Harvard M.B.A., he had been hired right out of B-school by Global Bank Corporation's high-powered International Sector. After a year in training at Head Office in New York, he got his first overseas assignment. But it was overseas in the broadest sense only; Kilgour was posted to Mexico City. He spent three years there learning the ropes. At the end of their stay, he and his wife, Sally, had two small daughters and the polished assurance of members of an international community who were used to living on what by local standards were very large salaries. While he was there, he worked on a financial accounting and information system for his area that would clearly be the best in Latin America someday, and his name went into "the Book."

The Book's official name was Corporate Estate, although no one could remember exactly why. It was a list drawn up twice a year by the senior managers in every area naming the "fast-trackers": young people, early in their careers, who had caught the corporate eye, who were good and ambitious and willing to work hard, and whom management wanted to keep at Globe-Bank — at almost any price.

So instead of Malaysia, which would have been his next assignment had he been a more ordinary officer, Kilgour was sent to Sydney, Australia. Better for the family, of course. Globe-Bank's Australian lending subsidiary was a real opportunity for a bright young man. This was a chance for Kilgour to show what he could do. If he failed . . . Well, they would see.

He did not fail. On the contrary, he succeeded brilliantly. And apart from his own talents, which were considerable, the reason was Paul Gregson, the subsidiary's head man and Kilgour's new boss.

When Kilgour met him, Gregson was in his early forties, already completely gray, tall, hollow-chested, and snaggle-toothed. Kilgour could never understand why Gregson hadn't done something about his teeth. He came from a large Mormon family in Salt Lake City, but had been stationed in the Pacific for more than fifteen years. Gregson's wife, his third, was a still-beautiful former actress in her late thirties who faded from the social scene for months at a time during bouts of depression. They had one child, a spectacularly beautiful boy of nine, who was brain-damaged. Gregson, Kilgour quickly learned, was an alcoholic.

He was also invaluable. No person in the Pacific area, perhaps even anywhere in the bank, knew more than Gregson about the back office, about investments, cash letters, funds transfers, letters of credit. When his mind was clear, he was an encyclopedia.

"But how does he last? I mean, I really don't understand it." Sally and John Kilgour were in bed, their cigarettes the only light in the dark room. The girls had finally fallen asleep, and they could hear the cicadas in the trees outside their window.

"I'll tell you, Sal. He lasts because nobody knows anything. Not compared to him. Everyone's scared stiff that if he goes, it would take years to get back up the curve on what Paul carries around in his head. The place would fall apart."

"But all the time he's not there? Isn't that held against him?" Sally Kilgour faced her husband in bed. He could just see her face in the glow of her cigarette.

"It doesn't work that way, Sal. Sure, everyone knows he's a drunk. Maybe Regional Office knows it. But they won't know *officially*. They have no way of doing without him — yet." He took a long drag on his cigarette.

In his ironical way, Gregson seemed to take to his crisp, young colleague. And Kilgour had realized at once that he could learn a great deal from Gregson. He learned fast. On the weekends when Martha Gregson was well enough for company, the Kilgours and their two little girls would often be invited to the Gregsons' for lunch that extended to dinner. Paul Gregson would meet them at the door with a water glass of gin that, refilled through the day, never left his hand. He seemed to enjoy having the little Kilgour girls climb onto his lap and pester him with questions and with stories about nursery school. Perhaps, Kilgour surmised, it was a way of feeling like a father. Gregson's son had never learned to speak.

But Gregson was fatherly to Kilgour, as well, and seemed not to resent his burgeoning success. And of course Gregson was perfectly happy to leave his young assistant in charge when he was "ill," as he often was, for two days or three days a week.

29

During one of Gregson's longer absences, Kilgour hired a new young man, a local boy, Maurice Allison, who had returned home after five years in Chase's Education and Training Department. Kilgour stressed his firm's need for a comprehensive management training program in all the subsidiary's operations.

"We've been running this place like a Mom 'n' Pop store," he said. "Gregson has been holding everybody's hand. That simply won't do."

Allison agreed. He also agreed to have the training program in place and working at the end of five months.

"You report directly to me, of course," Kilgour told Allison. "Whatever you need, you let me know. And come to me for the nuts and bolts information." To Gregson he explained that Allison was there to develop some communications programs, work on an orientation package, and "maybe do some management training." It would require a lot of information, Kilgour said; "I may be bothering you a lot, picking your brain." Gregson asked very few questions. His periods out of the office got longer and closer together; Kilgour covered for him.

When Gregson was in, Kilgour plied him with questions about operations. Gregson warmed to the topic, one he clearly loved, and openly showed his pleasure at his young assistant's interest. Kilgour and Allison met on an as-needed basis, often three times a week, almost always after office hours. Allison came prepared with checklists of topics, and Kilgour fed him the information as he learned it from Gregson.

Sally was the only one in whom Kilgour could confide. She followed Allison's progress as he got his cross-training plan together, and she made several suggestions that Kilgour passed on to Allison, not mentioning that they came from his wife.

Allison did better than expected; at the end of four months, he had operations manuals outlining every process in the subsidiary, step by step. It was as though the information stored so long in Gregson's head had been transmitted directly through the air and into a book. The training program was staffed and ready to go.

After a lengthy meeting with Allison one afternoon, going over the details again and again until he was certain that nothing — absolutely nothing — was missing or out of order, Kilgour closed his office door and wrote a long memorandum by hand. It was directed to Head Office, with copies to the Pacific Regional Office, GlobeBank's head internal auditor, and, as an afterthought, to the medical and personnel departments. The memorandum first set forth the details of Gregson's alcoholism, the times it had affected the operation, the times he had been unable to come to work. The second part was a report on how no provision had been made at the subsidiary for cross-training operations managers or for disseminating to the staff what only Gregson had known. "Fortunately for our operation," the memorandum said, "his periods of incapacitation have never been extremely long. But if this should change, we have no staff of managers fully conversant with *all* the operations of the subsidiary to fall back on. The present head has allowed the full picture to be lodged only with him and with whomever his current assistant may be. But the assistants typically are rotated out of the position after only a few years. Thus, any hope for management continuity has depended on the presence of Gregson. The manuals prepared under my management direction constitute the single back-up repository for carrying on essential activities throughout the region."

Sally Kilgour typed the memorandum that night at home. Attached were the details of Allison's plan. The next day, Kilgour put the copies for New York into the overseas pouch in envelopes marked Confidential and mailed the regional office's copy directly. Then he waited.

He did not have to wait very long. By the end of the month, Head Office had sent a team of investigators to Sydney. They reported that matters stood just as Kilgour had described them, and commented very favorably on the unobtrusive but knowledgeable help Kilgour had given them during the investigation. Soon after, Gregson was asked to report to Regional in Melbourne. He came back three days later; he was drunk when he stepped off the plane and immediately went into seclusion. An Eyes Only memo to Kilgour followed in the next pouch. Gregson had been given a year's salary and instructions to clear his desk by the end of the week; and Kilgour had been promoted to head the subsidiary.

◇ ◇ ◇

The *buzz-buzz* of the intercom startled Kilgour out of his reverie. "Yes, Barbara?"

"A Mr. Gregson here to see you."

"Yes. Show him in." Three sharp. Right on the dot.

The door to Kilgour's office opened and Gregson stood in the doorway. His hair was now completely white and he stooped a little more, but otherwise he looked the same. Kilgour noticed that he still hadn't done anything about his teeth.

"Paul! Good to see you!" He advanced toward Gregson, his hand outstretched.

"Hello, John."

"You're looking great. Time doesn't touch you, I see. Not like the rest of us." He motioned Gregson toward the couch. "How is Martha? . . . And the family?"

"She's all right, John. We're all right."

"Good to hear it, Paul. Good to hear it. And what have you been up to these — how long has it been? — fifteen years? You haven't kept us posted."

Gregson's face was expressionless. "Holding my own," he answered. "I ran a little consulting firm for a while, but it was hard to keep it going. A one-man operation, you know?"

Of course. Drunk half the time. More than half, Kilgour thought. "It's amazingly unpredictable how some firms seem to take off and others have rotten luck," he said. "But that's a shame. Well, Paul, what brings you to New York?"

Gregson looked down at the floor.

Shit. This is going to be bad, Kilgour thought. Painful. "My son," he said finally. "There's a place in Connecticut we got him into. Supposed to do wonders. He's a grown man now, you know, John," he said. "A grown man. We have to start thinking about what will happen when we're gone, when I'm gone. Not that I'm planning to go any too soon." This was added hastily. Gregson smiled, but his eyes looked bitter.

"Well, and we also thought it might be the time to make a new start. Something fresh. A new country, a new house. I wanted to come back to the States. Look, John," he said, speaking louder and faster, "I'll level with you. I need a job."

Here it comes, Kilgour thought.

"I know what you're probably thinking. But I've been on the

wagon for years now, for five years. Not a drop. And I know operations, John. Nobody knows them better. I learned them from the ground up. And I trained you, didn't I? I'm proud of your success. I mean it," he said a little wildly, looking around Kilgour's office. "If I may say so, I feel partly responsible for it."

"You are, Paul. You are," Kilgour replied smoothly.

Gregson leaned back on the couch, exhausted by his effort. "Martha hasn't been all that well," he said.

"I have to tell you, Paul," Kilgour said after a minute, "that I'm not too sure you'd be happy in our present environment. Operations have changed a lot since your day — since the early days." He corrected himself. "I'm not too sure we could fit you in.

"Look," he said, "you leveled with me and I'll level with you. There's a younger breed around now. We old-timers have to take a back seat. The fellows now are all technical guys — heavy industry, financial analysts, marketing guys. The heyday of the walking encyclopedia is past, Paul. That went the way of the green eyeshade. Everything now is automated, controlled. No more flying aces. I'll tell you what, though" — Kilgour leaned forward in his chair — "I'll have you shown around our Wall Street plant. You'll have a chance to look around. Who knows? Maybe something will turn up. But I wouldn't get my hopes up."

"My hopes are not up, John," said Gregson after a moment.

Kilgour pushed a button on his console. "Barbara? Get Lippert and have him set up a tour of 176 for Mr. Gregson. Just a second." He covered the mouthpiece with his hand. "What's a good day? Tomorrow?" Gregson nodded. "For tomorrow. All day. And have Lippert take him out to lunch. Tell him this is special; tell him that Mr. Gregson is my old boss, that he taught me everything I know. Right. Right." He hung up. "Lippert's a great guy, you'll like him. Well, Paul, be sure you and Martha touch base with Sally and me before you leave town. We four really have to get together sometime, talk about the old days."

He stood up and shook Gregson's hand. "Great to see you, Paul," he said. "Be sure you keep in touch."

◊ ◊ ◊

33

For the years that Kilgour was in Sydney, and for many years before that, the annual statement of GlobeBank showed one number that rose out of proportion to inflation, out of proportion to all other corporate expenses, out of proportion to the bank's annual growth. That number appeared under Operating Expenses.

It included many separate items: building maintenance — the lights, air conditioning, repairs, and heating; and equipment — typewriters, adding machines, brooms and mops, paper towels, a mural for the employee cafeteria, stationery and forms, and the motor pool, among others.

But the biggest number, the one that kept climbing year in and year out, was the Payroll number: the thousands of clerks in every department of every sector of the giant bank, the people who processed all the transactions — the back office.

Each sector had a front office, the elegant half of a floor where customers could be received — customers like corporate treasurers and chairmen of other banks, central bankers from Europe and finance ministers from Asia. In splendid offices with wide windows, carefully tended plants, and the best in low-key modern art, account managers and lending officers from good schools would adjust their horn-rimmed glasses and make deals over the phone or over a handshake, would declare to customers that "the paperwork will be handled quickly, and let's have lunch soon."

Whatever the transaction — a thirty-dollar withdrawal made at a branch, a ten-dollar check deposited by mail, movement in the millions on a corporation's line of credit — it had to be processed: the account at GlobeBank had to show a debit or a credit; a corresponding account elsewhere had to show a mirror-image credit or debit. Statements had to be prepared and mailed. The transactions had to be recorded in the bank's books. Auditors had to know about them. Regulatory agencies had to know. Lending officers tracking their bottom lines had to know. Branch managers and area managers had to know.

It was an extraordinary record-keeping job. Billions of dollars in transactions flowed through GlobeBank's back office in a single week — as checks, letters of credit, loans, and as funds transfers. They flowed in and out of every corner of the world — in different currencies, in different languages, from vastly different

34

kinds of customers. Billions of dollars. Billions of pieces of paper. All pushed along by the rubber-covered fingers of the back-office clerks.

And the back office kept growing. Eight years before Kilgour introduced Autotran, the operations requirements of GlobeBank had spread to half of twenty-nine of the thirty floors of Head Office and all of its three basements, to three rented floors in a large green office tower near Times Square, and to ten rented floors in a large blue office tower on Third Avenue. All of the bank's real estate in New York — everything but the elegant thirtieth-floor aerie on Park Avenue, where the top management had its offices — was given over partially or totally to operations.

As business boomed, more people were hired to do the additional paperwork. Every year, as a matter of course, 12½ percent was added to the previous year's figure for clerical expenses.

The people in Personnel tried to keep accurate employee records. "How many people," one of them asked a vice president in the Metropolitan Sector, "do you have full time in the back office?"

"Do you want today or last week?" was the answer. "Nobody knows the exact figure. I have bodies scattered on at least ten floors. I have an overflow at Third Avenue and at some of the branches. I have part-timers and I have temps. Whatever I need that day, less 4 to 5 percent, is what I have." He ground out his cigarette in the brass ashtray on his desk. "Nobody knows the figure," he repeated.

And it was true. What they *did* know was that the clerks got paid, somehow, and got raises and fringes — pensions and sick days, vacations and medical benefits. And that they used up a lot of paper and needed a lot of equipment and a lot of space.

By the best estimates, over ten thousand people worked as clerks in the New York operation, with thousands more in GlobeBank branches and subsidiaries around the world.

For managers, the back office was Siberia. It was where deadwood was sent, a receptacle for old men, worn out and washed up. For the problem people, drinkers or "crazies." For the nephews, as they were called, people who couldn't accomplish much or who didn't fit in, but who had to be kept on the payroll because somebody somewhere owed them something. They sat in plasterboard offices, returned from lunch at three smelling of

35

Jack Daniel's and Wrigley's Spearmint, and kept business cards in their wallets.

The clerks paid no attention to them. The clerks knew why they were there, knew how little they understood and how much less they cared about letters of credit and lock box accounts.

The bank's account officers knew it, too, and they knew how to go beyond the managers to the clerks. It was the only way to get anything done. "Call Henry in Lock Box on that one," they'd say. "He'll take care of it for you." Or Zach, the letter of credit expert. Or Louise, who could find anything in the files.

But when Louise or Zach or Henry went on vacation or had the flu, chaos reigned. There were mistakes, delays. Transfers and vouchers were lost.

And then customers would complain to the officers. "What are we paying your bank for, Art?" they would ask half in jest, knowing that other banks were just as bad, maybe worse, that there was nowhere else to go.

And meanwhile, year in and year out, the cost of operations rose between 10 and 18 percent.

This, finally, was the reason that, at a certain October Globe-Bank senior officers' meeting, Chairman of the Board Charles Hardesty announced that he was forming a special Task Force on Account and Operations Control. "I'll give the task force eighteen months to find out how to cut out the fat," Hardesty announced to rows of men sprinkled with a few women in the fifth-floor auditorium. "As we have grown, adding new customers, new kinds of financial instruments, gone into new markets, new countries, our back office simply hasn't kept up. And, gentlemen and ladies," he added in his dignified voice, "since we can't tell what needs to be measured anymore, our costs have gotten away from us."

The task force would be given all the resources necessary to do a thorough job and make recommendations. Archie Dale, GlobeBank's comptroller, was put in charge, reporting directly to Hardesty. But the real manager, the person who would run the show, was Kilgour.

◇ ◇ ◇

After four years in Sydney, Kilgour had been called to Melbourne as chief of staff to the regional senior vice president. His reputation as a brilliant planner and systems man had earned him the job. Most people held it for two years before moving on to something big. It was reserved for fast-trackers, and Kilgour was at the top of the list in International.

So, as he expected, his next assignment was at Head Office, heading the financial staff for the International Sector. The bank found a house in Pound Ridge for the Kilgours, and they settled in happily before the school year began. They were glad to be home.

Home in the United States, at least. Kilgour was rarely at home in Pound Ridge. He was usually at his desk between six-thirty and seven A.M., reading mail, dictating assignments for his staff, reviewing reports. And then, all day, meetings, presentations, and more presentations. He became known in New York, as he had been known in the field, as a clever and tireless manager, a martinet. The members of his staff were afraid of him, but they produced. That was what mattered. They hated to be seen going home at night. No matter how late they stayed, Kilgour was nearly always still there, his door open, his slim frame erect in his chair, his fair head bent slightly to read a report. He never missed seeing any of them go by, and he would always call out "Good night" before glancing at his watch.

When Kilgour was nine months into the job, Archie Dale called him into his office and offered him a spot on Hardesty's new task force. He said he would think it over for three days, talk it over with his wife, but that was just to keep Archie Dale on edge. He knew his reputation, and he knew that Dale wanted him badly. He also knew that close proximity to Hardesty could be useful. So, after letting Dale wonder for seventy-two hours, Kilgour met with him again and agreed to serve if he could be in charge.

The large conference room on the twentieth floor was turned over to the task force for meetings, and each member was assigned a decent office on the Park Avenue side of the building. Kilgour recruited three people. Fred Deveny, who had come to the bank from a brokerage house, was their logistics expert. Dave Alessio was an accountant and actuary whose myopic eyes shone with pleasure behind his thick glasses only when he had spread before him financial tables and reports, which he read like so many magazine articles. And from International, like Kilgour himself, was Ray LaRocca.

LaRocca had been a finance major at Northeastern and had a master's in operations research from B.U. A dark-skinned, dark-haired Italian from South Boston, he had brown eyes and a prominent, proud Roman nose. He was a quiet man, but his nervous manner and busy silences betrayed him. When LaRocca talked, he illustrated everything in diagrams, word fragments, dotted lines and arrows, his gold Cross pen moving skittishly across the paper. The son of a shoemaker whom he visited regularly, he made no bones about his intention to rise far above his origins. His nervousness made him seem forever poised on the edge of flight, as though he felt the past at his back.

From business school he had gone to a synthetic leather plant — shades of his father — where he learned financial control from the whiz-kid technocrats who ran the Finance Department and operations techniques from the men who managed the assembly lines. From there he went to GlobeBank. He was proud of working for a powerful bank, of working his way up from the position of an analyst in International to a key staff position.

The team met daily at seven A.M. Kilgour would ask each of the three men to report on the previous day's events and raise any issues that had come up. If there was nothing to report, they met anyway, for the discipline. Two assistants, management trainees, made sure there was plenty of coffee and croissants from the Brasserie.

"I've gone over your separate assignments with each of you," Kilgour had said on the first day, "and outlined what I expect this team to accomplish. Let me say it now to you as a group. Since operations is where the fat is, our task is to study operations in each of the sectors. This means, as we all know, that we have to understand the current situation down to the micro level. For each division within a sector, for each group within a division, for each operations desk in the group, each transaction at that desk. Down to the penny. We are going to know how the transactions are processed from the moment they come in the door and how much each step costs.

38

"If you have a problem getting close to anybody's area, remind him that we report to Hardesty. The chairman's Task Force on Accounting and Operations Control. Hardesty's name will open doors. Use it. Also, if you have trouble with anyone, let me know. You should understand that I intend to report weekly to Archie Dale on how we're doing as a group" — he looked around — "and how you are doing individually."

He smiled, tight-lipped, and looked again at his team. At Alessio, squinting through his glasses; at Deveny, his arms crossed, rocking slightly back and forth; at LaRocca, drawing lines and arrows across his pad.

The Four Horsemen, as the trainees quickly dubbed them, seemed to be everywhere. They went to meetings, talked to clerks, hovered over operations managers and operations heads. They went from building to building, from floor to floor. They ate lunch at odd desks or in the company cafeteria, talking to clerks. At the end of each day, they put all the facts together in files and notebooks, ready for the seven o'clock meeting.

They stayed late. But Kilgour stayed latest of all.

More than any of the others, he kept at it, talking to the people, asking amiably if he might pull up a chair and observe them at their work. The clerks were nervous but flattered as he asked questions and watched them clip papers together, fill out forms, answer calls from customers. "What are you doing now?" he would ask. "What does that stamp say? Why did you call for the credit file? What's next?"

He tried to be one of the boys when he was on the floor. Sometimes at the end of a day he would stay to help reduce the backlog. Jacket off, shirtsleeves rolled up, he learned operations at the ground level.

Often, when he had stayed late, he would take one of the clerks out for a drink. "Let's go celebrate," he would say, "now that we've whittled down your In basket so it won't topple over." He'd take them to the bar at the Summit — they seemed to like it there — and ask questions about their children, about their commute, and laugh at their jokes. And, always, he talked about the work.

Only LaRocca came close to Kilgour in stamina. One night, after Kilgour had put an exhausted and slightly drunk clerk in a cab to the Bronx with three ten-dollar bills in his hand, he went back to the office to make notes on what he had learned. He found LaRocca in the conference room, bent over papers on the long table, his gold pen held like a cigarette between thumb and forefinger.

"Still at it, Ray?" Kilgour sat down and reached inside his breast pocket for a cigar. He offered the case to LaRocca, who shook his head.

"No, thanks."

"What are you working on?" Kilgour asked between the short sucking sounds of lighting the Don Diego.

LaRocca leaned back. "Funds transfers. A mess." Kilgour saw that LaRocca had covered the pad with branches of lines and arrows, like a great family tree.

"There's no pattern," LaRocca said quietly. "Not a damn thing. The procedures are chaotic, ridiculous. I can't imagine how anything gets done. The cost figures obviously show it. More volume, more clerks. That's all we know. Bring them in, put them wherever there's room, shoot them at the work. Somehow they do it." LaRocca wrote "somehow" on the pad. "Look at this."

He opened a file folder and pulled out a piece of paper. It looked like a floor plan. "I followed a single transfer today. An easy one. From our Paris branch, to transfer an amount from the customer's New York account to a correspondent bank of ours in Montreal. Simple, right? But look at this, John — I mean, look at this."

Kilgour looked down at the paper.

"The instructions come in the door and go to a desk on the sixth floor. International Sector, Europe Division, French Group. OK so far."

LaRocca was using his pen as a pointer.

"The clerk at the sixth-floor desk does screening and receipt. Then she sends it down to five for translation. Why five? Because the clerk knows — she told me this — that the best French translator at the bank happens to sit in the back office for the Canada Group, which happens to be part of the North American Division, which happens to be in the National Sector. She just *happens* to know him; she's lucky."

LaRocca's voice got shrill. He was talking quickly.

"Back to six. To the original clerk. She generates the debit and credit tickets and the customer and beneficiary advices. OK. Then copy up to nine for encoding and to ten for input to the computer. Then back to nine for reading and sort. After that, back to the original clerk on six for reconcilement and dispatch, with a copy to the twenty-ninth-floor data center for capture on the on-us tape. And then down to the mailroom in the basement." He shook his head. "Crazy."

"I know," Kilgour said. "It's the same in letters of credit; it's the same in the branch work."

"How many miles a day do you think the pages actually walk? It would be an interesting figure." LaRocca wrote "m/day" on his pad, remembering the young girls, many of them still in high school, who wore the orange GlobeBank page's uniform and carried mail from floor to floor. Some of them attended in-house classes and eventually were turned into secretaries. President Pruitt's secretary had started as a page.

"And that isn't even the end of it," LaRocca went on. "Because I've been there when the customers call. The account officers put them right through to the clerks, saying they'll know the answers to their questions. What are the questions? The usual questions. Most of the time, their questions amount to 'What's the status of my transfer?' or something like that. Big deal, right? But typically, the clerk has to tell them she'll call back, then get up and race around all those different floors, chasing it down. I went with one of them today. We took about eight different elevator rides, John. Crazy." LaRocca leaned back and threw his pen down on the table.

"I know, Ray. It's bad," Kilgour said, looking over the diagram, cigar in hand. "Can you imagine what your synthetic leather plant would have been like if the assembly line had been on thirty different floors? If they had to have messengers with chemicals and grommets and metal fittings running up and down elevators all day so you could crank out one pocketbook and one belt and one shoe?"

LaRocca shook his head.

"But that's it, Ray. Don't you see?" Kilgour clasped his hands on the table. "Is there really that big a difference?"

41

"What do you mean?"

"What I see is a manufacturing plant. People always think of banks as godlike, abstract institutions. Well, they're not. You and I both know it. Especially in the back office. What we've got here is not a clerical operation exactly, and certainly not a temple of Money with a capital M and Investments with a capital I. That's just how it looks to the outside world. What we've got here is a manufacturing plant."

LaRocca nodded, biting his lower lip. He pulled the pad closer and started taking notes.

"And the transactions are products," Kilgour went on. He was warming to the speech he had been rehearsing in his mind for months. He had already decided that LaRocca was going to be his chief man in whatever he got out of this. And he expected to get a lot. Ray LaRocca was a hard worker — and a very loyal man.

"There's a loan product, there's a letter of credit product, a check product. The customer asks for a service, thinks he's getting a service. But what we really deliver is a product.

"When you produce products," he said, "you should do it along product lines. The old Henry Ford number. Industry learned that a long time ago. A product line for each separate product. Just like shoes." He watched as LaRocca winced. "Just like Fords. Just like lathes.

"The problem we've got, Ray, is that floor plan you drew. That's no straight line. You couldn't make a goddamned corkscrew that way." He sucked on his cigar. "We've got to have straight-line processing. Not a goddamned flow that goes all over the place."

LaRocca nodded briskly. "How are you going to do it?"

"Get our own building. Put the whole back office in there, line them up straight by product. We'll have to cost it out, Ray, but I'm betting that what we save on labor will more than cover the rental of eighteen, twenty floors somewhere."

LaRocca's expression reminded Kilgour of his daughters' look when they were small and he had taught them how to tell time. Grave, attentive, unsmiling. "But how are you going to *do* it?" LaRocca insisted.

"Go right to Pruitt and Hardesty. Give them a plan for a

wholly new sector, an Operations Sector, in its own building.

"Look at it this way," he went on. "There are all these operations functions scattered all over the bank. And it's all called the back office. As if it were a single structure, a single entity. But it isn't. And there's no single management over it. And the flows go all over the goddamned place. It's like a" — Kilgour groped for an image — "like a river," he said finally. "Like a great big river. And all the transactions get poured in to make their way downstream somehow. Whatever kinds of transactions they are, wherever they come from, they're just dumped in — from here, from there, upstream, downstream, all around."

LaRocca grasped at the image. "And if a log gets thrown across the stream — if someone takes a sick day or goes on vacation — the whole river backs up. A flood." LaRocca drew two parallel lines on his pad and put a slash mark across them.

"Exactly." Kilgour nodded. "That's when we drown. Someone comes back from vacation and he has to run like hell to catch up. He never really does. He's always running, always on a treadmill. And even if that person *never* went on vacation, we'd still drown. Suppose the encoding room is understaffed. That happened last week; remember, I mentioned it at the meeting? Everything flowed along smoothly — or at least as smoothly as it could, given our crazy layout — until the stuff went up to encoding. *They* were slow. So every damn transaction in this big, powerful bank got held up." He stubbed the cigar out in the ashtray.

"And Ray, it's not like anyone can do anything about it, given the present chaos. The front-office guys are helpless. They've got a bunch of clerks they know personally, sort of, whom they rely on, and they're theoretically responsible for the pieces of paper those clerks push. So when things back up, when something gets lost, they blame the clerks. But the clerks say, 'Look, it's not us, it's the encoding room, or a machine at the data center is down, or Lucille is on vacation. What do you want from me?' What I'm saying, Ray, is that everyone's involved, but there's no control. A lousy situation. But I think I — the bank — can do something about it."

Kilgour took LaRocca's pad and started drawing as he spoke. "Straight lines. A straight product line from the customer's in-

43

structions to the final advice that goes back to the customer. A single line. A funds transfer line. A letter of credit line. And at the top of each line, a single manager. A single product line manager. We make him responsible for the whole transaction, but we give him control. We give him everything he needs. We give him a preprocessing function, a translator function, an encoding desk — his own encoding function — an accounting desk, an investigation desk. Everything but his own data center. That we can't do. Obviously. But everything else."

"That will do it," said LaRocca, looking at Kilgour's sketch. "Make the guy absolutely accountable for his line, for the whole product, from the minute it comes in the door till the minute it leaves. One hand-off and one only: to the computer."

"It's going to save us money, Ray. I know it is. Despite all the equipment we'll need. You know why? Because we replace the people with machines. That's the key. The technology continues to get better, but the people are always lousy, they always make mistakes. We'll have to automate over time, knock off some human heads and install machines instead. But first" — Kilgour smiled — "first, we get control. And to do that, we linearize, lines across the environment."

"That's the sequence." LaRocca began quickly to tick off the items on his fingers. "I get it." He reached for his pad from Kilgour. "Linearize to get control. See where the financial fat is and start cutting away. Find out exactly what we're doing. Once we know, we can manipulate. We can streamline. Knock heads. Consolidate functions. Give the Lucilles of this world two simple tasks. Then three. Then ten. Then, when the technology gets developed, put all of Lucille's functions into the machine and get rid of her. John, I'll bet we can get flat costs the first year we do this program. Maybe keep them flat until we're really ready to bring them down."

Kilgour brought his fist down hard on the conference table. "Exactly, Ray. You think we should commit to Charlie and Toby on that?"

LaRocca shrugged. "The man who runs the new Operations Sector, if they buy it, will make commitments. You make recommendations. But, well" — he looked hard at Kilgour — "I'll go along with whatever you recommend."

Kilgour smiled. LaRocca was smart. He understood what was between the lines as well as what was on them. "Let's see what we can do," he said.

◇ ◇ ◇

At the morning meeting, Kilgour announced that they were ready to start their analysis. LaRocca was going to finish up the loose ends of the operational details. The others were to hand him all their notes and work papers. LaRocca no longer came regularly to the morning meetings, but he surfaced occasionally to send one or the other of the assistants on complicated errands — to get floor plans, information on the latest technology in envelope-stuffing machines, data on new, mechanized filing systems. His real assignment was to design assembly lines for GlobeBank operations.

Kilgour seldom walked the floors anymore. He was usually in meetings with account people from the sectors or with group and sector heads or even with the managers of single accounts. He prodded them: What kind of service were they looking for? What were their complaints? What did they depend on?

One day Kilgour had lunch with Dick Chatwin of Chatwin and Dant, the most influential market researchers in the financial industry. Over veal *francese* at Giambelli, Kilgour hired Chatwin to do a poll for him, to rate the leading American banks in terms of overall service quality. To Kilgour's delight, GlobeBank came in seventh in the Overall column. In some of the specifics, it came in dead last.

After he got Chatwin's results, Kilgour held a seven o'clock meeting for the first time in over a week. It was short. "Crash time," Kilgour announced. "I go to Hardesty and Pruitt three weeks from today. Let's get those reports produced."

The conference room quickly took on the look of a publishing house. Two temps were hired. Everyone was frantically busy — writing, rewriting, proofreading, Xeroxing, re-Xeroxing. The assistants joked that nobody would ever again vacation in Maine because all the forests would be bare.

A graphics firm was hired to do the charts. The conference table was covered with open looseleaf binders; the assistants were responsible for monitoring the contents. Seven sections, twenty-two schedules, seven graphics. They punched holes, prepared tables, and hounded the typists and the chartmakers for corrections. Small crises made tempers flare. One page was punched and inserted upside down; a proofreader spotted it. Kilgour was icy for several hours, and everyone triple-checked all the other pages. The Xerox machine broke down twice and the secretaries had to wheedle time on other machines.

Finally it was over. The day arrived when Kilgour carried into a meeting with Hardesty and Pruitt four shiny looseleaf binders, a manila folder containing LaRocca's separate sixteen-page report, and a business envelope from Chatwin and Dant, with its conclusions.

The meeting started with the usual amenities. John Kilgour believed that Hardesty and Pruitt owed their jobs in large measure to their affability. A uniformed waiter served coffee in the fine porcelain stamped with GlobeBank logos. Kilgour ate a Danish. Hardesty said at last, "Well, John, you've got a lot of paper here. Let's get started."

Kilgour pushed one binder over to Hardesty, one to Pruitt, and one to Archie Dale, who was invited as a courtesy. "Charlie, Toby," he began, "Archie, I can read over these books with you if you like, but I think that would be a waste of time. The books are clear. They tell you that we have an outdated accounting system and they recommend a better one, a very good one, tailored to the business needs that the Executive Committee laid out in the strategic plan. The books also tell you that we have no consistent MIS system, and they recommend a very sophisticated but simple-to-use one that I believe will capture the right data for the right level within the corporation in the right way." Kilgour paused and sipped his coffee. "That means that at your level, you'll see only the data you need to do your jobs. The vice president running the Paper Industry Group in the Midwest Division and the account manager handling four customers in the Petrochemical Group of the French Division see only the data each of them needs, and none of you has to be bothered with a lot of extraneous detail.

"The recommendations are based on the facts we've culled and on an analysis of those facts, which is Part One of the book. They are the work of my staff, and frankly, I think those guys did a hell of an outstanding job. I hope you'll decide to implement the systems we've recommended."

Kilgour took a breath. This was it. "But even if you do, it won't do a damn thing for GlobeBank if you don't do something else at the same time."

Hardesty's eyes widened slightly. Pruitt leaned into the conference table. He smiled. "What have you got to say, John?"

Kilgour opened the binder in front of him. "I'll direct your attention to Part One, Section Two, page one, the first bullet. And I quote:

'Operating expense figures in this institution are typically buried in the front-office budget of each lending department. GlobeBank has never isolated out the cost of processing transactions from its other operating costs. Our team has achieved this breakdown, and our analysis reveals that since 1960, the actual costs for processing transactions, independent of other operating expenses, have risen at the rate of 17 percent a year. With GlobeBank growing at 14 percent a year, this trend represents a potentially significant adverse impact on bottom-line profitability over time.' End quote."

"Well, well!" Hardesty said.

And Pruitt: "How do you get a figure like that, John? How do you get that 17 percent?"

"With all due respect, Toby, it was easy. We just counted it up. We looked at the costs of literally every operation, every part of every operation, and this is in fact what it's costing us." He paused. "And there's something else."

At that moment, the phone on the conference table buzzed. It was Hardesty's special line for urgent calls. "Yes, Helen?" the chairman said.

"It's Rosenfeld."

"Excuse me, John. An irate customer."

John Kilgour later joked that Hardesty's call had made him believe in God all over again. He listened as his boss tried to soothe the president of one of the city's biggest brokerage houses. Hardesty winked at Kilgour as he told Rosenfeld, "Phil, I'm sorry as hell your statements are late. I'll deal with it personally right away. And Phil, let's have lunch soon. Regards to Pearl."

Hardesty buzzed Helen and told her to "put Nichols on it."

"Rosenfeld's an excitable little Jew," he explained to the group, "but he runs a hell of a business, and we want to keep him. Go on, John. You were saying there was something else."

"Actually, Charlie, the something else is just what that phone call was about. Service. Twentieth-century service." Kilgour pulled out the white envelope.

It was nearly six o'clock when the meeting ended. The others would have to wait until tomorrow morning to hear the news. Let them anticipate it, Kilgour thought. By anyone's standards it had been a good day's work. He put in his attaché case the contract giving him absolute authority over all GlobeBank operations. A big budget. The promotion to senior vice president. He would form a new sector, the Banking Operations Sector. It's going to be called BOS, he thought. I wonder how many jokes are going to be made about that before the name just seems to sink into the language? He was very tired, but elated. Call Sally and see if she'd like to drive somewhere for dinner. Celebrate.

GlobeBank immediately negotiated to buy the two-year-old, twenty-eight-story office building at 176 Wall Street. Kilgour showed his staff the floor plans and told them to begin planning the move of all GlobeBank operations. "We have a unique opportunity here. We can lay things out from scratch, from the walls in. Some plants make washing machines or cars. We make letters of credit or canceled checks. But the principle is the same. You set up an assembly line. Break the processing into separate tasks, easy tasks. Specialization of labor — that's what we're aiming for."

He leaned back in his big leather chair. "Right now we're in the nineteenth century. Before the Industrial Revolution. We may look like a big bank, but we're really a village market. Ten years from now I expect us to be in the twenty-first century. Ray will give you your assignments."

All of them worked hard, although the effort seemed to flow from LaRocca. He was designing a linearized transaction, laying out processing steps, specifying how many people and how many and what kind of machines he needed. The others became architects, movers, purchasing agents. They allotted space in the new building, chose and contracted for furniture and partitions, planned the logistics of the move. And as soon as a floor was filled on paper, they began to fill it in reality.

Slowly, people began to notice that Head Office was full of breathing space, elbow room.

LaRocca's linearization plans came faster than the others could make them happen. He had gotten the hang of it.

First he defined the product: checks, for example. In a single day, GlobeBank processed two million checks, give or take a few, a stack as tall as a Manhattan skyscraper. LaRocca separated all the checks used by individual customers from those used by businesses. He broke down the individuals' checks by borough — checks from the Manhattan branches, from Queens, the Bronx, Brooklyn, Staten Island. Then he divided each borough into regions. For Manhattan he did the split by neighborhood; it was the way people thought of the city. So there was a Lower Manhattan region, an Upper East Side region, Greenwich Village, Washington Heights — all the others. A region's checks were broken down further into sets of accounts: 8001–12000, 12001–16000, and on up.

Within each set of accounts, he decided what volume each line should handle. So the lowest common denominator for all customer checking was a certain number of checks from a specific set of accounts from one region of one borough.

This lowest common denominator, a small molecular cluster of the enormous total of customer checks, became a "line" at 176 Wall Street.

And the line *was* an assembly line, a series of endlessly repeated tasks. If it took ten separate activities to process a check, then the line had ten positions, each with one or more clerks. The pattern was standard: Receive. Record. Sort. Wire. Encode. Read to tape. Post. Dispatch advice. Over and over again, until all the transactions had been moved down the line.

Even the layout of the floor echoed the litany. LaRocca and Deveny had thought of having separate spaces for the separate steps. So Receive had one room, Record the next, Sort the next. Each room had its own Mr. Coffee machine, surrounded by little towers of paper cups and containers of sugar and coffee lightener. The rooms were lined up in the standard pattern and connected by windows. Every fifteen minutes or so, the clerks "batched" the papers and put them in baskets on the window-sill.

Alessio, the numbers man, was in charge of the functional transfers that brought the people and equipment to their new jobs. If two clerks were removed from the National Sector, Northeast Division, Petrochemicals Industry Group, the cost of those clerks — their salaries, fringe benefits, and other over-head — had to be transferred from the National Sector to the new Banking Operations Sector being created at 176 Wall. Equipment had to be moved or purchased. ECs, Expense Categories, had to be set up to match the organization LaRocca was designing. Alessio was creating a new quantitative model for BOS, and he loved it.

Deveny headed up the overall coordination. LaRocca was the planner, Alessio, the accountant, but Deveny made it all real. "You guys do it all on paper," he would chide the others, "but I've got to deal with real people, real machines, and real space in a real building. Slow down, will you?"

They didn't slow down, and Deveny managed. He managed to get the right clerk to the right task in the right line at the right time. He managed to get the clerk trained. He saw to it that a line was complete — in planning, equipment, and in dollars — before a single transaction started its way down.

Linearization. A brilliant concept. Utterly simple. But John Kilgour had to rip the back office to shreds in order to make it work.

The hours began to be brutal. Wives complained. "I never see you; the children never see you," they said.

But Kilgour made it clear that he wasn't interested in anyone who was "soft"; he meant anyone whose attention wasn't un-swervingly on the project at hand. *His* wife never complained; she kept herself busy with her work for the hospital and her li-brary fund drives. Wives, he would have said if he had thought about it at all, shared their husbands' goals as they shared in the material rewards. And with no whining.

So the men who were creating GlobeBank's Banking Operations Sector kept to the long hours their boss expected. And the truth was that they loved it. The commuters learned the late train schedules and got used to the bleak and shabby look of Penn Station and Grand Central at ten and eleven o'clock at night. Often they stayed overnight at a hotel. They kept fresh shirts and shaving gear in their desks.

More staff was hired: management staff; a new kind of manager for GlobeBank. In another era, many of them would never have dreamed of seeing the boardrooms and offices of any bank. They were second-generation Italian and Irish, born in the Bronx and raised on Long Island, boys who were thick in the chest from pasta, beer, and high school football. In colleges near home, they had majored in business. They had gone on to business school at St. John's or Fordham, working at jobs during the day, nodding over their books long after midnight on the subway back to Queens. There they shared one-bedroom apartments with the girls they had met in their senior year and married after graduation. After business school, when the Globe-Bank job was lined up, the wives became pregnant. They were hungry, and Kilgour liked that. They considered themselves lucky to be at GlobeBank. They were prepared to work hard for the promised rewards.

Some of the other new managers were cut from a more traditional cloth and arrived at GlobeBank in a more traditional way. But despite their credentials and tailoring, they too were a new breed of manager. In a way, they were like Kilgour, smooth and well connected. In another way, they were like LaRocca, impatient and hard. At Harvard Business School, at Stanford, at Wharton, they had known all along that they would choose GlobeBank; there was never any question about GlobeBank choosing them. But they were going to choose their own Globe-Bank, not the one that might have satisfied their fathers. They were not going to be content with the entry-level trainee job based on a degree in international finance, with the regular two-year stints in approved slots, with the predictable vice presidency at forty. They wanted the vice presidency at thirty or at twenty-five. If that meant a little dirty work for a few years, they were not unwilling to soil their well-manicured hands — even if it meant taking orders from Ray LaRocca.

51

The very top line of managers was hand-picked by John Kilgour, and he didn't look for them in the classroom. Instead, he plucked them from other companies at inflated prices. They had already proved themselves in manufacturing trucks, or cans, or steel. They already knew how to streamline operations and cut costs. Only a new jargon had to be learned: Linearize. Knock heads. Automate with computers.

And the nickname, Killer Kilgour, picturesque and appropriate. Kilgour and his men, his breed of tough guys new to banking, went about their business like executioners.

Over the next five years, 60 percent of the ten thousand employees at GlobeBank became "extraneous": if they couldn't be placed elsewhere in the bank — and most couldn't — they "went away," as Kilgour's men put it. Of the four thousand who were left, only thirty-one hundred performed clerical jobs. The rest were the new breed, all fiercely loyal to Kilgour and formed to his mold. In those five years, operations costs remained flat. And John Roland Kilgour was rewarded.

MEMO TO: All GlobeBank Officers and Professionals
FROM: Charles Hardesty, Chairman of the Board of Directors
RE: BOS Reorganization

It gave me great personal pleasure to announce to our stockholders at last week's annual meeting that the institution's operating expenses were flat for the fifth year in a row. As you know, this remarkable achievement is due to the Banking Operations Sector's efforts and to that organization's fine management team.

I am very pleased, therefore, to announce the following new appointments. Raymond T. LaRocca, formerly chief controller for BOS, is named senior vice president of the corporation, effective today, and moves from the controllership to a new assignment as head of the Transfers Division in BOS.

Also named BOS division heads are: Frederick L. J. Deveny, head of the Trade Operations Division; David J. Alessio, head of the Demand Deposit Accounts (1) Division; and Thomas R. Randall, head of the Demand Deposit Accounts (2) Division. Frank R. Phillips, a vice president, has been named BOS chief controller.

In addition, I am very gratified to announce that the Board of Directors has also approved the appointment of John R. Kilgour as executive vice president of the Global Bank Corporation. The

Executive Committee welcomes John to the team, confident that he will be an extremely valuable addition to the institution's policy-making body.

I know all of you join with me in wishing the very best to John, Ray, Fred, Dave, Tom, and Frank.

C. M. Hardesty
Chairman

The BOS organization chart was attached to the memo.

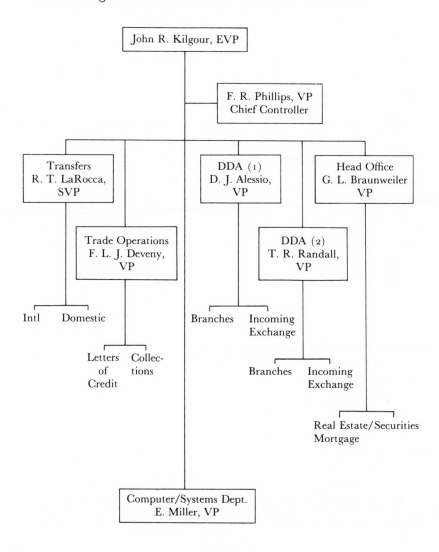

6

THE TAXI CARRYING LISA GOULD stopped in front of the GlobeBank tower, standing tall among the forest of skyscrapers that lined Park Avenue from Grand Central to Fifty-ninth Street. Corporate headquarters for one of the most powerful institutions on earth, the building was virtually anonymous. Its smooth face of stone, steel, and tinted glass gave no hint of the activity within. Only a modest sign, etched into the glass above the center set of revolving doors, gave away the mystery: Global Bank Corporation. The three words were set in a pale orange color. Quietly. But then, Lisa reflected as she flashed her I.D. and stepped into the wood-paneled elevator, no noise was needed in the case of GlobeBank.

It was what it was: the fastest, fattest, smartest bank in the world. "We are first with the best," Charlie Hardesty liked to say when he opened stockholders' meetings. "We like being first and we like being best, and we intend to continue to be both." Lisa sometimes thought about Charlie Hardesty up there in his enormous office on the thirtieth floor, which the chairman shared only with Ronald Dobelle, his very private secretary, with Toby Pruitt, with a platoon of typists and administrative assistants, and with three armed guards. She had been on thirty twice: once when Pruitt had asked her to represent her area in a meeting with him and Hardesty, and once for a special cocktail party hosted by the chairman and president for the secretary of commerce. She had glanced into Hardesty's office on both occasions and had decided then that she would like to sit there someday.

◊ ◊ ◊

Until she was in her third year of college, Lisa had wanted to be a doctor, "like Daddy," an obstetrician in Westchester County. Harold Gould sometimes took his little daughter to his office when he had paperwork to do and no patients to see. She would dress up in one of his white lab jackets, the sleeves rolled up, the hem hobbling her around the ankles. Sometimes she would bring along a doll and examine it gravely, her father's stethoscope dangling from her neck.

By the time she was in junior high school, she realized that New Rochelle was not at the center of the universe and that her tired, kind, ironic father with the pepper-and-salt mustache was not the medical profession's shining glory. Still, she wanted to be a doctor. She was a serious student, always prepared for tests, always ready with her homework. Her friends used to tease her, a little spitefully, because her term papers were always ready days before they were due. She got A's in biology, chemistry, and physics.

Her mother made sure that she was dressed well and that her adolescent acne was looked at by "the biggest dermatologist" so it would not "ruin her chances." Lisa was pretty enough and popular enough. She knew that grades alone would not get her into the best colleges, and she pursued the right assortment of extracurricular interests: She was president of the French Club and picture editor of the yearbook; she even sang Yum-Yum in the school production of *The Mikado*.

When the time came, Lisa applied to Vassar, Smith, Bryn Mawr, and Mount Holyoke, which was her first choice. On her application, she said the reason was its excellent reputation in the sciences, but the real reason was that she met a young female colleague of her father's at the hospital one day and she thought that the lady was very nice. They had a cup of coffee together while Lisa was waiting for her father. When the conversation turned, as it always did those days, to "Where do you plan to go to college?" and young Dr. Lauren Hickok mentioned that she had graduated from Mount Holyoke, Lisa felt a sudden determination to go there as well.

In April she was accepted everywhere except, strangely, at Vassar. Years later, when she had two or three Vassar alumnae on her staff, she always wondered whether her attitude toward them was colored in any way by the slightly miffed feeling Vassar always evoked in her.

Her science grades at Mount Holyoke were not as uniformly impressive as they had been in New Rochelle. Lisa realized that the good colleges were full of pretty, smart, ambitious young women who were just as eager to get to medical school as she was. But Lisa wanted to shine. She had always shone. By the end of her sophomore year, she realized that she would not shine in medical school, and for the first time in her life she considered what else she might do.

Spring in South Hadley was no time for decision-making. The old apple orchard on the campus bloomed into thousands of perfumed puffs. Lisa and her friends would amble down the hill to the Connecticut River to watch it rolling into the misty distance or paddle around the weedy campus lake in canoes. Sometimes, when the weather was very fine, they would take their books down to the town graveyard and study among the friendly spirits of Massachusetts farmers long deceased. Lisa was courted that spring by an Amherst junior, a history major from Bloomington, Indiana, with a passion for John Adams. He called Lisa "Abigail" and told her she was beautiful. They made love on Saturday nights in her dormitory room while her roommate was similarly occupied at nearby Hampshire College.

That summer she shared a sublet in Manhattan with three college friends. All four registered with a temp agency and filled in for vacationing secretaries and administrative assistants. All spring, Marge Gould did her best to discourage Lisa by sending her clippings about street crime in New York and the expense of housing. "Why can't you stay in your lovely room, in your own home, and be taken care of?" she asked. But Lisa was excited about being on her own, and insisted.

Her second assignment that summer was a three-week stint at Citibank, as secretary to a vice president in International Operations. Lisa was suddenly thrown into the heady atmosphere of international funds transfers, letters of credit for huge amounts, the sureness and determination of decision-making at the senior level. Her boss liked her and immediately assigned her administrative tasks, which she handled smoothly. Since his wife and children were out in Amagansett for the summer, he flirted with her over drinks at the Four Seasons and took her to little dinners at La Cocotte. He told her that she showed talent, she had promise. And he suggested that she look into graduate school in business when she graduated. "Go for an M.B.A.," he advised over Bloody Marys. Lisa felt herself shining again. It felt good, and she determined that her future would not be spent in the corridors of a hospital but in the corridors of a corporation. One sultry night, her boss locked the door of his corner office against any intrusion by the cleaning lady and made love to Lisa on his long beige couch. He smelled of Aramis and perspired profusely. While they were making love, Lisa fantasized about having an office just like the one she was in, all light woods and nubbly fabrics.

In the fall she received a few postcards from him, but she never replied. She changed her major to economics, with a minor in history, and studied harder than ever, especially for her statistics courses. Numbers came hard to Lisa, but the aesthetics of economics and history thrilled her — the ebbs and flows of prosperity, the moving of money, the manipulations, the changes in the public mood, the inexorable push into the future. She ran for student government president and won. Other students started coming to her for small favors, and she realized that she had acquired a modest amount of power.

The following summer, before her senior year, Lisa worked for a brokerage firm that hired promising undergraduates in the hope of attracting a few of them to the firm after graduation. She capitulated to her mother's pleas that she live at home, assuming it was the last time.

Her senior year was a triumph. She was elected to Phi Beta Kappa and accepted by the three business schools to which she had applied. She chose Stanford over Wharton and Harvard, partly because she thought it would be exciting to try a few years in California, but more because she had read an article that called Stanford "the business school that impressed boardrooms most — more now, even, than Harvard."

As a graduation present, her parents gave Lisa a summer in Paris. She stayed with a college friend, Constance Moret, whose father, an official in the French government, was willing to let "two mademoiselles" share his empty pied-à-terre on the Right Bank. That summer stamped forever on Lisa's mind the idea of pleasant idleness. She wandered up and down the streets of Paris, continually startled by tableaux shockingly familiar from her art history classes at Mount Holyoke. She and Constance were teasingly squired about all summer by two students from the University of Iowa, who, like them, were spending three months in Paris and, like Lisa, were delighted by everything and not afraid of being trite. They went to the top of the Eiffel Tower, took the boat ride on the Seine, and drank wine in sidewalk cafés.

Lisa's bedroom, when she came home from Paris, was full of boxes and bags from Saks, Lord & Taylor, Bloomingdale's, and Bergdorf Goodman — "almost," Lisa complained, "like a goddamned hope chest." Her mother had decided that the perfect California wardrobe included half a dozen silk shirts, velvet jeans in black, burgundy, and midnight blue, three Charlotte Ford suits ("for professional meetings"), and four Evan Picone skirts. She had also bought Lisa seven sets of matched John Kloss undergarments, one for each day of the week (like the panties I had as a little girl, with "Monday," "Tuesday," and "Wednesday" on them, Lisa thought, half-amused), and three long cotton nightgowns deemed suitable for dormitory life. "You're not going to have enough time to take care of yourself, you'll be so busy learning to be an executive," Marge Gould said.

Marge and Harold Gould drove Lisa to Kennedy Airport, three Wings suitcases in the trunk of the car. Lisa's mother smiled stiffly as they sat in the boarding lounge and wept a little when she kissed Lisa good-bye. "Don't forget you have parents," her father called out as Lisa rose to board the plane.

◇ ◇ ◇

Lisa's first impression of Palo Alto was that she had fallen into a Parisian flower bed and was looking up at the cobalt blue sky through profusions of blossoms. Her idea of a campus, formed by South Hadley and New England winters, had not prepared her for the golden shock of California. The long line of palms on Stanford's main street, the odors, the brilliant contrasts of light and shadow, all left her with a sense of excitement and possibility. In California, anything could happen.

This excitement carried over to her classes. Lisa was satisfied in a wholly new way. She felt that she had found her niche. She shone. There was something in the way people looked at her, at the respect she was given in class, even by the faculty. Some days she virtually took over the discussion; she seemed to know everything, to ask all the right questions. She felt heady as power flooded into her fingertips like electric current in the vivid California air.

◇ ◇ ◇

Marge Gould called her daughter twice a week, on Wednesday nights and Sunday mornings. The night calls came at around eight, just after eleven New York time, when the rates went down. "Why throw away hard-earned money?" she would say.

"Hello, darling, how are you?"

"Fine. Really OK."

"How's school? Are you being brilliant?"

"Oh sure."

"Are you eating enough, sleeping enough? Do you take the vitamins I sent you? Libby Rosen told me that her son at Harvard Medical School takes them."

"Yes, Ma."

"And how about the social life?" Marge Gould's voice would grow sly. "Is any handsome California man romancing my girl?"

"Twelve or fifteen," Lisa would say. "All blonds. Listen, Ma, how are you? How's Daddy?"

"You know your father. That man is *so* dedicated, never thinks of himself."

Then would come the engagement and wedding announcements.

"Do you remember Denise Katzenbaum, who was in your nursery school? She got married; I ran into her mother in Saks. She married a lawyer for a big firm, a very nice boy." Or, another time: "Guess who's buying the house in Croton that Uncle Julius told us about? Barbara Resnick and her husband — you remember, the one who started at Yale and then went to Goddard to become a poet and now works for Exxon? They're expecting."

"Yes, Ma. Yes, Ma. Yes, Ma," Lisa would say patiently.

One day in November, she was sitting in the Union poring over a marketing text, a tall glass of orange juice at her elbow. Outside, students were riding bikes, jogging, tossing Frisbees back and forth. But Lisa had a paper to do for 240, Marketing

Management. When someone sat down across the table from her, Lisa looked up for a moment. Next to the stranger's tray was a stack of oversize art books, large and glossy. Behind the stack Lisa saw a faded blue workshirt and, as her eyes moved up, a dark beard, a straight, prominent nose on a bony face, light-colored eyes, and masses of glossy brown hair curling over his ears and down the back of his neck. The stranger smiled.

"It looks like a coffee table, doesn't it? With all these coffee table books? But I've never actually seen a coffee table with coffee on it." The stranger smiled again. "Hi, I'm Joe Barclay." He stretched out a long, slim hand.

"Lisa Gould. Hi."

"Am I interrupting? You seemed so absorbed."

"Yes, you are." Now Lisa smiled. "But it's time to quit anyway. I'm about cross-eyed."

"Are you an undergraduate? Wait a minute," he added hastily, "let me guess. You're a graduate student in, hmm . . ." He looked her up and down with exaggerated interest. "In linguistics."

"Not even close. I'm at the business school."

"Oh, my God," said Joe Barclay. "A budding lady executive."

"I'm surprised to hear you say that," said Lisa. "Don't you know that these days you don't say 'lady' anything except maybe 'lady' bug? Just 'executive' will do, thank you." She stood up and put her book into her canvas bag. "Good-bye, Joe Barclay," she said.

"Where are you off to?"

"Just the bookstore. I thought I might treat myself to a new ball-point pen."

"Just a second, I'll walk you over." He gulped down his coffee. "Let's go."

Josiah Pollitt Barclay was a visiting professor from Kenyon College, thirty-two years old, now teaching two studio courses and two art history courses. He was originally from a small town in Connecticut near the coast, where his ancestors for many generations had been ship's captains and merchants in the China trade. From them he had inherited a steely will and a strong, lean frame. Lisa fell in love with both. Three weeks after their walk to the bookstore she moved in with him.

The studio apartment in the Oak Creek complex near the medical school was small for the two of them. It came with a separate dressing room and a rectangular kitchen that looked over carefully groomed lawns and knolls. From the bed she could see banks of flowers around the steps leading to a small pool.

They often began the day there, cold in the early morning, running down the steps and diving in, shouting back and forth, coming out a few minutes later shaking drops of water from their hair and running back up to the apartment for coffee and rolls. Most days they were back before sunset to set off for Oak Creek's larger communal pool, a five-minute walk that they took wrapped in matching blue terrycloth robes. The big pool was heated to just below body temperature, but it felt cool after the hot Jacuzzi in which they boiled first.

Between their morning and evening swims they usually went in separate directions, each to class or to the library. Sometimes they would meet for lunch at the Oasis, looking at one another with desire over their hamburgers and beer.

In the evening Lisa would study, sitting in the dumpy black beanbag chair in front of the large window, while Joe sprawled on the bed, reading, sorting prints, making notes.

It was golden, just like California, until spring.

Joe had been married twice, first to a "fellow student named Anne Ash" and then, five years later, to a Japanese textile designer. That marriage had lasted for six years. Their child, Mariko, lived with her mother in Montreal.

He was as easy as a cat with women, languid and assured, and Lisa began to feel jealous. "This is nonsense," she would say to herself as she watched him at the Oasis with his arm around someone else, looking straight into the other woman's eyes and laughing. Misery washed over her. No matter how many times Lisa watched him or how many times she told herself it meant nothing, the pain was real. It drove her down like a nail into sullen silence. She wanted him to notice and comfort her. But even if he noticed, there was no comfort coming.

Lisa was not used to jealousy — or to any other loss of control. It bewildered her that she could neither keep herself in hand nor manage the events around her. Nothing had ever prepared her for losing. And she *was* losing, a little each day.

Joe liked everything to be easy, loose, free. With women he was a conquistador, not an administrator. Only new territories appealed to him. Once he had learned the terrain, he was bored and ready to move on. It was too instinctive with him to be considered deliberate cruelty, but the effects were cruel.

The more jealous and frightened Lisa became, the harder she clung to him. A cool, detached Lisa seemed to be looking down from a great distance at the panicky, red-eyed Lisa, the mewling, begging Lisa who struck poses, hoping that one of them would work. The Indignant Lady, high born and haughty, too proud to notice. The Big Kidder. Ha-ha. The Wimp. Lisa felt that the Wimp was the real face behind every mask. Pay attention to me. Love me. Look at me. Stay with me. If I get sick will he feel sorry for me, take me home, touch me? Am I prettier than, sexier than, more interesting than she, or she, or she? Lisa felt that she was sitting alone in a corner at every party. Joe, laughing, would always be hugging someone.

He was gone a lot. More and more, his absences were unpredictable. Each time, Lisa determined that when he finally walked through the door she would say, "Hi," just like that, and "Did you have a good day and are you hungry?" But when he actually walked in, she felt big lemony tears squeezing out of her eyes, and she heard the Wimp say, "Where were you? I was worried, I was alone." She knew she was disgusting, and that each time she drove him a little further away.

She would lie next to him in the dark, waiting for him to turn to her full of love and reassurance, but she only saw his back. Then she would try to sleep, lying on her side, looking unhappily at the back of his neck. Sometimes she woke up, groaning from one bad dream after another.

"What is it?" he would say. "What's the matter with you?"

"I had a bad dream." She would wait. "Hold me, Joe," she would say, "I'm scared."

"Easy, OK? Take it easy." He would cluck with exasperation.

"Put your arm around me." Her voice in the dark was small.

"Just a minute, will you?" He would go to the bathroom, putter into the kitchen for a drink, turn on a light, and sit up for a few minutes leafing through a book. When he finally came to bed, he would find her sobbing, thoughts running through her head: I hate him. I need him. I love him. I would hold *him* if he needed me.

"Where are you going, Joe?" she would ask, hating herself, when he went out after dinner.

"Why the hell are you so anxious? I don't understand these rules." Once he called her "adhesive." But sometimes he softened a little: "Don't worry, you know I love you."

Lisa allowed nothing to interfere with her work, and she threw herself more relentlessly than ever into her studies. But at home she could not recognize herself. After crying in the bathroom for an hour, two hours, sitting on the toilet, her face pressed into the toilet paper roll, she would finally get up and look at her swollen, blotched face in the mirror. Can this be me? she wondered.

She began to press Joe to marry her. "Are you kidding?" he would say. "I've been married twice already. Twice is enough. How many ex-wives do you want me to create?"

"But you've never been married to *me*," she would say, laughing woodenly. "What about me?"

Occasionally he didn't come home all night. At first he would tell her in advance: "Look, I've got this big project, don't worry, OK?" Later, he didn't bother. Once he drove into his parking space under the building at seven A.M. and found Lisa shivering, sitting on the concrete in her nightgown and a sweatshirt, her knees drawn up to her chin. "I told you not to worry, didn't I?" he said in a hard voice. But he took her upstairs and made tea for her.

Her mother sensed that something was wrong and called four or five times a week.

"Lisa, darling, how's my baby? How is Josiah?" she would ask.

Mrs. Gould hoped that Lisa did not realize how shocked she was that her daughter was living in sin. She realized that she was not being very modern, and she was sure she would feel differently if it were somebody else's daughter. But the idea that her Lisa shared a bed . . . well. She turned away from the thought.

"Are you eating enough or are you too worried about that glamorous California look?"

"I'm fine, Ma. OK, Ma. Everything's fine," Lisa said over and over. Her voice was tight, eroded by tears.

63

Her work took on an added brilliance. She was so sharp in class, answered so incisively, that some wag nicknamed her "the Gould digger." Her eyes felt baked, from studying and from crying. She knew that something was about to happen, and it did, a month before the end of the semester.

"Let's go out to dinner," said Joe. He put on a coat and tie — the only ones he owned — a worn Harris tweed coat and a bright orange tie. He looked marvelous, his hair glistening with chestnut highlights, his angular face handsome and severe. He took her to the Faculty Club.

Lisa had no appetite and came back from the buffet with a few olives and some three-bean salad. Why the Faculty Club? she thought. Why here? It's because he knows I can't cry or make a scene in a place like this.

"Not hungry?" he asked her cheerfully. He seemed in better spirits than he had for months. "Are you comfortable? Can I get you anything else? How about some wine?" She shook her head and tried to eat an olive.

"Well," said Joe, "I want to be honest with you, Lisa. You're an honest person, and we've had some wonderful times together. But this relationship is over. It's been over for a while." He waited for a few seconds for her to say something. "Well," he said. "Anyway, I think we both feel that when a relationship gets strung out past its natural time, it gets hollow, and both people suffer. I care too much about you, Lisa, to want that for you, or for me either." He smiled brilliantly and bit into a roll. "I think at this point it would be best if you looked around and found somewhere else to live. The term just has a couple of weeks, anyway. Maybe a friend from school . . ." He took another bite of his roll and buttered what was left. "I realize that this may cause you some financial problems . . ."

"Don't worry about my financial problems," she said. She sounded bitter. "If you want to worry about my problems, worry about the real ones."

"Well, anyway, I wanted you to know that I'm prepared to help tide you over." He took out his wallet. "You may have to spend a little time in a hotel or something." Lisa watched, dry-eyed, while he counted out two hundred dollars. Her mind raced. I don't believe this is happening. I can't believe it. Everything around her seemed to have slowed down. People were talking and laughing very slowly, as if they were underwater. The sounds came from far, far away. Lisa looked down at the table. A fifty, two twenties, some tens, some fives, some ones, all spread out. I'll take it, damn him. Damn him. Oh Joe. She got up to go to the Ladies' Room. The tears were coming, and they would never do in the Stanford University Faculty Club.

She spent her last night in Joe's apartment on the couch. Rectangles of light made by passing cars sailed across the ceiling all night long. The next morning she dragged her big suitcase out of the closet and packed her clothes — the velvet jeans she had never worn, the John Kloss underwear, the blue terrycloth robe Joe bought her for walking to the pool. She stuffed books all around the edges and put what was left into an empty liquor carton. Then she called a cab and went to the Tiki Motel, using the first of Joe's five-dollar bills to pay the cabbie.

◇ ◇ ◇

"Hello, Ma?" She called them from the motel that night.

"Lisa? Darling? Is everything all right?"

"Everything's fine, Ma. I just — "

Lisa heard her father's voice. "Marge? Is it Lisa? Let me speak." He picked up the phone. "What is it, sweetheart?"

"Oh, Daddy. I wish I were home." She looked at her watch. She had subtracted three hours instead of adding. "Oh, God, it's two-thirty. I'm sorry I woke you up, Daddy."

"It's OK, sweetheart, you know I never sleep much anyway." He tried to make a joke. "Always ready for one of my early A.M. babies." His voice was tender, solicitous. "Did something happen?"

"No. Well, yes, Daddy. Joe and I have split up." She took a breath. *Split up. That's a good one.* "I've moved out."

"Oh, sweetheart, oh, I see. Uh-huh. Yes. Well, where did you move to?"

"The Tiki. It's a motel." She started to cry.

"Don't, sweetheart, don't," her father said.

She heard him telling her mother, "They broke up. She's at a motel."

Marge Gould took back the phone.

"Lisa darling, don't worry, Daddy and I will take care of everything." She paused. "Is it a *nice* motel? Clean? Is there a decent restaurant?"

Oh my God, she thought. Even now. "Don't worry, Ma, I'm all right, I'll be fine. It was just a, well, you know, a shock. But I'm really fine, I'll be OK."

Lisa returned to New York and Citibank that summer as an intern. She was assigned to do a marketing survey on the feasibility of developing a preauthorized electronic payments system, which would be processed through a network of automated clearinghouses. It was an exciting project, and it suggested the paperless, cashless environment of the future, when people would be paid in electronic beeps. Lisa pictured oceans of numbers rolling up and down in accounts large and small all over the country. "I'll take this dress." Beep. "My account down by a hundred." Beep. "Saks' account up by a hundred." Beep. Beep.

She was too tired even to think of an apartment, so she lived at home. She felt, and was treated by her parents, as though she were recuperating from an illness. She felt somehow refined by it all, a little lighter than she had been, as though her spine had been pumped full of helium. Her mother or father was always waiting for the train at night; a hot meal was always waiting on the table. Outside of work, she saw few friends.

In September, she went back to Palo Alto. She wanted to live by herself, and with a stipend from her father ("Here's a little pin money for you; you don't have to mention this to Mommy"), she rented a small studio as far as possible from the Oak Creek complex and still within walking distance of the campus. Her life was monastic. She got out of bed every day at six, did the Canadian Air Force exercises, and ate breakfast — a cup of coffee, half a cup of cottage cheese, a slice of toast, and an orange. Then she went to class, returning home to a dinner as spartan as her breakfast. By the end of October, at just about the time people stopped inviting her out since she never accepted, Lisa was beginning to feel like herself. In the bookstore she ran into a classmate, Ann Hutchinson, who impulsively invited her to a party that Friday night. She accepted. "It absolutely floored me," Ann told her husband later over dinner.

66

Ann and Fred Hutchinson lived ten miles from Palo Alto under one of the approach patterns for the San Francisco airport. They were both students, she in Lisa's class and he at Stanford Law School. Their first year in California, they had supported themselves by living rent-free above a funeral home, taking calls for the funeral director at night. They hated the job, not because it was macabre or because they got depressed, but because someone always had to be near the phone. This year they had a little more money, saved from a summer waiting on tables at Yellowstone, and they felt lucky to have found a pleasant little house — even if it shook every few minutes and the planes seemed to fly directly through their living room.

Ann was tall, rangy, and red-headed — not pretty, but with a candid face that invited trust. Her husband, Fred, was a head shorter and madly in love with her. Lisa was glad to be invited to their party.

"The only problem," she told Ann on Wednesday over a shared tuna fish on toast at the Union, "is that I don't know how I'm going to get out there. I'm probably the only living soul in California who doesn't have a car. Is there a bus or something I could take?"

"Not to worry," said Ann. " There'll be several people driving. You can probably come out with Barry."

"Who's Barry?"

"Barry Berman. He's a classmate of Fred's. Nice guy. Funny. *Very* smart."

Barry Berman picked her up at five o'clock in front of her apartment. Exactly at five o'clock. Lisa had been standing downstairs, enjoying the air and the *swoosh, swoosh* of cars going by. October. She had a vague pang as she remembered the bright fall colors of New England and the East, and she was just trying to visualize the view from the top of Mount Tom when a voice said, "Hop in."

Hopping was out of the question. Barry drove an old and dirty two-seat Triumph into which one dropped, like a coin in a vending machine, and rode along tilted at a forty-five-degree angle. Thank you, Marge Gould, for the velvet slacks, thought Lisa, wondering how anyone in a skirt could have made that maneuver with any grace.

She studied the driver. Nice face. Not handsome. Pleasant.

Barry Berman, Lisa realized, was one of those young men whose tendency to get bald early only emphasizes how hairy they are. She was to learn later that it was almost arbitrary for Barry where he stopped shaving. He was fuzzy on his back, his chest, his arms. On important days he shaved twice, but still his cheeks were always bluish.

"You're a classmate of Ann's, aren't you?" he was saying. Lisa asked him how he knew Fred, how he liked law school. Conversation was easy. By the time they arrived at the Hutchinsons', she had learned that he had grown up in Brookline, Massachusetts, was an only child, had graduated from Harvard with a major in economics and a minor in French, and loved California but "not forever; it's too laid back, too smooth, too lacking in the sense of urgency that seems normal on the East Coast."

She teased him about his absurd little car. "It's a matchbox truck," he said, laughing. He had bought it for five hundred dollars plus his beat-up blue Chevy from a friend at Harvard whose wife had just had a baby and refused to ride in "that goddamned astronaut capsule."

The party was very pleasant, with most of it spent outdoors in the small backyard. Ann had set out big bowls of bulgar wheat with almonds, chicken stew, cucumbers in yogurt, a spinach, sprout, and walnut salad, an avocado and tomato salad, bean curd in brown sauce, seven-grain bread, and a grape and strawberry dessert. There was lots of white wine and Perrier for the nondrinkers.

"What do you think of this California food?" Barry asked, sitting down next to Lisa with his plate.

"I don't know; there's something a little pushy about it."

"You're right. It's like eating a political position with every bite." He spooned up a few dripping cucumbers. "Still, it's a meal. I'm sick of cooking for myself." A plane thundered overhead. "American," muttered Barry. The Perrier in Lisa's glass danced in tiny waves. He lived, it seemed, in a small room carved out from the top of a garage. At one end it had what he described as a "cook-in closet, with a contraption that's a stove on the right, a sink on the left, a refrigerator at the bottom, and plumbing in between." His current favorite dinner was avocado mashed up with anchovy paste. Lisa wrinkled her nose. "The California Special," he declared. "I've decided to cook my way through the alphabet, and have gotten as far as the A's. Next week it's bulgar wheat." He looked at his plate with distaste.

Barry Berman made Lisa laugh, but he could also listen. She found herself telling him about New Rochelle, about Mount Holyoke, about wanting to be a doctor when she was small. And about business school, about what it felt like to shine, to need to shine. Am I really telling him these things? she wondered. A United plane, then a TWA, then another United roared overhead, one after the other. The plates on the redwood table shivered and moved; spoons rattled on saucers. He drove her home and parked outside her house for a minute. "Can I see you again?" he asked. Before he drove off, he leaned out and shook her hand.

On Wednesday night he took her to dinner at the Good Earth in Palo Alto. When they ordered, the young waitress leaned over them, looked deep into their eyes, and murmured, "Yes-s-s. I know what you mean."

He asked Lisa about her courses and listened with what seemed to be unfeigned interest to a rather complicated story of classroom politics.

"... so if I let him take that topic, I'll be putting myself out into the cold."

"What do you think you'll do?"

"I don't know, really. No matter what I do, someone is shafted. I guess my first choice is that it not be me," she said, "but all things considered, I wish it weren't anyone else either."

"Well, this is one thing you might consider." He struck directly to the heart of the situation. Lisa was fascinated by the way his lawyer's intelligence sorted out all the threads and then laid out the best solution among the alternatives. It was a startling performance.

He took her out again on Saturday, to the movies and then to a Mexican restaurant somewhere on the highway. "Thank God, the food is terrible there," he said. "Everything looks like a map of the Balkans. You get your basic tamale, your basic enchilada, your basic refried beans. But I have never been able to figure out which is which." Lisa laughed. Even a bad meal — and it *was* bad — was cheerful and fun with Barry. She was beginning to feel that when he wasn't around, something was missing.

"How about a swim tonight?" His voice on the phone was

deep and even. If I didn't know what he looked like, Lisa thought, I'd picture someone like Al Pacino — but taller. "I can borrow a friend's pool," he was saying. "Well, maybe not the whole pool, but enough of it to cover the two of us."

Barry swam like an injured whale, coming up for air every few minutes to snort and spout and shake water in every direction. Lisa looked at him from the side of the pool; she had never seen his body before. It was covered with curly dark hair. I want to hug him, she thought. He's not good-looking and he's cheerful all the time and he's always sweet and he's terribly smart and I want to hug him.

She slipped into the water and swam over next to him. "Barry," she said. He stopped his wild sidestroke and treaded water, looking at her. She put her arms around his neck and, treading water, they kissed for the first time.

"Well," he said, his voice hoarse, "maybe we'd better get into shallower water."

They swam to the shallow end of the pool and stood up. Lisa put her arms around him again. He felt good to hold. She ran her hand the wrong way against his cheek to feel the bristles. He held her closer, and she could feel him growing hard against her.

"Nobody's here," he whispered. "All we have around us is this big privet hedge."

Lisa climbed out of the pool on the ladder. Barry vaulted up over the edge.

"Just a minute," Lisa said. She spread out her striped beach towel over the grass. Then she stripped off the top, and then the bottom, of her bathing suit and lay down.

They decided not to live together officially. Lisa still felt a little raw from her affair with Joe, and Barry was reluctant to make big changes in his life on the basis of impetuous decisions. He liked to think things over. But it was all formal because they spent every night together, either at his place or hers.

Lisa tried to be home for her mother's semiweekly calls. By the end of February, she felt confident enough to mention Barry.

"I tried you last night. You weren't home." Marge Gould could make any statement sound like an accusation. "Were you out?"

"Well, yes, Ma," Lisa said. "I had a date."

"A date? And who was the lucky young man?"

Ma probably thinks she's fooling me by trying to sound jaunty, Lisa thought.

"A friend. Someone I've known for a while. His name is Barry."

"Barry?" Her voice shifted gears. "Barry what?"

"Barry Berman. He's a lawyer. Well, actually, a law student."

"Barry Berman? A lawyer? Has he ever been married?"

"Oh, Ma. For Heaven's sake. No, he's my age. Look," she said rather crossly, "let me answer all the questions right now. He's my age. Single. Never married. Yes, Jewish. No, homosexual. He will probably make an excellent living. *When* he gets a job. I'm not sure yet whether he wants to work on the East Coast or somewhere else. Yes, taller than me. What have I left out?" She giggled a little, her mood rising.

Her mother sounded hurt. "Well, sweetheart, you can't blame a mother for looking out for her only daughter."

Lisa immediately felt contrite. "No, Ma, I'm sorry. I think you'll like him. I'm hoping to bring him home for spring vacation. He comes from Massachusetts — Brookline — so he'll probably fly east anyway."

Lisa felt it was premature to mention that both she and Barry were planning to spend spring vacation job hunting. Silly phrase, she thought; the jobs are hunting us. Barry had decided to work in New York. "Never lived there," he said. "I want to try my luck in a real city." So he replied to the letters he had received from Shearman and Sterling, from Davis Polk, from Milbank Tweed, from Proskauer Rose Goetz and Mendelsohn, from Hayden, Markham and Bialecki, and from several smaller firms. He was being wooed like a star, and he planned to go from one firm to another during vacation "to try to get a feel for which offer it is that I can't refuse."

Lisa was also being courted. Recruiters, almost always sleek alumni who were doing very well, arrived like armies in the spring. Installed in small, airless rooms, they interviewed candidate after candidate after candidate, trying to guess by inflection, dress, boldness or reticence, perspiration, and the number of umm-m-ms per sentence how well this person or that might succeed with the bank, with the company, with "our organization." Of course, they had all heard of the remarkable Lisa Gould, and they were not disappointed when they saw her. She was perfectly dressed, brown-haired, smiling — too pretty, the men thought, for someone with such a saber-toothed reputation. But sharp. Oh my, yes. Very sharp indeed. Each person who interviewed her wanted to hire her for his firm but was secretly determined to make sure that there was no way she could possibly be working for him. She shone — like a laser.

Within a month, she had eighteen letters inviting her for an interview. She eliminated all the companies not in New York City. That act told her clearly for the first time that she intended to marry Barry Berman. As a consequence, she made tentative appointments for April with Citibank, her old summer employer, Manufacturers Hanover Trust, and GlobeBank, along with several brokerage houses and American Express.

◊ ◊ ◊

After two days with his family in Brookline, Barry moved into the Goulds' guest room. He and Lisa would breakfast together, each in a suit.

"My God," he said to her over biallys and cream cheese, "you look like *The Women's Dress for Success Book,* doesn't she, Mrs. Gould?" He flirted with Lisa's mother, who already looked on him with full pride of ownership.

Lisa and Barry would ride into the city with the other late commuters, separate for the day's appointments, convene again around four for a drink and to rehash the day's events, then make the trip back to New Rochelle.

The brokerage houses were out, she told Barry. Too limiting. She wanted more room. They were in the Oak Room at the Plaza drinking Perrier. "I think American Express is going to be out, too." She had been made an offer, $23,000, but she didn't like any of the people she'd seen. "Maybe I'm being silly," she said to Barry, "but I don't want anything that doesn't grab me right away. I don't feel like dawdling around in some nothing area waiting to be given a chance."

Barry had already made up his mind and was going to start with Hayden, Markham and Bialecki in mid-July. "From what I gather not too deep between the lines," he told Lisa, "there's a full partnership in ten years. *If* I work out." Old Mr. Bialecki, now in his nineties, still came into the office once or twice a month, leaning on a cane and nearly blind, but as keen as ever. He had been taken to meet Leland Stanford, Sr., when he was a little boy and was partial to Stanford men ever after. "Women, too, when I can find 'em," he would say in his flat, midwestern voice.

It had come down to the banks for Lisa. "I feel at home there," she reflected. "Maybe because of those summers at Citibank." She suddenly had a flashback of herself on the beige couch with her old boss, and she shuddered, thinking, What would happen if I ran into him? Would we even recognize each other? "Next to GlobeBank, Citibank certainly has the reputation for being the first with the most, you know, Barry, but I'm not sure . . . Maybe I spent *too* much time there while I was in college." She narrowed it down further to Manny-Hanny and GlobeBank.

Her appointments at GlobeBank were scheduled for Thursday. It was warm enough for her beige linen suit, and she tucked a pretty lace-edged handkerchief in the breast pocket. She pulled her hair behind her ears with a pair of rose-colored combs Barry had bought from a street vendor on Third Avenue. Barry had asked the vendor why he was selling them for three dollars each when there had been an ad in the *Times* for the same combs at Bergdorf's for fifteen dollars. "Why, we *steal* them," the vendor said in a cultivated voice. Barry just couldn't get over it.

Lisa arrived a little before nine-thirty, after walking up Park Avenue from Grand Central. Nondescript. It could be anything, she decided. Corporate headquarters for an oil company or a toothpaste conglomerate. The personnel office was on the second floor. Corporate Recruiting. They gave her a neatly typed agenda of the day's appointments and, in an envelope, a form to record any expenses connected with the interview. I should charge them for the combs, she thought. Then for the rest of the day, there was one forty-five-minute appointment after another, all in BOS; its recruiter had found her first.

The appointments seemed all alike. The yellow questionnaire. Her résumé on the table. The list of "probing" questions: What is the hardest decision you have ever made? What was the most rewarding experience of your life? What do you see yourself doing in five years? In ten? What are your strengths? What would you call your weaknesses? I see, Lisa, that despite the policy at Stanford to have no majors, you have a heavy marketing background. How do you feel about Operations? Would you be interested?

She was escorted from interview to interview. International Transfers. Domestic Transfers. Letters of Credit, a big-ticket area at GlobeBank. Collections. The Demand Deposit areas, Branches and Incoming Exchange. Each floor was throbbing with energy. She wished she could simply be taken through and ask questions. But, no, more of the same. How do you see yourself fitting into Operations? What would you do in this hypothetical situation or that?

Lunch at the Shun Lee Palace was interesting, though. She had been taken out by Ray LaRocca, head of the Transfers Division, and by his personnel manager, Marvin Feinberg. Feinberg was a C.C.N.Y. psychology major, full of lightbulb jokes. But LaRocca really interested her. He was impressive. Inarticulate, but an expert, a real one. He knew his stuff inside out. She asked a lot of questions and got real answers, although every now and then she had to swallow a giggle at LaRocca's vague little diagrams.

"Kumquat? No?" Feinberg offered as the last course was served. The conversation became more general. LaRocca talked more easily about the early days at the bank, before Kilgour, and the changes after Kilgour. He scraped BK and AK into the tablecloth with his chopsticks. Feinberg hinted to Lisa that the corridors were buzzing over her interviews and that BOS wanted her.

The phone rang during her four-fifteen interview with Rick Schmidt. "What is it?" he said crossly into his intercom. "What? Oh. Oh, yes. Of course."

He hung up. "Do you suppose you could manage to stay for one more interview, Lisa? John Kilgour would like to see you." He smiled conspiratorially. He was impressed. Almost no new hire candidates got such an audience. This was extraordinary.

Kilgour, the famous Kilgour, the Kilgour whom Lisa had read about in *American Banker* and *Business Week* and in the *Wall*

Street Journal, turned out to be a rather small man with graying hair and a smooth face. Superb clothes, though, she noted. Farther up the line than New Rochelle. He spoke in a very low voice and made very few gestures. His office confirmed the impression of power. Lots of leather. Almost no papers. They sat in armchairs. On the wall between them hung a LeRoy Neiman.

"As you must know, Lisa," Kilgour began, "your school seems to regard you as a student of exceptional promise. I gather they think highly of your analytic abilities."

She thought fast. Should I be modest and demur politely? No, not with him. He likes confidence. "I certainly would expect so," she said. "I worked hard for it."

He smiled. It had been the right answer. "We're looking for people with good analytical skills, Lisa. However, I see that you have a very heavy background in marketing as well."

"Yes, I do," she answered. "It's my impression that marketing *services* — the way goods are marketed — are going to be something that service organizations are going to be doing more of very soon."

He smiled again. He has a pleasant face, she thought. I gave him another good answer. Good girl, Lisa.

They talked about Stanford, about New York. Very friendly. She could feel her heart racing. She had been in Kilgour's office for forty minutes and he was still chatting. She knew the offer would be good, that it would be made before she left the building, and that she would take it.

"How would you feel about coming to work for us, Lisa?" Kilgour asked. "We would like you to start as soon as possible, maybe in July."

She and Barry were married at the end of June by Sherman T. Kane, who had been the Goulds' rabbi since they moved to New Rochelle. After much long-distance pleading from Palo Alto, Lisa convinced her parents that she did not want a big or even a medium-sized wedding. Just the immediate family. Her brother, Jeff, and his wife. Barry's parents and his grandmother who was still alive. That was it. An afternoon wedding in the rabbi's study. Marge Gould held out for something bigger for an hour and a half. Finally Lisa heard her father's voice in the background: "Listen, Marge, this is what the kids today want." Thank you, Daddy. And that was it.

7

WHEN JESSICA RETURNED from lunch, she found a note from Lisa waiting for her on the dial of her telephone. "Bravo!" it said. Brava, she edited unconsciously. "Let me buy you a drink after our meeting." Great, thought Jessica; nice of her.

Lisa enjoyed spending time with Jessica Moser, regarding it as a form of recreation that she could allow herself occasionally. Jessica, who had taken a degree in Old English and Old Icelandic after she graduated from Bryn Mawr, had come to GlobeBank rather by accident. Divorced after twelve years of marriage, with custody of her precocious ten-year-old girl, she had never held a nine-to-five job, though she had written pieces for library journals and two scholarly articles on the Old Norse sagas. Her total income between graduating from college and coming to the bank was $365. At the time of her divorce, the Public Relations Department was looking for a talented but cheap writer for their consumer relations project. Jessica was recommended to them, and they were happy to get her qualifications at an entry-level salary. And she was happy to get a paycheck twice a month.

Very little of that paycheck went for clothes. Jessica always looked as though she had just returned from a bargain vacation in an underdeveloped country. Very often she had. She wore long filigree earrings, cheap cotton skirts in vivid colors, T-shirts from Woolworth's, and canvas shoes. She seemed to have absolutely no corporate ambition, and it was this disinterest that allowed Lisa to relax with her. Jessica was no threat. She was funny and honest. She said things no one else would dare to say. Even so, she was spectacularly good at her job. Lisa had decided long ago that the secret was Jessica's uncanny mimicry. Jessica could rattle off little speeches in half a dozen European languages, whether she knew them or not, and could "do" most of her colleagues at the bank, not to mention Humphrey Bogart, Bette Davis, Henry Kissinger, and Diane Keaton. And she was just as good at imitating, on paper, what everybody at Globe-

Bank thought great business writing should sound like — a little Peter Drucker, a little technology, a little advertising, with a special added dash of Jessica Moser.

Jessica's official title at GlobeBank was internal communications manager. This meant, she would cheerily explain, that she wrote a newsletter. It appeared monthly, full of good news of successful division projects. "No exposés this month," she would comment in her mocking way. But she produced much more. She wrote speeches for Lisa. She wrote glossy pamphlets on the division's more permanent contributions to the bank, and she had achieved some renown as the author of a booklet, entitled *The Hollow Floor,* on construction work to accommodate computer cables. She had hung the first paragraph of this treatise on her wall in her own Old Norse translation. She had also produced a short film on GlobeBank's evolution from a green eyeshade environment to its present futuristic technological razzle-dazzle. The film was shown everywhere in the bank, to the Board, and to interested parties all over the country, and had earned Jessica a two-thousand-dollar bonus that she blew on a trip to Peru.

◇ ◇ ◇

Although Jessica and Lisa Gould had long since established an easy relationship, there were many things that Jessica never discussed. One secret she kept was that she had been an early *Business Week* contact for the magazine's article on Kilgour. Though Lisa knew Jessica's irreverent attitude toward the bank, she would still consider feeding unflattering observations about Kilgour to the press as mutinous. But the episode had tickled Jessica.

She had routinely showed the *Business Week* reporter around National Services West. He took her to the Blarney Stone for drinks afterward and asked her to speak "not for attribution." When the article appeared, two weeks later, there was a boxed sidebar paraphrasing her comments and leading off with a direct quotation:

"BOS is kind of like the Green Berets. People here take a lot of pride in telling 'war stories,' and the idea is to top the other guy by having had a tougher 'war' experience. It's a little weird."

The office was abuzz the morning the article appeared. In the Xerox room, where people were lined up waiting to make copies, everyone wondered aloud about the "BOS official" featured in the sidebar.

The talk continued in Jessica's own office, where a steady stream of visitors made it impossible for her to read the piece through until ten o'clock.

She had just finished and was thinking what a fine job the reporter had done when Linda Glover walked in. "What do you think about the article, Jess?" Linda asked, setting an armful of looseleaf binders down on Jessica's table.

"It's very well written, I'll say that," Jessica answered.

"You think Killer will be pissed off?" Linda sat down opposite Jessica.

"Why? They spelled his name right."

"Come on, Jess. I mean, it's not exactly a completely flattering portrait."

"He's not exactly a completely flatterable man. Has Lisa seen the piece?"

"Yes. She's got a call in to Kilgour. Apparently, so does everyone else in the bank."

Jessica was nodding. "Actually, you know, he's probably secretly flattered by all of it. He's probably the kind of guy who likes the idea that people think he rides roughshod over his employees' personal lives. Come to think of it, Linda, wouldn't Lisa secretly be flattered by an article like this — or you? It's kind of admiring, really, once you accept the assumptions."

"I don't think *I'd* be flattered."

"Oh, come on, Linda, this is *me* you're talking to."

"No, I mean it."

"Wouldn't you want to be thought of as a 'tough' manager?"

Linda thought fast. What was the right answer? There was always a right answer, one that advanced, if only minimally, whatever your particular goal was. What answer did Jessica want? What would make Jessica think well of her? "I wouldn't mind being thought of as tough," Linda said, "if I were also thought of as fair."

Jessica made a face. "Oh, Linda."

◇ ◇ ◇

Jessica was still looking at Lisa's drink invitation when a blue-jacketed porter wheeled in a dolly stacked with small cartons.

78

"Looking for J. Moss," he said. "Stuff from Central Printing."

"Oh," said Jessica, signing the crumpled delivery sheet, "these must be the Productive Environment booklets. Let's have a look."

She pulled a shiny blue brochure from the top box. "The Productive Environment," the title read in a computer-like typeface, "Processing in the National Services West Division."

Jessica thumbed through the booklet. "Goddamnit," she murmured, "this stinks." It really stinks, she repeated in her head. She pulled the phone to her and punched some numbers. Christ! This is what happens when we print in-house. Just because it's free. You get what you pay for in this world. "Milt?" She had reached Milt Saltzman in Central Printing. "Jessica Moser. The books arrived, but we've got problems. I really can't accept them as they are . . . Well, the color's off," Jessica continued. "Everyone looks like they've just had hepatitis. You've got broken type. You've got a slant on the straight line on the front cover. Jesus, Milt, it's just no good. And I think you guys ought to get it straightened out fast. I mean, we have a pub date on this. And if Lisa starts asking questions . . . Right, Milt," she said finally. "I'll be right there."

She spent forty-five minutes with Saltzman in the glass office in the basement that shielded them from the noise of the presses, collators, binding machines, hole-punching machines, and staplers.

Back in her office, it was time for her meeting with Lisa to write up the confidential reports on the fast-track "stars" in the division. The reports would go into the Sector Estate section of Kilgour's Manpower Monitor report. The names of the chosen would be on record with Hardesty and Pruitt. Lisa picked the names, but it was Jessica who had to write up the reports — the Strengths, Areas for Improvement, and Improvement Plans for each person on the list.

Jessica enjoyed this assignment. She was not unaware that because she was privy to Lisa's assessments of her people, she had a very solid base of power around the division. Jessica Moser has Lisa's ear, people said. Lisa really *talks* to Jessica. The perception of power, Jessica knew, was almost the same thing as having the power itself.

"OK," Jessica said. "We're up to Tony Maresca."

"Tony," Lisa repeated, pursing her lips, inwardly analyzing her right-hand man. "Tony. Strengths: reliable, meets his commitments, that sort of thing. Areas for Improvement: needs to be more of a self-starter; he doesn't initiate enough. Lacks confidence." Jessica thought Lisa looked sad as she said it. "Plan: I will personally work with him to improve confidence level."

Jessica scribbled notes. "OK," she said. "Next is . . ."

They covered three more names before they came to Linda Glover's. Jessica was interested to know what Lisa would say about Linda.

"Linda Glover," said Lisa, as if the name were a question she was pondering. "Well, Linda's got excellent managerial skills, obviously. Highly motivated. Highly organized. Outstanding analytical ability."

Lisa paused. Jessica waited.

"But," Lisa said finally. "Well, I don't know, what do you think, Jess? You and Linda seem pretty friendly. I mean, how would you put it about Linda? What do you think about her?"

Jessica lowered her pen. "To tell you the truth, Lisa, she reminds me a lot of you."

Lisa started. "She does? In what way?"

"Her ambition. Her focus on what it takes. Her understanding, even her instinct, for the power game. Her manipulative ability."

"Thanks a lot. You mean we're both real snakes."

"Not really. No, not at all. I just mean that you both see clearly what you want and you know how you intend to get it. And I think you both will. It's not an unenviable trait, really."

"Well, I think we have to say something about Linda's interpersonal skills; I think she needs improvement at interpersonal skills."

Jessica winced at the word "interpersonal." "Yeah, I know what you mean. She lacks your smoothness, your maturity, your — "

Lisa interrupted. "I just think she's trying to move too fast. She has to slow down, pay her dues first. Don't you think? I mean, there's nothing wrong with ambition, but you have to learn to manage it."

Jessica nodded slowly. "Yes, I see what you mean. I'll think of some way to word it."

"Tomorrow, OK? Let's go have that drink now. I could use one."

They went to Laurent. Jessica picked all the Brazil nuts out of the bowl on the table while Lisa watched, amused.

8

SANDY LIPPERT WOULD LATER look back on his last year at Wharton as the last time he had had fun. He had no classes on Friday, so on Thursday nights, he drove to New York.

Kathy shared a two-bedroom apartment on East Seventy-second Street with three other Finch students. The girls' fathers, all golfing partners in Greenwich, paid the rent. Sandy made a deal with Allison Winter, Kathy's roommate, paying her $50 a weekend to sleep on the living room sofa so he and Kathy could have the bedroom. The four girls convinced him that this was a legitimate business expense, one their fathers would certainly write off. Sandy listed it on his weekly expense report to Globe-Bank as a "host gift."

On Fridays he reported to 176 Wall Street. His programming project took him only four months. In January, he got a new assignment; in March, another. He got to know the people and allowed them to get to know him.

In June, following graduation, he and Kathy were married in Greenwich. Their honeymoon trip to Bermuda was a wedding gift from her parents. The "basic furniture" in their one-bedroom apartment on East Eighty-ninth Street was a gift from the Lipperts.

On a hot July day, Sandy arrived to work full time at Globe-Bank as an assistant financial controller in the Transfer Operations Group. He reported to Rick Schmidt, one of five operations managers in the International Transfers Department. Six levels away from Kilgour, Sandy still felt the excitement of the man's power.

There was a style that Kilgour had stamped onto the back office, a style that had "changed the face of banking forever." The managers in the Banking Operations Sector were bred to that style, and Sandy loved it. He loved its speed and its toughness, loved the conspiratorial pride in admitting that self-interest was what drove every individual everywhere, especially in BOS.

Isolated at 176 Wall, different from the uptown "bankers," the sector's M.B.A. generalists, analysts, operations researchers, and technocrats knew themselves to be a breed entirely new to banking. They were young, fast, well paid, ambitious, and impatient with the dusty obstacles that dared to block their way. Sandy hoped — expected — to belong, to be one of them.

On his first day at the bank, he heard the term "binary management." It meant that a manager's performance either won or lost. There was no gray area, no halfway. Sandy meant to win.

He crunched the numbers, mastering the BOS budget style, the form and substance of FRAC — Financial Report and Costing — the sector's accounting sheet, its basic method of control. In BOS, control was everything.

He was there for the planning cycle and learned the style of what was called the Midget-Mod — from MGT-MOD, the Management Model. It was Kilgour's own design, "a way," the sector head had written in an introduction to the manual, "to manage anything — from a dinner party to a dynamic organization like BOS." It had three parts: Current Situation, Ideal Future, Path of Motion. First, you described the Current Situation in crisp, quantitative terms. The manual laid out ten "indicators" that had to be described, yardsticks by which the manager's situation was measured.

Then you identified the Ideal Future for that situation. The same ten indicators were made better and described in equally crisp, quantitative terms.

Finally you laid out your Path of Motion. How, precisely, to get from the Current Situation to the Ideal Future. How to "cross the delta," as they said in BOS.

It all gave a kind of clarity Sandy's engineering mind appreciated.

He was there every morning at seven. They said Kilgour was often there then, that he often had his driver take him to 176 early so that he could wander around his empire, see it all "in the flesh" before being deposited uptown on Park Avenue. It was how Kilgour kept in touch, they said. But Sandy never saw him there that early.

After six months, the group head three levels above Sandy "went away." That was the way they put it at 176; Sandy hardly listened to the whispers. Everybody moved up. Schmidt became an operations head — an OH. Sandy was named an operations manager — an OM. He was on "the line" now. He was a boss: twenty-six international transfer clerks reported to him.

Shirtsleeve work. Firefighting. Sandy's "office" was a desk under a window on the nineteenth floor. Through the window he could see the lacy Brooklyn Bridge, snub-nosed tugs plying their business up and down the East River, the downtown Brooklyn skyline. Sandy hardly looked out. He spent his time on "the floor," the great space dotted with desks, watching his clerks.

Fifteen thousand transfers arrived each day. Sandy's line was responsible for nearly seven hundred of them. They all had to go through the litany of tasks devised by LaRocca when he linearized the process. The tasks were consolidated somewhat now, but they all still had to be done. Receive. Record. Sort. Wire. Encode. Read to tape. Post. Dispatch. Seven hundred transfers. All those tasks. All day long.

The first stop was the mail desk. Telexes. Order sheets from account managers uptown. "Transfer $6 million to credit disbursement Barclays London." "Eight million from General Account via Chase to Mitsui branch 14, Manila." Log it in. Move it on.

To Preprocessing. Type the information on fanfold forms. Split the forms. Pink copy to files. Blue into the box. Yellow to Out folder for customer advice. Other eight copies to processing.

Processing. Nine clerks at REDI terminals, teletype machines hooked to the computer on the twenty-seventh floor. Translate the information from the forms into machine-readable lingo, REDI format.

Reject and repair. The computer spits out 40 percent of the instructions. Specially trained clerks fix them. What input is missing? Where the hell is the file? Who typed this anyway? Resubmit to REDI.

Customer service. Keepers of the files. Thousands of pink copies. REDI tapes. REDI printouts. Phones ringing all day. What happened to my transfer? Did the payment get made? One moment, sir, I'll check for you. I'll get back to you. Please hold. Just a minute. Sometimes the phones kept ringing and nobody answered.

Hectic, exasperating, high-powered work — Sandy loved it. He loved the steady *clack-clack* of typewriters and teletypes, the refined clicking of the REDI keyboards. The shoptalk buzzing around the floor. Great names. Very big deals. Over and over. Twenty million. Union Carbide. Bank of America. General Motors. Banco de Chile. Bank of Tokyo. Sandy was conscious of his unit as a focal point on the globe, the planet spinning to the harmonies of different currencies, time zones, the huge, unreal sums that drove colossal corporations.

Schmidt was not only his boss, he was his model. Broad-shouldered, sturdy, square-jawed, and with an ungiving expression, Rick Schmidt could have been an ad for the Special Forces. He had, in fact, been decorated in Vietnam, and often described himself as "a *former* captain," the emphasis so boldly self-effacing as to be false.

GlobeBank actively recruited from the armed forces and the military academies — officers only, of course. The corporation believed, as one personnel officer told *MBA Magazine,* that "the kind of discipline and results orientation the military breeds makes people flourish here. They do very well for us." Like all corporations, GlobeBank had patterned its organizational structure on the military to some extent, such as in the distinction between line and staff. The notion of support functions and the reporting hierarchy itself all came from the military tradition.

So did the military lingo that coursed its way through the conversation of a man like Schmidt and the attitude that lingo represented. Schmidt once told his OMs that the thing he was proudest of was achieving the highest kill ratio in his outfit for six weeks running. "I'd like to feel equally proud of the speed and accuracy measures we achieve here in International," Schmidt said. Sandy found the analogy a bit disturbing, but the other OMs were nodding solemnly, so he nodded, too.

Schmidt took him to lunch to go over his MBO for the year. GlobeBank was a strong believer in Management by Objectives. You "commit" to goals for the coming year. Then you either succeed or you fail. This was binary management. It made the supervisor's job easy. And the way the chain of command worked, almost everybody had a chance to practice binary management on somebody. Except the workers — they didn't manage at all.

Sandy's MBO committed him to book savings of \$121,960 over the year. He would have to knock eight heads to do it, reducing the number of clerks working for him to eighteen.

It was a big year for Alexander Lippert. Kathy gave birth to a daughter. They named her Blair for no reason except that Kathy liked the name. Blair Laura Lippert. They bought a house in Chatham, New Jersey, an hour's commute by train and tube and only a short drive to the horse country in Somerset County, where Kathy could ride regularly. Kathy's father provided the down payment for the house, but he let them know that he would rather have seen them in Connecticut and hoped that they would soon "move up" to Greenwich.

Sandy knocked eleven heads during the year, three more than he had committed to. When Schmidt was promoted to International Group head, reporting directly to the division head, Ray LaRocca, he took Sandy with him. Sandy became an OH and was named an assistant vice president of GlobeBank.

Schmidt and the guys took him out for drinks to celebrate the promotion. They got a table at Michael 2 and started with beers. Guys began peeling off at about seven, heading for trains that would take them home to the Island or out to Jersey or up to Connecticut. Finally, it was just Sandy and Schmidt. They moved to the bar and started drinking Scotch.

That night at Michael's, Sandy saw a new Schmidt. The bluff, tough Schmidt melted away in the Scotch. He started talking loudly about personal growth and his own special feeling about God. It all came together, he said, in the way Kilgour had changed the back office. One leader, Schmidt said, with vision. And the will to make his vision a reality. And the power to make it happen. You needed all three, Schmidt said, vision, will, and power. A little string of spittle hung from Schmidt's lower lip. This is bullshit, Sandy thought. What the hell, the guy is drunk.

The day Autotran went live had been hectic for Sandy Lippert. And long. He woke up at five-thirty to run six miles around Central Park as a dim, gray dawn spread over the city. He had hoped the exertion would calm him for the press conference, but

85

he felt as excited as a child to mingle with the press, to stand on a podium with Kilgour, to deliver his prepared talk and answer questions about Autotran. His Autotran.

The call from Kathy had wrecked all that. Shit, what a downer. Why the hell did she have to call me today of all days, Sandy thought, with her goddamned nagging voice and her goddamned money, money, money. Her shit alimony, which she doesn't even need with her sonofabitch rich daddy. "Daddy doesn't think our house is entirely suitable." "Daddy feels I should keep up my riding." He imitated her in a mincing voice. And she has the kids most of the time. After all, they're my kids too. Expensive raising kids. Not that I would begrudge them anything. Not anything in this world. The kids love me. He softened for a moment, thinking of his children in feet pajamas, the two of them ready for bed, round and stumpy like little fire hydrants, with flushed faces and sleepy eyes. He felt better. He suddenly remembered how sweet Kathy's voice had once sounded to him, and he winced. What the hell; she calls, she calls. Might as well get used to it. He tried to concentrate on how good he had felt that morning. Get it back, he thought.

He almost got it back as the afternoon wore on. There were phone calls from the other division heads: When could they come see Autotran at work? There were rumors, which proved false, of a surprise visit from Hardesty. And the constant checking of the floor — the people, the machines. It was all moving smoothly. Sandy thought of the transfer control working away in the darkened closet on the twenty-seventh floor, just a simple store-and-forward switching device. It seemed alive to him. *Chut-chut-chut,* the sound of a gearshift. The only sound in the darkened room. Like a heartbeat, really, and that's what it was, the heart of the system, the core of Autotran.

His own heart seemed to beat to the same rhythm all day.

Five-thirty. Frank was still there, and Marie, but most of the Autotran workers would have gone home. Sandy walked out to the floor to have a look.

Walter Noble was at his station, sending film flying across the microfilm reader.

"What's up, Walt? Problems?"

"Sandy! Hi. No. I'm just making sure the files are on here OK. I don't want to get behind at all."

86

Sandy moved on. Clara Palomares was there, yawping a rapid-fire Spanish into the phone as she maneuvered a ton of makeup into a small plastic case.

Vince Palumbo and Don Osterman, coats on and imitation Samsonite briefcases in their hands, were coming toward him down the central corridor.

"Great day, Sandy!" Don said as they approached their boss.

"You better believe it!" Sandy responded. "And you guys helped make it happen."

"No," Vince said, straightening his collar, "you know what Kilgour says. Managers make things happen."

"Well, it really went great," Sandy said. "I really want to thank you guys. I hope you know I'm really grateful, on a personal level."

Vince, who was twice Sandy's age, slapped his arm. "See you tomorrow, Sandy."

In the old world, Sandy thought, the world before Kilgour, Vince and Don wouldn't have had a prayer of ever becoming anything but clerks. But now they're professionals. They know how to operate sophisticated technology. They have direct customer contact. They contribute in a real way to the institution. They're well paid and in line for promotions. In a year or so, they could be officers. Four weeks vacation. Perks. Their signatures on file with the Federal Reserve.

"Night, Sandy!"

"Night, Clara! Thanks for today!"

Now only Walt Noble was left, still running film through his reader. Sandy walked to the window and looked up the river to the lights of the bridges. A renaissance, a rebirth. That's what Kilgour calls it, and he's right.

"See you tomorrow, Sandy."

"Right, Walt. Good night."

Jesus. I sound like the goddamn press conference this morning, Sandy realized. I sound like Kilgour's PR. Me, of all people.

He turned around to the empty floor. His floor. Lippert's floor. It still felt good to think that way, to hear those words. Almost as good as when he had first heard them. Lippert's floor.

That was long ago.

◇ ◇ ◇

He was a GlobeBank AVP then, an OH in LaRocca's International Division, reporting to Rick Schmidt, and with four OMs reporting to him. He had "big troops and a big budget"; he had asked for and gotten big responsibility.

LaRocca had dubbed that year "the year of REDI enhancement." They were going to beef up the transfer system, give it fancy embellishments, make it do new tricks. Sandy had asked Rick to assign him the biggest part of the effort.

"This is a two-and-a-half-million-dollar task, Sandy," Rick had answered skeptically. "You don't just have technical and systems enhancements here, you also got a shitload of saves to make. I've committed to LaRocca to knock half the heads we own. I intend to make that save."

Rick leaned forward a little, his eyes glittering. "Between you and I," he said, "I'm just not sure you've got the combat experience to hack it."

Sandy argued. He made the promises Rick was waiting for, and they cut the deal. Rick was in fact delighted. He had told LaRocca he couldn't possibly knock a third of the heads in the department and still make the enhancements. Now he had gotten Sandy to commit to cutting half. Rick couldn't lose.

Sandy left the house in Chatham every morning at six after kissing a still-sleeping Kathy and straightening the invariably knotted blanket wrapped around Blair. He stopped at the Chock Full O'Nuts on Wall Street for a fried egg sandwich and coffee to go, then proceeded to 176. He became a completely hands-on manager. There wasn't anything that went on in his line that he didn't know about. He held daily meetings with his four OMs and he approved every action personally.

He had selected a team of consultants — software writers — to design the enhancements. It was an education, like M.I.T. and Wharton rolled into one. New capabilities. Consolidating functions into the machine. Streamlining. So that the computers did more and the people did less. The technology, after all, was more reliable — and certainly cheaper — than the people.

He traveled. Zurich. Hamburg. London. Abu Dhabi. Hong Kong. Finding out from customers what they required. Coming home to tell the consultants. Forcing them to design and redesign so that the enhancements were yet better, so that they knocked yet more heads. It was thrilling stuff. Scarves and perfume for Kathy and costume dolls for Blair piled up in the house at Chatham.

But he rarely saw Chatham. Most nights he didn't leave 176 till eight. A crisis, a major step in the enhancement, would keep him even later. Often he never got home at all. He slept on the couch in Rick's office and shaved in the Men's Room.

Even when he went home, his mind stayed at the office, always churning over the work. How to make REDI better. How to streamline. How to knock another head.

Kathy was often napping when he got home. She had learned to drink beer when she was nursing Blair. Now she kept a shelf full of it in the refrigerator, drank it through the day, and was often sacked out on the sofa when Sandy walked in the door. They would have a light supper together in front of the television. Then he'd look over some papers before bed.

They never went out anymore, apart from the occasional Saturday night at a neighborhood restaurant, followed by groggy and predictable lovemaking. In those tender moments, they would talk of how it was going to be. When the year of REDI enhancement was over. When he was vice president. When they could go on vacation.

But they didn't go for a long time. And Sandy continued to leave the house at six in the morning and get back home at ten at night. He continued to meet with the OMs and the consultants, continued to be a hands-on manager, a tough manager. When he did relax, it was on Friday night at Michael 2, sometimes with Rick and always with three or four other regulars. On those nights he didn't get home till midnight.

He never noticed when Kathy switched from beer to Scotch. Never really noticed that her evening naps were not naps at all. Never really paid that much attention to the increasing scorn with which she commented on their Saturday night sex.

He wanted her out of his way so he could finish the job. "Go up to Greenwich for the weekend," he would say. "Let your parents spoil Blair for a few days."

By early summer he was beginning to wind down. "I hope you're planning some vacation," Rick told him one day. "You look like hell. And you're the only guy in the shop who's not tan."

Sandy was wary. "My combat color," he said to Rick. "I'm not resting, so why should I look rested?" Why did Rick want him out of the way? Or did he? This place is making me paranoid, he realized.

They finally went to Nantucket for two weeks. At Kathy's insistence, he left his papers home. The first few days, he would sneak down to the inn's pay phone and call the office. After a while, to his surprise, he lost interest in all that. The sand and the water soothed him, and the sight of Blair digging purposefully, hour after hour, with a little Popsicle-colored plastic shovel, filled him with a happiness painful in its intensity.

He and Kathy jogged, swam, and bicycled around the island, with Blair sitting up tall in a little seat on the back of Sandy's bike. The inn provided baby sitters, so each evening they dressed to go out. They felt elegant and strong in their clean, rustling clothes after the long, salty days in bathing suits. Nantucket was romantic.

When he got back to the office after Labor Day, he was sorry he had gotten so far away.

Rick Schmidt called him in. "I think you may be carrying too much," he said. "I'm thinking of giving a piece of your shop to Bob."

"What in hell for?" Sandy asked. He tried to think fast. I'm learning. Running a tight ship means throwing a lot of bodies overboard. He remembered, to his chagrin, admiring Rick's style a long time ago. This guy, this place. It gets away from you so fast. He got rid of me for two weeks. Somehow he thinks I'm going to step in his way. "Bob's a financial guy. He doesn't know shit about the line. You'd be running a training program."

"Hold it," said Rick, "it was just a thought. Fletcher's numbers were lousy while you were away, and I'm a little concerned."

Be calm. Sandy breathed deeply. "Obviously you need me."

"Now just a minute," said Rick. "I don't call it control when the place blows up the minute you leave."

Sandy dug in again. More time at the office. More numbers. More work to take home. More procedures to streamline and functions to consolidate. More staff meetings.

90

Kathy started drinking again, really drinking, and he never noticed. On Christmas Eve she passed out at a party in Madison. Their embarrassed host helped Sandy get her into the car and tried to make a joke of it when she threw up all over the driveway. On New Year's Eve it was almost the same, except that the party was next door. "Let's go," he said to her when she started to get raucous. "Fuck off," she said in a loud, hoarse voice. "Fuck off, Sandy, I'm finally having some fun." When she passed out, he half carried her home. This time she vomited on the couch. A month later, Sandy was promoted to vice president.

Three weeks after his promotion, Sandy went to see LaRocca. It was a tough decision, since he still reported to Rick — on paper, anyway. When Rick got wind of Sandy's going straight to LaRocca, that would be it. Forever. But he decided to risk it. With Rick Schmidt, he was only going to make Rick look good. With Ray LaRocca, he might get more. LaRocca had been around for a long time. Kilgour had already made room for him. LaRocca had less at stake. It was worth the gamble, Sandy felt. He had a lot to win. If he lost . . . Well, he wouldn't lose. He wasn't a loser.

"I'm ready for a new assignment, Ray. I feel that REDI is as far as I can take it."

LaRocca praised him for the job he'd done, a job with results better than planned. "A hell of a job, Sandy," he said. "I personally am very appreciative. I've expressed this to Kilgour, by the way, and he said a few interesting things about you, asked a few interesting questions. I wouldn't do anything right now, Sandy," he said. "I think something will break in a week or so."

Two weeks later, Alexander Lippert was named chief controller to John Roland Kilgour, and he moved to Head Office on Park Avenue.

POSITION DESCRIPTION
Chief Controller, Banking Operations Sector
Goals and Accountabilities

- Manage and control all sector budgets and expenses.
- Act as chief of staff to sector head.
- Manage and control strategic planning for the sector.
- Matrix-manage all systems managers within the sector.
- Matrix-manage all personnel officers within the sector.

Chief controller was the hot-ticket job in BOS. The division heads had to come through you on everything. And it carried the weight of Kilgour's favor; it meant you had been touched on both shoulders by his sword of state.

Sandy and Kathy spent a weekend in New York to celebrate the new job. They agreed that things had gone better than they had dreamed, that now they couldn't lose.

"Jesus, Kath. When I think back, I used to think it would be heaven to be where I am now, where we are. A vice president at GlobeBank, pulling down big bucks, with a nice house in a nice suburb and a beautiful wife who's pregnant with my second kid. That would have been the ultimate, just a year or so ago. And now here we are, with the toughest job in the sector. Lots of exposure, very high viz. You gotta figure they've been watching me, talking about me. It means they've got their eye on me. Kilgour's got his eye on me. I'm his man, now, Kilgour's controller. Kath, I'm a comer."

She smiled at him and automatically patted her stomach. It was true. The house, the manicured lawn, the shrubbery and flowers, the smell of country air. This summer, they would join the club. Sandy could golf, and she could swim with Blair. They'd "do" a nursery for the new baby. Sandy would come off the golf course, wave at her, then shower. They would dress in bright summer clothes and join other successful couples for cocktails in the lounge. "My husband? A vice president at GlobeBank. Well, right now he's chief controller to John Kilgour, the EVP there." Daddy would be so pleased. Things were definitely going to be better now.

It was a good weekend.

Sandy was happy for a long time. The hours were more grueling than ever, of course, but it was all worth it. There were the early morning meetings, just him and Kilgour huddled over coffee, going over their agenda of items and issues. There were the public meetings when Kilgour would say, "Hey, Sandy, can you stick around for a few minutes after we're through? I've got a couple of things."

Sandy became slightly intoxicated by the small conspiracies he shared with Kilgour. His posture changed slightly and so did his walk. He tended to glide a little where he used to lope. He bought himself two very expensive ties at Paul Stuart and a set of colored shirts with white collar and cuffs. He got used to having people jump quickly when he asked for something. If he needed a report in the morning, he expected his staff to stay up all night getting it ready. *He* had, hadn't he? "Here at sector level," he liked to say.

He loved it all and did it all well — at first.

Later, and for a long time after, Sandy would try to pinpoint the moment, the episode, the choice — the *something* — when it had all gone wrong. Like a lover when the affair is over, his mind played and replayed reel after reel of his time with Kilgour. Where, how, did it go off the track?

Little by little, the feeling of power had disappeared. He realized that Kilgour wasn't leaning on him — Kilgour was using him. He was a glorified secretary, a gofer, a faithful dog kept happy with occasional scraps of power from the master's table. What had once seemed intimate he now saw as contemptuous. "Make it happen," Kilgour always said. Sandy was working his ass off, and all Kilgour had to say was, "Make it happen." Sure. Easy. Nothing to it — except his time and his sleep and his whole life.

He gradually realized how much of Kilgour's strength came from having somebody else to do his work. And then there were the servile details. "I don't like the way the monthly book looks," he might say to Sandy. "See if you can work with those people on the format." Which meant that Sandy had to scramble around, worrying whether they had a Courier 10 element for their machines, or whether the type was 10 or 12 pitch, or whether the captions were centered properly. It was Sandy who had to hassle the building people when the air conditioning in Kilgour's office went off at five P.M. Sandy who had to fire a guy from the data center who came in drunk one day. Sandy who had to stay until God knows when every night just in case Kilgour needed him. Not *when* Kilgour needed him. In case. And the more he did, the more he stayed, the more he heard an unmistakable note of scorn in Kilgour's voice. Sandy realized that Kilgour used people, then despised them for being used.

One night, just before midnight, Sandy looked out his office window at the other lighted windows around Manhattan. It had rained hard, and the air now had a special clarity. A sudden kinship for the people behind all those lighted squares rose in him, people making love, or coming back from the theater, from elegant dinners, from visits with friends. Husbands and wives talking quietly. Mugs of coffee being poured, bakery boxes opened to delicate pastry horns studded with almonds. A brush running through shining hair and the crinkling sound of tissue paper being pulled away from a new satin nightgown. Everywhere people together, their breaths rising like feathery clouds to swirl and mingle in the air.

His heart seemed to stop for a moment. In Chatham, in his house, Kathy was alone. God knows what she is doing, he thought. I certainly do not. He berated himself all the way home, sharing his railroad car with a few other men who, like him, had worked halfway through the night. Five or six dreamy couples swayed to and fro on their way back from their nights out in the city, the wives with raincoat collars turned up, drowsing on their husbands' shoulders. *I'm going to save it. I'm going to save it. Save it. Save it. Save it.* He leaned against the filthy train window, exhausted.

He worked on that as systematically as he worked in his job. He delegated more work to his staff and got home early. Kathy was heavily pregnant now, and he treated her with elaborate formality, asking what she needed, what he could bring her. He played with Blair so she could get some rest, brought her tall, cool glasses of iced tea, did the household chores. He forced himself to be calm, to make small talk. He kept her from drinking.

June came, and with it the first heat wave of the summer. Sandy was as irritable with his staff as he was calm at home. He snapped at everybody, and more than half the time when Marie came out of his office, she would roll her eyes up in comic despair.

At home Kathy bored him, and his boredom made him feel guilty. Then he would be calmer, more courteous, more thoughtful than ever. Only Blair could make him happy. In bleak moments he would hug her fiercely. "Daddy loves you, Daddy loves you," he would cry, as if that certainty could save him from drowning.

One hot evening, Kathy lay on a lawn chair in the backyard.

94

The yellow mosquito-repellent candle cast moving shadows all over her, lighting up her damp hair and the shining beads of sweat on her upper lip. Sandy brought her iced tea.

"God," said Kathy, "it's too hot to breathe." They were quiet for a while, listening to the rasping of the cicadas. "I'm so sick of being pregnant," she said suddenly. "I feel hideous. Look at me," she said, pulling up her cotton maternity top. Sandy looked. In the yellow light her stomach was enormous, distended. Her navel bulged like a mudpie on the beach, and all around it was a network of white streaks, stretch marks. He looked away. "Well, anyway, I hope we have more luck this time than we had with Blair," Kathy went on.

"What?"

"Well, it's just that she's such a homely little girl. I always thought I'd have a pretty daughter. Of course, it's not as though I would love her more if she were pretty. But she really *does* have that face everyone talks about, doesn't she? I mean, the face only a mother could love."

Sandy stared at her. He felt his eyeballs burning; he felt he would scream. Then his eyes flooded with tears, and he walked to the edge of the yard. He could hear a sprinkler somewhere down the block. The air was thick. A flash of lightning briefly lit up the sky, silhouetting his neighbor's house and the expensive, calculated shrubbery in his yard. Up and down the street were identical hydrangeas, dogwoods, holly bushes, identical grasses, identical geraniums in pots on front doorsteps. He drooped under the weight of the heat. His shirt stuck to him and he could feel drops running down his sides. He licked his lip, and it tasted salty. On an impulse, Sandy took off his shirt, standing bare to the waist under the flashing night. His torso gleamed with sweat, shining in the eerie light. His chin lifted and a cry came from deep inside, starting as a groan, snapping Sandy's half-naked body as though it were a whip, becoming a long howl.

But the marriage was a long time dying. Kathy's dream of that summer — a golden time of sport, of tall, cool drinks, of club buffets where the tables twinkled with platters of poached fish and crisp salads and fresh fruits — that dream died early. Sandy was never home. He had slipped back into his GlobeBank regimen of long hours. The club was an ordeal of muggy heat

95

exacerbated by her heaviness and Blair's two-year-old whining, which did not end when she drove home at five o'clock, when the other women were waiting for their husbands to come off the golf course.

Evenings, she tried to keep cool. The tall drinks were gin and tonic now. Only by lying very still could she be comfortable.

For Sandy, the summer was a time of panic. At the office and out of it, he was scared all the time. Kilgour began to snipe at him at meetings, to be unavailable, to drop him. So did everybody else. No one at the upper levels of BOS wanted to be within smelling distance of a failure.

He analyzed it again and again. Perhaps, he thought, he was not perfectly suited to financial control or to the management of a large staff. But he was doing all right. Things got done, and they got done on time. Maybe not as smoothly as one would like, but results were what counted, weren't they?

LaRocca once suggested he try being more creative. Creative about monthly financial reports? About personnel matters? About making sure Kilgour signed what needed to be signed and saw what needed to be seen? He didn't understand.

In the fall, Kathy gave birth to a boy — eight pounds, seven ounces — named Blake after Kathy's favorite uncle, the chairman of the board of a big insurance company in Hartford. When Sandy returned from that brief moment of joy, he was more panicked than ever.

Then it all fell apart.

A Wednesday in mid-December. LaRocca's monthly review with Kilgour. Scheduled from nine to twelve. But it may go longer, Sandy remembered thinking; LaRocca's numbers had some big snags.

"Denny?" he called to his top aide.

Not in yet. Damn him.

He went into Denny Kyle's office. On the desk was the black looseleaf binder with the monthly data. Sandy took it back to his desk and began to go over LaRocca's numbers.

Got to be prepared for the meeting. Get in gear. He pushed his hair back off his forehead and concentrated.

The meeting began promptly. Kilgour's meetings always did. LaRocca handed out the usual three looseleaf binders: one for

Kilgour, one for Sandy, one for himself. Sandy opened his copy to follow along. LaRocca reported on the major events of the previous month. Transaction volumes in his processing shops. Dollar amounts. Average turnaround time.

LaRocca sat back. It had been a straightforward presentation. It was eleven A.M.

Kilgour turned to Sandy. "OK, Sandy, any sector-level issues for Ray?"

"Got some numbers I want to check through with you, Ray," said Sandy. He pulled his binder toward him and riffled the pages. "You're still eighty-six thousand outstanding in travel advances. Also, you're still two heads over budget held over from last month. And you have two functional transfers into Schmidt's area that have to go into this month's budget. So your running rate is off a bit and the year-to-date numbers show that you're probably not going to make the year-end forecast." He waited for LaRocca to answer.

LaRocca was silent for a moment. When he spoke, his answer stunned Sandy.

"Sandy, you're way out of line on this one. You're wrong. You're dead wrong."

There was a heavy silence in the room. Kilgour's face was impassive. Sandy stared at LaRocca for a minute, closed his book, and got up and walked to the window. "Those are the numbers, Ray. These are sector-level issues." He sat down again, opened his book, and jabbed his finger at the pages. "This is *my* job."

"Then do it right," LaRocca said. His long Roman face suddenly looked sinister.

"What do you mean?"

"I mean for one thing that you have one hell of a nerve springing this stuff on me here. Even suppose you were right about those numbers — and, believe me, you're not — is this a professional way to report it to me?" LaRocca stopped for a minute, then got up to pace up and down the room. "Sandy, we've worked together. I never pulled rank on you, but you don't do that to a division head." He jabbed his Cross pen in the air as if he were drawing one of his charts. "You just don't." Sandy couldn't speak. He felt his heart pounding, and he opened and closed his fist.

97

LaRocca continued. "I went over all those numbers with Denny; they're all fixed, straightened out. We did it last week so the book would be ready, correct. You should have known that, Sandy."

Nobody said anything. Sandy sat and waited; he put his hands in his pockets.

Finally, Kilgour spoke. "OK, I think we're through for the day." The three men got up and gathered up their papers. Then Kilgour said, "Sandy? Can I talk to you for a minute?" His voice was very smooth.

They went into Kilgour's office. He motioned Sandy to one of his big leather club chairs. "Sit down a minute, will you?" Kilgour went into his private bathroom, leaving the door open halfway. Sandy could hear the sounds of Kilgour urinating, flushing the toilet, washing his hands. He stared stupidly at the picture of Sally Kilgour on the windowsill. She was wearing a short leather jacket and standing in front of a fence. The country, he supposed. Her hair was blowing to the left.

Kilgour came out of the bathroom. His hands were still slightly wet. He sat in one of the chairs facing Sandy and spoke in his flat, even voice.

"Sandy, we've worked together for a long time. You know my style, and you know where my priorities are. My only concern is whether I get a job done in the way it needs to be done. That's what they pay me for. When I can't deliver, they'll find someone else who can."

Sandy said nothing. He kept his eyes on Kilgour's face. Don't flinch, he told himself.

"I think, Sandy," Kilgour went on, "that you've lost control at your end. You're not the first one. But I can't sit in this chair and report the things Pruitt wants to hear while I play nursemaid to my chief controller.

"Sandy, I'm going to think of a new assignment for you, and I want you to think about it, too. Go home, get some rest, come back on Monday, and see me first thing in the morning." He stood up. The interview was over.

"Barbara," he called through the door as Sandy was leaving, "get me Denny Kyle on the phone, will you please?"

◊ ◊ ◊

98

They gave him to LaRocca. A special project: designing a new funds transfer system. "Engineering stuff," LaRocca said, "more your style. You'll report to Rick Schmidt on the organization chart, but you'll be talking to me. Schmidt has a space for you down at 176."

Under Schmidt again, Sandy thought. LaRocca has to be doing this especially to gall me.

"I'd like you to shoot a report up to me on the fifteenth every month," LaRocca continued. "Status sort of thing. What you're up to. This is the usual Management Model project. Current Situation. Ideal Future. Path of Motion. OK?"

Projects — GlobeBank's no-man's-land. Projects were the lowest rung on the ladder, the outhouse. Projects were what you did when you were between jobs and they didn't know what to do with you, or when you were washed up and they didn't know how to tell you. And they hoped you'd get so fed up you'd want to go away. Then your "project" was to call up everyone you knew at the other banks, the brokerage houses, the software shops, the headhunters — expecting, then hoping, then trying not to beg for a job at close to your old salary and close to your old prestige. When you worked on a project you didn't exist.

He took it. He had no choice, so he took it. It was bitter to go back to 176 and Rick Schmidt. He could hardly believe Rick hadn't had a hand in it. Now he had to beg paper, supplies, secretarial help from the man. Rick told the typing pool that Sandy's stuff had "low priority." That sadistic bastard, Sandy thought. Just in case there's a doubt in anyone's mind.

It was the dead of winter when he and Kathy, strangers now for months, had the talk they both knew was coming. When he moved out the next day, it was anticlimactic. At least, he said to himself as he killed a cockroach on the hotel bedboard, there's no place to go but up.

◇ ◇ ◇

It was a slow ascent. It took a month to find an apartment, a one-bedroom on East Eighty-fifth with a view all the way downtown. Jessica Moser gave him tips on where to buy furniture and household stuff. It was all new to him, a role he had never thought he would play.

He got used to it, though. Except for alternate weekends with

99

the children and the heavy burden of checks to Kathy, he had no responsibilities. He spent lavishly, if guiltily, to build a sound system — speakers, receivers, tape deck, cassette deck, a headset. I deserve it, he reassured himself.

At the office, he worked in concentrated isolation. He was aware that people pointed to him as an example of failure, that many found his fall from grace entertaining. He still yearned for power, and trying to put the yearning out of his mind isolated him even further. He lunched alone. Sometimes Jessica would be working at 176 and would drop in. His secretary, Marie, had stayed uptown at Head Office but phoned him regularly, asking about him as if he were newly bereaved. Perhaps he was.

Summer came again. He began going to bars. It was different now, not the way it was when he met Kathy. The crowd was older, his age, and many of them were divorced, like him, eager to have a few drinks and take each other home to bed.

He submitted his Current Situation paper to LaRocca, then waited. Nothing. He submitted his Ideal Future paper and waited again. Rick suggested that no response meant to keep going. In the autumn, he sent up his Path of Motion paper. He waited.

In mid-November, Kilgour held one of his quarterly meetings for all BOS managers in the auditorium at Head Office. Afterward, everyone headed for the Executive Lounge and the obligatory cocktail party. Sandy told himself he'd stay for one drink, wondering if anyone would talk to him.

"Hi, Sandy. How're you doing?" It was LaRocca.

"Fine, Ray." He was surprised. "Enjoyed your presentation."

"Thanks. Look. I've been over your stuff. Like to talk to you. Can you give me next Tuesday?"

"Sure. What time?"

LaRocca sipped some white wine. "All day," he answered.

At two-thirty on Tuesday, Kilgour walked into the room where LaRocca and Sandy were meeting. The long conference table was littered with papers full of flow charts, boxes, solid lines, dotted lines. "You guys hard at it?" Kilgour asked as he walked in. Unannounced as usual, Sandy thought. He walks in here without even a knock on the door, as if he owned the whole damn place. Which I guess he does. When he had fired him from the chief controller's job, Kilgour hadn't even bothered to shut his bathroom door. He makes the rules, Sandy thought. It may be a jungle, but it's *his* jungle.

"How are you, Sandy? How's it going?"

The first thing he's said to me in over a year. Sandy wondered for a brief moment what would happen if he got up and left the room, or spit in the bastard's face. Fuck you, John. "Going good," he said. LaRocca nodded.

Kilgour sat down between them. "Sandy, how about catching me up on what you and Ray went over today?"

Sandy told him, his recitation polished by now. Kilgour listened very carefully, nodded, asked questions. Smart questions, very smart. Sandy had to hand it to him. Kilgour was at his best, seeing the vision of a new automated network for the transfer of funds for corporate customers. He put a few marks on the flow chart. "Better this way, I think." He was right. It *was* better.

When they were through, Kilgour stood up. "OK. That's good. You and Ray finish up with this, then you'll want to do a detailed action plan. Ray, you see him twice a week." He turned to Sandy and smiled. *Smiled.* Sandy felt a flush of pride and pleasure. It was like the warmth that returned when he looked at the pictures in his high school yearbook. "I want Ray to track this pretty closely just so we have a division-level input to add to the technical base," Kilgour added. He checked his watch. "I'd like to have your plan by January 15th, Sandy. Does that sound workable to you?

"Good," said Kilgour when Sandy nodded. "You'll send the plan to me, copy to Ray, no other copies. Let's keep this to ourselves for a bit."

Getting through the next two months was tough but exhilarating. Sandy stopped going to bars, stopped going to lunch. Thanksgiving Day, he treated himself to a turkey TV dinner and worked at the kitchen table. On Christmas Day, he went to one cocktail party in his building and stayed an hour. The hostess was an older woman, maybe in her late forties, Sandy thought, who seemed to be after his ass. Sandy didn't want to be rude, but he had no time for that at the moment. He hardly had time for the kids. Luckily, Kathy had taken them to her parents for the holidays. Maybe I should have insisted on a few days here, he wondered, then bent back over the plan.

At night in bed he considered all the possible scenarios when

Kilgour reviewed the plan. He wouldn't like it and would suggest that Sandy look for another job. Or, no, he *would* like it and would get someone else to implement it. Sandy tossed from side to side. What if he thinks the plan is great? What about that? He'll think the plan is great. Sandy felt Kilgour touch his arm. You're there, Sandy, I want you to build it and run it. You're in control. He mustn't think of that scenario. He should be prepared for the worst. Then Sandy would pad into the kitchen and get a beer. It helped him sleep.

During the day, he drank gallons of coffee. The system. It's mine. Nobody knows as much about it as I do. Nobody knows it inside out. Only I do. Only I can make it happen. I know the business and what it needs technically. Even Kilgour doesn't. The hardware. He's not an engineer. Sandy crumpled up a flow chart and pitched it into his wastebasket. It's going to be the best. The most powerful bank in the world will use it to transfer funds for the most powerful corporations. And I, Kilgour's whipping boy, am putting it together. It's my baby.

He had already named the baby. Automated transfer. Autotran.

9

LISA GOULD'S FIRST JOB AT GlobeBank lasted only three months, the "probationary period" for new hires. Lisa sensed that the trick was to establish your reputation early and never lose it. She was committed to proving herself quickly, and she was committed to proving herself a star.

The Task Force on Product Management had been divided into three teams. One was asked to compile a list of all the possible products in BOS. Another was to study corporate impact. The third, to which Lisa was assigned, was to research product development and implementation.

All those specialized marketing courses at Stanford had given Lisa a solid background in the techniques of the team. As at Stanford, she became a leader of small study sessions, and her sharp views were conceded to have "added value" to the team's work. She learned her first corporate lesson there, too, when the team leader took credit for all the work the team produced. Her own carefully written reports, neatly packaged — another result of her marketing studies — all bore the name of George Grizzuti.

She had some fun in those first few months, meeting and sizing up her coworkers. Her favorite was Danny Faber. He had been hired the year before, straight out of NYU Business School, and was an operations manager for a Collections line. Lisa had decided it would be helpful to learn line operations. Her study team's stated objective gave her an excuse, she realized, so she set up "tours" for herself among the product lines at 176 Wall.

Danny took her around himself. Jacket off, shirtsleeves pushed up, he kept talking despite the people who were constantly giving him forms to read, authorizations to initial, problems to resolve.

"Just pull Luis and Elaine out of dispatch till you get the backlog worked down, Henry," Danny said. "It's not a big deal."

"You don't want me to get some temps?"

"Nah, you don't need temps. You don't need to lean on temps at ten-thirty in the morning. At four-thirty this afternoon, if we're still behind, we'll think about temps. OK?"

Danny turned to Lisa. "It's a firefighting job. There's always something. Or like being a traffic cop. The point is to keep the traffic moving."

"I get the feeling you love it," she said.

"I do," he said. "I also love griping about it."

Their friendship solidified over lunch. Danny's helpfulness put her at ease.

"Listen," he said, "when you're ready to tour IFT, tell me. I've got a buddy there."

"What's IFT?"

"International Funds Transfers. Big volume, big bucks." They were at Wolf's on Lower Broadway. Danny was eating an overstuffed pastrami on rye with gobs of Russian dressing. Some of the dressing was oozing out the side of the sandwich.

"Also DFT — Domestic Funds Transfers. Larry Klein works there. We were at business school together."

Lisa got to know Danny's friends and the line operations they managed. She submitted regular reports to George Grizzuti. She came early and stayed late and made sure George knew it.

She had been on the job for six weeks when she attended the day-long Orientation for all new hires. It was the second time she saw John R. Kilgour. His presentation, complete with color slides, told the story of the renaissance he had worked in bank operations. The story was already well known outside Globe-Bank; the case history of a fictionalized bank back office had figured in Lisa's Organizational Behavior 270 course at Stanford.

Lisa hung on his words. Linearization. Assembly-line concept. Controls of speed and accuracy. Forecast-based financial control. A proactive management style.

It was not, she realized, the words alone that excited her, or the elegantly simple ideas behind the words, or even the actions that the ideas had set in motion. It was, rather, the power behind it all. To be the moving force behind a change this big, this deep, to take a blank slate and draw your own vision, whatever you wanted — that was what stirred Lisa.

She felt it as a physical sensation as she sat in the large, darkened auditorium, watching the charts and the graphs on the giant screen, listening to Kilgour's faint midwestern twang. "So the net result is streamlined operations. Some people around here call it the Kilgour catechism . . ." He waited for the laughter, which tripped lightly through the audience. "But the idea is that it's basic stuff and it's all one color. Now what that means is that if anything doesn't fit, it shows up as a brightly colored flag. We can manipulate it out of existence. We have streamlined for control — *control of the process*," Kilgour hissed, "in terms of costs, which are a barometer of how the process is moving, in terms of quality control, in terms of performance. With that kind of control, we can mold the process to our own objectives. And that's what managing is all about."

Lisa shuddered. Yes, that's what it's all about. You control the process, and you mold it to do what you want. But first you need control.

"Now this Kilgour catechism is really only our first step," Kilgour was saying. "Phase One. Because there's an inherent problem in it. With everything all one color, every service is uniform.

That's fine for now, and it's necessary, as I've said, in order to get the process controlled. But our customers are not uniform. So what we're actually moving toward is the ability to manipulate the process in such a way that we give every customer exactly what he requires.

"We're beginning to think about this now. We're talking to a lot of equipment vendors about our needs for transaction-processing technology that will enable us to fine-tune our process. We are now studying the possibility of a product management capability within BOS" — Lisa felt a rush of pride — "with a view to an eventual new kind of revenue stream for the corporation.

"But I have to emphasize that, for the present, our objective is still control. We want to produce financial transaction services faster and better and with fewer errors than anyone else in the business. I believe we're doing that now, and I invite each of you to go down to 176 Wall and see it for yourself."

◇ ◇ ◇

At the cocktail party that evening, attended by all the new hires and all the members of the Executive Committee, Lisa sought out Kilgour. He, in turn, was making it a point to chat with anyone there from BOS. He moved through the crowd, smiling, staring at the nametags over people's hearts, looking for the boldface BOS.

Lisa found him standing against the floor-to-ceiling window of the great reception court. The court, on the twenty-ninth floor, commanded a vista of all of Upper Manhattan, river to river. Kilgour seemed small against the view, Lisa thought; how deceptive appearances can be.

Three other BOS new hires were crowded around him — all men. "The really outstanding achievement," one of them was saying, "is that the costs were kept flat during a highly inflationary period. I mean, it's one thing to keep costs flat in operations anyway, but when you plot that against the inflation rate for the period, then the total save in *real* dollars is just amazing."

"That's right," Kilgour agreed. He rattled the ice in his Scotch. "Oh, sure. That's a key point. And we're really hedging against any future inflation by getting off the people-intensive curve and on to the capital-intensive curve. The technology is going to significantly lower our costs over time."

Kilgour noticed Lisa. "Hello. Nice to see you again." He extended his hand.

"Hello," she said, returning his handshake. "I enjoyed your talk."

Kilgour thought her pretty. He quickly noted that her clothing was expensive and that it fit well. Kilgour was not usually comfortable with women in the office, except for secretaries and the wives of his staff. But he had recognized that it had to happen; GlobeBank, fearful of government scrutiny and eager to avoid the kind of feminist organizing that had plagued Chase, had been vociferous in its commitment to Affirmative Action. Kilgour intended to meet his quotas — as he met all his goals — and, if possible, to profit from them. And, of course, this girl was an exception anyway. Her name had come up while she was still in school.

"Your team about ready to report?" he asked.

Lisa nodded. "I think so. Yes."

"Want to give me a preview?"

"Well, what we've done is basic research. And what we'll report is basic research results. Nothing striking. Just confirming what we, what you already suspected. That the services side of banking is growing in importance over the credit side, and that GlobeBank is way ahead on that. Because of automation and also, *I* think, because of management style."

She meant to flatter him. She believed it. Then she decided to plunge. "But basically, I don't see that the report is going to be particularly important in a management sense."

"Oh? What *would* be important?" Kilgour asked, one eyebrow raised. "I mean, in a management sense."

Lisa smiled, thinking, You don't have to patronize me, you know. She knew what she was going to say — it was what she felt. She had discussed it with Danny and had gone over it with Barry evening after evening when they did the dishes. She didn't have to rehearse anymore.

"A process," she said. "A management process for making it happen."

"Making what happen? Precisely." She's sharp, he thought. Like a knife. Reminds me of me.

106

"Precisely? Well, *precisely* to get the services developed, get them packaged, get them marketed, and get them sold. That's not only a big job, it's one that will require a matrix-management process."

"Oh? How much do you know about matrix management?" Kilgour had only heard the term for the first time the week before. Hardesty had gone up to Harvard and said it was "all the rage at the B-school."

Lisa shrugged. "Theory. What I've read. It's got to be very difficult to implement. And the political implications ... I mean, as opposed to linearization, with matrixing you've got management responsibility for functions over which you don't have management control."

Politics, too, Kilgour thought. Razor sharp. "Think it's workable?"

"Frankly, no. Conceptually, it's a great idea, but I don't see it working. Do you?"

Kilgour raised the other eyebrow. "I'm interested in *your* thinking."

Lisa looked down into her wine. There was no point in going on. She had accomplished what she had set out to do — gotten John Kilgour to notice her, to pay attention. Score one for the home team.

A week later, Kilgour and his division heads went off to a conference room in the Waldorf for an all-day management development session. Around BOS, this was known as the player draft. It was the meeting in which Kilgour and the division heads allocated the personnel in the sector. Each division got some stars, and each had to settle for some turkeys.

The Human Resources staff had put together a big looseleaf binder containing all the ratings for professional staff in BOS. The assessments came from each division head's Manpower Monitor, the confidential personnel file. The book began with the section called Corporate Sector. The sheets in here, dossiers complete with photographs, were few in number; these were the shining stars, the people who were to be moved along, promoted, rewarded, kept happy. There was a section for High Potential/Good Performance, the people who showed promise. There was a section for Stable Performance, the people who had probably reached their level of competence and responsibility. A final section was called Dispensable; these were the people who didn't fit. Part of the purpose of the meeting was to devise paths for removing these people — getting them transferred to other sectors, finding places for them within BOS where they couldn't do much harm and would eventually resign, or, if necessary, documenting their bad performance "with a view toward termination of employment," as Personnel put it.

Kilgour had a private breakfast with LaRocca the morning of the meeting.

"Ray, I'd like you to take Lisa Gould into your shop. The new hire from Stanford; you took her to lunch; remember? She's working on the Product Management Task Force. Smart girl. The Task Force is about to be a flop and I don't want her in on that. We'll get to Product Management again in a while. Meantime, she could use some broadening. Give her a line position, will you? Maybe an OM slot. Good and tough. Let her get her hands dirty. See if she can hack it."

LaRocca gave Lisa a small line in Letter of Credit. Twenty-two clerks reported to her, as well as a financial analyst, Tony Maresca, who was working his way through Pace Business School at night.

Lisa loved being the boss, solving problems by what she called "the decision-making process" and watching her directives being carried out. Two images stayed in her mind. One was of Kilgour as he had appeared at Orientation, standing at the lectern on the stage, at ease and in charge, a man accustomed to seeing hundreds of people react to his word. The other image was of Danny Faber managing his Collections line, the taut wrestler's body, the rapid-fire answers in language deliberately laced with "street talk."

Lisa was aware that her images of managers held no pictures of women. I break the type, she thought, I set the style.

She calculated and shaped that style from the first. Her strengths, she knew, were her intelligence and her ability to learn quickly. Lead from strength, she decided. Show interest and curiosity but never ignorance — and never weakness. Numbers were a weakness. So she cultivated Tony Maresca, favoring him, to win his loyalty.

Her confidence increased with the length of her work days. At the end of twelve hours, her hair, carefully blow-dried into its soft layers in the morning, would hang limp around her face. The lipstick and pale gray eye shadow she had reapplied after lunch would have faded. Only the color in her cheeks shone — not with rouge but exhilaration. She would go home to Barry, energized by her work.

"I don't know how you do it, sweetie," Barry would cluck in admiration. "On your feet all the time, racing around, all that administrative stuff. You're terrific!" He believed it, and so did she.

Once she was up the learning curve on Letters of Credit, she began to institute some changes in the operation. She did it very carefully, slowly, after much meticulous planning. That, too, became her style.

She had committed to knock three heads in eight months. She knocked seven, and she did it in six months. "A startling achievement," Kilgour called it, and he asked LaRocca to find out her method quickly.

It had been simple, in her view. Logical. She spent three months watching, observing the work every step of the way. It occurred to her, almost at once, that a simpler, more streamlined method existed. At the end of three months, she felt confident enough to draw up a detailed plan. Then she implemented it. Eight tasks were consolidated into one, and seven workers were shifted into GlobeBank's Availability Pool.

Kilgour called the move the Lisa Gould formula; he directed all his division heads, who directed all their group heads, who directed all their operations heads, who told all their operations managers, to implement it in their lines. Lisa became an assistant vice president and received a bonus of 12 percent of her salary. She and Barry spent it on a two-week vacation in France.

Kilgour now took personal charge of Lisa's career. She was *his* woman M.B.A., and she would not be allowed to fill some dull slot in one of the usual corporate female ghettos like Personnel or Public Relations. She would have a major line position, in time becoming perhaps the highest-ranking woman in a major money-center bank. And she would owe it to him.

His first impulse was to name her a group head at once and prepare her for a division head slot, reporting directly to him. LaRocca talked him out of it. "It might be fairer to Lisa to bring her along somewhat more slowly," he said over breakfast one morning. "She has enough resentment aimed at her now. She's come along quite fast already. And she probably has some burdens because she's a woman. I'm not saying she can't handle it; I'm just saying to go a bit slower."

Kilgour acquiesced. But he took her out of LaRocca's division and gave her an operations head slot in Frank Phillips's Trade Operations Division. It too was a Letter of Credit operation, with six separate lines. In the previous two years, no one among a succession of OHs had managed to bring in the six lines at budget. The cost overruns had been substantial, and Kilgour had decreed the operation a "knot," sector jargon for a difficult problem that he himself wanted to keep an eye on.

"Go in there and unravel it," he told Lisa when the assignment was announced.

But Barry had a better idea.

"Alexander the Great!" he announced at dinner that night. They were celebrating with an enormous meal at Nanni's. "Remember the Gordian knot? Everyone had tried to untie it, and when it came Alexander's turn, he sliced through it with a sword. I think you're going to be Alexandra the Great."

Though she liked Barry's metaphor, she spent the first three months in her new post observing quietly. After all, there were six people reporting to her now, and some twenty reporting to each of them. The six OMs had been on the job for a while. They knew the process and they knew the score. Each of them had tried, without much success, to implement the Lisa Gould formula. All of them were stymied by the complexity of the processing. It was just a slow procedure; the clerks worked as fast as they could, but it was never fast enough to keep up with the volume or the customers' demands. They were all stumped. So was Lisa at first.

◊ ◊ ◊

"Will you both please stop talking shop?" Harriet Lipmann squealed, pretending to tear out her hair in mock despair.

Lisa and Barry, Danny Faber and Harriet Lipmann, his new girlfriend, were at Gene's in the Village, having just seen *The African Queen* at a rerun house. It was the eleventh time Barry had seen it, and he sang "There was a bold fisherman" all the way to the restaurant.

Lisa looked sheepish. "Sorry, Harriet. This thing at work is on my mind all the time, and Danny's the only person whose brain I can pick without fear of finding a knife in my back tomorrow morning. Can you just give us one more second? I've just got to finish this one thing."

"It's actually great for us," Barry assured Harriet. "I can tell you this joke Lisa's heard eighty-seven times." He put his arm companionably around Harriet's shoulder. "So there's an economist, a poet, and a politician in a trench in World War I . . ."

Lisa returned to her question. "But don't you think there could be a quicker way to log in there? Some kind of code?"

"Maybe. But you still have to open a book and write something down. So you're susceptible to human error and slowness."

Lisa shook her head. "That just doesn't sound right to me when I think about it."

"And as you've just admitted," Danny said, "you think about it all the time."

When the solution occurred to Lisa, it *was* like slicing the Gordian knot. The problem was the set of transaction forms, the ten-part fanfold the clerks had to fill out as soon as the transaction instructions were received. A major purpose of the paperwork was tracking, keeping a fix on where the work was and its status. Lisa simply removed the entire tracking task from the processing, took it away from the clerks, and gave it to the OMs themselves. And she designed a huge Plexiglas board on which each OM would personally keep hourly track of the work. It would succeed, she thought, in adding a competitive thrust to the operation. Not a bad thing at all. She might even reward the winning line of the month.

For the processing itself, she developed a simplified, clean-looking, three-part form. The entire plan, Lisa estimated, would eliminate so many workers that she could consolidate the six lines into four.

She knew it was a bold and aggressive plan, and she worked at it, on paper, for two months. Besides Danny, only Tony Maresca, whom she had brought along as her operation controller, knew about it. Together, they went over every detail again and again. Just presenting the plan to her group head and to Phillips, the division head, had its dangers. If it was workable — and Lisa was certain it was — Kilgour might want to know why *they* hadn't thought of it. Its very excellence could then become an incentive for them to shoot the plan full of holes. On the other hand, everyone knew that Lisa was a personal favorite of Kilgour's. Not to push her plan up the ladder might be equally dangerous.

If the situation was a minefield for the two men who were her bosses, it was equally so for Lisa. She intended to tread carefully, but she also knew that she held the big guns. Kilgour was watching out for her. If necessary, she could go directly to him. And she also knew that if anyone else should try to take credit for the plan, she could convince Kilgour otherwise. After all, it had the stamp of the Lisa Gould formula.

The group head, Mike Loomis, and Phillips himself listened attentively as Lisa made her presentation — or seemed to listen, anyway. In fact, Phillips had already figured out how he was going to handle the situation — that is, if the plan was any good at all. And it was — he could see that just by riffling through the handout.

"Good," Phillips said as Lisa finished. "Super. Very well done, Lisa. I do have a couple of issues, though. Let's go back over some things."

So Phillips asked for some changes, and Lisa made them; Phillips ordered the plan implemented and sent the report on up to Kilgour with a cover memo.

"I think Lisa has done a superb job on this plan," it read. "Her quick grasp of the problem and her careful approach to its solution are reflected in her own document, which I have attached. I suggested certain changes, which are now part of the plan, which reflect the scope and maturity of my perspective out of my level of management."

Six months later, with the six operations consolidated into four, with a total of forty-three heads knocked, with the transaction processing working more smoothly than ever before, Phillips, prompted by Kilgour, put Lisa in for a promotion to vice president.

She was, indeed, a shining star.

It was said that Kilgour had told Hardesty and Pruitt about this "fantastic gal I've got working for us down at 176 Wall, doing an outstanding job on the line."

It was said that she was next in line for a group head slot and that even the division heads were beginning to worry.

It was said that she couldn't be stopped.

Whenever uptown people or visiting customers went to 176 Wall to see for themselves what a renaissance in bank operations looked like, they were given a tour of Lisa's shop.

Whenever junior officers were put on display at sector-wide meetings, Lisa was among them.

That year, she was chosen by Corporate Public Relations to be one of six young managers profiled in its annual recruiting-book-cum-puff-piece. A writer and a photographer from the PR office came downtown to "do" her profile.

"Hi, I'm Jessica Moser."

The writer looked absolutely out of place at GlobeBank. With her frizzy dark hair and dangly earrings, a bright, vaguely Mexican dress, and a heavy leather shoulder satchel stuffed with papers, she reminded Lisa of a certain crowd she had known at Mount Holyoke.

"Hi," said Lisa, "did you go to Bronx Science?" She was sorry the minute she said it and blushed fiercely. She simply hadn't been able *not* to ask it.

Jessica smiled. "Music and Art. Did you?"

"Did I what?" asked Lisa through her embarrassment.

"Go to Science?"

"Oh, no. It's just . . . You reminded me of someone."

"Right. I remind everyone of someone — usually of their old boyfriend."

"God," said Lisa, "I hope not."

They both laughed. Jessica interviewed Lisa while the photographer took pictures.

"Come and have lunch," Lisa said as Jessica was packing up her enormous satchel. They went to the junior exec dining room, where Jessica kept Lisa laughing continually while everyone else in the room wondered who on earth was that odd woman who was having lunch with the famous Lisa Gould.

The pictures came out fine, and the draft of the profile

that Jessica sent down made Lisa sound as good as she was supposed to.

She was appointed vice president the same day the recruiting book came out. This time, Barry took her to Lutèce and then home. "I've always wanted to make love to a vice president," he said dreamily.

"You sure you don't just mean you've always wanted to screw one?" she asked laughingly as he tumbled her on the bed.

She became a group head the following month. Even she sensed that from here on in, she couldn't lose. "A good reputation is as hard to shake as a bad one," the saying went. She had a good reputation, and there was no imaginable circumstance that could take it away from her, short of disastrous failure. And she didn't consider that possible.

She could, of course, glide, but she didn't intend to. She intended rather to continue to shine, to continue to make important changes, big changes, changes that would gain her attention and advancement. She knew — everybody knew — that she could go all the way.

She began to build her staff, an entourage of trustworthy advisers, "her" people.

There was Tony, of course. Tony Maresca. His fealty was absolutely secure. He had advanced as she had advanced, carried upward by her. He knew that he could not have risen on his own, and he was content to have hitched his wagon to her very bright star. He would never cross her, and he would do anything she asked.

Lisa also needed a first-rate secretary. She had already gone through six.

Flo Taretsky had been at GlobeBank for seventeen years, "since the pre-Hardesty days," she liked to say. She had spent her entire career working for one man. He had been an AVP in the National Banking Sector when she went to work for him; then he became a senior vice president and retired early to move with his asthmatic wife to Arizona. So Flo Taretsky found herself, at the age of fifty-six, jobless and afloat in the organization she had served faithfully since the day her youngest child had entered first grade.

Fifty-six-year-old secretaries, she found, weren't easy to place.

The old guard, like Flo's own boss, had loyal secretaries who had grown along with them. The young men tended to want flashy young women who knew how to use a Dictaphone. "At least I can spell," Flo said ruefully when the third young AVP in a row turned her down.

All of Lisa Gould's six secretaries had been young and flashy, and all had known how to use a Dictaphone, though Lisa herself couldn't stand "those contraptions," as she called them. All of her secretaries had found her manner brassy and her treatment of them intimidating; two said she had reduced them to tears. Among the secretarial pool in BOS, Lisa had been put on a kind of blacklist. No one even wanted to interview with her.

"Would you mind an older woman as your secretary?" the personnel manager asked timidly.

"No," Lisa answered. "Why should I?"

"Would you consider working for a woman, Flo?" the same personnel manager asked Flo Taretsky. "She's only a VP, but they say she has a bright future."

"Mind? Why should I mind?" Flo thought it was a silly question; she herself was a woman.

"What do you consider your strengths for this job?" Lisa asked at the interview.

"What? Strengths?" Flo shrugged. "I'm a secretary. I can type, I can file, I can answer phones, I can keep track. Also, I can spell." She smiled. "I sound like my husband when he talks about a ballplayer. 'He can run, he can hit, he can field.' "

"Well, BOS is something of a new organization. New methods, new technology. It's not much like banking in NBS."

Flo took a chance. What the hell? She seemed like a bright girl. So young, though. "Listen," she said, "you take care of the banking and technology. I'll take care of you."

Lisa thought for a moment. "It's a deal," she said.

As things turned out, it was a good deal for both of them. Flo did indeed take care of her, even to the point of scolding her like a mother when she thought Lisa looked tired or wasn't dressed warmly enough. Flo was, in addition, a woman of remarkable organizational ability, and she put Lisa's office in order.

And working for Lisa seemed to put new life into Flo. She loved being in the "young" BOS, loved being around all the clever young managers, and loved knowing that in all of BOS, none of the clever, promising young managers was quite so clever or quite so promising as her young boss.

One day, when Lisa had gone uptown on one of her more and more frequent summonses to meet with Kilgour, she dropped into Jessica Moser's office. She had visited there frequently since the episode of the recruiting book. Jessica Moser made Lisa laugh, even at herself.

"Jesus, you're uptown a lot lately," said Jessica as Lisa peered around the door of her office. "Come on in."

"You're not busy?"

"Just a canned speech for one of the EVPs. I can do this stuff in my sleep now."

"What's it about?"

"Reg Q. You know, the basic party line. The interest differential between commercial banks and thrifts is unfair to us poor commercial banks. It destroys competitiveness and undermines the free enterprise system on which this great country of ours was built."

Lisa giggled, though she really believed the argument. "It's true, you know," she said at last. "Regulation Q *does* destroy competitiveness."

"Blooey." Jessica spoke with finality. "What brings you up here to the land of overpriced restaurants?"

"Not the restaurants, I'll tell you that. I don't think I've eaten anywhere but at my desk for three weeks."

"All the more reason to break away in time for lunch on your next trip, instead of at" — Jessica looked at her watch — "Jesus! Four forty-five. Quittin' time!"

"Not for me." Lisa sighed. "I've got to stick around and see Killer. We had a four o'clock appointment."

"Boy, everybody's seeing Kilgour today. Do you know Doug North? Sort of suave. WASPy. Works in the Multinationals Sector. He spent the morning with Kilgour for some reason. Then he came up here to check on this speech I'm doing, which is for his boss, and he mumbled something about big changes coming and he hoped soon to be speaking to me on his own behalf."

Lisa looked up sharply. She had just had an interesting

thought about Jessica, probably the same one Doug North had had. "What did you say?" she asked.

"I asked him since when had he perfected his John Alden act, but he didn't get it." Jessica shrugged.

Lisa smiled again, but she had no intention of letting the moment pass because of Jessica's wit. "Listen, Jess," she said, "there *are* big changes coming. Quite big. I mean it."

"But, of course, you are not at liberty to divulge the nature of those changes," Jessica said drily.

"Corny, but true. Promise me something, though. That if Doug North talks to you, or if anybody talks to you, you'll listen to me first before you tell them anything."

One side of Jessica's mouth turned up in a sly smile. "Goodness! Let me guess. Killer Kilgour is going to reorganize. North, you, some other Young Turks, are about to be elevated to positions of power. It has occurred to North, and to you, and to who knows who else, that what is laughingly called a corporate communications program would be a big plus in your new role. And since I am what is laughingly called a corporate communicator . . . Well, it stands to reason, doesn't it?"

"Jessica, nothing is definite yet. Nothing."

"You are, Lisa. You are a definite comer."

Lisa looked at her watch. "Got to go," she said as she stood up. "But would you consider it, Jessica, if it all works out?"

"Work for you? I'd jump at the chance."

10

IT GETS SO DARK SO fast, Sandy thought as he stood, alone now, on the platform of Autotran terminals. Before him was the glass control booth, its consoles and telephones quiet in the cold, silent hub of computers.

All this in eighteen months. From a piece of paper and a few lines drawn in that little closet — to this.

He surveyed the silent floor, which seemed poised on the point of electrifying speed, ready at the touch of his hand to send money whirling headlong around the earth.

So much of himself had gone into the creation of this system. What was that bird — the phoenix? — that rose from its own ashes? Autotran was Sandy Lippert's phoenix. He had built it on the wreckage of his life. And it worked — as nothing else in his life had ever worked. It responded to him, to his touch, soft as a caress.

His mind wandered back to the press conference that morning. A big win with Kilgour. Like I had always been the fair-haired boy. No hard feelings allowed. No feelings of any kind. Sandy shook his head. Praising me like a favorite son. A credit to his father. Everything comes back to him in the end, doesn't it? Even Autotran. I should have said something at the press conference when Kilgour started going into that "our system" stuff.

Our system. Sandy sat down at a terminal and flicked it on. It's *my* system. Nine months in the making. Like a baby.

Nine months before, Sandy had arrived almost half an hour early for his meeting with Kilgour. Sitting on the red velvet sofa in the reception area, he thumbed through the Action Plan again. Oh, Jesus. He spotted a typo that must have eluded him fifty times, "reccomned." Oh, Jesus.

Kilgour arrived. "Come on in, Sandy. Sorry to be late. My daughter flew in from Sweetbriar for the weekend and, of course, she expects Daddy to drop her off at the airport come Monday. Coffee?"

Daughter. Coffee. Small talk. Is he softening me for the kill? Sandy wondered.

The secretary served coffee in porcelain cups. Kilgour took one sip and set the orange folder neatly before him on the desk.

"The plan is great, Sandy. I've got one or two small issues I want to pop with you in a bit. But it's an outstanding job."

Relief, pride, elation coursed through Sandy. A year ago, behind the same desk, this man had shattered him. Now, with a few words, the pieces came flying dizzily back together. He felt like a movie running backward. What a whore I am, he thought.

"Thanks, John," he said.

Kilgour leaned toward him. "There's a big change coming,

Sandy. I'm about to do a very big change in BOS. Let me tell you very simply: Linearization is over." Kilgour leaned back, a satisfied look on his face.

"And it's over in this sense: that the technology exists to handle the work of the lines electronically — with minicomputers." He leaned forward again, gesturing now. "Take an accordion. Pull it out to its full width — that was linearization — then collapse it. That's what we're going to do. We're going to squash the lines, consolidate the functions into the machines. We've got to get off these big-box maxicomputers, anyway. Cost reasons alone. You saw that in your first paper, Current Situation. And you called for minicomputers in your Autotran Action Plan. That's what we're going to do. Put the whole BOS on minis. So instead of seven hundred people doing assembly-line tasks, we have a hundred people. Each of them at a terminal, hooked to a minicomputer." Kilgour's eyes glittered.

Why, the bastard's excited, Sandy realized.

"And the system we go with is Autotran. Your system for transfers. You saw the correct path, Sandy — you just didn't go far enough, that's all. Autotran isn't just going to be Automated Transfer; it's going to be Automated Transaction. Everything's going that way. Got to. But we're going to be first, as Charlie Hardesty says, and we're going to be the best."

Kilgour took another sip of his coffee. "I'm reorganizing the whole place. No more product lines. Customer groupings. Just like you said in your Ideal Future paper. Only we're going to implement that future the first of the month."

He handed Sandy a sheet of paper. It was an organization chart. At the top was John R. Kilgour, executive vice president, sector head. Underneath, eight direct reports. Two staffies, chief controller and chief human resources officer. Donovan and Green. That figures, Sandy thought. Six line slots. Five boxes in a row, labeled International Services, National Services West, National Services East, Metro Services, Multinational Services.

Jesus, except for LaRocca, it's all new names. Sandy was stunned. All the comers. They've arrived. Division heads. Kids! Christ, Faber's not even thirty. Doug North's never processed a transaction in his life. O'Connor. Gould. Smooth sailing for some people.

"What do you think?" Kilgour asked.

Sandy swallowed. "Well, this is clear. I mean, a clear signal that we're a market-driven, customer-focused organization." He paused. "What's Utility?" A sixth box, with no name on it, stood alone under the others, a black line connecting it directly to Kilgour.

"What do you suppose? I mean, the reorganization into market-driven divisions is a management task that I know very well how to do. We make it happen. Current Situation, Ideal Future, Path of Motion to cross the delta." Kilgour tapped his finger on the blank box. "But somebody's got to drive the technical effort. Get all those divisions up on the system. On Autotran. Carefully, without blowing the place up and losing customer records, somebody's got to get all that system stuff configured."

Sandy's pulse raced.

"I'd say it was maybe the biggest systems job in the industry today." Kilgour stood slowly, aware of the drama. "Want the job, Sandy?"

Want it? Did he want it? To pull the levers and turn the knobs that made the whole bank run? Did he *want* it?

It was there again, the feeling of power, raw and alive. God, he had missed it. *His* system the basis of GlobeBank's back office. The name he had given it on everyone's lips. Access to Kilgour again. Division head meetings and the division head lunches. Presentations to Hardesty and Pruitt. Travel again — first class. An army of troops waiting for his orders.

"John," Sandy said, "I want the job."

Only nine months ago. Sandy remembered. I was excited then and I was excited this morning, but now I'm just tired. What does it all mean, anyway? Head of Utility. It still means that. That feeling had never left him. He loved leading GlobeBank into its undisputed preeminence. And the system, Autotran. To have built it all from his own speculation into this. The dark terminal screens twinkled slightly, precious gems of commerce. *He* knew that it was Autotran, his system, that would keep GlobeBank in its leadership position, keep it there for years. None of the other banks was even close.

But now what? he thought. So GlobeBank is the first with the best; so maybe Kilgour eventually gets Hardesty's job. He imagined himself in ten years. His hair might be gray, he still might be dragging out to Chatham every other Saturday to pick up his kids, still sleeping occasionally with Pam or some other woman just to have a warm body next to him. *Pam.* He looked at his watch. Was I supposed to see her tonight? Seven-thirty already. Too late to call her for dinner.

He turned back to the terminal. I'll just run some functions, he thought, just put it through the paces. He keyed in the security password. Access. Main Menu, the screen said. Choose function. He keyed in the code for his father's company, Midwest Canning, then asked for the Profitability Report/Month End. Jesus, were they raking it in. Good for Dad. He called for the Transfer Activity File. Page 1 of 11 came on the screen. One page alone held some twenty transfers. Date, Time, Dollar Amount, Beneficiary, Remitter, for each. Big numbers for an ordinary man to look at, he thought. Look at that line, $574,308 via Banco Nacional for Account of Stanley and Sowerby, Inc. He paged further, the screen flickering as he touched buttons on the terminal. Here's a big one. Over two million. Raw materials, he guessed.

The funds that corporations moved had never been real to Sandy Lippert. At GlobeBank, the word "money" was hardly used. People talked about "big-ticket items" or "high-net-worth individuals" or, in the more mundane areas, "big bucks." Now, as Sandy paged through Midwest Canning's transfer activities, he realized that he was looking at money.

Two million dollars. He tried to imagine what he would do if he had two million dollars, how his life would be different. Kathy, of course. He could buy her off. Here, take this two million and don't call me for a couple of months. He pushed the hair back off his forehead. Or trust funds for the kids. They *have* trust funds, he reminded himself. Kathy's father wouldn't think it suitable if his grandchildren didn't have trust funds. Like tricycles when they're little, trust funds from Granddad when they're big.

He pushed another button and the Midwest Canning records disappeared from the screen, replaced by Main Menu. Let's see, a big company this time. Ensold, maybe. One of the biggest. They had used Ensold this morning at the demonstration. He programmed a recall of the demo transaction. There it was. A modest one, for Ensold. He called up their Transfer Activity File for the month. Pages and pages, billions moving back and forth between San Francisco and London, Riyadh and Tokyo. A few million out of its publishing company account into its paper plant account. A few million more from its television station account to a film company in Rome.

He imagined the sky full of dollar bills, the money racing across the sky as though fired from rockets. Pow! Two million to Avanti Films, Rome. Pow! A million-five to Barclays Bank for the account of Morgan Cross Ltd. Pow! Thirty thousand to the Minerva Group, Special Account, for the GlobeBank demo.

Hell, he could do it too. Fire Ensold's money to Donald Duck, if he liked. He had all the codes. He'd *invented* the codes.

He pressed TRNSFR on the keyboard. The Ensold information disappeared, and the Transfer screen came up. Remitter, it said. Sandy typed in "Ensold Corporation." Beneficiary. He typed in "Donald Duck." At Amount, he put "12 billion."

Lucky Donald. Lucky Ducky. He yawned. God, he was really punchy now. He erased Donald Duck and typed in "Alexander Lippert." He looked again at the screen. Jesus Christ, he thought, it would be so easy. He erased "12 billion" and entered "1 thousand." His heart was racing.

They would never miss a thousand bucks when they reconciled. Christ! Even a few thousand to them was just a few dollars dropped between the cracks. They would just write it off. He knew for a fact that corporations the size of Ensold tolerated a percentage of their monthly transfer activity as a write-off; it simply wasn't worth their time and effort to track down a few thousand dollars.

No. It's crazy. No. How do you do it? You can't do it. Transfer money to Sandy Lippert? They'd find it. Easily. Autotran helps them find it. No.

Not to Sandy Lippert. Who, then? Someone else. Make up a person. Get a GlobeBank I.D. He could do that. He was a division head. He could authorize temporary I.D.'s for temporary staff, staff working on Autotran. He had that power. One I.D. Get that, and the rest follows. You get charge cards, a bank account — you're real.

But where do you open an account? Chatham? He could open

an account in New Jersey and pick up the money when he went out to get the kids. No. No good. He got the kids on Saturday mornings. The banks there were closed. And Jersey was no good. Too close.

London.

He would be in London next month. And two months after that. And two months after that. Anytime he wanted to go until Autotran was up and running. I need to review their final specs, John, he could tell Kilgour. Need to check their acceptance testing. Need to go over their procedures for parallel operation. Need to get some cash.

Sandy hit CLEAR WORK and Ensold's Activity File disappeared. He stood, looking around one last time at the silent terminals, imagining the money that lay buried within them.

No. It's insane.

But it would be so easy.

Part Two

1

"FLO, CAN YOU FIND ME some coffee?" Lisa called over her
shoulder as she dropped her coat and headed for the Ladies'
Room. In front of the mirror, she brushed her dark brown hair,
fluffing the layers and waves that hung to just above her shoulders. She stealthily dabbed at each armpit to see if the fast walk
to work had possibly caused a stain on her coral silk blouse. She
thought not, but she reached into her purse for a spray bottle of
Norell just to feel refreshed.

Tony was waiting in her office, and steam was rising from the
coffee mug Flo had brought.

"I want to hold off on the allocation issue," Lisa said, settling
into her swivel chair. "Let's just do a line-by-line on expenses.
Did Linda get the consolidations done?"

"Yeah," Tony answered, "they're here."

"Did you have a chance to review them, or should we get
Linda in here?"

"I've got the numbers OK." Tony looked unhappy. There was
tension between Lisa's two top aides; she knew it, and she enjoyed fostering it. She felt it kept them both on their toes.

"OK. What have we got here?" The papers read like a glos-
sary of buzzwords, anagrams, nicknames. Yearly comps. Fringes.
OT. Consolidations. Temps. Severance.

"I'd like us to cut this overtime number, I'll tell you that,"
Lisa said. "That's a hell of a big number. How did Linda get
that?"

"That's the consolidated number from each of your group
guys."

Lisa shook her head. "No. Absolutely not. Unacceptable.
Take the consolidated number down by half and have Linda
task each of the group managers to get their numbers down.
We'll discuss it at the meeting with all the guys, but get Linda
started." Tony scribbled on his pad.

"And I don't think this severance number ought to be that

high," Lisa went on. She shrugged helplessly. "I thought we all decided we weren't going to outplace. I thought everybody had gotten the message that they have to reassign within the bank. Everybody signed up for that."

Tony said meekly, "I think they're having trouble finding transfer slots."

"And the solution is to blow their numbers?" Lisa's voice grew steely. "Absolutely not. You go back and tell the guys they're going to have to meet their commitments. That's what a commitment is. That's what they signed up for, and if they fail, they face the consequences. And make that an agenda item for the meeting also. OK. Let's go on."

Tony left at twelve-fifteen, loaded down with directives, memos to write, calls to make, follow-ups to track. The meeting had irritated Lisa. Had she been lax lately? She thought back over the past several months. Had she been preoccupied? Had she slowly been giving up control? Why did the guys think they could get away with blowing their numbers?

"If Taddeusz arrives, tell him I'll be right back," Lisa said to Flo. She headed for the Ladies' Room. There might have been something. Or some accumulation of things. She had evidently given out the message that it was OK to renege on a commitment or two. Well, it was not OK. No fails allowed. Fail and you're out.

◊ ◊ ◊

Taddeusz Walkowicz was in the office when she returned. It was to be a working lunch. Lisa saw the rolls of floor plans on the table and felt a new burst of energy. Layout. Design. Change. She liked this. The conversion to Autotran became real when the layout of the floor changed to accommodate the new machines and the ever-decreasing number of workers.

Taddeusz had been trained as an architect in Cracow and he did not suffer fools lightly. It was fortunate that Lisa had learned to read floor plans like the ones now spread before her as part of her earlier job in the old Trade Ops Division, when she had consolidated six lines into four. It was there she had learned about the Hawthorne Effect: make a change — any change — and production workers will think it's an improvement. That was important, she thought, especially now, when the fear of job loss, of not being able to "make it" in the new world of Autotran, was spreading among the workers like a chill wind.

"Let's see what you've got, Tad," she said.

It was a good plan. The straight product lines of linearization had been shifted into half-moon clusters, each a set of CRTs — cathode ray tubes — hooked to a minicomputer, each processing transactions for a single set of customers.

"I'm thinking to make each cluster in another color," Taddeusz said between bites. "Also posters from the region the cluster is serving. You know: wheat fields, Chicago, whatever it is."

"I like that," Lisa said. "That's good. Give people a proprietary feeling. You know, though, there's a lot of empty space." She traced the white areas with her plastic fork. "I really don't want the place looking empty. Spacious, but not empty. You know? Because people see their coworkers disappearing, they see all this empty space, they worry."

Taddeusz shrugged. "You think you are fooling these people?"

Lisa shook her head while she swallowed some tuna. "Not trying to fool them, Tad. Look. These changes are real. These are external changes that mirror substantive changes in the way we do business. And we *are* reducing the work force. But I want everything we do to be moving us toward the goal of greater productivity. And I want — I just think that great gaping empty spaces are going to make people feel isolated. And that's counterproductive."

Taddeusz sighed. "Well. Plants. And they have those nice round tables, Lucite. You can put things on them. Keep the color-coding pattern. That could do it."

"Right." Lisa nodded and buzzed for Flo. "Ask Jessica to come in, will you?"

"I want to communicate this right up front to everyone," Lisa said after Taddeusz had explained the changes to Jessica. It was something else Lisa believed. "What we're doing, why, when, how." Jessica took notes. They agreed that Lisa would hold a breakfast for all the workers, regular bulletins would be posted on the progress of the work, a party given when the new floor was finished. "Let's make this a positive thing," Lisa told them both. "Generate some excitement. Keep the morale up."

◇ ◇ ◇

Once a month, John R. Kilgour held a review with each of his division heads. Everything was reviewed: financials, production figures, personnel numbers, status of the Autotran conversion. The division head presented the data in the two-inch looseleaf notebook called simply the Book. It was a performance, and Kilgour rated it.

Lisa Gould always shone in her monthly reviews. Her Book was always the most complete; Tony Maresca's main assignment was to put it together. It was also the best produced; Jessica edited for format and language. And Lisa always knew her stuff. She rehearsed her Book so well that she could answer from memory whatever Kilgour asked.

The review was always scheduled for two hours. Lisa and Kilgour invariably got through the Book in one, then sat opposite one another in the spacious conference room, talking about GlobeBank.

"Why don't you try to come to our division meeting on Wednesday, John? Martin Camden is speaking." Camden, a management consultant, was the man behind Directional Control Management, which he had explicated in his new book, *Control Through Goals*. Lisa was sold on DCM and had been after Jessica for weeks to line up Camden for a divisionwide lecture.

"I'd like to," Kilgour said. "I'll see how the calendar looks. I've got a lot going on here. We're having the usual trouble with O'Connor." He often fed her these tidbits of intimate gossip. "The guy is so damn well liked by Metro's account managers that I can't really touch him. But he's in way over his head on this conversion."

"Can't you let Lippert handle most of it?"

"That's what I have to do. But Sandy's overloaded now, and he's going to be really racing on the London Autotran." Kilgour paused before confiding further. "What I may do is bring in a good techie and slip him in as a kind of staff person to O'Connor. Keep an eye on things. Push through the technical effort. Keep me informed. I don't want to ruffle any Metro feathers right now."

130

They talked on, making the circuit of personalities, issues, gossip around the bank. Rumors had circulated at the highest levels that Pruitt was being courted by an aggressive California bank to be its chairman. Kilgour could report that Pruitt was absolutely staying put. "What does he need a challenge for at this stage of the game?" It had also been suggested that Vernon Ramback, who had been sleeping with his secretary for sixteen years, was about to make an honest woman of her. Kilgour could report that Ramback's wife had definitely left him.

Five o'clock. Kilgour's secretary rapped on the conference room door. There was a cocktail party in Multinational and Kilgour had promised to stop by.

"Any issues, Lisa?" he asked.

"No," she said. "Everything's under control."

2

DINNER WAS A GLUM affair. Lisa and Barry had decided they could not go back to France this year. There was too much work for both of them. They would take some time off, of course; go up to the house in the country, perhaps. They had bought it a year ago as a retreat — and so it was. But France — *their* country, where they had honeymooned — was out. It enchanted them too much, took them out of time, took them too far away from the things they needed to be close to this year of all years — the Autotran conversion, Barry's big case.

"Next year," Barry said. "For a long time and leaving no forwarding address. And we take the Concorde."

As they did the dishes, Barry wondered aloud, "What's on the nine o'clock movie?"

"I can't, Barr'. I've got lots of paperwork to get out of the way."

"Really? Well, go do it then, sweetie. I'll finish up here."

Lisa kissed him on the bald spot at the very top of his head and went to the study–guest room, where her brown leather attaché case waited on the desk. She rubbed its creamy finish lightly. It was Barry's present to her when she was named division head. It still smelled fresh, like the aroma when you entered Mark Cross. Her initials shone, burnished below the handle.

The first thing to go over was the methodology paper from Sandy Lippert's division, describing how his consultants intended to go about aiding National Services West in the conversion to Autotran. Lippert had written the covering memo, a reassuring sign that he approved the contents of the report.

To: Lisa Gould, VP
Re: Methodology for Preliminary Conversion Analysis

Attached is a description of the methodology we propose in performing a preliminary operations analysis to aid National Services (West) in its conversion to Autotran. This preliminary ops analysis will then be reviewed with you and your staff. When all issues are resolved, the Utility consultants will prepare a detailed proposal in which we will fully spec out hardware and software configurations as well as organizational dynamics. Once the detailed proposal has been agreed upon, it will be up to your managers to implement the plan, with full assistance and support from me and my staff. In this regard, let me assure you that the team assembled at the beginning of this process will be ongoing throughout the process to assure continuity of focus and to maintain the support relationship.

(Signed) Alexander Lippert, VP

cc: A. J. Maresca, VP, F. R. Kozlow, VP

Lisa frowned and wrote a note on the memo: "Tony: Reply that we will handle org issues. Want tech support *only* from Utility."

"Cocoa?" Barry interrupted, handing her a cup.

"Great," she said. "Boy, this is the life. You're very good to me, you is." She smiled at him. He was wearing the plaid flannel shirt he had bought in Oregon the year he hitchhiked across the country, when he was in college. It was soft with hundreds of launderings. For a moment, she wanted to reach under it and fondle his chest. "Of course," she said, "you're very good at a lot of things." She winked.

"I am shocked," Barry said, leaping backward, "shocked at the lewd and lascivious implications of your tone, Ms. Gould. I would remind you that I am an attorney-at-law, a counselor-at-law, a lawyer, and an esquire." Lisa nearly fell from her chair, laughing. "That was the dumbest wink I ever saw. I'm leaving."

The second document for review was a directive from Kilgour. He wanted her to head a Task Force on Interdivisional Issues. She didn't really know what he was up to with the task force, but she knew it was a high priority for him because he had taken her to Le Lavandou to discuss it.

"You must be about to fire me, John," she had quipped as they turned in on East Sixty-first Street and entered the restaurant's cool, dark elegance. "You fattening me up for the kill?"

Kilgour laughed heartily, as she knew he would. "Just taking my favorite division head to lunch," he said. "A meeting with you at a nice restaurant is very appropriate. If I took LaRocca here, he'd be drawing diagrams on the tablecloth." Lisa chuckled discreetly. "If I brought Danny Faber," Kilgour went on, "he'd try to order a corned beef and tongue on rye." Kilgour enjoyed his own humor. "But I do want something from you," he admitted.

The task force, he told her, would be "to make sure we're all on the same wavelength in the conversion. The chairmanship requires some diplomacy. I want the slower divisions to catch up to the faster ones; I don't want the fast ones held back. The standard here is going to be set by the fastest kid in class."

"Isn't that Ray?" she asked.

"I said diplomacy, Lisa. National Services West is almost up to International, and you're a hell of a lot smoother than Ray LaRocca."

Now, in his memo, Kilgour was formally creating the task force: "I would like it to meet once a month and resolve any issues that may be outstanding. The Task Force should consist of all the division heads and their chief controllers. The primary difference between the Task Force meetings and our weekly division head meetings is that I will never be present at Task Force meetings. This should enable all of you to work out policy from your level and present your recommendations, as a unified body, to the sector head. The Task Force, then, will focus on issues at the division level that should not concern the sector head."

Kilgour had put it more bluntly at their lunch: "All of you can call me names and complain about me and come up with a united front. I've got too many other things on my plate to be bothered by fights among divisions."

Talk about diplomacy, Lisa thought. Killer Kilgour, you con man, this is a crock of shit. For she, Lisa Gould, would be asked to report back to Kilgour regularly, perhaps over elegant meals like this, featuring the finest wines, accompanied by the most obsequious service. True, the task force might be able to keep some bothersome things from reaching Kilgour. But its real purpose, Lisa clearly saw, was to keep an eye on the division heads. Another eye — Lisa's. She owed Kilgour everything, including this. She knew it, and the division heads knew it. They'll be falling all over themselves trying to look good to me so that I will tell Kilgour how great they are. And they're going to hate me for it.

"Sounds like a sort of hot spot for me, John," Lisa had said as she sipped some Cabernet.

"You can handle it. That's why I picked you."

Attached to Kilgour's memo was a copy of the memo he intended to distribute at the Friday morning division head meeting. It announced the creation of a Task Force for Interdivisional Issues, with Lisa Gould as chairman. Jessica had once said that corporate writing was like "some pre-Socratic first principle. It has the virtue of being nothing in particular and everything at once." This memo certainly filled that bill. Not that anyone would be fooled.

Lisa lifted her shoulders and sighed. This was going to be a bit prickly. How do I play it? she wondered. Straight. I just play it straight. I run the meetings as if they were important. I pop the issues and get them out on the table. I keep minutes. That will be Tony's job; I'll have him sit in to do the grundge work after each meeting. I'll defuse it.

Then I'll lay it on straight with Kilgour. Act like it's real. Pretend it's an involvement that interests me. Who knows? Maybe it will.

I'll make it mine, she thought with a slight smile. I'll make it work for me.

Lisa moved on to the next item, Jessica's copy for the division's monthly newsletter. *The National Services Manager* went to all the managers and professional staff in the division. Lisa edited lightly. She was impressed by Jessica's ability and was loath to touch her sentence structure, punctuation, or word choice. But when she came to her own bylined column, "From the Corner Office," she decided that a fundamental change was necessary.

The column was Lisa's chance to sound off to her troops about whatever was on her mind. It might be a pep talk, a thinly veiled warning, or information she wanted them to have. This month, she had told Jessica she wanted the column to be about Directional Control Management. She wanted, she said, to describe the theory in terms of National Services West and to recommend some specific initial actions. All this Jessica had done, but it was still way off.

Lisa pulled a sheet of paper from a pad headed Memo from . . . Lisa Gould and wrote: "Your sarcasm is showing. Redo."

She moved on.

Next was a detailed policy memo from Corporate Public Relations about the cautions that should be exercised in speaking to the press. Lisa made a note to Flo, ordering copies to be distributed throughout the division.

There were two memos from Elaine Green. One announced that Corporate had forbidden the use of the word "employee" in any written material. They were to use "human resources" or "staff" — nothing else. The other was a reminder, "in light of some of the inquiries being made to this office," that there was a strict policy against hiring any temporary workers. Lisa wrote a note to Tony: "Check with Linda on how our technical consultants are being listed. Follow-up to me Monday."

Wearily, Lisa picked up a six-page memo from Linda Glover.

To: Lisa Gould, VP
Re: Strategic Plan: Format for Financial Planning Section

Lisa was surprised to feel her pulse suddenly racing as she thought, Going around Tony and right to me. Ballsy. The tactic was hardly subtle. The contents of the memo, as Lisa forced herself to read it, were excellent. Bucking for stripes, Lisa thought. Bucking for stripes. But damnit, she's good. The stuff is good. Cuts right through. Slicing the old Gordian knot, all right.

"Want to see the news?" Barry had reappeared.

"Is it eleven?"

"Just about."

They watched the news side by side on the sofa. Barry had a habit of doing a running commentary on every story. It was a habit that annoyed her. But tonight her mind was on other things — the Autotran conversion, Linda Glover, the task force.

Can't let this stuff get away from me. Too much going on to get bogged down in this stuff. The conversion is the key thing. Let Tony handle this task force. Got to slow Linda down a little, keep an eye on her. Maybe Jessica would. Got to keep control here.

"I'm for bed," Barry said.

They locked up and turned out the lights. One goal at a time, Lisa was thinking. Control toward the conversion — that's the goal.

When she came out of the bathroom, Barry lay on the bed in his briefs and undershirt. He had neatly folded the bedspread down to the bottom. It always nauseated her slightly.

She sat down next to him on the bed. "Hello, sweetie," he said. He took her hand and put it on his groin. He liked her to rub him through his underwear, liked the cloth moving against him. Lisa heard the wail of a distant siren and wondered if it were a fire engine or ambulance.

Barry reached over. He untied the sash on her robe and pulled at the front. Lisa took her hand off his groin, stood up, and removed her robe. She went to the closet and hung it carefully on its hanger. Then she went back to the bed and lay down next to Barry. They lay still for a moment, not moving. Lisa could hear the *whoosh* of traffic on the street outside, the faint clanking of the elevators, the sound of ticking. She realized that Barry was wearing his watch. He rolled over to her, kissing first one breast and then the other. Lawyer. Always fair.

She noticed how clean his hair was. Nice Barry. She kissed him on the forehead. Barry stood up, pulled his undershirt off, and stepped out of his briefs. Then he pulled the duvet all the way down.

"Are you ready?" Barry asked in a thick voice. She said, "Mmmmm." He got on top of her and pushed in. Pushed. And pushed. "Do you like it?" he kept asking. "Is it good?" Lisa wished he wouldn't ask questions. *Everyone asks me questions.*

136

She patted him on the back. She was aware of a faint erotic tickle somewhere deep inside, like the intimate confidence of a neighbor. "Give it to me," Barry said in an urgent voice. Then he grunted. Barry lay still on top of her, then pushed one more time. A drop of sweat rolled down his chest and onto Lisa.

She lifted her pelvis and pressed it against him. The erotic tickle was coming closer. She knew she was shifting into gear. She kept her pelvis thrust upward and pulled Barry's buttocks down against her. Her eyes closed and she could feel the blood rushing in her ears. "Don't move," she said as it started. Bump. Bump. Then, more faintly, bump-bump-bump. Another drop of sweat fell on her, and she opened her eyes. She breathed deeply, patted Barry on the arm, and kissed his shoulder. Barry rolled off and lay next to her for a minute.

"Hello," he said again.

"Hello, sweetie," said Lisa.

"Going to sleep now?" Barry asked.

"Mmmm," she murmured.

"Good night, sweetie." He leaned over and kissed her cheek.

"Night, Barr'."

Lisa closed her eyes. She heard Barry blow his nose. I've got to keep an eye on Lippert's guys too; I don't want those guys touching my org chart. Technical support is what I want from them, period. Support. Got to keep control of my own organization.

And this task force. Can't let it interfere with the conversion to Autotran. A lot to do there. Can't let the task force get in my way. Got to keep control. Can't lose control . . .

3

SANDY LIPPERT ARRIVED at 176 well before eight A.M. He flashed his I.D. at the guard and went immediately to the security office on the glass-walled mezzanine. Captain Frank Crowley was there, reading the *Daily News*. The captain made it his business to know all the big guns in the building.

"What can I do for you, Mr. Lippert?"

"I need some temporary I.D.'s, Frank. We have some software consultants coming in for a few months."

"No problem." Frank handed him blank staff passes. "Just let me log in their names and you initial them."

Three consultants were due in from MinCom. Sandy added a fourth name, Thomas Putnam. Thomas Putnam. I like it, Sandy thought. Distinguished.

No one was in yet at BOS Utility. His coat still on, Sandy sat at Marie's typewriter and, inserting one of the blank passes, typed "Thomas Putnam" on the line marked Contractor Identification. Beneath it was another line, Signature.

Sandy sank back into the chair. Of course, Thomas Putnam would need a signature for everything. It was almost as foolproof as fingerprints. He would need it to open and activate any bank account anywhere to verify him in official eyes. Without a signature, Thomas Putnam did not exist. And a signature could not be forged, not by Sandy, not without a signature to forge *from*. Even then, learning the forgery well enough to write it effortlessly, while clerks looked on, would be nearly impossible.

Sandy leaned forward and gloomily turned the typewriter carriage until Thomas Putnam's I.D. card rolled free. So that's that. Thomas Putnam dies for lack of a signature. He swiveled around until he was hunched over Marie's desk. There was the carved soap windmill that her six-year-old had made for her for Mother's Day. Her pencil holder was a mug that read: "Best Mom in the World," a gift from her daughter, aged nine. The GlobeBank internal phone directory and GlobeBank's *Secretaries' Manual* stood upright on one side of the desk.

Sandy began to doodle on the pad in front of him. He wrote his signature: Alexander R. Lippert. Funny about signatures. They were something you never thought about. They were second nature.

He wrote his signature again and considered the process. Interesting how I automatically slant the paper to the left and slant the writing to the right.

On an impulse, he tipped the pad to the right and set his hand to write slanted to the left. He wrote "Alexander R. Lippert." He wrote it without thinking about it, without strain. It looked entirely different from his real signature. Then he wrote "Thomas Putnam" the same way. He looked at the signature. It looked impressively authentic.

Hurriedly, he took the I.D. card, tipped it to the right, slanted his hand left, and wrote "Thomas Putnam" on the line marked Signature. He took his billfold out and inserted Thomas Putnam's temporary I.D. in a tuck.

A photograph. He could use one of those passport-type pictures the bank had made him get for that special visa for Japan. Marie had ordered dozens, saying he "looked cute." Moving into his own office, he shuffled through his desk. There was a whole page of them — six identical Sandy Lipperts looking earnestly at the camera. He cut one off and left his office, walking across Wall Street to the camera store, where a laminating machine completed the job. A plastic-wrapped temporary pass for Thomas Putnam lay safe in Sandy's billfold.

"Great day yesterday," Frank Kozlow said as Sandy returned to the office. "We're in *American Banker* this morning" — he tossed the tabloid onto Sandy's desk — "and Jessica thinks the *Journal* will have something next week."

The story, "GlobeBank's Automated Transfer System Live," had merited two columns on the front page.

"That's great," Sandy said. "Listen, though, we've got a shitload of stuff starting today. I'm going to be really holed up doing stuff for London, but I want to get rolling on the conversion for Gould's world. See if you can set up a meeting with her and her guy, Maresca, OK?"

It was just nine o'clock. Outside Sandy's open door, the office was coming to life. Marie and the other secretaries were filing back from the Ladies' Room, where they had retouched makeup and recombed hairdos. People moved across the doorway carrying mugs of coffee, white mugs emblazoned with AUTOTRAN in bright blue. Sandy leaned out the door. "Marie, I'm holing up. No calls, OK?" Sandy closed his door.

He opened the *Times* to Classified, Office Space, and began making phone calls. Half of the people said he would have to come in to the real estate office to discuss his needs. "My needs are a single office space," Sandy insisted, "basically just a mail drop." "Sorry, sir, you'll need to come by personally; we have a variety of floor plans," they answered. He decided those ads were come-ons. The other half were for long-term leases in spaces that would require complete furnishing. Too risky, he decided, and too costly.

What a bust. Instinctively he patted the billfold containing Thomas Putnam's I.D. No address, no existence. Just as well. An insane idea, anyway. Probably. Ah, just forget it.

He dialed Pam Shipley's number. "Sorry about yesterday. Things got crazy here. How about tonight? Martell's? Six?"

"Should I get a sitter?"

"Oh, absolutely." He felt a stirring in his groin at the thought. That's probably what I really need.

It was a busy day, the kind of day he liked. He was on the phone, out on the floor, in the control booth. Yesterday's excitement still hung over the floor. Sandy forgot Thomas Putnam, forgot everything as he wandered his domain. At their cockpit-like desks, workers tapped at keyboards and screens answered with lights. In their specially cooled, walled-off area, the mini-computers chugged away. Disks whirled, stopped abruptly, whirled again.

◊ ◊ ◊

The patrons at Martell's were three deep at the bar. "Why don't we just go up to the apartment?" Pam suggested. "I'll make us some dinner *afterward.*"

They headed out into the cold evening, moving uptown on Third. "Wait a minute." Sandy stopped in his tracks.

"What is it?"

Between a newsstand and a Korean vegetable store was a narrow doorway, 1473 Third Avenue. A sign hung on the glass door: Studio. Sublet. Short term.

"Nothing," Sandy said. "I just thought I saw something. Let's go home."

4

SANDY AND PAM SHIPLEY LEFT his apartment together in the morning, kissed, and separated at the corner of Third. Sandy then made a small detour on his way to the Express bus. He stopped in front of 1473 Third Avenue and wrote down the phone number, placing the piece of paper in his billfold, next to the I.D. for Thomas Putnam. Maybe we can find you a home after all, Tom. He chuckled to himself.

At his desk, he waited until he had had his second cup of coffee with Frank; then he closed the door and dialed the number. A woman's voice answered. "Hello?"

"Hello," Sandy said. "I'm calling about the studio for rent. Fourteen seventy-three Third Avenue?"

"Oh, yes," the woman said. "Can you hold on a moment?" He heard her turn down the volume on a radio. Classical music. "Yes. Sorry. It's a studio, and it's only available for six months. And it's four-twenty a month."

"Uh-huh," Sandy said, writing down the information. "And is it furnished or what?"

"Semi. The basic stuff." She sounded impatient. "It's really small. Look, is the six-month thing going to be a problem for you? Because if it is, we're just wasting time."

"Actually, no," Sandy answered. "I'm a consultant on assignment." Was he telling her too much? "A short-term rental is just what I need."

"Oh," said the voice. Then, in a friendlier tone: "What kind of consulting do you do?"

"Banks. Financial and data processing. I'm in New York for a while."

"Uh-huh," she said. "Well, maybe you want to come over and see it."

"Yes, I would," Sandy said. They made an appointment.

"OK, then," the woman said. "Listen, I didn't catch your name."

"Putnam. My name is Thomas Putnam."

◇ ◇ ◇

He got to the studio promptly at six o'clock. It was up two flights of narrow stairs that creaked a little as he climbed. He was nervous. Take it easy, he commanded himself. He rang the bell.

The voice on the telephone belonged to a small woman in blue jeans and a forest green sweater. Late twenties, he guessed. "Brooks Harris," she said, extending her hand. "You're Mr. Putnam?" He was surprised at her friendliness; she had sounded so brusque on the phone. She wore no makeup or jewelry, and her reddish hair tumbled frizzily around her face.

The place *was* small. A counter divided it in two. One side was a kitchen containing a refrigerator of late forties vintage, a metal-topped table, and a sink with the dishrack set inside. The other room, which looked out on Third, held a large table and a bed covered with an Indian spread and several large pillows.

"Well, this is it," she said.

"Seems fine," Sandy said. "It's four-twenty?"

"Right." She smiled, relaxing now. "Look, I hope you didn't think I was awful or anything, but I've had a lot of creeps here who made me show them the place and then told me that they had to have something for a year. You know?" She shrugged.

"It'll really be OK," Sandy replied. "How come you're able to sublet it for six months?"

"I'm going to Idaho," she said. "I'm a potter, and I got this job at a college out there as a kind of artist in residence. I was lucky. But anyway, I don't want to give this place up."

He thought he should ask some questions. "Is the neighborhood quiet?" He waved his hand toward the window.

"Pretty quiet. I work mostly in the day, and the street sounds aren't too bad for the city. On the other hand," she said, looking up at Sandy, "I'm a native New Yorker, and I find city sounds restful."

"A New Yorker? No kidding. I would have pegged you for a Midwesterner come east to seek your fortune."

Brooks Harris laughed. "Just the opposite. I'm an Easterner heading west to be recognized."

He filled her in: Consultant. Abroad for six years. Assignment to GlobeBank. He showed her the GlobeBank I.D. for Thomas Putnam.

"If you need a reference, you can contact one of the vice presidents at GlobeBank. I'm sure he wouldn't mind vouching for me." He wrote "Alexander Lippert, VP, 176 Wall Street" on a piece of paper and handed it to her.

"Thanks," she said, folding it. "But I doubt I'll use it."

"So," said Sandy. "I really think this place will do. Can we shake on it and make it official?"

She thought for a moment. "Yeah. I think we've got a deal." She pulled a piece of paper from a drawer. "I've got this lease agreement. A friend of mine who's a lawyer drew it up." She pushed it toward Sandy. "It's really to protect both of us, you know? So why don't you look it over, and if it's OK with you, we'll both sign, and then you can, you know, give me a check."

A check. Jesus. A check. For the rent. Now what?

"You'll see that the monthly checks are to be made out to Gordon Oliver. He's the guy I live with. He's staying on in our apartment, although he'll come out to Idaho a couple of times. At least, he *says* so."

He was thinking fast as she talked. "Gee, I didn't even think about the check. The fact is that I don't have an account yet; I mean, the checks haven't been issued. Can I pay you by money order? I can drop it by tomorrow."

"Oh, sure," Brooks said. "Except maybe you can leave a deposit? I don't know. How much cash have you got on you? I mean, leaving some for getting home and all."

"I can give you at least seventy-five." Sandy reached for his wallet. "And let me sign this now." He squared the lease in front of him, then tilted the paper to the right. He signed "Thomas Putnam" smoothly and rapidly.

The next day, he waited until after lunch to go to the Department of Motor Vehicles, hoping to avoid the lunchtime crowds. But at three o'clock it was still packed. He stood in line for nearly an hour, trying to read the paper as he waited. The hell with this, he thought at one point. Why does Thomas Putnam have to drive? But he waited, finally emerging from 155 Worth Street with his application for the written test and the New York State driver's booklet. He would also need a certificate from an accredited driving school that he had had the benefit of three hours of refresher training.

5

THE DIVISION HEAD meeting, Kilgour's formal staff meeting, was held every Friday morning — all morning — in his conference room. Early arrivals picked up printed agendas, like playgoers getting programs, and gathered in the reception area.

Lisa had been there since eight-thirty. She felt good after her walk to work, and she was warming up on coffee, warming up talking to Danny Faber, who sat next to her on the red velvet sofa.

"You performing today?" Danny asked.

Lisa shook her head, then scanned the agenda. "It doesn't look like anybody's got a formal today. You?"

Danny made a face. "Hey, we went to a great new restaurant last night." Danny, newly married to Harriet Lipmann, was still enjoying the whirl of New York nightlife. Lisa remembered it well — the dream of New York's young professionals — when she and Barry had subscribed to theater groups and the City Opera and the ballet, when they had gone to every museum opening and every event in town, eaten out three nights a week, thought nothing of driving to the Village or Chinatown or City Island or Brooklyn, for a meal, a movie, a jazz club. They were never tired then. Lisa also remembered how they used to make love after work. "We have time before the curtain," Barry would say.

Brian O'Connor pushed through the glass doors. Red-haired, Irish, laughing loudly at every opportunity, O'Connor was perfectly suited to be Metro division head, processing the transactions for the GlobeBank branches in the city. Born and raised in Queens, the product of parochial school, Fordham, and Fordham Business School, O'Connor was the image of the "sharp, hungry operations analyst" Kilgour had once predicted would come into his own in the back office renaissance.

"Hey, you guys." O'Connor came over to the sofa. "Hey, who's doing minutes today?"

Danny raised his hand.

"Better watch your spelling this time," O'Connor joked as he walked off.

Doug North followed O'Connor to the coffee machine. No two men could have been more different. North's dull blue eyes flanked a perfect nose. His brown hair, Lisa was certain, was professionally shaped. He looks like an anchorman, she thought. North had gone to Yale and wore his Calhoun College tie at least once a week. He had gone on to Stanford Business School and had married a daughter of one of San Francisco's finest families. His manner was suave, his voice smooth and quiet. He was just as suited to the carpeted hallways of the world's great corporations, for which his division processed transactions, as Brian O'Connor was to the ethnic hurly-burly of the city's neighborhoods, as Danny Faber was to the fast, rough-and-tumble world of old manufacturing corporations, as Lisa herself was, she realized suddenly, to the sleek, marketing-oriented businesses of the Sun Belt and the new West. Or do we all just take on the personalities of our jobs? she wondered. Even Ray LaRocca, hardly a cosmopolite, had smoothed his rough edges and learned phrases of a few languages since he took over the International Services Division.

"Did Ray and John come up yet?" North asked. Kilgour and LaRocca had breakfast together almost every working day. Privately. Often they ate in the employee cafeteria, in a corner of the barnlike hall. Sometimes Kilgour felt like going to the Brasserie or the Regency Hotel. These breakfasts went on the expense account as business meetings. And even though no one ever knew what, precisely, the two men discussed nearly every morning of nearly every day, all were sure it was strictly business.

"I think they're in John's office, actually," Danny said.

Sandy Lippert arrived last, as usual, his coat still on, his cheeks red from the cold.

"Good morning," he said.

Lisa noticed that his vivid green eyes and his ruddiness seemed to bring energy into the hermetically sealed, overheated building. "Morning, Sandy. Chilly out, isn't it?" She imagined him bounding to work. Down Park? she wondered. Or weaving among the crowds along cramped Lexington?

"I'll say." He gave her his most winning smile.

Lisa was reminded of Flo's comment about Sandy Lippert: "A doll, that boy, a living doll — and a real looker."

Kilgour's voice reached them from the conference room. "Let's go."

◊ ◊ ◊

Friday was an easy day for the rest of BOS. The division heads were safely closeted away for the morning; then they usually went on to lunch in knots of two or three. This meant that the managers could pretty much count on not seeing any of their bosses until one-thirty or two in the afternoon. And even at GlobeBank, two o'clock on a Friday afternoon was a little late to start any really demanding project.

So on a Friday morning, Linda Glover could spend time in Jessica's office, drinking coffee and talking.

Tony was there, too, this morning. The three of them lounged around the small table, its surface concealed by the *Times* and the litter of Jessica's work. It was a cozy office, in Linda's view. The smell of hot coffee rose from the Styrofoam cups. Tony was in shirtsleeves — so he looks like he's working, Linda thought. She was leaning back in a posture that her mother would have discouraged.

"So what's going on in the meeting?" Jessica directed the question to Tony. He was notorious for spilling all of Lisa's confidences, although Jessica was certain that Lisa knew it and only gave out those confidences she wanted spilled.

"Well, you know about the new task force Kilgour's creating? Lisa's going to head it up."

"What task force?" Linda's posture instantly improved.

"Interdivisional Issues."

"Interdivisional Issues," Jessica repeated, sounding arch. "What the hell does that mean? What the hell is that supposed to mean?"

"Yeah," Linda said.

Tony shrugged. "Well, I think Killer feels that he has to deal with too much of the nitty-gritty on the Autotran conversion. You know, like where one division wants some special thing, or then one copies the other. Stuff like that. So he's letting them all get together once a month without him and work it out. Then Lisa's supposed to buck the real issues up to him." Tony sipped his coffee. "I sit in. I'm kind of the chief controller for the task force."

"Sounds like it might be a lot of work for you, Tony," Jessica said sympathetically.

"For you too, Jess," Tony replied. "We've got to do minutes, reports, stuff like that."

"Oh shit," Jessica said. It was the kind of work she disliked. Memos, reports, follow-up notices. Moving commas, she called it.

"Is it a big deal?" Linda was alert to any possibility.

"Well, I don't think anyone knows yet. I think even Lisa's not really sure. I mean, we've got bigger things on our plate than that." He glanced at Linda, hoping the "we" had registered with her. "The conversion is the top priority. Absolutely." Tony ventured one leg onto the table, then the other. "And the off-site's coming up soon. In fact, that's what they're doing at the meeting over there right now."

Off-sites. Jessica had once thought she might write an article — under a pseudonym, of course — about off-sites. She had gotten as far as the first line: "In a sea of three-martini lunches, padded expense accounts, and corporate 'perks,' the off-site conference is the crest of all boondoggles." She would go through the history of the thing. How it started as a simple idea: Take everybody off-site — i.e., out of the office, away from interruptions — to hole up and tackle difficult issues in an intense way. How it grew. The distances getting longer — from a nearby hotel room to a resort along the shore to Paris, Rome, Tokyo — until the IRS clamped down on overseas meetings. How meeting times grew shorter and play times grew longer. Hell, here we are in Palm Beach; might as well get in some tennis, some golf, some sunbathing. Some good meals. Some cocktail parties. Hell, might as well have the wives along, let them get to know one another while we're meeting all day. Hell, silly to meet *all day;* we'll just hold meetings in the morning, have the afternoon free to refresh our brains. Hell, we're down here for five solid days, let's make one of them a real rest day, loosen up with tennis, plan an excursion.

With Kilgour, of course, it was different. He expected solid performance and scheduled less play time than most. But he too believed that having his people relax together built good teamwork, very important to corporate thrust. So even play at a Kilgour off-site was a performance. Tennis, golf, swimming, line management. They were there to win.

"The resort is supposed to be gorgeous," Tony was saying. "Palmas del Mar. It's . . . I don't know where in relation to San Juan but not too far. I think it was built by the Hilton Head people. So there's lots of tennis and golf. And — get this — a swim-up bar in the pool."

"You're kidding," Linda said.

Jessica had a mental picture of Kilgour, LaRocca, and Doug North treading water furiously while they waited for drinks.

The phone rang. "Hello?" Jessica said in her emphatic way. Linda made a mental note to tease her again that she had once more failed the answer audit. The corporate manual required that "in a service organization, we must all be representative of the service we provide. In answering our phones, this means that the proper method is to answer: 'GlobeBank!' and then your name." Jessica never did.

"Um-hmm," she said. "OK." She hung up. "Tony, it's Flo. Crisis on the customer service front."

Tony sighed and got up.

"Run and jump," Linda said, glad that the crisis was at service and not at numbers.

Tony turned quickly and walked away. I know about you, he thought. I know all about you, loose and lucky Linda Glover. You're loose in bed. You and Rick Schmidt. That's how you got lucky and got ahead. I have to serve customers; you just service Schmidt.

◇ ◇ ◇

Lisa, in her accustomed place between Danny Faber and Doug North at the huge conference table, looked down stealthily at her watch and decided it was just about time for Kilgour to call the midmorning break.

They had been through the numbers, Al Donovan taking the whole group through the financials for each division, pointing out the ones that were in trouble — who needed to update a forecast, who was blowing their Operating Expense budget, who had outstanding travel advances. They did it every week. Kilgour had come to believe that hearing your misdeeds said out loud before your peers was good for the soul. A toughening-up measure. Kilgour believed in toughening people up.

Elaine Green was droning on with her usual pep talk about Affirmative Action. Lisa tuned out. She had met her numbers for blacks, women, and Hispanic surnames early. She stole a glance at Kilgour and caught him assessing Elaine's cleavage.

Everyone knew about Kilgour's "crush" on Elaine, assuming, correctly, that it was benign, that there was nothing going on between them; but wasn't it amusing — cute, some people said — to see the great, puritanical John R. Kilgour actually smitten? He invented excuses for summoning her to see him, and at the sector cocktail parties, he grew wide-eyed and playful in her presence.

Had he known that "everyone knew" and that his infatuation was the subject of general gossip, he would have been furious. He would have forced himself, in his disciplined way, to become disenchanted.

For Elaine, Kilgour's flirtatiousness was a bother. For all her self-confidence — helped along by her good looks, her smartly tailored wardrobe, a degree from Skidmore, and two up-and-coming stockbroker boyfriends — it was still galling to know that a couple of thousand people were laughing about you behind your back.

Still, Kilgour's favor, whatever its source, had done a lot for her. She was human resources director for the sector with a staff of five division human resources officers, her own chief controller, a secretary, and an administrative assistant. She was an insider, privy to confidential knowledge about who the stars were and who was in trouble. Her salary was excellent, and Kilgour allowed her a long leash on expense account lunches. Elaine occasionally asked herself what she would do in the unlikely event that Kilgour made a move in her direction. She didn't know, really.

Headstrong Sandy Lippert was her problem division head today. He had not met his quotas. "Elaine, two of the people you sent me had no technical background whatever. None. The others were just not qualified." Sandy appealed to Kilgour. "Autotran's too sensitive to go with untrained people right now."

"Sandy," Elaine said, "the point is — "

Kilgour interrupted. "OK. Hold it, you two. This issue isn't for this meeting. Sandy, I want you and Elaine to try to renegosh this on your own time. If it can't be resolved, do a memo, co-signed, and I'll handle it." He smiled at Elaine. "OK. Let's break."

Lisa headed for a phone to check in with Flo. Nothing going on. She poured a fresh cup of coffee for herself and one for Danny. "Want to have lunch?" she asked him.

Danny nodded. "Wolf's?" he asked hopefully. Danny's favorite lunch was a pastrami on rye and a quick walk through Tiffany's.

"Great," Lisa said.

She paid little attention to the rest of the meeting. North was proposing some change in the financial reporting system. It bored her. I'll get all this from Danny later, she thought. Numbers had never been her strong point. She had mastered finance, as she had mastered computers, because she had to. Numbers were an abiding passion with Danny Faber, whose hand could move over the face of a calculator with lightning speed, just as computers were an abiding passion with Sandy Lippert, who loved building systems and watching them flow. For her, she reflected, the real joy was in juggling everything, "driving the process," she liked to call it, "managing all the variables in the equation."

Especially the people variable. Lisa was proud of her ability to sense instantly what made people tick and then to motivate them in the special way each one required. With Tony, it was money and a sense that he was on the inside. With someone like Linda Glover, it was power and all the trimmings. A label next to her name. A ride in the limousine reserved for division heads. A chair at high-level meetings.

North proposed on. Danny interrupted with a question. "Good point," North conceded, and the table erupted into a general discussion.

What are we doing this weekend anyway? she wondered. She couldn't remember if she and Barry had any special plans. I wouldn't mind just loafing; I wouldn't mind sleeping late, maybe going somewhere nice for lunch, maybe taking in a movie.

She tuned in on Kilgour's voice.

". . . tell you about the plans for the off-site. Very roughly: Tuesday and Wednesday are the presentations of this year's plans. Thursday and Friday are presentations by each of you on special assignments. Wednesday afternoon is free time, by the way. OK. Al?"

Donovan handed out schedules and the special assignments for Thursday and Friday. Lisa quickly scanned the list. Lippert: Autotran Update. North: World Economic Trends. Faber: New Techniques in Financial Reporting. Gould: Directional Control Management Theories. O'Connor: People Motivation. LaRocca: Overseas Branch Back Offices.

The division heads looked warily at one another, wondering about their topics. And Kilgour looked ostentatiously at his watch. "OK," he said. "That's it. Any questions?"

6

ARMED WITH HIS LEARNER'S permit from the motor vehicle bureau, Sandy walked quickly back to 176 Wall. He felt buoyant. It must be lunchtime, Sandy thought. Nassau Street became a pedestrian mall every weekday at lunch hour. People streamed through the street, covering the sidewalk, blazing diagonal trails from one side to the other to enter the shops and lunchrooms and fast-food stands that lined the thoroughfare.

Sandy enjoyed being tall in a crowd. He liked the feeling of being able to see over the heads of the people around him. Especially the women — he liked looking down at the women. Black secretaries in bright coats and shiny boots who moved out of nobody's way. Middle-aged clerks traveling in knots of three or four, women who had worked on the Street for years, handling more money in a day than they would ever earn in a lifetime.

Young executives carrying briefcases — lawyers for Wall Street firms or vice presidents at the banks or maybe assistant commissioners at the city agencies, whose offices clustered around City Hall and the Municipal Building.

He liked weaving through this female world, sure of his body, moving jauntily, feeling strong.

Sandy's eye instinctively sought out the most attractive woman, and he fell in step with her. She wore a camel's-hair coat with a fur collar. No hat. Brown leather boots that matched her brown leather bag and her brown leather briefcase. He followed her up Nassau, trying to guess where she worked, what she did, who she was. The woman kept her stride. She turned eventually into the William Street door of the Chase headquarters. He whispered good-bye. Maybe she's Chase's Lisa Gould, Sandy thought. Jesus. I've got that meeting with Gould this afternoon. I'd better get back fast and go over her stuff.

The meeting was scheduled for three o'clock in Lisa's conference room. Sandy and Frank arrived carrying armloads of black looseleaf notebooks. Lisa took her blazer off carefully and hung it on the back of the chair. She really looks great today, Sandy thought.

"Those books appear fairly intimidating," Lisa said. "I guess we better get started."

Sandy realized that he knew very little about Lisa Gould. Her performance in division head meetings, her presentations, were always perfect.

Many people resented her. If she had been a man, they said, she would never have gotten this far. People said she was all showy staff work and no substance. People said she was Kilgour's "token woman" — just a showpiece, not really competent.

Sandy didn't agree. The proof of the pudding, after all, was in performance. National Services West was no easy assignment. She had kept costs flat in a group of shops that had consistently gone over budget. Kilgour knew what he was doing when he gave her the division. But then, Kilgour almost always knows what he's doing, Sandy reflected wryly.

Frank was giving his presentation, but Sandy continued to focus on Lisa.

Does she really look that good or am I just in a great mood? he wondered. Even in profile, she had an intense look. Her brow was furrowed, as if she were setting her mind to draw in everything Frank Kozlow was saying, sending each bit of information to her brain's proper quadrant.

So serious, he thought. But soft. He wondered what her husband was like. Barry Something. A different last name.

Lisa shifted in her seat. Her left arm, hidden by her body, jerked almost imperceptibly. Adjusting her bra, he quickly thought. His eye moved to her bosom. Soft, he thought again. She was a small woman, with small wrists and a slender neck. There were no hard angles.

I'm staring, he suddenly realized, and he shifted in his chair.

". . . design the final specs based out of your macro plan plus the way we resolve things in these frequent meetings . . ." Kozlow was wrapping up.

7

"FLO, WE MISSED YOU last week," Jessica said. "How was the training course?"

Flo's mouth turned down at the corners. "Not easy. I'm too old to go to school. You can't teach an old dog new tricks, that's what I say. Let me tell you, there's so much to remember. Correcting. Justifying. Shmustifying. Who needs it?"

Jessica tried to appear sympathetic. "Come on, Flo, it's state-of-the-art technology at GlobeBank. Listen, you'll get used to it. You're brighter than any twelve people around here. Just relax. You'll catch on."

Flo rolled her eyes upward. "I hope so."

A lined pad under her arm, Jessica entered Lisa's office. Tony and Linda were forcing themselves to make small talk at the long table. The meeting had been called to go over the proposed formats for the Strategic Plan.

"Flo sounds a little rattled by her training course," Jessica said as she sat down.

"Oh, hell, she'll catch on." Lisa dismissed the issue with a flick of her wrist. "Flo's great."

"Yeah. Well, be patient with her, Lisa."

The meeting began in earnest, punctuated by Flo's fretting noises. "Damn!" they heard her say, muttering at the machine. "Mode 1. Where the hell is Mode 1? Pushed the wrong — damn!"

Linda started giggling, and Tony looked as though he was about to join her. Lisa peered over Tony's head to the open door, poised like a pointer.

"What should we do?" she finally whispered to Jessica.

"What are you asking me? What would *I* do?" Jessica demanded.

Linda stared, her mouth open. No one, but no one, ever talked to Lisa Gould this way.

"What I personally would do," Jessica was saying, "is laugh her out of it."

"Oh, that's great," Lisa said, "just go out there and laugh at her."

"Not *at* her, Lisa. There's nothing to laugh at. Flo is an intelligent grownup lady faced with something strange and new. She feels that her work, which she understood perfectly up until last week, is now alien territory."

"What do *you* think, Linda?" Lisa asked.

Linda blushed. "I don't really know Flo very well. I don't know what kind of motivation she responds to."

Jessica groaned.

Lisa said, "Let's get back to the issue at hand, I think."

They continued their discussion. Flo buzzed Lisa that Kilgour was on the phone.

"Hello, John," Lisa said. "Mm-hmm. Right. OK."

Lisa hung up and buzzed Flo. "Can you come in?"

Flo appeared, steno pad in hand. "What?" she inquired, with the crashing final *t* that marked her Bronx origins.

"Kilgour wants this morning's numbers right away. He also wants to test the Ardec network. Can you send them by electronic mail transmission?"

Flo's face fell. "I'll try," she said.

The Ardecs — Kilgour and all the division heads now had them — were hooked together in a network so that they could

154

communicate with one another. No paper, no phone calls. Messages would appear on CRT screens or on the Ardec printer. Flo sat at her machine, opened her manual to the notes she had made at the training session, and began muttering.

"Excuse me," Jessica said. She walked casually to Flo's desk.

"So nu, Buck Rogers," she hailed, "how's it going?"

"It's not going," Flo said. "I'll never get it, Jess."

"Baloney," said Jessica.

"I'm too old to learn this — or too dumb."

"You're not old and you're certainly not dumb. Come on. What is this? It's a toaster. It's an electric can opener. It's just a gadget."

"A toaster I can work. This I can't." Then she blanched. "Oy. I pushed PRINT by mistake."

Behind her, the printer started moving. *Chug-chug-chug-chug.* Then it began to print — rapid clacking sounds interrupted by a sudden *whoosh* as the mechanism moved to the next line.

"It's going crazy," Flo said. "What's it saying?" Jessica picked up one end of the print-out and began to read: "Hello. I am your Ardec print-out demonstration. The material you key in next will appear as print when you activate the print mechanism. To do so, you should push the button marked PRINT on the lower left of your keyboard. Remember" — Jessica shouted the word — "first you must store the data you have keyed in. To do so — " Jessica broke off, laughing. "Jesus," she said, "I hope to hell this is coming off Kilgour's printer."

Flo began to laugh.

"And of course Barbara is so brilliant she'll probably take it in to him and say it's from Lisa," Jessica continued.

Flo was laughing hard as Lisa, Linda, and Tony emerged from the office.

"What's going on?" asked Lisa.

"Listen," said Jessica, "high technology is going on out here."

"What happened?" It was Tony.

"What happened," Jessica replied, "is that Flo's finger slipped, and John Kilgour's printer is now getting a lesson in how to work John Kilgour's printer."

The phone rang. Lisa picked it up. "Yes, John, we pushed the wrong button or something. We'll get it up to you." Lisa looked

155

at Flo and nodded. "Listen, John, don't hold your breath. We're not quite ready to transmit."

Jessica read to Flo from the manual in a German accent, with embellishments: "You vill now push ze button marked STORE! You vill!"

Flo pushed the button.

"It iss done? Gut! Pushing now ze button marked SEND! Iss pushed? TORPEDO LOS!" Jessica shouted. "Zehn, neun, acht, sieben, sechs."

Flo laughed from her stomach, leaning forward over the keyboard.

The phone rang again in Lisa's office. "I'll get it," she shouted. "Oh, hi," they heard her say. "You got it? Good. Right. OK then."

Everyone applauded, and Flo bowed in her seat.

8

"SANDY!" MARIE YELLED THROUGH the wall. "Pick up on two-four."

He had not even heard it ring. He was concentrating on the detailed specs for the London Autotran.

"Sandy Lippert," he said absently.

"Hi." It was Kathy.

"Kathy. Oh. Hello. Is anything wrong?"

"No. Not with the kids." Her voice was icy. "But I'm calling about the check. Did you send it?"

Oh, Jesus, he thought, the check. Again. I've forgotten it again.

Sandy hated this scene, which had been played many times. It seemed that no matter how firm his resolve, it would only be a month, or two months at the most, before he would forget the check — and hear from Kathy again.

◊ ◊ ◊

"I just don't understand myself," he said to Pam Shipley. They had made love and were lying in Sandy's bed, sipping wine

156

and sleepy enough to exchange confidences. At that late hour, they could hear only occasional traffic sounds below. "I just don't know why I keep doing that when I *know* she's going to call."

"And you feel . . ." Pam said.

"Stupid. Guilty. Like a lousy father."

"I don't know," Pam said. "I went through something like that with Bob. He was always late with his payments. Always something."

Sandy grimaced.

"And either he would call me or I would have to call him. This happened nearly every month. I was really upset for a long time."

"I don't know if you could call Kathy 'upset,' " Sandy said. " 'Vindictive' would be more like it."

"Listen, Sandy, don't sound hurt," Pam said, reaching for his hand. "Let me tell you, a whole lot of divorced couples I know are not exactly big buddies. After a *lot* of time with my shrink, I finally figured it out."

"And?"

"And what I realized was that all those calls were just a way of not breaking the ties. And not just the ties of affection — do you know what I mean?"

"Not really."

"Like power. Like dominance. Like, 'You may think you got rid of me but you still have to beg me for money.' That kind of tie."

"I don't want to be tied to Kathy," he said stiffly. "I'll have Marie put the check on my calendar for the rest of the year; she'll *make* me do it."

◇ ◇ ◇

The day scheduled for Thomas Putnam's road test was gray and fiercely cold. Sandy was tempted to cancel the appointment and drop the whole idea. It was totally insane, he said to himself for the hundredth time.

The truth was that in the last month, except for making out a money order to Gordon Oliver for rent on the studio at 1473

Third Avenue, Thomas Putnam had been out of sight and nearly out of mind. The moment of signing the money order had caused him no small amount of alarm. What in the hell am I doing? he had wondered almost aloud as he reminded himself to tilt the stiff paper when he signed the name. This is not only crazy, it's expensive. And for what? I'm not really going through with anything.

The pressure at the office was fierce. He was preparing for several conversions at once, juggling machines and programs and people and budgets. He was preparing for the off-site, gathering status reports and working nights on his special assignment. He was also preparing for a trip to London, spending most of his mornings on the phone to his staff there, people he had not yet met, people who seemed not to know the meaning of a due date, people who maddeningly went home promptly at 5:00 P.M. London time. His desk was piled high with papers he couldn't even get to until evenings or weekends. He just couldn't seem to catch up.

Lying in bed, he wondered what would happen if he just threw in the towel. Start fresh at another bank — Chase, maybe, or Citibank. They'd probably jump at the chance to get him. He knew several guys who had gone from one bank to another, or to Merrill Lynch, and always with a big hit in salary. Same work, but twenty or twenty-five thousand more. Jesus, the new hires at GlobeBank right out of B-school were getting twenty-seven, twenty-eight, to start with, a hell of a lot more than his starting salary. He thought of how much easier it would be for him to get along if he had twenty, twenty-five thousand more. Supporting two households, with Kathy nagging him for higher child support all the time. "Cost of living, you know," she said. What about *his* cost of living?

He remembered taking Pam out to a movie the other night and then going for cheeseburgers. Not exactly a big deal. After he took Pam home, he counted the bills in his wallet. Eighteen dollars. And he'd started with fifty. Thirty dollars and change, just for a lousy movie date.

Thomas Putnam, he thought. A consultant. If I were really Thomas I'd be pulling it in. Big billings. He knew what consultants charged the bank. They made out like bandits. Shit. I'm a vice president at GlobeBank and a division head and I'm working my ass off, and I still can't buy a woman a cheeseburger without worrying about the meter running.

He decided to take the road test.

At nine o'clock he called Marie and said that he had a bug. The road test down on Delancey Street was short and easy, a very different landscape from the one at his last test, right after high school driver's ed. What would Dad think of this? he mused, making right and left turns, stops and starts, among the lingerie shops and pickle stands, the cheap shoe stores, the odors of the Lower East Side.

He was elated as he walked west on Delancey. He'd passed, of course. He'd been driving half his life. Why does it feel so good, Putnam? New York State was issuing a license to Thomas Putnam, 1473 Third Avenue, New York, New York 10028, height 6–1, eyes green.

Thomas Putnam, Sandy said to himself as he hailed a cab. "Where to?" the cabbie asked. "Good question," Sandy replied. I'm not going home yet, he realized. Not yet. I'm going to keep going for a while. "Donnell Library, please; Fifty-third between Fifth and Sixth."

By midmorning he had a library card, a Museum of Modern Art membership, and a Vanderbilt YMCA card. He walked uptown to the Metropolitan Museum and joined: an individual membership. He felt pleased, warm. He decided to walk across the park and join the Museum of Natural History, too. Thomas, my boy, you are one very cultivated person. He was happy. It was worth spending all the money.

He walked down Columbus Avenue from the museum, amused by all the renovated town houses and stylish restaurants. A day off in the middle of the week was wonderful. Putnam lived the good life, didn't he? He realized he was hungry and stopped in at O'Neal Bros. for a hamburger and a Molson. Good, too. He was very mellow.

Sandy decided to walk some more, though it was definitely getting colder. He turned the collar of his coat up over his ears. Brisk. Bracing. He continued along Seventy-second Street, stopping to look in Kreeger's window. Should I get that wool hat? he thought. It tickled him, the idea of pulling a wool hat down over his ears like a sailor on watch. But he decided against it and headed downtown again, along Amsterdam. Suddenly he stopped in front of a large gray building on the corner of Sixty-fifth. Why not? This would be a great way to seal Thomas Putnam's good name. He went inside and volunteered to give blood. An hour later he had a donor card from the Greater New York Blood Program and an admonition not to drink alcohol for three hours.

That's too bad, Sandy thought. A drink to celebrate would be just the thing.

The next day he decided to face the final hurdle. He had to open a checking account for Thomas Putnam. It had all been easy, ridiculously easy, he thought. It gets easier each time. Why wouldn't this be easy too?

Sandy picked the branch of Century Trust at the corner of Eighty-sixth and Lexington. He was pretty sure he didn't know a soul at Century. They asked a few questions. He told them he was a consultant and had been abroad for six years. No other accounts, and he was depositing five hundred in cash.

"You're a consultant, sir?" the platform officer asked. "May I ask the name of the firm you're working for at present?" He was very correct.

"Yes, certainly. GlobeBank. I can give you a reference there if you need it."

The platform officer relaxed into a smile. "GlobeBank? What's the matter, afraid they'll mess up your account?"

"No," Sandy said. In this setting, he felt oddly protective of GlobeBank. "Not at all. I just prefer banking near home."

The officer handed Sandy three cards and marked an *X* on the bottom line of each. "Now if you'll just sign each card where I've indicated, Mr. Putnam . . ." Sandy left the branch with a package of temporary checks and a check register. Thomas Putnam's personalized checks — black printing on blue, Morocco leather–style cover — would be sent to his home.

Part Three

1

LISA HAD LOOKED FORWARD to being in Palmas del Mar.
Late winter in the city always depressed her — sleet mixed with
snow, dirty slush to wade through at every intersection, days of
tugging boots on and off and on again. She was even grateful, if
a little guilty about it, that Barry was off on his own business
trip. Though the Paris case tired him, she thought a little time
apart was probably good for them both.

She was also looking forward to something else besides meetings. She expected to come away with a bigger piece of turf,
taken out of Danny Faber's shop. Nothing was definite yet, but
she thought she had it. She had been hinting about it to Kilgour
for some time and he had not discouraged her.

She was glad too that she had asked Tony to come. He'll make
me look good, as usual, she thought. Her first presentation would
be a breeze, and the special topic wasn't until Thursday. She
could relax.

"Moo-oon over Miami," she hummed. She unwrapped two
Calvin Klein silks from their plastic bags and hung them up in
the closet. She changed from her suit into a wrap skirt and a T-
shirt and tied her hair back with a ribbon. Then she went across
the lawn to the main building for a drink.

The air was warm and a little damp with the sea breeze. The
light was just beginning to fade, turning the ocean purple and
the sand a shade of pink. Lisa imagined Barry asleep now in his
hotel room after a day of meetings in Paris. Maybe I'll try to call
him tomorrow.

She spotted Tony and his wife at a table near the bar and
went over to join them. The wives always surprised her. Perhaps
it was a jolt to see her colleagues as halves of couples. Some of
the older wives, expensively dressed and jeweled, were big social
drinkers and immediately ordered Scotch, neat, or double gins
on the rocks. The younger ones, Lisa knew, would be out the
next morning, trim and confident in running shorts, and would
spend most of their days cultivating creamy tans.

Lisa ordered white wine and looked around the room. The men wore sport clothes — loafers, slacks, polo shirts with alligators. Lisa smiled, remembering Jessica's joke about the alligators in Palm Beach who wore shirts with little golfers on them.

From the bar, open on all sides to the warm, sweet air and the palm trees, the GlobeBank group had a view of the check-in desk. "There's Sandy, late as usual," Tony Maresca said. He waved. "Sandy! Hey, Lippert!"

"You know my wife, Terri, don't you?" Tony asked as Sandy strode to their table and offered his hand.

"You've got a lot of catching up to do," Tony said, holding up his drink. "We're way ahead of you."

"Come sit with us," Terri said, giggling. "You can be Lisa's date." Lisa looked out at the palm trees, thinking, I wish Barry were here.

"Did you take the noon flight?" Sandy asked her as he sat down.

"Yes. You came on the three o'clock?"

"Yes."

"Did you have a good flight?"

"Very good. And you?"

"Fine." Lisa was impatient with the stiff, polite chitchat. She thought longingly of the large bed in her room and the book she had started on the plane.

"Where are the Kilgours?" Terri was asking. "I haven't seen them."

There was a long pause. "I think John told me that he and Sally would be in San Juan until late tonight," Lisa finally said.

"Hitting the casinos, probably," Sandy guessed.

"Do you play tennis?" Terri asked eagerly. "Maybe the four of us could play doubles. Of course, I am absolutely *awful!* But if you don't mind putting up with a bad player . . ."

Lisa took a last sip of her wine. "Well, we'd better see how much time there is."

Terri persisted. "Well, I was thinking of Wednesday afternoon. That's free time, isn't it?"

"We'd better wait and see," Tony said. He had registered Lisa's wishes. He always did.

◇ ◇ ◇

The first session started promptly at eight the next morning. Everyone was dressed informally. An elaborate breakfast was laid out on a sideboard along one wall of the meeting room. Lisa knew that "the issue" — whether or not she would get more of Danny Faber's turf — would not come up until tomorrow or the next day. She nibbled at her pastry and pretended to listen as Brian O'Connor made feeble jokes in a loud voice. She noted with satisfaction that Tony was taking everything down.

Sandy Lippert wasn't paying much attention, either. His presentation would be tomorrow, when everyone would be tired of listening. They would probably be behind schedule by then, and Kilgour would undoubtedly ask him to cut it short. Fine. For once, he wasn't on trial.

The meeting went on through lunch. Lisa forced herself to pay attention to Ray LaRocca's unsmiling, straightforward presentation. He was, after all, ahead of her in performance and in the status of his division's conversion. She had learned a lot from Ray LaRocca in the past and might learn something from him here.

Her right arm suddenly felt weary. She rested it on the back of Sandy Lippert's chair. "Is my arm in your way?" she whispered in his ear.

"It's a pleasure," Sandy said. He surprised himself by blushing.

Kilgour called a halt to the session at two-thirty. Lisa found herself heading back to her room in the company of Elaine Green and Sandy Lippert, whose rooms flanked her own. The afternoon sun seemed blinding after the drawn curtains of the meeting room.

"I feel like I'm back in high school," Sandy said, "walking home with books under my arm." Each of them had a two-inch orange looseleaf binder, the cover embossed in blue with the legend: Shaping the Future: Banking Operations Sector Off-Site Planning Session, February, Palmas del Mar, Puerto Rico. "Except in high school, I never had *two* attractive girls near me at once." Elaine giggled; Lisa managed a smile.

"What are you guys going to do this afternoon?" Elaine asked.

"Nothing much for me," Lisa answered. "What about you?"

"I'm going to the pool," Elaine replied, "to work on my tan."

Lisa changed into a swimsuit and stuffed a canvas bag with beach gear. She ran into Sandy just coming out the door of his room. "Going my way?" he asked.

Lisa looked at a Sandy Lippert she had never seen before. He was in a brief pair of swim shorts and an old gray T-shirt that read: Property of N. Y. Knicks.

She realized she was staring. He looked taller than ever and even more boyish. And he was staring back. He had of course never seen her dressed that way, either.

She wasn't at all sure that she wanted to spend her time making conversation with Sandy Lippert. Probably nothing but Autotran. But she couldn't think of a polite way to walk off.

At the beach, they spread out their towels side by side.

"Swimming?" he asked.

"Not yet. I think I'll get hot first."

"I think I'll go for a run. I need it after that long session." He pulled off his shirt. His shoulders were broad, and his muscles rippled. Lisa registered the smoothness of his chest. She could see the muscles in his calves and thighs stretch and flex as he loped down the beach. His soft, brown hair bounced up and down. She watched until he was just a dot in the distance, then leaned back and closed her eyes.

◊ ◊ ◊

She looked up to see Sandy heading into the surf. She watched him prance into the water, then seem to leap into the air before disappearing under a high wave. For a moment she was frightened. But then he emerged on the other side of the wave's crest and began to swim hard out to sea. In the sun and water, in the hot, flat tropical colors, he seemed to shimmer.

She watched him for a few moments, then turned resolutely onto her stomach and lay down, her head resting on one arm.

She didn't move when she heard him return. He lay down beside her, red and panting, glistening with sweat and the sea. He turned his face toward her, closing one eye against the sun. Through his skewed vision, Lisa Gould's body was the biggest thing he could see. The horizon was distant. The curve of her shoulder, the hollow of her neck, her rising breast, filled his gaze. The tiny beads of moisture on her arm were magnified. He no-

166

ticed a small, dark beauty mark just at the crease of her armpit.

"You're getting burned," he said. "Better be careful."

Lisa realized he was looking at her and began to feel even hotter.

"How about a drink?" Sandy said. "I'm going to ask the guy for a piña colada."

"What time is it?" she asked.

Sandy looked at his watch. "Four."

Lisa rarely drank before five. "Why not?" she said.

He hailed the attendant. "Could we have two piña coladas, please?"

The attendant nodded and walked solemnly away.

"That's some watch you've got there," Lisa said. It was a diver's Rolex. "Can I see it?"

She had assumed he would take it off, but instead, he held out his wrist. She took it in both her hands. The dark brown hair lay straight and smooth along his arm, not at all like the unruly waves of hair on his head. She noticed that he had long fingers and a wide palm.

"Is this one of those watches that does everything?" she asked.

He smiled at her. "Almost. A gift from my parents. When they heard I'd taken up jogging, they gave me this. The card said: 'Good luck with the racing.' "

"You race?"

"No, I don't." Sandy lay down. "I just like to run. I like to stretch. I like to sweat. Competitive running doesn't interest me."

"I'm surprised. I figured you for a very competitive type." She rummaged in her canvas bag for a comb and began combing her hair.

"No," Sandy said carefully, "winning doesn't interest me much. Not anymore." Then he added: "I guess the GlobeBank experience and a failed marriage have something to do with it."

Lisa was startled by the sudden confidence. Their drinks arrived, and Sandy signed for them. They watched the sky change color as they sipped their drinks.

"Is there some big dinner thing happening tonight?" Sandy asked.

Lisa shook her head. "Tomorrow's the big shindig. I'm having dinner with the Fabers tonight." She paused. "Why don't you join us? About six?"

"Thanks. I will."

As she walked back to her room, she turned to see Sandy swimming easily out to sea. He hadn't said a word about Autotran.

The Fabers, Sandy, and Lisa ate dinner in a corner of the dining room, near a window. Sandy could see beyond Harriet Faber's pretty head to the golf course. Lisa had a view of the other GlobeBank tables in the dining room. Everyone seemed relaxed.

After dinner they settled in the bar. Lisa felt Sandy's hand at her elbow as she sat in one of the easy chairs around the small table. People had ordered cognac and were getting giggly.

Elaine Green, who had dined with the O'Connors, found a chair and joined them. The LaRoccas and the Norths took a nearby table. It had become a party. The Kilgours soon arrived, having taken the Donovans to dinner. Everyone straightened up slightly and tried to shift into Kilgour's line of vision. Lisa noticed that the group's loud laughter had driven other people away. She also noticed that Sandy had hardly said anything the whole evening.

It was almost midnight when Sandy, Lisa, and Elaine walked down the gently lit ramps to their rooms.

Lisa's alarm went off at six-thirty, and she crawled out of bed into her swimsuit. Dropping her towel on the beach, she set off at a slow pace toward the tree on the curve. Her legs felt stiff. She bent her head and pushed against her desire to stop. The muscles loosened.

A man wearing only a pair of brown-and-white-striped trunks was coming toward her, running on the hard sand. She knew it was Sandy.

He waved and jogged in place until she reached him. They ran together in silence. The sweat trickled down her face. She could feel rivulets of it under her swimsuit, down her stomach. Her stride was easier now.

"Turning here," Lisa said.

He turned with her and they started back along the beach. With a short distance to go to her towel, he asked, "How about sprinting for the end?"

Lisa felt strong. "Let's do it!" She bent her knees and ran.

He outpaced her easily. When she arrived at her towel, she stripped off her T-shirt — the one of the London Underground that Barry had given her — and they both ran into the surf.

Lisa felt as if she were bursting with the sea. She dove under a wave and forced her body into a straight line, pushing down until her lungs ached. Then she thrust herself up, breaking the surface of the ocean with a splash.

Sandy followed her back to shore.

They breakfasted together under the shed near the pool, a thatched-roof structure that was meant to suggest an ancient beach cottage. Lisa, barely managing to drink half her orange juice and eat half her croissant, was amused to watch Sandy. For a lanky man, he really packed it in, wolfing down a meal of melon, two eggs with bacon, four pieces of toast lathered with butter and jam, and a tall glass of milk.

"I'll have my coffee at the meeting," he said.

◊ ◊ ◊

Kilgour decided to change the order of things. "I know you all want to have a nice long afternoon," he said, "so we're going to try and speed things up. I'd like Sandy to give us just fifteen — maybe twenty — minutes on the conversion and on the London Autotran status. Then we'll go on to Lisa and Danny."

"This is just a schematic of the basic system," Sandy began; a picture of blue boxes and orange circles connected by yellow lines flashed onto the screen. He explained the "flow" and showed the design for Autotran in London. Colors and shapes flashed in the darkened room. Sandy, pacing, occasionally walked through the projector's beam. Flow charts widened across his shirt and appeared creased along his face.

"So it's a very, very big job, a very complex effort," he continued in a faraway-sounding voice. "It means very careful meshing of a lot of different activities on a lot of different fronts. It means that we in Utility have to exercise very tough control to make sure all the gears mesh in the right way at the right time." He paused and seemed to sigh. Lisa wondered if the sigh was one of disgust at the amount of work involved or of pleasure at the complexity of the task. It was certainly an enormous job, one only an engineer's mind could embrace, she mused.

"We also have to have your absolute cooperation in every way," Sandy went on, his voice hard now. "We have to know you're going to make your due dates, or if you're not, we have to know well in advance that you're going to miss. And by how much." Lisa recognized this as the pep talk.

"John?" Sandy said suddenly. Lisa was surprised he had stopped so soon.

"Right," Kilgour said. "I'm just going to add to what Sandy said there at the end. He and his people are going to be tracking your cooperation and how well you meet due dates and how well you meet with them and so forth. But you'll be answerable to me on this." He looked around. "If we blow the system anywhere along the line, it'll be big losses for the bank and big losses for whoever is responsible. Understood?"

No one spoke. It was understood.

The first half of Lisa's presentation was a slide-show summary of the main points: her proposed budget for the year; four different organization charts, representing the phased head-knocking she planned for the year; the final floor plan sketched by Taddeusz; and the final hardware configuration planned by Sandy.

Then she switched off the machine, turned on the lights, and asked Tony to pass out the specially prepared tooth-edged booklets that contained all the details and Issues for Consideration.

The elegant booklets made an impression, which she had intended. As she watched Kilgour thumb through his copy, as she saw him appreciate its professionalism — the charts and graphs, the special laminated tabs, the clean look — she inwardly gave thanks for the fact that Jessica Moser belonged to her.

She went on for an hour. The presentation was informal and almost everyone asked a question. Throughout, she was aware of Sandy beside her, leaning back in his chair while she leaned forward in hers. Out of the corner of her eye, she could see his long legs disappear under the table.

After a break, it was Danny Faber's turn. Danny's presentations were like Danny himself, completely relaxed and a bit disorganized — there were three slides out of order and one upside down. Danny could get away with a few mistakes and the tone of hokiness because he was very good at his job and his plan was excellent, with or without elegance.

Kilgour broke things up promptly at noon. He and Sally were giving a luncheon at twelve-thirty by the pool. "Let's wrap it up," he said as he stood. "Lisa, you want to see me for just a second?"

The others left. Kilgour was stuffing papers into his attaché case. "Good presentation. Fine piece of work," he told her.

"Thanks, John."

"You remember that discussion we had in New York about a month ago, market perception. You brought up the point that you thought some of Danny's turf might more properly be in your shop because of the style of doing business. Remember?"

Of course she remembered. She had brought it up again with Kilgour just last week. He had told her then that he hadn't forgotten and would try to give her an answer in Puerto Rico. She was waiting for the answer now.

"I remember, John."

"I've made a decision, and I'd like to talk to you about it. Will you have breakfast with me tomorrow? At the pool?"

Breakfast? Why did she have to wait till breakfast? Why couldn't she hear the decision now?

"Sure I can have breakfast, John. I'm curious, though. Can't you tell me now?"

"It's more than just a yes or no, Lisa. It's a matter of what pieces go where." He clipped the attaché case shut. "And I want to get to Danny about it also. And I want us all to forget business this afternoon." He flashed his charming smile and steered her outside into the sunshine.

They stood together for a moment, looking out across the beach to the ocean.

"Don't worry, Lisa," Kilgour said. "You'll get what you want. You always do." He turned and walked away.

Lisa turned in the opposite direction and started down the slope to her room.

"Hey, Lisa! Wait up!" Sandy was running after her. "Where are you headed?"

"Back to change. I want to swim some laps before the lunch. Where are you coming from?"

"I was up at the desk, checking on plane schedules. My . . . friend arrives this afternoon."

They walked together in silence for a moment. "Your presentation was excellent," Sandy said. "Very interesting. You've set yourself some hard tasks."

"I can handle it." She smiled coldly.

Her statement surprised him. Gravely, he said, "I never doubted it. What was Kilgour's private word with you? Or can't you say?"

"Oh, just something we've talked about before. It's unofficial right now, Sandy, but it looks like National Services West will be taking on more turf."

"Really? What? What turf?"

Lisa paused. "Well, John and I agree that some of Danny's customers more properly belong to West."

"Hmm . . . Good you're getting a bigger slice — nobody can handle it better. Still, I guess it's too bad it's got to come out of Danny's shop. I mean, you and he are such good friends. I think Killer sometimes forgets the personal factor when he makes decisions."

Was he thinking about his own case? Lisa wondered. But this was entirely different, not the same thing at all. Her voice kept its hard edge. "No," she said. "Danny and I *are* friends, but this is business. He knows it and I know it. The issue is what's good for the corporation, what's beneficial to the bank."

Sandy stopped. She stopped too, turning back to face him. He looked at her blankly. She had no idea what he was thinking, but his look made her uncomfortable. His eyes were very green, very piercing, as he stood tall and straight in the bright sunlight. She considered what to say, then shrugged and walked on. As he turned off toward his room, he said, "See you soon."

In her room, Lisa stepped into her swimsuit and pulled it up. She felt uneasy about her talk with Sandy, a bit off center, a little annoyed. Oh, the hell with it. It wasn't worth bothering about.

It was just a few days anyway. She was stuck here for a few days with a bunch of people. That was all. No need to get worked up. Especially since she had gotten what she came for.

It was, as always, a satisfying thought. Lisa put on the white and navy beach tunic that went with the navy swimsuit and her white canvas espadrilles. She brushed her hair, picked up her canvas bag, and started for the pool. The next thing on the agenda is a swim, she thought decisively.

Sandy had said he would see her soon. She wondered suddenly about his "friend" from New York. She had to admit she was curious about Sandy's private life. She wondered what kind of woman was attractive to him.

All at once she remembered Barry. Of all the times to have to go to Paris, she thought unhappily. Oh, Barry.

Sandy had done ten laps when he saw Lisa approach the pool. He waved, but she seemed not to notice. She found a chaise, set down her things, and slipped out of her tunic. Her feet did a little dance motion; Sandy guessed she was getting out of her shoes. She started to tie her hair back in a knot.

Just then, a soft red ball whizzed past his head. Two boys had been playing water catch. Now one of them moved swiftly through the water toward it. Sandy grabbed the ball and tossed it to the boy. "Can I play?" he asked. "How about monkey in the middle? I'll be the monkey."

The boy looked at his pal. "OK," he said tentatively and without joy. A few minutes later, however, the three of them were laughing and playing easily together. "Toss it!" "Go wide!" "Beat him. Get it! Get it!"

In the deep end Lisa swam laps, a slow, sculptured crawl. She was only dimly aware of the raucous game going on in the shallow water. She switched to the breaststroke. Now she could see Sandy's shiny body leap and gambol in the blue water, could see him as the boys closed in, grabbing him, their bodies a set of awkward limbs against his grace and strength.

She could hear only the swish of water that she made, so she was surprised when she saw Sandy beside her.

"Hey, Lisa! John's calling us to lunch."

She had taken on a copper hue, he noticed. Her teeth seemed very white against her face when she smiled at him; her brown eyes seemed darker and softer. She motioned him to precede her up the pool ladder. When he turned to give her a hand, he found himself staring unabashedly down on the tops of her breasts just under her suit, a soft white contrast to her reddish-brown tan.

"I'm going over to that rain forest after lunch," he said quickly. "Want to come?"

"When does your girl arrive?" Lisa asked.

"Oh. Not till later."

"Sure, I'm game. I was going to walk over there anyway."

After lunch, Lisa dressed in faded blue jeans, her plain white T-shirt, Bernardo sandals, and a broad-brimmed floppy straw hat. They had arranged that Sandy would "call for her," as he jokingly put it. Now, as she waited for his knock on the door, she prowled through the kitchen — the room was more like a self-contained condominium — opening drawers and cabinets.

Her flash of annoyance had faded quickly. She couldn't understand why she had been provoked — he was really such a nice guy. He had been the saving grace at the luncheon, where she found herself at a table with the Norths and the Donovans. Al Donovan was telling his wife all about the morning session — verbatim, it seemed to Lisa. The Norths, on the other hand, made it clear that they felt extremely uncomfortable in the company they were keeping. Lisa wasn't sure which couple she disliked more. Sandy's arrival, with his plate heaped with food, was like a ray of sunshine.

He kept up an easy flow of conversation, deftly turning aside all talk of business and engaging both Betsy North and Louise Donovan in repartee. He amused the group by eating everything on his plate, everything left over on Lisa's plate — which was most of the meal — and almost everything on the plates of seconds that he gallantly fetched for himself and Doug North.

There was a knock on the door. Lisa opened it to see Sandy dressed in a pair of khaki shorts and a light blue cotton shirt, the sleeves rolled up above his elbows. He had sandals on his feet and a Pentax slung over one shoulder.

"You really look like you're ready for the jungle," she said.

Laughing, they set out across the golf course. Sandy told Lisa about his disastrous attempt, when he was chief controller for Kilgour, to learn to play golf so he could hobnob with bank executives. "I was a total flop," he said. "I just haven't got the patience for golf."

"Well, you're a runner, anyway," Lisa said.

"I'm not serious enough about it," Sandy answered. "I am serious about audio, though. Oh, you know — stereo equipment."

"Oh. What's the hobby? I mean, what do you *do?*"

"Read about it, talk about it, build it, listen to it."

"What kind of music do you like? What do you listen to most?"

Sandy smiled. "Mostly I've been listening to Tubby the Tuba. When my kids come on weekends."

Kids, thought Lisa. "You take your kids every weekend?"

"Every other, actually."

They had arrived at the starting point of the rain forest walk. They both took descriptive folders from a wooden rack and stepped into the forest.

A silence surrounded them, and the forest ceiling blocked the sunlight. Lisa removed her hat. The silence was humming with sounds that had no source: tiny cracklings, popping noises, moist, lapping sounds.

"Is it hard, seeing your kids so infrequently?" Lisa asked.

"Yes." His voice grew tight. "I miss them all the time. I resent not being able to watch their growing up. Two days out of every fourteen. It isn't a lot. It makes for a kind of distorted view of them, I think."

"Where do they live?"

"Not far, thank God. In Chatham, New Jersey. With their mother. It's not a big trip. But it's not like living with them."

"Has your wife — has their mother — remarried?"

"No." They had stopped at station number four to read their pamphlets. A slight breeze riffled along the boardwalk.

"How long were you actually married?" Lisa asked.

"Four years. A fair piece of time." There was a bench along the boardwalk railing up ahead of them. "Why don't we sit for a bit," Sandy suggested. "I'll have a cigarette. Plus we hadn't been close for about a year before that."

She realized he was still talking about his marriage.

"That's hard, too," he went on. "Breaking up is hard to do, as the song says. It's amazing, you know. Kathy and I didn't have the most amicable parting of the ways. Sometimes I try hard to remember that I once loved her." He looked at Lisa and then at the ground. "Once she was all I could think about. And now I can't even remember it. Sometimes, when I get really lonely, I try to recreate in my mind some of the times we had. When things were good. But I can't get back the feeling." He dragged on his cigarette and stared straight ahead.

It's so quiet here, Lisa thought. It seems so tranquil. But actually it's teeming. Underneath us and in all those branches and vines, insects and lizards and even plants are feeding and struggling and killing and coupling like mad. The thought made her melancholy. Sandy felt close beside her. She resisted an impulse to stroke his hair. Her heart went out to him. She didn't know why he was confiding in her, but she felt as if the confession had shattered him. He's so damn boyish, she thought; she had a quick vision of his head on her breast, like a baby's.

"I guess there's not much danger of fire in a rain forest," Sandy said. He tossed his burning cigarette over the railing and stood up. They walked on.

"Do you like your job?" Lisa asked. "I mean, do you enjoy it, do you *really* like it?"

He looked at her quizzically. "No," he said, as if surprised to hear himself say it, "I guess I don't. I love to build systems, that's the thing. I love Autotran. I know that sounds dumb, but it's true. A system has logic, purpose."

"And it doesn't turn sour on you," she added.

"Right. When the system talks back, it's because you've programmed it that way." He stopped. "I guess I love the systems I build because" — he hesitated, searching for the right words — "because I control them."

She nodded in understanding.

"But the rest of the job — all the administrative stuff, all the meetings, all the paperwork, all the responsibility of hiring and firing and promoting and demoting — that I hate. To me, it's just pressure that keeps me away from building systems and making them run."

"Yes," Lisa answered.

"What about you? You like your job, don't you?"

"Yes, I do." Her answer was straightforward. "I like it very much. I actually like all the administrative stuff, as you put it.

It's fun. I'm good at it. I can dispose of it quickly and easily, so I guess that's why it doesn't bother me. But the main thing, I guess" — Lisa almost sighed — "is just the process itself. Just having all those variables to juggle. Just coordinating all of it and driving it as a single process toward a single goal. I guess that's the turn-on for me. You like to control systems, you said. I like to control processes."

"I think," Sandy said, "that you have to share the goal. You have to believe in it, care about it."

"Yes," Lisa agreed. "Yes, I think that's true."

"I guess I just don't care as much as some people about the goal. Not anymore. I'm not even sure I ever did. It's not real to me. When I think about Autotran, I think of its power, and sometimes even about the power and prestige of the bank. But not of GlobeBank's bottom line or its corporate goals."

"I think I can understand that," Lisa said. "But even if your goal is not necessarily the corporation's goal, it can still work in the right direction."

"What's *your* goal?" Sandy asked.

They were on a loop off the main course of the boardwalk that rose to the level of the treetops. Below them was a brackish canal, its surface rippling sluggishly. An older couple passed, wearing matching hats and with identical binoculars hung around their necks.

"Myself," Lisa answered. "My goal is myself. Doing something I like and am good at. My advancement, for that matter. It just happens that right now my goal can be achieved best by furthering the corporation's goal." She turned up her chin defiantly.

"That's an honest statement," Sandy said.

"But not very pretty or noble."

Sandy smiled. "Honesty is fairly noble, I guess. Anyway, I think it all depends on your methods. I think that somehow we both will further GlobeBank's goals, whether we mean to or not."

They walked on in silence, past huge cattails, wide ferns, mangrove, mottled flowers drooping under the heavy air. Lisa felt slightly uneasy. It was all too gorgeous, too sweet, too unreal. They stopped before a night-blooming cereus. Sandy read aloud from the brochure.

"I've got to be getting back," he said finally. "Pam's arriving soon." Their eyes met, and they both felt the need for a small ceremony to seal the intimacy of their talk and this place; but the moment passed and they hurried out of the forest, striking off across the golf course toward their rooms.

"Is this a serious girlfriend?" Lisa asked — and instantly regretted her choice of words. She sounded just like her mother.

"No, not really," Sandy answered. "I'm not even sure why I had her come. Except that Killer Kilgour was so gushingly generous about inviting her . . . while making it very clear that he would be happy to get her 'her own room,' as he said."

Lisa laughed. "He was evidently a lot less gushing to Elaine. Her friend is coming tomorrow, I think. I bet Kilgour's jealous."

"Jesus Christ!" Sandy gasped. "There's the airport limo. I bet Pam's in it." The long, steel blue Cadillac was winding along the drive toward the reception building. "I'd better run," Sandy said. "Lisa, could you take my camera?"

He handed it to her and sprinted across the rolling golf course to greet Pam Shipley.

2

LINDA GLOVER was angry.

She had lived for this week with Rick Schmidt, the week of the off-site, when all the bosses would be in Puerto Rico. Sometimes the mere thought of it, of five days in the anonymity of a hotel room alone with Rick, had made her squirm with anticipation. At the office, on the train, at home with Charley, she had had fantasies of the things she and Rick would do together. At such moments, she would feel the hot wetness start between her legs; then she would think quickly of something else.

But the week was turning into a big disappointment. It had been fine, at first, when she arrived on Monday morning. They had grabbed at one another hungrily. On the floor, limbs askew, her bra over her face, her pantyhose ripped, Linda had gasped with pleasure at Rick's frenzied bucking. Afterward she whispered to him, "Later, I want you to try and hurt me again."

But Rick had barely been able to sustain the more gentle

lovemaking of the late morning while they waited, in what Linda found thrilling suspense, for the room service tray with their lunch. Rick excused himself by saying he had really been worried that the room service waiter would knock "just at the most important moment." They had tried again, late in the afternoon. He was tired, he said — jet lag — and his performance was weak. Linda told him to get a good night's sleep. Her own rest was troubled by more fantasies, and when she arrived this morning, she was tense and anxious.

They made it once, and they had been trying to make it again ever since. But Rick was just not able to get it up.

Now, as Linda dressed to leave, moving about the room with her lips in a tight, thin line, Rick was apologizing. "I'm so sorry, babe," he said. "I think you make me nervous when you tell me to 'sleep well' so I can be prepared. I keep worrying about how I'm doing."

"You ought to worry," Linda said. "You're doing lousy."

She turned to him, one shoe on her foot and one in her hand. She pointed it at him. "Look," she said, "I'm taking a risk coming here. I'm away from the bank, and there are calls coming in and people wondering where I am. I do have managerial responsibilities, you know." She put the shoe on. "I frankly can't afford to run this risk for nothing. If I wanted to spend a week with a man who can't get it up, I could stay home with my husband."

Linda thought quickly of Charley, poor, sad Charley, a failure at everything — job, marriage, friendship, sex. He both worshiped and resented her, hating the success she achieved so easily, needing her just the same. These days, Charley was at least half drunk by the time he got to bed, a snoring lump beside her. It had been over a month since they had had sex. She hadn't even tried to prod him much, knowing that Rick was coming, that this arid period would end.

She put on her coat. "I'm going into the office in the morning and I'm going to have lunch there. I'll be here in the afternoon sometime, I don't know when. Did you get me the extra key?"

He pointed to the dresser. She took the room key.

Rick got up and walked over to her. "Please, Linda," he said, "it'll be better." He slipped his hands under her arms and moved them up and down her sides.

She grew tender and put her arms around his neck. "I thought you said I was all you needed to get hot," she whispered. "You said you wanted me all the time."

"Maybe I want you too much," he said.

"We'll get you something to relax you and turn you on. Not booze; something else." She pulled away from him.

"How about a room full of naked dancing girls?" he asked lightly. "Just ask a bellhop where you can get some. That might turn me on."

She smiled at his joke. "Oh, is that all? Easy." She turned and walked out the door.

Maybe it wasn't such an outrageous idea after all, Linda reflected as the elevator took her down to the St. Magnus lobby. Not dancing girls, of course, but a prostitute. After all, wasn't a prostitute just another kind of professional, an expert at sex? At GlobeBank and everywhere else, when you needed professional expertise, you went and hired it. That's what consultants were; they were always hiring consultants in BOS.

The elevator doors opened, and Linda walked into the ornate lobby of the hotel. It was almost six o'clock. Businessmen were heading back to their rooms to "freshen up" after a long day of meetings. People were streaming into the cocktail lounge; Linda peeked in to see elegantly dressed men and women, to hear the clink of ice against glass, to smell the unmistakable aroma of liquor and peanuts.

She stood for a moment putting on her gloves. A knot of bellhops stood in the corner of the lobby. What had Rick said? Just ask a bellhop . . .

Linda fished in her wallet and found a twenty-dollar bill. She folded it so the number showed and made a mental note to remember to get it back out of petty cash.

"Excuse me," she said to one of the bellhops. God, he was young; maybe she should find an older one.

"Yes?" the young man said, almost snapping to attention.

"I wonder if you might help me." She stepped back a few paces to draw him toward her. He followed dutifully. When they were out of earshot, she said, "My firm has a client visiting from out of town. He's staying here."

She nodded toward the twenty. "This gentleman, our client, has expressed an interest in having a girl sent up to his room and

I have no idea how to go about finding one. Perhaps you can help. He's an important client."

The bellhop took the twenty and slid it into his pocket. "Do you have a piece of paper?" he asked calmly.

Linda pulled a leather notebook out of her purse. A slim gold pen was tucked inside. She handed them to the boy, who wrote down a phone number and a name, Mrs. Evans.

"This is a very fine house," the young man said. "Most of the girls who are brought in here are from Mrs. Evans."

"Thank you," she said, closing the notebook.

Linda was stupefied by how easy it had been. No smirks, no innuendo. She left the hotel and headed for Grand Central. In a phone booth along one of the corridors off the great hall, she placed the call.

A woman's voice answered. "Forty-one eighty-eight."

"Mrs. Evans?" Linda asked tentatively.

"Yes?"

Linda realized suddenly that she had no idea what to say next. "I'd like to order . . . that is, a client of my company would like to . . ."

Mrs. Evans took over. "Would like to avail himself of our services?"

"Yes," Linda said gratefully.

"You wish to arrange an escort for a gentleman?"

"Yes," she said again.

"What is your company?"

"Oh. It's . . . it's GlobeBank."

"Oh, yes," Mrs. Evans said, "we do a lot of business with your company. What precisely do you require?"

Linda explained that the client was visiting from out of town, was staying at the St. Magnus, and had asked for a white woman who looked like Jacqueline Bisset, the actress Rick had once told her he'd "like to fuck."

Mrs. Evans laughed. "I'll see what I can do," she said.

It was arranged that the "escort" would arrive at the room at one-thirty the next afternoon. Payment in cash would be required. The charge for the afternoon would be a base price of $300, with additional fees for specific services. Linda was quick to mention that if it worked out, she might want to engage the services of the escort through Friday. Mrs. Evans said that an overall sum might then be arranged. Would the escort be serving just the one gentleman? she asked.

"Well, no; that is, yes, one gentleman, but someone else might be there." Linda felt herself blushing as she answered. The fee would then surely be larger, Mrs. Evans said. The escort would, however, discuss all this at the start. "One-thirty tomorrow, then, that's set," she concluded.

◇ ◇ ◇

Linda got to the hotel room shortly after one o'clock. She had spent a successful morning at the office. She had managed to put through an early call to Tony, in Puerto Rico, to assure him that everything was going along smoothly. She talked Jessica into joining her for a quick lunch in the cafeteria, where she was seen by most of the people she knew at the bank.

Rick had been at Head Office that morning too, she heard, then had gone downtown to keep up his contacts at 176 Wall and to check up on the latest technological developments.

She felt both nervous and excited as she waited now, alone in the hotel room, for the escort. She wondered briefly when Rick would show up and what he would say. She had a feeling he would like it.

There was a knock on the door.

"Who's there?" Linda asked.

"Mrs. Evans sent me. My name is Julie."

Linda opened the door, and Julie quickly came inside. She does look like Jacqueline Bisset, Linda thought. Rick will like that.

"The man?" Julie asked, looking appraisingly around the room.

"Rick. He'll be here soon," Linda said.

"What am I expected to do?"

Linda decided to play it straight. She told Julie that she and Rick had been carrying on an affair for some time; that they had not seen one another for a while; that they had this opportunity this week only; that she, Linda, really needed this week; that Rick was good for only twice a day, if that — he had no stamina.

"So basically you want me to turn him on but you want him to get it off on you?"

Linda hesitated. "Yes," she said.

"It's five hundred dollars to do a couple," Julie said. She held out her hand. Linda counted out a stack of twenties. She had withdrawn $600 from her savings account that morning; she would get it back from Rick later. Julie put the money into an elegant leather wallet.

She began to undress. "You'd better undress and get into bed," she said.

Linda somehow felt shy in Julie's presence. She went over to the bed and undressed quickly, dropping her clothes on the floor, then slipped hurriedly under the sheet. Julie still stood near the table, lighting a cigarette, absolutely at ease in her nakedness. And why not? Linda thought. She has an incredible body.

Julie came over to the bed carrying the ashtray, the cigarette protruding provocatively from the middle of her mouth. She sat down at the end of the bed, near Linda's feet, and crossed her legs yoga-style. She smiled at Linda.

"So how did you, you know, get into this business?" Linda asked.

Julie blew out smoke. "It's something I know how to do, know how to do well, and it commands a good price." She shrugged.

"Do you . . . do you like your work?" Linda put her hands behind her head to show she was at ease.

"Do you like yours?"

The question surprised Linda. "Yes. Mostly. I don't love every second of it, but on balance I like it."

"That's the way I feel," Julie said. She put out her cigarette and set the ashtray on the floor. "I never really dislike it. Sometimes I enjoy it very much. Mostly, it's just a job." Then she asked, "Where's your boy?"

"He really should be here any second," Linda said, blushing. "He's probably coming from Wall Street, and there may be traffic."

Julie pulled the sheet down Linda's body to her feet. "Let's see what you look like," she said. She surveyed Linda from head to toe unabashedly.

"You're nice," she said. She began to caress Linda's thighs. "You have lovely soft skin. Smooth." Her hand moved lightly up and down Linda's thighs. "And you have nice tits." Julie's hand continued to caress Linda's legs, up and down, in an automatic motion.

"So do you," Linda said.

Julie smiled. "Yes," she said, "so I'm told." She took her breasts in her hands, as if presenting them to Linda. "Why don't you feel them?"

Gingerly, Linda put out one hand. She set her palm against Julie's right breast. She held her hand there for a moment, tentatively, then gently tweaked the nipple between her thumb and forefinger. It seemed to spring forward under her touch, a hardening pink center in Julie's creamy breast.

Julie smiled. She leaned forward suddenly and cupped her mouth over Linda's right breast. Linda felt the weight of Julie's long, thick hair as it tumbled onto her chest. Julie was sucking at her breast as a child might, then licking it, her tongue and lips and teeth all moving in wet, lapping movements. Julie moved her mouth to Linda's other breast. She made small popping, sucking noises.

Quickly, Julie's mouth traveled down Linda's stomach to between her legs. Linda stared in amazement at the top of Julie's head. Julie was parting her with her fingers. Now she bent deep over Linda, setting her tongue inside her. Linda could hear Julie swallowing. She put her hands on Julie's head.

"Don't stop," she said urgently. She threw her head back against the pillow.

The door opened; Rick Schmidt walked in.

Linda, her eyes closed, heard the door as if from far off. Her body heaved and jerked on its own. Her head was flopping from side to side. Her eyes opened, and she saw him. She looked at his wide-mouthed face with triumph. "See what I've brought you?" she said.

Julie looked up. "Come on, Rick," she said breathlessly. "Join us."

Linda pushed Julie's head back between her legs and groaned.

Rick closed the door and walked over to the bed, around to the other side, closer to them. His eyes were riveted on the two women. Linda's eyes were shut tight; her mouth was pulled wide, almost distorted. He could not really see the face of the woman crouched over her, but he noted the smooth, shiny limbs, the full breasts pushed against Linda's legs, the back beaded with sweat, the twitching buttocks high in the air.

He realized that he was rubbing himself, growing hard under his own touch. He yanked at his belt buckle, unzipped his fly, and pulled down his pants. He held himself in both hands now, his eyes still on the two women. Linda was gurgling softly, a kind of rhythmic, pleading cry.

Rick came around behind the woman hovering over Linda. He knelt behind her on the bed. With his hands, he parted her buttocks. Funny, he thought, I've always wanted to fuck a woman in the ass. Then he pushed his way in.

She seemed oblivious to him. He pressed himself against her, curving his pelvis to fit her back. He reached over her back and under her arms to grab her breasts. Straight before him, he could see Linda. Her eyes were open now, but she wasn't looking at him; she was looking at the woman.

Suddenly Linda yelped. Her body seemed to lurch, propelled by a power of its own, shuddering. She sighed deeply, then lay back.

Julie lifted her face, smiled at Linda, then stretched toward her and rested her face on Linda's neck. Linda looked dreamily at her. Then she noticed Rick, his face contorted with effort.

He grunted above them, swayed, pitched, and was still.

3

AFTER THE WALK IN THE RAIN FOREST, Lisa spent the afternoon on the beach. She took her beach towel away from the pool and bar area, away from people, alternating between lying on her stomach to read and lying on her back to sunbathe.

At five o'clock she went up to her room, warm from the afternoon sun, and bathed in cool water. Stepping out of the tub, she looked at herself in the full-length mirror on the bathroom door and smiled. The tan marks were evident. She seemed to be wearing a pale, flesh-colored swimsuit. She turned, then twisted to see her back in the mirror. Good. A smooth tan down her legs and across her back.

Lisa dressed in a long skirt and her apple green silk blouse. I look terrific, she thought, making a final appraisal of herself in the mirror.

Kilgour had reserved a corner of the open-sided cocktail lounge from six to eight. Lisa got there at six-twenty; the party was in full swing. Her eye immediately picked out Sandy, taller than almost everyone, in a navy blazer and white trousers.

The woman beside him came to his shoulder. She *is* attractive, Lisa thought, in a hard sort of way.

Kilgour greeted her enthusiastically. Sally Kilgour kissed her cheek and set a piña colada in her hand. "We're all drinking these tall, gooey things, my dear," she said.

Lisa listened to Terri Maresca talk about the tennis pro and heard all about the Lilly Pulitzer dress that Louise Donovan had purchased that very afternoon.

"Lisa, this is Pam Shipley." It was Sandy. The two women shook hands. Lisa wondered briefly if Sandy had told Pam how much time he and Lisa had been spending together. Then she wondered why she thought of that.

"How was your flight?" she asked politely.

"Oh, fine. No problem." Pam smiled, showing a line of white teeth.

"Cold back home?"

"I'll say."

Kilgour waved them in to dinner.

It was a noisy meal, with most of the laughter coming from the table at which the Fabers and Sandy sat. I'm always at the wrong table, Lisa thought, like always driving in the wrong lane. She looked toward the others. Sandy, smiling, was staring at her. She turned away.

Afterward, the party continued by the pool, where Kilgour had reserved a group of the small tables. The band wore flowered, wide-sleeved Cuernavaca shirts open to the waist. They played "The More I See You" with a slightly Latin beat. Kilgour asked Lisa to dance.

He danced like her father, she decided when they were out on the floor, like he's had ballroom dancing lessons. Probably the only thing Harold Gould and John Roland Kilgour have in common.

Kilgour made small talk, gliding in the correct pattern over the dance floor. Did she miss Barry? Hadn't the sessions gone well? She sensed he was counting. Having fun? Two, three, four.

Kilgour asked Pat LaRocca to dance and Lisa sat next to Ray. "Barry's in Paris?" he wanted to know.

She was tired of questions about Barry, tired of chitchat about how well the sessions were going, tired of having to talk at all.

"I've always wanted to dance with a division head," Sandy said, coming over and offering his hand.

Kilgour, Lisa saw, was dancing with Louise Donovan. He's going to dance with all the women, she realized, so he can have an excuse to dance with Elaine. She was thinking that this was a bit repellent when she felt Sandy's arm around her waist, his hand in hers.

The song was slow, romantic, familiar. What was the name of it anyway? "Evergreen"? It sounded different here somehow, more sensual, perhaps, with the maracas. Or maybe it was the tall flowers that lined the dance floor or the colored lights that hung over them, soft blues and greens and orange. Beyond the flowers, the ocean rhythmically swooshed up on the shore. Lisa could see the night sky shot through with stars over Sandy's shoulder. She said, "You see so many more stars down here than in New York."

Sandy looked up at the sky. "Yes," he said. Then he lowered his gaze to her. "This *is* a pretty place, isn't it?"

"It is." Lisa was aware of a faint shift. He was holding her closer, she thought. She let it happen, folding against him, resting her face ever so slightly against his chest.

Lisa's eyes closed involuntarily. Silently, in her throat, she hummed along with the song. She was aware of a rich fragrance in the air. Those flowers, she thought. This air.

The song ended. Couples applauded.

"Well, thank you very much," Sandy said. He seemed so tall and lean to her, his dark jacket blending with the dark night, his face seeming to swim above her.

She wouldn't wait to see Kilgour get his dance with Elaine. She excused herself and went to her room.

She was vaguely uneasy as she lay back on the huge bed. Maybe because this off-site is almost over and I just want to get on with things, she thought. Maybe because Barry's not here, and everyone else is all coupled up. She had a quick mental image of Sandy and Pam in bed together. Through the hum of the air conditioner, she could hear, very faintly, the dance music from the pool area.

I'll go for a run in the morning, she decided, get the *agita* out of my system.

She forced herself to sleep.

◊ ◊ ◊

Lisa was early for her breakfast meeting with Kilgour, refreshed after a long run and a hard swim.

Kilgour wore an Izod polo shirt over a pair of remarkable green pants and carried an attaché case. The eternal preppie, Lisa thought, trying not to smile.

Kilgour ordered a large breakfast. Lisa asked for half a grapefruit. "Nice party last night," she said.

"Sorry you left so soon," Kilgour replied. "It got nicer as the night went on. *Everybody* was dancing."

"I guess I was just really tired. Too much sun yesterday, maybe."

Kilgour helped himself from the basket of croissants the waiter set down. Lisa watched as he spread butter and grape jelly on and inside the delicate roll.

"I suppose it's hard for you without Barry." It was a statement, not a question.

Lisa's temper flared for a moment. She decided to say nothing.

"I suppose it isn't easy to be a single when you're used to being part of a couple," Kilgour went on. "Have you ever met this guy Elaine's bringing down?" He took a bite of his croissant.

Why, you coy old fox, Lisa thought. "No," she answered.

"I wonder what he's like," Kilgour said. Then, as if to dismiss everything else, he exclaimed, "Well, to business," as his eggs arrived.

"I have, of course, decided to break up National Services East," Kilgour said, "and give the relevant portion of the southern market to your shop. I'm compensating Danny by giving him a few of Brian's operations." Kilgour chewed. "There's no compensation for O'Connor." He smiled, then mopped up some egg yolk with a piece of croissant.

"How are those account managers going to feel?" Lisa asked, not caring at all. "I remember your saying how much they love Brian and want him to serve their markets."

Kilgour chewed and took a sip of his coffee. "Tough," he said. "This is the way I'm cutting it." He signaled for more coffee. "Well, Lisa, what about it? What do you think?"

This was what she had wanted, of course. It meant more budget, more troops, more responsibility, more variables in the equation, more buttons to push. "I'm glad there's something in this for Danny," she said.

"What about you?" Kilgour asked. "You're glad for yourself, aren't you?"

"Of course," she answered. "It means some changes. My premises guy is going to have a cardiac arrest. Although, in all honesty, I sort of warned him that there might be less space than we originally anticipated."

Kilgour laughed. "I'll bet you did, Lisa Gould."

They finished breakfast discussing details. She would be getting a block of people, machinery, and functions valued at just about three million. She had a lot to do — meetings to set up, plans to spec out. People issues. Cash issues. Tech issues.

She and Kilgour arrived together at the morning session. Lisa signaled to Tony, who joined her. "We've got it," she told him. "Can you come by my room before dinner tonight — say, about five? I've got some items to go over."

Tony nodded, all smiles.

She looked for Danny. He waved and came over. "I think we should get together as soon as we get back to New York," he said, "and go over the transfers."

"Good." She nodded. "Let's get the paperwork out of the way." Was it the wrong thing to say? She had never wanted to hurt Danny, of all people. She had hoped and expected that he would be businesslike about the whole thing. That's how she had to play it too. Danny was still her friend, wasn't he? The only one of the division heads she could talk to as a friend. She had never before won something at a friend's expense, she realized, and she was surprised to find that it felt no different from any other win. It felt good.

Her special presentation was first. She went through it smoothly, almost automatically. There was a sandwich lunch, then more presentations. In the darkened room, Lisa made notes on the coming changes, savoring her triumph, deciding how she would manage it.

She spent the rest of the afternoon alone, then met with Tony as they had planned. Impatient to have the evening over with, she excused herself right after dinner. "Got to pack," she said.

On her way out of the dining room, she passed Elaine Green and her friend. Elaine was bubbly. They had gone to a restaurant in town, "one that Stephen knew about from a previous trip." It was, Elaine reported, "wonderfully authentic."

◇ ◇ ◇

Sandy and Pam walked back to her room.

Another starry night, Sandy thought.

They went inside. Pam kicked off her shoes and began to undress. "Pammy, I think I'm just going to take off," Sandy said. "I am beat!"

She was standing, shoeless, in her slip. She looked astonished. "You're kidding," she said matter-of-factly. "You mean you're going back to your room?"

He walked toward her, smiling. "Yeah, I'm just no good tonight." He slipped his arms around her, burying his face in her hair. "You know I've been working here, really working," he whispered, "and I'm tired." He stepped back. "Tomorrow, Kilgour will be gone and it'll really be a party. We'll all relax."

There was a sour, mocking look on her face. He recognized it as the look Kathy had worn in the dying days of their marriage. He realized he didn't care. Pam Shipley had been attractive to him for her body and her willingness. Right now, her body didn't interest him and her willingness didn't matter. But he saw no reason to be unkind, and he hoped that she would not be unkind, either.

"OK," she said. "Lucky I brought something to read."

He kissed her on the forehead. "See you tomorrow. You'll come to *my* room. Night."

He walked out into the night air and back to his room.

Next door, Lisa stood before her packed suitcase, ticking things off in her mind. She had opened the sliding door to the balcony so she could hear the band, playing again by the pool. The warm, sweet breeze floated in. It felt good.

She stepped out onto the balcony. The band was playing "Evergreen" again. Automatically, she looked up. Another starry night, she thought. She remembered the colored lights that had hung over the night before when she danced with Sandy. She breathed deeply, a yoga breath that raised her bosom high under her loose robe. A breeze lifted toward her from the golf course, coming straight at her. She tilted her head back to let it catch her hair, then she went inside and closed the sliding door.

On the next balcony, deep in a white wicker chair, Sandy Lippert struck a match to light the cigarette he had been holding in his hand while he watched Lisa Gould watch the night.

4

NORMA EVANS FINISHED COUNTING the money Julie had collected from her three days at the St. Magnus. She counted out Julie's cut, handing it to her, and slipped the rest neatly into the metal cash box.

"That's good," Norma said. "How did it go?"

"Fine. No problem. It was the first time either of them had done a threesome. I more or less had to choreograph the whole thing."

"The woman who called me. She was part of it, wasn't she?"

"Yes indeed." Julie shook her head from side to side. "She's a real winner, that one. Very hot. Evidently she's got some dud of a husband and she keeps this guy around for service, but he hasn't got a hell of a lot of stamina. She'll take anything, though — man, woman, or object. I don't think she cares what's on the other end so long as she gets hers." Julie smiled. "A practical woman."

"And the man?"

Julie wrinkled her nose. "Weird. One of these religious fanatics, you know. A *real* hypocrite. Lots of repressed heat. I can't say I liked him much."

"Why not?" Norma Evans rested her chin on her clasped hands. She enjoyed these "shop talk" discussions, as she called them, and particularly with Julie, whose comments showed good insight. An intelligent girl, Norma thought, except for the pills. That was dumb and rather a shame, since it meant Julie could only last a few more years in the business. Already, her body was hinting at the neglect and fatigue that the pills produced. Still, the intelligence counted for something. Norma had occasionally thought about helping Julie set up her own place when the time came, a satellite of Norma's own operation. When the time came.

"... just not a very nice guy." Julie had been answering Norma's question. "And then he was forever praying, for God's sake. He'd go over to the window and get down on his knees and look out, like he was having a private conversation with heaven." Julie smiled. "We did an interesting little combination on that theme," she said.

"Tell me," Norma urged.

"Well, I lay down on my back on the floor facing him, with my legs wrapped around his knees. He's kneeling, as usual. Then she kneels also, sort of over my face, so they're facing one another." Julie smiled broadly, remembering. "So when he was ready, he wanted to get it off in her. But she preferred what I was doing. So she pushed him away and said, 'Spit it out somewhere else!' " Julie laughed. "He got so panicked!"

Norma smiled.

"You know something?" Julie leaned forward. "They're somehow charging this whole thing off to that bank, to GlobeBank. They both work there, you know."

"Don't knock it," Norma said. "If it weren't for GlobeBank, neither of us would be here today."

"Why is that?"

"The chairman of GlobeBank is a guy named Charlie Hardesty."

"You know him?"

"I know him. Charlie's pretty clean now; I guess it would be dangerous not to be. But in the old days he was quite a swinger." Norma sat back, ready to tell her story.

"Charlie and a guy named Paul Bell used to be good buddies. They came up through the ranks together. Poor Paul dropped dead one day a few years ago, just before Charlie was named chairman." Norma's eyes stared past Julie to some memory. "He was a nice guy, Paul Bell.

"Anyway" — Norma lit one of the dozen cigarettes she allowed herself each day — "Charlie and Paul used to work closely together. And play closely together. Once a week, at least, they'd go out to lunch and they'd get smashed. Then they'd give me a call and I'd get a few girls, and we'd all go to a hotel somewhere and party. And I mean party!"

Norma smiled at the recollection.

"So when I got ready to set this place up, I asked Charlie for advice and seed money. And he came through with both." Norma leaned forward. "In fact, through me, Charlie Hardesty used to have major investments in this house, in two other houses I helped start, in a couple of Eighth Avenue massage parlors, and in a club on East Forty-fourth Street."

Norma dragged on her cigarette. "When they made him chairman, he sold out to me totally. We both got rich."

"Do you ever see him?"

Norma shook her head. "No. He phones sometimes, just to chat. And every now and again he asks me to set something up for some customer, very quietly. The whole association is something Charlie has kept very quiet."

Norma's face brightened. "Once there was this girl named Sandra — great redhead, but a junkie. Anyway, one day Charlie calls me from Fraunces Tavern, downtown. He's there with Paul, they're tight, they want a little action. So I get Sandra and the two of us go down there, and Charlie is really turned on by Sandra. He says we're all going to go out to the Island, to Southampton, where he has a house. So he calls Carey for a limousine and we all get into this car and start heading up the F.D.R. Drive. Charlie and Paul have a couple of bottles in the car, and we're all drinking and not caring because we've got a driver. Then, a little way up the drive, Charlie tells the driver to pull off. He gets the driver to park underneath the drive, near some big apartment houses, and he asks us to get out of the car. So the three of us, the driver and Paul and I, are standing near the car, and inside we see Charlie's bare ass bopping up and down. Charlie is hooting and hollering and his ass is going up and down" — Norma motioned with her arm as Julie began laughing — "and he's still wearing his fancy suit jacket, which is pushed up his back. I swear that car was rocking. The poor chauffeur looked like he was going to faint!"

Julie was still laughing, trying to picture the scene.

"Oh, boy," Norma sighed, "those were the days!"

5

LISA WAITED FOR HER luggage, waited for a taxi, waited in traffic during the ride into town, unhappy to be out of the warmth of the Caribbean and amid the raw chill of New York.

She was on edge. It had been an unsettling week. But why? The off-site had gone well — very well, in fact. She had performed smoothly, had gotten her win.

The cab inched forward. "Some traffic," the cabbie said. He shook his head. "This is some traffic." He turned around to face her. "OK if I take the Triborough?"

"That's OK," Lisa answered, thinking, God, how I want to get home. The trip seemed endless. She thought she might sleep on the plane, but couldn't. And now this traffic on top of it.

Why am I so jumpy? she wondered. The cab crawled through Queens. She couldn't wait to get inside the apartment, take off her shoes, and dump all her dirty laundry into the hamper. Maybe a bath would help. I'll take a long bath and have something hot to eat. Maybe split a can of soup with Barry, she thought automatically, then corrected herself. What's the matter with me? Of course. Barry's still in Paris. Of course.

Maybe that's why I'm so jumpy. Coming home to an empty place. That's it. I miss Barry. The apartment would seem gloomy without him; it always did. Alone there. I'll be alone again. Come sit with us, Terri Maresca had said. Sandy can be your date. She thought of him now, probably dancing with his girl. Pam, that was her name.

Lisa tried to relax. Use the time, she thought. Don't waste it. Think about the new market segment. How to mesh it in; communicating the change. Tony will do the numbers. Sandy can be your date, Terri had said.

The taxi moved toward Manhattan in spurts. The radio system crackled, the dispatcher's voice giving instructions, reciting numbers, locations.

"I been in this business thirty-two years," the cabbie said, his elbows on the wheel. "When you hit this kind of traffic, there's nothing you can do about it." He turned on the radio.

Lisa leaned back against the seat, trying to unwind. The music. She thought of the flowers around the dance floor at Palmas del Mar. Bird of Paradise, bougainvillea.

Tomorrow I'll shop, get some fresh food, flowers. Straighten the place up. Barry will be back Sunday. A real American breakfast for him. Ham and eggs, maybe. Seeded rolls from the Cake Master. Oh, Barry. I miss my husband. Everybody was a couple. Except Sandy. Dancing with him, my cheek on his navy jacket.

The phone was ringing as she opened the apartment door. She pushed her suitcase in with one foot and lunged for the telephone. She hoped it was Barry.

"Hello?"

There was a pause, a click. "Hi, sweetie!"

"Barry! I was hoping it would be you."

"How are you doing?"

"I'm fine. I just this minute walked in!"

"I know. I've been calling for a while."

It was a tonic to hear his voice, steady, familiar, loving. "Sweetheart! It's good to hear your voice!" she said. "Where are you?"

"Paris. Where should I be?"

"I know, but where?"

"In the hotel. We just got back from dinner. You OK? How was Puerto Rico?"

"It was fine. I got that extra market segment I wanted. I'll tell you all about it when you get here. When *are* you getting here?"

"As scheduled. Sunday. I figure I'll be in the apartment by four or five unless the plane's late."

"I'll be here. Are you exhausted?"

"Très, très fatigué."

"How's Paris?"

"Beautiful," he said with feeling. "I wish you were here."

"I wish *you* were *here*. Oh, Barry, I missed you. I miss you."

"Likewise," said Barry. Barry always said "likewise."

They both laughed.

"OK, love, see you Sunday," he said. "Try to get some rest."

The apartment smelled musty. She opened the windows, and a blast of cold air blew the top of a pile of mail off the desk.

She was hungry, she realized, as she took some crackers from the pantry shelf. Opening the refrigerator, she was assaulted by the unpleasant odor of spoiled food. *Christ!* she thought, angry now. Couldn't Carmela throw this stuff out? There was mold on the cottage cheese. A chicken leg — it had to be two weeks old — looked gray in its Saran Wrap. The milk had soured days before. "Damnit," Lisa said aloud. "Goddamnit." She could feel tears rising.

Stop this, she told herself. You're just feeling sorry for yourself, and it doesn't even make sense. "It's just because it all seems dismal without Barry," she said aloud. Nonsense, she reproached herself. Everything went well in Puerto Rico, even a little better than you expected. No hard feelings, even, from Danny. She felt good about that. And Barry would be back on Sunday. Try to get some rest, he had said. She really should. God knows, there would be plenty to do at the office. On Monday it would start in earnest. The prospect excited her. Meetings, memos, activities. Changing things; making things happen. The conversion. She sat down and buttered some crackers.

She supposed she'd be seeing a lot of Sandy now. They'd be working closely together on the Autotran conversion. Once again she had a quick memory of dancing with him, her cheek brushing against his jacket. I don't even come up to his shoulder, she thought.

Well. She leaned back and took a deep breath. Tomorrow, I'll get the place cleaned up and think about the conversion. Sunday, I'll read the paper and relax. And of course Barry would be arriving.

6

SANDY HAD NOT ENJOYED the final weekend in Puerto Rico. Pam was annoyed, and she let him know it. Her idea of a good time — lying on the beach all day, dressing up for dinner at night, "just relaxing" — made him feel on edge. On the beach blanket next to her, with one set of her Sony Walkman earphones over his head, he found himself thinking about the things he had to do back in New York.

The London trip would require a lot of preparation, both for the Autotran conversion and for Thomas Putnam. He had to get down to some serious supervision of the conversion for National Services West, Lisa Gould's world. On the blanket beside him, Pam flipped over the cassette. Sandy hadn't noticed when it ended. He looked down the beach where he and Lisa had run that day. He ought to have a meeting with her as soon as he got back.

◇ ◇ ◇

She wore gray flannel to lunch in the senior officers' dining room at Head Office the first day after the off-site. Sandy wanted to know more about the added market segment she had won in Puerto Rico in case his technical horsepower requirements were impacted. More CRTs would be required, of course; but they had agreed it would all have to be specked out, and that they'd need to keep in touch.

"So how was the weekend?" Lisa asked over coffee when the business discussion was over.

Sandy thought quickly of Pam, of the almost silent plane ride home and the quick, cool good-bye. That romance is over with, he realized. "Oh, OK." He shrugged. "Why didn't you stay?"

"Well, you know, without my husband . . ."

Sandy was sorry he had asked. Was she going to talk about her husband now?

"I had a lot to do up here," she went on, "and my husband was due back on Sunday."

"Where was he?" Sandy decided he ought to ask.

"Paris."

"Oh. Well, that's great, a great city." He sipped his coffee.

"Yes, although in February, Puerto Rico is probably a better business trip to pull off."

"It has its compensations."

"Aren't you off somewhere yourself pretty soon?" Lisa looked at her watch.

"London. Next week." Sandy shook his head. "Could be a sort of knot over there. The London guys — Fenton and Bennett — are feeling a little *agita* over this Autotran thing. You know, these guys still think of us as the enemy a little bit. Like who the hell are we to tell them how to run their data centers and set up their processing. I don't know. Could be a knot."

Lisa was interested. "Yes, that's a tough variable. A little matrix-y. I mean, you have accountability but no real authority over them, is that it?"

Sandy nodded.

"Well," Lisa went on, "diplomacy should work, I think. You've got a lot of charm." She blushed, adding quickly, "I mean, you've got a friendly personality. Just wine them and dine them a bit, and try to win them over on the personal side."

Sandy thought this over. "Yes, I should set up a nice dinner or something. Who knows that stuff? Who knows about nice London dinners?"

"Jessica," Lisa said immediately. She looked down at the table. Even his hand was darkly tanned, the smooth brown hairs still gleaming a reddish blond from the Puerto Rican sun. She realized he was staring at her.

"I've got to run," Lisa said.

Jessica knew several places in London. "It used to be," she told Sandy by way of introduction, "that the guide to English cuisine consisted of three words: 'Cross the Channel.' No more."

They were at Brownie's, a vegetarian place, surrounded by health-food freaks, Orthodox Jews from the novelty and ribbon workshops in the neighborhood, and a few wide-eyed construction workers from a nearby high-rise site. Jessica plowed through a salad bowl topped with shredded carrots and went down her list of London restaurants.

"What do I get for this valuable consulting assistance, anyway?" she asked. "I mean, besides this lunch."

"What would you like?"

Jessica considered. "Something in a tin from Fortnum and Mason. It doesn't matter what — it's the tin I'm interested in. I need it for a sewing box."

"You got it. I'm surprised you sew. I thought women like you didn't do that sort of thing." He was smiling.

"Women like me?" She feigned a look of horror.

"You, Lisa. Superior women is what I meant, of course."

"Oh, of course," she said, matching his bantering tone. "Well, I do sew, although badly. I don't know about Lisa, but if she sews, she probably does it well."

"She does everything well, doesn't she?"

"Seems to. She has an aura of competence."

Sandy seemed thoughtful. "Yes. Not that she's unfeminine. I mean, she's, well, very feminine."

"You've noticed."

"Hard not to." His tone became hearty. "I mean, at the offsite, when everyone's in a bathing suit, you sort of notice these things more." He tried to hail the waitress to get some more coffee.

"So what did you all do down there? Was there any fun at all?"

"Oh, a little. Wednesday was our big party day. Kilgour threw a lunch, and then everybody went off and played. Then Kilgour threw a dinner, and then we all danced."

"What did *you* play? Tennis? Golf?"

"No, I'm not much for that stuff. I went for a walk, actually, with . . . your boss. They have a tropical rain forest kind of thing there. Very interesting place."

"Oh?" Jessica noticed that Sandy was looking past her, still trying to find a waitress. That was unlike him. "Did you talk business?" she asked.

"What?" He jerked his head back to look at her. "Oh. Yes. A little. More or less."

"I thought your girl was down there with you."

"She's not my girl, and she didn't arrive till Wednesday night," Sandy replied, almost snappishly, Jessica thought.

The waitress arrived. "Check, please," Sandy said.

◊ ◊ ◊

Linda Glover was on the six-twenty train home to Tarrytown, thinking.

"That's the way I want to cut it," Lisa had said to her. She had rejected Linda's proposal for a new format for the financial section of the Strategic Plan. "We'll do it my way," Lisa had said. Then she smiled. "I'm still in charge here."

So she was, Linda thought ruefully, very much in charge. She refused to consider the rejected proposal a failure. It had just been a test of how far Lisa could be pushed, and it had yielded a result. Now she knew that Lisa Gould, for all the scope of her position, for all the responsibility she had, still paid attention to detail.

That was important to know. It was important to Linda to know all she could about power. There had been a lecture in her management course at B-school: "The Five Bases of Power." She had taken careful notes at that lecture; she still had them somewhere. But she didn't need her notes. She remembered what they said.

Coercive. That was Kilgour. He just gave orders. He sat at his big desk and punched his Ardec and talked into his Dictaphone and people acted. He was secure in his ability to force people to do his will.

Reward. That was the kind of power she wielded over Rick Schmidt. The thought of him shot a sudden heat through her groin. She squirmed in her seat as she remembered the week before, remembered Rick, and Julie. They had kept Julie through Friday. She had devised all sorts of combinations for the three of them and new ideas for Rick and Linda to try alone, while she watched. When Rick went to the bank to get the two thousand in cash to pay her, Linda and Julie had stayed in the room. Linda closed her eyes at the thought of it. The two thousand would go on Rick's expense account, spread out over time. So would the five hundred Linda had already paid, which Rick reimbursed. Linda had showed Rick ways to bury the amount on the expense sheets. "You think LaRocca will sign it?" he asked her. "Make sure he does," Linda had answered, caressing him between the legs.

Legitimate. Well, that could be anybody, really. Tony, for example, in her case. The truth was, she found Tony a bit of a drip. The only reason he had power over her was his position in the hierarchy. She reported to him. He reviewed her performance. That was the base of his power. That, and nothing more.

Expert. Sandy Lippert was probably a good example of that. Even after he had failed, his superior knowledge of the Autotran system had given him a base of power, and he had been able to build a return to hierarchical power. Even Lisa deferred to Sandy. At the staff meeting that morning, she had told them all in no uncertain terms that they were to give him their fullest cooperation. She would, she said, be spending a lot of time with Lippert over the next few months, working very closely with him on the conversion. And she would be asking him how well her people were cooperating, just as Kilgour would be asking Lippert how well National Services West was cooperating. It looked like Sandy Lippert was the man of the hour as far as Lisa was concerned.

Referent. You had referent power by dint of personality. It was like charisma — you just had it. That was Jessica's power, Linda decided. Jessica couldn't coerce, couldn't reward; her position in the hierarchy was not very high, and her expertise didn't have much impact on the bottom line. But Jessica had a kind of power, anyway. People liked her, trusted her. Lisa trusted her. Jessica had Lisa's ear and an ability to persuade Lisa to a point of view. She used this power sparingly, only when she cared. So it was important to have Jessica care about you, important to be on her good side. And very important, Linda realized, not to be on her bad side.

Then there was Lisa. What base of power did she have? All of them, actually: coercive, reward, legitimate, expert, and referent. And she used them all. She used them all well.

That was what Linda Glover had to learn from Lisa Gould. She knew well enough how to get power. But using it, and using it well — that was something Lisa Gould could teach her. And Linda was determined to learn.

The train pulled into Tarrytown. It was just after seven. She would be in the house by seven-thirty. It was important, this week, to get home late, when Charley had already started drinking. She didn't want him lucid enough to notice the red splotches and scratch marks that Rick and Julie had left on her body.

◇ ◇ ◇

Barry had cooked dinner while Lisa was running. The jogs along the beach in Puerto Rico had gotten her started again. She really thought Barry ought to take up some exercise too, "particularly in the winter, dear." He needed to tone up; he was putting on weight, and he lacked energy. "You'll work better, Barr'. You'll feel better, and you'll look better."

But Barry complained that he didn't have time. "I've just got to get through these few months," he said.

They set the table together. Wordlessly, like a well-rehearsed drill team that knew one another's moves perfectly, they passed knives and forks and napkins as they bent over the table, forming a comfortable arch.

"Leifer came in to see me today," Barry said. He reached for a piece of bread.

"Oh? What did he have to say?" Lisa was chewing delicately at a chicken wing.

"Just that he thinks I'm doing a great job on the Paris thing."

"Well, that's great, that's super. Sweetie, don't put so much butter on the bread."

"Lis', will you just let me eat?" His tone startled her. Barry took a bite of the bread. "Anyway, yes, it's nice to hear. But the subliminal message was: more pressure. You know. Leifer was full of little subtexts about 'the importance of this case' and 'value to the firm' and all that."

"Well, we knew this was your big one," Lisa said.

Barry set down his knife and fork. "I know, but I'm tired." He looked at her, almost pleadingly, she thought. "I just haven't stopped for a while. I need . . . a break. Or something."

Lisa looked away. Her heart went out to him. "Listen," she said. "We both need something. We both need a break. This weekend. We're going up to the house and we're not taking any work." Something had to be done, and she was in charge. "I

202

mean it, Barry. Not a paper, not a law book, not even a French record. We need to just . . . cool out. And be together."

Barry smiled gratefully. "It sounds good, sweetie. It sounds good to me. And only two more days till we get there."

"Yes," Lisa said dully, "just two more days."

7

LISA HAD WONDERED WHEN she would have to face the resentment about her win in Puerto Rico. She found out pretty quickly, at a meeting of the Task Force on Interdivisional Issues.

North and O'Connor were ranged against her. There were issues that Kilgour needed to clarify, they said. Kilgour himself. Not an intermediary.

"That's challenging the very basis of this task force, Doug," she said as calmly as possible to North's steely, unsmiling face. "And it was John who created the task force."

North argued, supported by O'Connor. They're well rehearsed, Lisa thought bitterly. Must have practiced together on the golf course. She looked down the long table at Sandy, who was watching her, his boyish face serious.

I don't need this at all right now, she thought. A lateral attack by these guys is not something I need to add to the pressure. Lisa hated this kind of corporate politics. She flourished on contest, competition, head-to-head confrontation. Petty infighting — "squad squabbles," as Kilgour called them — were distasteful to her.

It was clearly a personal attack, an attempt to nip in the bud her steadily growing power. She didn't think they would succeed, but it was going to be a constant irritant. And it meant she would have to watch her flank at all times.

What an odd couple, she mused. North was still expounding, his speech a blur of corporate gobbledygook. Behind his well-bred exterior, she suspected, were some of the more unattractive human qualities. She also sensed for the first time that North wasn't really all that bright.

With O'Connor, there was no doubt about dull-wittedness.

He had taken up the argument, and even North looked embarrassed. What a jerk Brian is, Lisa thought. Why am I going nuts
over this? Just stay cool, she told herself; consider the facts.

The facts were that North and O'Connor, as individuals, were
not very formidable opposition. Their combined divisions, however, Multinationals and Metro, outweighed any other — in
budget, in people, in the clout their front office counterparts
could bring to bear. Even Hardesty and Pruitt would listen to a
joint statement from those two divisions.

On the other hand, her position seemed impregnable. Globe-
Bank needed her. She was their only female division head, and
one of their best. She was sought out by blue-ribbon government
commissions, by boards of directors, by charities and causes
eager to use her name. So far she had gone slowly, cautiously,
occasionally allowing her name to be used — after checking
with Kilgour — but accepting no active outside functions. First
she would get the conversion on its way, she told Kilgour. Then
she'd go on some boards.

She was, ironically, "one of the boys." A member of the club.
Well respected and well liked in the banking sectors.

And, of course, she was Kilgour's woman, nurtured and protected by one of the most powerful figures in the financial industry.

Impregnable, but not unassailable. That's what this move
from North and O'Connor was all about. You never really look
bad when you go after someone who's very strong. It wouldn't
be like going after — Lisa looked quickly down the table — after
Sandy, for example. He'd taken his lumps already; there would
be no profit in trying to stomp on him. She wondered what it
had been like for him when he was really down, wondered what
it felt like to lose that badly.

She wished the meeting would end. She had to get ready for
tomorrow — her meeting with Sandy and his guys about Autotran — and she had to pack for the weekend. Barry so badly
needed a rest. And Autotran counted. She wished things could
always be about substantive issues, not this kind of politics.

Lisa cut in on O'Connor. "Look, Brian," she said. "My char-
ter for this task force is to present John Kilgour with a consensus
agenda for his attention. Now if you guys can hash out a con-

sensus on this, I'll take it to John. Otherwise, let's go on. Because there are substantive issues here."

"Some of us think *this* is a substantive issue, Lisa," North replied.

She sighed. They were going to keep boring away at her. She wouldn't be able to relax for a minute.

Sandy was still watching her, stern and handsome, his green eyes attentive. He looks worried for me, she thought. That's . . . nice.

". . . and I'd like us to consider a memo out of this task force outlining the proper topics for its consideration." It was North. It was useless.

◊ ◊ ◊

Sandy had asked her if she wanted to walk home. "You're on Sixty-ninth, aren't you? I'm Eighty-fifth."

He looked boyish again, ruddy and vulnerable. She wanted to touch his face.

"I can't," she said. "I can't."

Sandy shrugged.

Lisa wasted time in her office until she was sure he was gone, then walked home briskly.

Barry looked even more down that evening. He seemed to be going downhill. He needs care, she thought.

"One more day to the weekend," he said, mustering a cheery tone.

"I've got to work tonight," she said in response. "I've got a meeting tomorrow afternoon with the Utility people to go over the first draft of specs, and I've got to . . ." Why was she bothering him with details?

She went into the study and closed the door behind her.

◊ ◊ ◊

Sandy sat in his imitation Eames chair, a drink in his hand, listening to Joni Mitchell on the headset. From the chair he could see his view, the long stretch of Manhattan a sea of sparkling lights.

Dumb meeting today, he thought. Lisa handled it well, she held them off. I'll take a walk, he decided. He felt tense.

The night was very cold. Sandy consciously took long, stretching strides, trying to work the flutters out of his body. He stopped at 1473 Third Avenue.

The mail's really piling up, he said to himself as he reached into the battered tin box marked Putnam. Some mailbox stuffers were addressed to Occupant, but there were several pieces specifically for Putnam. I should take these to London, he thought, as more proof. He wondered what lists had been sold where and by whom to account for the mail: an offer to buy life insurance, a solicitation from a conservation organization, a letter from the police community council. Brooks Harris had turned off her Con Edison account, so there was a bill for heat and light addressed to Thomas Putnam.

He opened a drawer in the kitchen and removed the Putnam checkbook to write a check for Con Ed. He put the checkbook and mail into the special billfold he had bought for Putnam's credit cards and I.D.

He wouldn't need to come back here again before he went to London.

◇ ◇ ◇

Friday morning, Lisa put on the most expensive dress she owned. It had been a gift from Barry, a wine-colored Perry Ellis with a low V neck. A bit sexy for the office, Lisa thought, and wondered if Barry would notice. But he said nothing.

Jessica, however, was full of comment when she came to Lisa's office at noon to pick her up for lunch. "You and Barry going out tonight?" she asked as Lisa reached for her coat.

"Hardly. No. We're driving up to the country, in fact. Why?"

"Oh. Because you're kind of dressed up. It's a terrific dress. Is it new? You have maybe a meeting with Paul Newman this afternoon?"

Lisa laughed. "I have a meeting with the Utility guys this afternoon. About as far from Paul Newman as you can get."

"Won't Sandy be there?" Jessica noticed that Lisa started slightly.

"I guess so, I expect so," she replied, busying herself with her gloves. "Where are we going today?"

It was always Jessica who picked the restaurant when they lunched together; Lisa always asked her to, and she was never disappointed at the choice. Jessica spent many of her lunch hours prowling the midtown area for interesting places to eat, all very different from the expense account restaurants to which Lisa was usually taken. Jessica always knew of a new Indian tandoori kitchen or a new source of enormous fresh salads; she had once even found a restaurant in the West Forties — requiring a short cab ride — called A Little Bit of Afghanistan.

Today she took Lisa to a Chinese place on Second Avenue. It was a cold day and they ordered a big lunch — broth with Szechuan pickled cabbage, slippery bean curd home-style, and, deciding to go all the way on the hot menu, chicken with orange flavor. "Remember to eat the orange rind but not the peppers," Jessica said.

The little restaurant had a cozy feeling. The lunchtime crowd was all enjoying the fact that it was Friday and that the restaurant was warm and the food good.

"Tell me about San Francisco," Lisa said. Jessica had taken the week before the off-site as vacation.

Jessica looked happy. "Well, it was great — just what the doctor ordered. I sat around with friends, saw some sights, had a lot of good laughs. Nice. Met some interesting people."

"Does that mean men?"

Jessica held up a chopstick. "One, actually."

"So tell," Lisa said, clearly interested. "Come on."

"Well, there isn't very much to tell. I mean, we spent time together, nicely, and now he's there and I'm here."

"No chance you'll see one another again?"

Jessica's Tsingtao beer arrived. "A fairly good chance, actually. He's a designer. Does a lot of hotel interiors. He's probably coming east next month. To Hartford, really, but it's close enough."

"Hotel interiors?"

Jessica shrugged. "Somebody has to. Actually, one day we went to see one he worked on, or consulted on or something. The Jackson Court. It's just wonderful. It's one of those small, elegant, quiet, homelike places that you wish still existed in major cities but have given up hoping for."

"Well, I hope the man was as good as the hotel," Lisa said with a smile.

Jessica nodded. "You bet."

Lisa laughed. "What about Abby? Did she have a good time while her mother was off looking at hotel interiors?"

"Oh ho. You're very sharp today, Ms. Gould. Well, yes. Actually, Abby had a great time. She's a real tourist, you know. I was pleased. I'm sometimes afraid she's going to be one of these jaded New York kids. But, nope, she fell for all the touristy things, all the hucksterism. Did me proud, she did."

The platters of food arrived.

"And what went on here last week, during the off-site? While the cat was away, did the mice play?"

Jessica looked up sharply from her bean curd. If only Lisa knew. If only Lisa knew what she herself knew but had no intention of telling. Should she tell Lisa, for example, that Linda Glover was hardly in the office all week, and that Linda's secretary nearly went crazy trying to juggle phone calls from Linda's husband and other people? The secretary had had no idea where Linda was. She had said she would be "downtown" or "at a meeting out of the bank" or "out to run an errand." *Where* downtown or out of the bank or on what errand, she never said.

Coincidentally, on the one day Linda showed up long enough to be seen at lunch, Rick Schmidt was reported to be wandering around at 176 Wall and at Head Office, asking people if he could look through their files. Should Jessica tell Lisa that Rick had pumped her about Lisa's conversion plan and had asked Jessica to get him a copy? That Flo had taken a two-hour lunch every day and that she, Jessica, had caught up with all her correspondence and had caught two first-run movies at the four o'clock show?

"It was quiet," Jessica said. "I don't think much of anything happened." She sipped some more beer. "Tell me about the off-site."

"A mixed bag, I'd say," Lisa began. "We did in fact get some stuff done, and I for one have a better feel for everybody's planning process. But there was also a lot of wasted time."

"Like Wednesday afternoon?"

Lisa's head came up with a jerk. "What about Wednesday afternoon?" she asked. Her face felt hot.

Jessica looked at her quizzically. "Nothing. I just ... I had lunch with Sandy, and he said it was about the only fun part of the whole week, that you and he had taken a walk through some tropical rain forest or something."

"Oh, yes." Lisa nodded vigorously. "There's a planned walk. You get a guidebook to the plant life. It's all numbered. Quite interesting."

Jessica looked hard at Lisa, who was staring past her — at the food, at the decor, anywhere but at Jessica.

"Sandy's a nice guy," Lisa went on. "He and I sort of got thrown together since we were the only people there without a spouse. And Elaine," she added. "Some girlfriend of his came down on Wednesday."

"Well, from what he told me, she's not much of a girlfriend."

Lisa reached for some chicken. "No? Really? Oh. Just how well do you know Sandy?"

"Pretty well. We have lunch together every now and then. Want some more bean curd?"

Lisa nodded as she said, "Did you ever go out with him?"

"Oh, hell no," Jessica answered. "We just sort of like each other. I don't know. We're both divorced. Maybe that produces rapport. Like you two spending time together in Puerto Rico because you were both single wheels." She spooned some bean curd onto Lisa's extended plate. "I think Sandy rather enjoys finding someone from GlobeBank who actually does not want to talk about the conversion or the thrust of technology or whatever the thrust is these days. I think he finds me a relief." She paused. "Like taking a walk with you in a rain forest and discovering you're not always a division head."

Lisa bristled. What the hell did Jessica know about the rain forest? What was there to know?

"Have you ever worked with him directly? I mean, I'll be working with him a lot on the conversion, and I was wondering what he was like to work with."

It was an odd question, Jessica thought. Lisa never needed to ask questions like that. "He's good to work with. Helpful. Nice. *Very* thorough. And . . ." She considered her words. "He's appreciative. You know? Always takes me to lunch when I do something involving Autotran. He's really a gentle guy. Inside he has a lot of sweetness."

"What was his wife like?" Lisa asked quickly. "Do you know?"

Jessica shook her head. Another odd question. "No, I gather she's one of the horsy set. Everyone knows she's really putting the screw into him for money." Jessica thought briefly of going into her speech that no woman capable of working should take alimony, but she sensed that this wasn't the time.

"That's lousy," Lisa said softly.

"No, but anyhow," Jessica said, "he's good to work with. He really loves his system, you know. He really cares about making it succeed, and he works hard at that."

Lisa stared into the middle of the crowded restaurant. "I guess there isn't much else in his life, really," she said.

Jessica broke open her fortune cookie. "Keep your eye on the goal," she read aloud. "I wonder if this guy knows John Kilgour."

◇ ◇ ◇

The Utility consultants sat around the table in Lisa's conference room, waiting. Sandy kept checking the door, looking for her.

He finally saw her coming from her office. A dark dress, cut low in front. Lovely, he thought. Oh, God. She's lovely.

"Hi," she said to everyone, not looking at him. "Who's taking us through this?"

"It's my show," Sandy said quietly.

He walked over to a large presentation easel and began to fiddle with something in the back.

Lisa watched him. His look was intent. His hands seemed to know exactly where to go. She suddenly had a sense of him as a handy sort of man. He was an engineer, after all. He could probably fix anything. He said he liked to putter around with audio equipment — probably with all sorts of machines and appliances. In her mind's eye, she saw him in old work clothes, bent over a broken steam iron, concentrating, contented.

"OK," he said, "here's what we've got."

It was a long, detailed presentation. Lisa leaned back in her chair and tried to take it all in. "This is a lot to absorb. I think you guys have done an outstanding job." She looked around the table. "I'll want to go over a few issues, probably just with Sandy, but I think I'd like to get going on phase one of the implementation."

The consultants, in unison, nodded.

"So why don't you guys get with Tony," she went on, "and start ordering the hardware; send me the bills."

Sandy walked her back to her office, talking while she stuffed her briefcase, helping her on with her coat. They left the building and started up Park together, heading east on Sixty-fifth, then north on Third.

"You in a real hurry?" Sandy asked. "How about a drink?"

She looked at her watch. Five forty-five. She and Barry were planning to leave for the country at around seven-thirty. Barry probably wouldn't be home until seven. She could stay for forty-five minutes, maybe an hour, tell Barry she had done some late work. "Sure," she said.

The bar was dark and quiet. Red-shaded lamps threw a soft light against the red-carpeted walls. Lisa squirmed out of her coat and Sandy forced himself to look away. Her soft bosom leaning toward him — he knew he would stare if he looked at her. A waitress brought a bowl of peanuts and took their orders: Heineken for Sandy, a Bloody Mary for Lisa. Both were silent for a moment.

"You seeing your kids this weekend?" Lisa asked.

Sandy nodded. "Yeah. I pick them up tomorrow morning. What about you? You have plans?"

"We're going up to our country place, a little house up in Connecticut. Nothing fancy, just a place to get away to, a place where we can rest and relax. My husband really needs to get away — he's been working like a demon."

"What's his field, anyway?"

"International copyright, mostly. Fascinating. But he does travel a lot, and he's often away for long stretches of time."

He looked hard at her. "That must be sort of a bore for you," he said softly.

The comment flustered her. "Oh. Well, of course, I have things to do, and New York is hardly boring. But I miss him, of course." Their drinks arrived. "How's your friend Pam?"

"I don't actually know," Sandy said, following the setting down of the drinks with his eyes. He took a long swallow of beer. "Nice dress," he said.

She glanced down at herself quickly. "Thank you."

They sat in uncomfortable silence. Lisa wondered if she should leave, but she had hardly touched her drink, and she didn't really need to leave just yet. Sandy had finished his beer and signaled for another. What did they have in common to talk about? Besides Autotran, which was talked out. And Puerto Rico. Not Puerto Rico.

"I had lunch with Jessica today," she said finally. She told him where they went and precisely what they ate. They both said how fond they were of Jessica before lapsing into silence again.

When his glass was empty, she said, "Well, I should be going. Can you tell me about those conversion issues next week?"

"Another drink?" Sandy gestured to the waitress.

"No, no. Really. I've got to do the driving tonight."

He looked at her, just looked, right into her eyes. She felt caught by his look, held by it. She told herself to look away but couldn't, felt herself redden, and, as he reached for the check, she blessed the darkness in the booth.

8

IT WAS JUST AFTER EIGHT when Sandy arrived at 176. The attaché case in his left hand was crammed with the papers he would need the next day when he left for London. He wanted to go over everything one more time.

His right hand held a Chock Full O'Nuts bag in which there were two fried egg sandwiches, a large coffee, and grapefruit juice. Sandy was hungry. He had been up since five-thirty, too restless even to hope for any more sleep; he finally went for a long run around the reservoir. The run made him hungry, and his uneasiness persisted. Was it the trip? He knew that the London Autotran installation would be difficult. As he told Lisa, there was always resentment of Head Office out in the field. Things could get hairy. That was it, of course, Sandy told himself. He had to be prepared, had to make sure the London people identified him with their best interests, their goals.

Lisa Gould. He pried the lid off his coffee and took a sip. He *was* uneasy. Maybe it was something she had said. He tried to remember, but he could only recall looking at her through half-shut eyes, lying on the beach, her breasts shifting inside her bathing suit as she moved slightly on her towel.

Conversion issues. That was it, he remembered. She had said she had some conversion issues she wanted to go over with him. He looked at his watch and again had a vision of the beach, Lisa holding his wrist for a minute in the brilliant sunshine.

Eight-thirty. Maybe she'd be in her office.

"Lisa Gould," she said, picking up the phone. Her secretary wasn't in yet.

"Lisa? Sandy." He decided to plunge right in. "You wanted to talk more about some issues? About the conversion?"

"Yes. Yes, I do."

"Well," he said, galloping on, "I'm leaving for London tomorrow, and it might be a good idea for us to review them before I go. Is there any chance we could get together today? Maybe lunch?"

There's nothing pressing, she thought, nothing that can't wait. She heard the slight urgency in his voice. She closed her eyes.

"You're on," she said. "Where?"

"How about a mini off-site? I have to be at 176 all day and I'm swamped. Halfway?"

It was only fifteen minutes by cab to the Gramercy Park area. Sandy had suggested Pete's Tavern. It was quiet and empty in the early afternoon, "a good place," he had said, "to talk." He was waiting when she arrived, a half-finished glass of beer in front of him.

Lisa slid into the chair across from him. It seemed a little awkward, somehow, sitting opposite him in this place, hearing only the faint *buzz, buzz* of a conversation between the bartender and an elderly couple near the door.

She noticed that his face was still reddish brown from the off-site and that the color emphasized the lightness of his eyes.

◇ ◇ ◇

"Your tan is fading," Barry had said. Yesterday? No, the day before. The long drive up to the country had exhausted her. The place in Connecticut was supposed to be a refuge, but there were times when it felt like a millstone around her neck. It was there, so they had to go. And frankly, she thought, with all the strain at the office, she would just as soon not have to add the strain of a three-hour drive each way almost every weekend — the headlights of oncoming traffic constantly in her eyes, the trucks roaring past them with only inches to spare. But Barry needed this.

Oh, darling Barry, she thought, darling, sweet Barry. I love him. But she was so irritable with him. And he so rarely protested. That made it worse. Even when she hurt him, he said little, remaining cheerful, wagging his tail like a big shaggy dog. Then she felt guilty, and it only added to the strain. He had wanted her the night they arrived, but she had been so tired. Too tired. His crestfallen look persisted through Saturday. She knew she had to make it up to him and planned how she would do it.

"Barry?" she whispered Saturday night in their bedroom. She stood very close to him. "I'm sorry about last night. I was so tired."

"It's OK, love," he whispered back. His arms went around her.

They stood for a moment locked together, quiet. She began to nibble his ear. I'm seducing my own husband, she thought. She stepped back from him and pulled the long-sleeved sweater up over her head. She was not wearing a bra. Then she sat on the edge of the bed and pulled off her shoes, her slacks, her panties. Barry's face looked confused.

She gazed up at him, put her hands up to hang on his belt, and brought one hand down between his legs.

Barry got out of his clothes quickly. She lay back on the bed waiting. He came to her and hugged her, burying his face in her soft, white breasts.

"Your tan is fading," he said, his words muffled against her chest.

She laughed, lifted his head, and looked at him. "Is that the only thing you can think of right now?" she asked him dreamily.

Barry smiled. He kissed her breasts in turn, kissed her neck,

kissed her mouth. She reached down and took him in her hand,
kneading with her thumb. Her legs spread wide. With both
hands she guided him into her. Her legs went around him, her
hands on his buttocks. They began to rock together. Drops of
sweat fell on her from Barry's forehead.

"Love you," he gasped. "Love."

"Yes," she said, urging him on. "Barry? Barry?" Her voice was
high.

◇ ◇ ◇

"Did you have a good weekend?" Sandy was saying in Pete's
Tavern.

"Fair. And you?"

"Kids," he said smiling. "All kids. It's tough to shop audio at
Sonnabend's with little kids."

◇ ◇ ◇

"These your kids?"

"These are mine." Sandy held onto Blair with one hand while
the other rested on the bar of the stroller into which Blake,
swaddled in his snowsuit, was wedged.

Mickey squatted down till he was nearly at eye level with
Blair. "Hiya, sweetheart," he crooned. "Hello, little doll."

"Say hello to Mr. Horowitz," Sandy urged. Blair tucked her
chin down into her neck and clung to Sandy's leg. Mickey stood,
and the two men smiled.

"And this is your boy?"

"This is Blake. And on my right leg is Blair."

"You got beautiful kids, Mr. Lippert."

"Thank you, Mickey. I couldn't agree more."

"So how is the analog bass system? Any problems?"

"No, no. I stopped in to tell you how much I like it."

"Good. Terrific."

"It's everything you promised, Mickey. Really makes a difference on the distortion."

"Yeah. It's a hell of a system. I sell you the KLH 2 or 3?"

"You? The 3, of course."

Mickey laughed. The truth was, Sandy Lippert was an easy
mark — a man in love with audio systems, as Mickey himself

215

was, and always curious about the latest improvement, the most exciting new development.

"So what's next for you?" Mickey asked. "You going to wait for digital?"

◊ ◊ ◊

". . . and then I realized that Blake had pulled all the brochures out of the rack and dumped them on the floor, and Blair was working the knobs of a floor sample," Sandy was saying, "and I realized that it was high time to get out of there. Kids are a menace in that kind of place."

"I did something like that to my father once," Lisa said. "I was in his office one day when I was little, and somehow I was left alone with his urine specimens. I guess he was called to the phone in another room, or something. But anyway, I found a nice shiny row of test tubes with liquid in them, and when my father came back into the lab, he found me stirring them all around in a big beaker. He never let me live it down."

She realized that it had stopped being hard to talk to Sandy, that he had drawn her out in a way that no one else had since the early days with Barry. He responded in a way that brought a rush of memories. She talked about the first male teacher she had ever had, in seventh grade, about her crush on him, and as she talked she felt vulnerable again.

He told her about the affair he'd had at M.I.T., and the time his sister was sent down to instruct him in his responsibilities. Jesus, I didn't even know I remembered that, he realized. "That romance was what soap operas would call bittersweet," he said. "I was very young. It was just as well."

The restaurant grew full of shadows and of the past. The only sound now was the bartender drying glasses and setting them on shelves.

Lisa glanced at her watch. "My God," she said, "do you know it's nearly four o'clock?"

"You're kidding," Sandy answered. He checked his watch. "You're not kidding."

"Sandy, I have to go. I can't believe it got so late."

"Neither can I." They stood, and Sandy held Lisa's wrist lightly for a moment. "Listen, we'll reconvene when I get back, OK?"

"OK," Lisa agreed. "And Sandy . . ." She didn't know what to say but wanted to say something. "Have a great trip," she finally told him.

◊ ◊ ◊

"Good meeting?" Flo asked her when she returned.

"Very good," Lisa answered, feeling uncomfortable. It was not until that moment that she realized she and Sandy hadn't said a word about Autotran.

9

THE BRITISH AIRWAYS 747 landed at Heathrow Airport with a gentle bounce, like a giant silver whale coming to rest on the ocean floor. The six first-class passengers were disgorged within five minutes of touchdown. Sandy Lippert, wearing a sweater and slacks, was happy to disembark. Not that the trip had been uncomfortable. He had rather enjoyed going upstairs for an elegant and time-consuming lunch. The movie had passed the time, and so had a steady diet of champagne.

Still, transatlantic flights were boring, and six hours in a confined space were not easy on a man over six feet tall. Next time, Sandy thought, I'll get Kilgour to send me on the Concorde. My muscles get too cramped in six hours.

Striding now along the wide corridors of Heathrow, with the customs and immigration check behind him, Sandy was limbering those cramped muscles with a vengeance, swinging his arms and stretching his legs so that they seemed to gobble up the polished airport floor. His elation seemed odd when he considered what he was about to do. When the immigration official had asked, "Purpose of your visit?" Sandy had been tempted to answer, "Embezzlement." He felt giddy at the prospect. The plan he was here to implement excited him as nothing had ever excited him before.

There was not a great crowd of people at Heathrow at nine o'clock on a Tuesday night. A fleet of green London taxis was lined up outside. Asking the driver to take him to the Inter-

Continental Hotel, Sandy handed his suitcase to the cabbie and entered the spacious back seat.

It was a good place to carry out his plan. Londoners were polite, but they were reserved. They did not pry into one's business. He could do what he had to do, he mused, and five minutes later he could be in a pub, deep in conversation with a total stranger who would probably offer to buy "a pint for the Yank." It was a reassuring thought.

The taxi was already in Ealing, and the surroundings, though still mostly residential, were beginning to seem like London. Sandy hoped he would be able to check in quickly and get to a pub near the hotel before closing hour at eleven.

The cab pulled into the drive of the Inter-Continental a little after ten. In the garish lobby, youthful Arabs in three-piece suits moved confidently within a halo of opulence. Sandy checked in quickly and asked that his bag be taken to his room while he "kept an appointment."

He turned into Down Street, hoping to find a pub. A round sign lit by a pink lamp announced the Rose. It was a quiet pub, with only a few patrons. A young couple sat entwined on a banquette along the far wall, a few sullen men lingered over drinks, and one cheerful fellow was engaging the barman in conversation as he moved up and down behind the counter, putting things away for the night.

Sandy stood next to the talkative man and asked the barman for a pint of bitter. When it was placed before him, he genially asked for another, saying he guessed it was "close to closing time and I'd better ask for it now."

Before long, the barman began to douse the lights. Sandy walked out. The rain had stopped, but the streets and air still held the permeating wetness of a British winter. He was high — high on bitter, high on London, high with anticipation.

In his room, with its view of Hyde Park, he unpacked, whistling. Then he showered and sprawled naked on the large bed. For a moment, he pictured Lisa Gould as she had looked on the terrace at Palmas del Mar, lifting her face to the ocean breeze. In the last second before falling asleep, Sandy Lippert realized to his surprise that he was happy.

◊ ◊ ◊

Simon Fenton and Arthur Bennett, the number one and number two men for GlobeBank's London operations, gave Sandy a cool and stiffly royal reception the next day. Tours, formal presentations, introductions, and a staged cocktail party took up most of the day. Sandy acted very interested, very impressed, evincing a kind of aw-shucks humility that he suspected the British felt appropriate in a colonial.

A large dinner at the Inigo Jones followed the cocktail reception. The entire Autotran London team was there. Sandy pointedly refused to be placed at the head of the table, opting to sit at Fenton's right. Relations warmed through several courses of superb food and several bottles of excellent wine.

The next day, Thursday, was the real "workhorse day," as Sandy put it. He, Fenton, and Bennett holed up in a conference room in the GlobeBank building in the Strand, took off their jackets, and went through every detail of the plan for implementing the system in London. In contrast to the day before, the three men used obscenities frequently. Sandy felt he could cut the resentment with a knife.

Over a lunch of sandwiches and bad coffee, he made the speech he had thought up in New York the previous week. "Look," he said, "the London Autotran is not just London's doing any more than the New York Autotran is just New York's business. It's a global system. London is one piece of it; New York is another. Tokyo is going to be bigger than either London *or* New York, for Chrissake." They were, Sandy noticed, listening carefully at least. "The role of Head Office in the London operation," he went on, "is strictly a support role. That's the word I've used in the draft agreement about division of responsibilities, and that's the word I mean. *My* role, however, my personal role, is as consulting engineer. Look, Simon, Arthur, I'm the guy who built Autotran. I'm the engineer on the system. I've got authority from Hardesty and Pruitt" — he might as well pull out all the stops, he decided — "to build and implement this particular system to these particular specifications." He punctuated his emphasis by slicing the table with the side of his hand. He studied them. Fenton looked expressionlessly back at him. Bennett, his chin on his hands, seemed to be dissecting the table.

"Nobody is telling you guys *how* to do it," Sandy went on,

opening his palm to them. "But the due dates have to be met. That's all."

There was a pause. Bennett moved his eyes to look at Fenton, who shifted in his seat.

"Right," he said. "That's all we're really concerned about. If that's the way the agreement reads, you'll have no problem from us." He turned to Bennett. "Arthur?"

Bennett's face came off his hands. "No problem here," he said.

Sandy breathed a sigh of relief inwardly.

Fenton said, "Right. Let's get on with it, shall we?"

They got on with it till nine that night. Then the three of them headed out into the Strand and found a pub. By closing time at eleven they were friends. They reeled out together to close the evening at Langan's brasserie.

Sandy had told Fenton he wouldn't be in the office until the afternoon on Friday. He was going to Harrod's, he said, to shop for his children.

In the toy department he bought stuffed animals. Then he walked out into the Brompton Road and turned left. He had decided he would stop at the third bank he came to. He wandered for several blocks, winding among the narrow side streets, until he found what he was looking for. He took a deep breath and went in.

He walked to the row of desks along one side. A blond woman about his age looked up from her papers and across the waist-high wooden barrier separating them. "Good morning, sir," she said. "How may I serve you?"

"Hello," Sandy said. "I'd like to open an account — a current account, that is."

"Yes, sir," she said as she stood up. She opened the gate in the barrier. "Won't you have a seat?"

"Thank you."

Her nameplate read Mrs. Blakely. She set some signature cards before him. "If you would just fill these out, please."

"Perhaps I'd better explain first. I'm an American, as you may have guessed." He smiled charmingly. "The thing is, in my business, I travel almost all of the time. But I'm in London quite often. I thought if I could deposit funds here, that would be helpful. But I have no permanent London address."

He was reaching for Thomas Putnam's billfold.

"That will be all right," Mrs. Blakely said. "You understand that you will need to fill out a check to draw your funds down?"

"Oh, yes," Sandy said. "Oh, uh . . . mostly, my funds will be transferred from the States, by my clients there."

"What business are you in, Mr. . . . . Putnam?" She was leaning over to look at his card.

"Consulting. Mostly for high-technology situations."

"Ah, yes. Well, no wonder you travel so much."

"Yes." He had finished signing and pushed the cards toward her. "But it's always lovely to be in London." He smiled again.

Mrs. Blakely smiled in return. "How much will you be wanting to deposit today to seed the account?" she asked.

"Will one hundred pounds do?"

"Quite nicely," she answered.

He gave her cash; she gave him a card identifying him by name and account number. The checks would be a problem. His personalized checks would not be ready before he left London. Could the bank possibly send them to his New York address, 1473 Third Avenue? He would be stopping there in a few weeks. Would it be possible to charge his account for the cost of the air mail postage? It would. It would all be quite possible. "And thank you so much for stopping in, Mr. Putnam."

Hefting his Harrod's shopping bag, Sandy stepped out into the steady drizzle of the London morning. He thought it a beautiful day. He looked at his watch. Eleven-thirty. The pubs are open, he thought. I think I'd like a drink.

◇ ◇ ◇

That evening, it was Sandy's turn to play host. He took Simon and Alicia Fenton and Arthur and Myra Bennett to the theater, to see the hit musical of the season, and then on to supper at Wilton's.

Sandy felt good about the trip and was more than willing to enjoy the evening. In practical terms, he had in his briefcase the memo of agreement about the responsibilities of the London Autotran team and the jurisdiction of the New York–based

BOS Utility. The goal Kilgour had set for the trip had been realized.

So was the goal he had set for himself, the goal of opening a current account in the name of Thomas Putnam. Sandy stared through the pale gold of the wine at Alicia Fenton's white, angular face and reflected that, to top off his week here, he really ought to win over the Fenton and Bennett wives.

It would not be easy with Alicia Fenton. Reserved, even cold, she seemed somewhat put out by her husband's volubility. From the jump seat of the taxi, Sandy had seen Alicia carefully tap her husband's wrist when, for the third time in as many minutes, he interrupted Sandy.

Myra Bennett was another matter. While it seemed as though he should probably play it absolutely straight with Alicia, Sandy felt he could banter a bit with Myra. Her high forehead and long neck gave her an arch appearance, but there was a shrewdness to her remarks and something in her smile that reminded Sandy a bit of Lisa. Not that Myra looked like her, not at all. Her tawny hair, parted in the middle, was limp and straight and pulled back along the sides of her head with brown barrettes, whereas Lisa's hair fell softly in dark layers and buzzed about her cheeks in little wisps. Myra was tall, robust, athletic-looking. Lisa, on the other hand, managed to combine delicacy with strength in a frame that was both small and full. Myra's eyes were gray, pale. Lisa's were very dark and very brilliant, and the whites of her eyes had seemed to Sandy, a few days ago in Pete's Tavern, to be pale blue really, not white at all. He suddenly wished very much that Lisa were there beside him to round out the party to a full six, three couples out for a night on the town.

He smiled at Myra as she told of a seaside outing the previous summer, when Arthur had saved an old woman from drowning, evidently at some risk to himself.

"Tell me, Sandy," Myra said, putting her hand on her husband's flushed cheek with affection, "did you ever suspect that this supposedly stolid engineer had such heroic depths?"

For a moment Sandy wasn't sure if Myra was being sarcastic. He decided to be serious, answering, "I always knew Arthur had it in him." Arthur blushed.

Myra leaned toward Sandy conspiratorially. "That's because you're an engineer too," she said. She raised her glass. "Here's to engineers," she proclaimed, "secretly the world's most daring and . . . passionate men."

The others raised their glasses. "I'll drink to that," Sandy said.

◊ ◊ ◊

Saturday, his last day in London, was all his. It didn't belong to GlobeBank; it didn't belong to Thomas Putnam. It was Sandy Lippert's.

He ate a large breakfast at the Ritz, then walked to Fortnum & Mason. He bought cookies for Jessica, a tea cake for Marie, and English jellies, English mustards, and tins of tea and spices. When he went back to the hotel to drop his packages, he found a message to "ring Myra Bennett at home."

Her voice sounded hootier on the phone than he remembered. "Arthur and the boys have gone off to the cricket match," she said. "I was wondering whether you would care to have lunch."

"Good idea. How nice," Sandy said. "Where would you suggest?"

"Well, how do you feel about a pub lunch somewhere near your hotel?"

"There's a place called the Rose — on Down Street, I think. How about one o'clock?"

"Splendid. See you then."

He changed into sweat pants and a sweat shirt, put on his running shoes, and headed for Hyde Park.

Wonder what she wants, he mused. Engineers are the world's most daring and passionate men, she said. Suppose that's it. Arthur at the cricket match, very British. Funny, he was worried that I'd take over his system, and here I am, about to take over his wife. Sandy ran for over an hour, smiling at children, waving at strollers. His stride was loose and easy; he felt he could run forever. Back in his room he showered and changed into gray slacks and a Harris tweed jacket. Anglo-American, thought Sandy.

◊ ◊ ◊

When Sandy arrived, the Rose was full. He looked around. There was no sign of Myra. He ordered a pint of light lager at the bar and stood against the wall near the door.

She arrived at one-fifteen. "Sorry to be late. There were

223

masses of traffic, and I've come all the way from Hampstead, you know."

"No problem," he answered. "What will you have?"

"Whiskey, no soda. Why don't I go get the food? What will you eat?"

"A shepherd's pie, please," he said.

Myra was back shortly with their meal.

"What do I owe you?" Sandy asked, pulling out a handful of unfamiliar English coins as she set the food before them.

She reached into his hand. "One of these, two of these, two of these. That does it," she said.

The conversation was pleasant; Myra talked most of the time while Sandy dug into his meal. He smoked a cigarette after they finished eating.

"Would you like to go somewhere for coffee?" he asked.

"No," Myra said, looking straight into his eyes, "I think we should go directly to your hotel room."

They stood. Arm in arm, they walked in silence to the hotel. She waited at the elevator while he got the key from the desk.

Sandy closed the door of the room behind them. Myra said, "You'd better hang the DO NOT DISTURB sign on the door." She began to undress, folding her clothes neatly on the extra bed. From the armchair, Sandy watched with admiration as she uncovered her body.

"Do you like what you see?" she asked.

"Oh yes. Very much."

"My turn now," Myra said.

Sandy smiled and stood up. He pulled off his jacket and began to unbutton his shirt, still smiling at Myra. She came toward him and ran her hand across his chest. "Nice," she said. Her hands reached down to his Dunhill belt and opened the buckle. "What else do you have for me?" she asked.

He sat again, pulled off his shoes, slipped his pants down, peeled off his socks, then stood and quickly removed his Jockey shorts. She took him in her hands. "You're almost ready," she said.

He followed her to the bed. She turned down the covers and knelt on the bed. "Come here," Myra said.

Sandy lay back on the fresh hotel sheets.

She leaned over and took him in her mouth, moving her tongue back and forth. "Lovely," Sandy said. "I like that, I like that."

He put his hands on her head in an affectionate gesture, then moved them down the back of her neck to her creamy shoulders. "You have such beautiful skin," he said. "Peaches-and-cream English." He heard her snort with amusement.

He moved his hands to her breasts, caressing them gently. "These are beautiful too. Come here." He lifted her under the arms and brought her toward him, filling his mouth with her breast. He licked her hard nipple. She moaned softly.

"Oh, do that," she urged. He ran his hands over and between her buttocks. "Oh yes," she said, "yes."

His hands moved under her, between her legs, feeling the inviting wetness. He began to shift her weight. She caught on, settled her knees on the bed, and lowered herself onto Sandy. He was very hard.

Half sitting, with her palms on his shoulders, her chin pulled in against her chest, and her eyes closed, she began rocking back and forth. "Oh, Jesus!" Myra said. She rocked faster, thrusting down hard onto him. "Big cock! Big cock!" Her voice got louder.

Sandy dug his fingers into the small of her back, then moved his right hand back across her wet thigh to the thrusting place between her legs. His fingers found her clitoris and stroked it. She gasped, yelped sharply, and fell forward onto his chest. He shoved upward, felt himself throbbing.

After a minute, she lifted her face to look at him. She smiled. "Well, we've certainly done our bit for Anglo-American relations." She climbed off him and sat next to him with her knees drawn up. She pushed her hair back, away from her face.

Sandy hunched back against the pillow and reached for a cigarette. "You were terrific!" he said.

"You were quite marvelous yourself."

"Apparently engineers' wives are passionate too."

They showered separately. At the door, she said, "That was so lovely. Perhaps I'll see you again next trip."

10

SANDY WAS STILL CHARGED up from London when he returned to the office. But life at BOS plodded along, slower than he remembered, than he expected. He was jittery.

He wanted to see Lisa — talk to her, have lunch with her. But she was in meetings all day, or tied up in conference, or had taken her group heads to a hotel for an all-day meeting.

Once Frank Kozlow learned that Sandy had "cut the deal" in London, he was only interested in passing along the detail work that had piled up, the decisions about day-to-day operations. Frank ticked off a list of items. "And Faber's people really want an answer on that special procedure," he said.

Sandy exploded. "Well, I want some answers too, Frank. I'm not about to make this decision until you do your job and give me the facts I need to make the goddamn decision!"

Jet lag, Frank said to himself as he left the room.

Damnit, Sandy thought. "Marie, I'll be on the floor."

He hadn't even had a chance to come in here in the two days he'd been back. The Autotran terminals were busy. He looked at an unmanned terminal, a jacket hung on the back of the chair. A transaction was coming in. "Jesus Christ!" Sandy muttered. He leaned over the keyboard to answer the order, a big-ticket item from Sanford Mining Corporation.

The operator returned and Sandy let him have it. "Where the hell were you?" he yelled, not waiting for an answer. "I am personally documenting you for this, Walter. And the rest of you . . ." He pointed an accusing finger at the nearby operators. "You *know* you are not supposed to let a phone ring off the hook like that! Jesus Christ!"

He stormed back to his office. "You want your calls?" Marie asked gingerly.

"For Chrissake, Marie! Can't you handle some of this yourself?"

Marie looked confused, then angry. She turned and left the office.

"Marie!" Sandy yelled after her. When there was no answer, he went to the door, only to see her fade down the hall toward the Ladies' Room. He noticed that the other secretaries in the area were scowling at him with disapproval.

He stayed late. He was weary but not tired. The wind blew with such ferocity that it came through at the edges of the sealed windows of 176 Wall. Sandy, in shirtsleeves, felt quick, cold drafts against his back. Here, at the bottom of Wall Street, the wind that had gathered on the ocean came off the river and was then forced into a narrow tunnel. It swirled up the constricted canyon flanked by tall buildings, past the Stock Exchange and Federal Hall, to be deflected north and south where Trinity Church stood in gloomy pride on the corner of Broadway.

The nocturnal bleakness of the financial district, emptied of its teeming daytime crowds, and the rawness of the weather were things Sandy was trying to forget as he pored over the detailed specs being considered for Danny Faber's conversion. Danny himself, Sandy reflected wryly, would be at home with Harriet, just as Ray LaRocca was at home with Pat, Brian O'Connor at home with his wife, and Doug North at home with his. The homes would be warm and well lighted. Children would be running around. There would be the noise of television sets, of dishwashers churning, of phone conversations. "Why don't you both come by Saturday night and have some cake and coffee with us? We'll be here."

So they would, all of them, "here" in their nice, warm homes, safe. All of them.

The phone rang. For an instant, Sandy hoped it would be his broker friend, asking if he wanted to meet for drinks.

"Sandy Lippert," he said, lifting the receiver.

"You *are* in your office!" It was Kathy.

Again. He groaned. I must have blown it again. "Hello, Kath. Anything wrong?"

"No, nothing," she quickly assured him, "nothing like that." She paused. "What *is* wrong, of course, is that I haven't received the check this month. You're late, my friend."

He felt anger rising and forced his voice to stay small. "I'm sorry, Kathy. I . . . I've just been so preoccupied. I've been away. I'll send it tonight."

But she wasn't going to let him off the hook that easily.

"Too preoccupied to remember your own children?" she sneered. "Too preoccupied to remember all those speeches you made about wanting to be responsible for your own children? Didn't you tell me that you'd have Marie put it on your calendar? Or was that a lie?"

Oh God, thought Sandy, I can't right now. It's not fair, not fair.

"You know," Kathy went on, "Daddy feels very strongly that I should go back to the judge on this one. He says if a man is not meeting his responsibilities, it's the court's business. Daddy has looked into this, and there are a lot of things that can be done, Sandy."

So Daddy had looked into it, had he? Sandy suddenly felt murderous toward Don Andrews, toward his groundless interference in his, Sandy's, life.

"I'll mail the check tonight, Kathy. Is that all?"

"No. What time is the car picking up the children on Saturday?"

"Eight A.M. The usual time. And they'll be back Sunday night *after* dinner. Be sure you tell your father." He hung up.

Sandy leaned back and lit a cigarette. He watched the smoke curl and feather and waited for the anger to subside in his gut. Goddamn, goddamn this life. Goddamn Kathy and her father. Goddamn Faber's conversion. Goddamn Wednesday night at eight o'clock with nothing to do. He mashed out the cigarette.

Despair, like a cold trickle, oozed through him. He put his head in his hands. He thought of that summer — how long ago was it? — when his life was falling to pieces. When his marriage was rotting, his career was failing, and only his daughter and his unborn child seemed real. Now he hardly even had his children. Nothing. Amid all this nonsense of Danny Faber's conversion, all the worries about money just to get by and keep ahead, amid all this, he had nothing to hold on to.

He walked out of his office and down the hall, onto the floor. The CRT terminals were quiet now. There was no one about.

No keyboards clicking, no lights flickering across the screens, no phones quietly ringing.

Yet the place seemed alive to him. He walked in the forest of terminals. They seemed somehow animate, their screens like dark and quiet faces, the keyboards their bodies, the casings like pale gray hoods.

How clean it was here, how uncluttered. Neat and simple. Quiet, obedient machines. Uncomplicated by desire, free of longings. There were no hatreds here. There was no bitterness.

He sat down at a terminal and punched in the code to activate Autotran.

GOOD MORNING! the screen said. THIS IS AUTOTRAN. CHOOSE MENU.

Sandy requested the screen for international transfers. The terminal flickered. SPECIAL ACCESS CODE REQUIRED.

The access code changed every day. Sometimes it changed in the middle of a day. It was a security measure. Sandy remembered how much time and thought he had put into designing a good, secure, special-code system. The one he had devised had been considered first-rate; *Datamation* had run a small news article about it.

The access code was controlled by Sandy. It was he who approved the code itself and any changes to it. It was his responsibility.

Quickly, he keyed in the code for the day. PROCEED, the screen told him.

Now a more important security measure was called for, the numerical code that was a customer's own personal password, the test key that authenticated the message.

Sandy's fingers darted over the keyboard. Jessica, watching him one day when she was writing a newsletter article about Autotran, had remarked, "You'd make a hell of a secretary, Sandy. You're a very fast typist." Then she had smiled and added, "A man of many accomplishments."

His fingers stopped. He looked at the screen to see the message he had keyed in.

VIA AUTOTRAN RTGC
19 MAR
09 42

REMITTER: ENSOLD CORP

BENEFICIARY: THOMAS PUTNAM CURRENT ACCOUNT 997 1849

                BEDMINSTER BANK #16

                LONDON

AMT: USDOLLARS 11,000

11

SANDY SLEPT UNTIL EIGHT-THIRTY the next morning. He had not even bothered to set the alarm clock.

When he arrived at the office, it was almost ten. Wordlessly, he set before Marie a huge bouquet of flowers with a note stuck prominently in their midst. It read: "I'm a rat, and I apologize. You're the best lady around, and if you stay mad at me, I don't know what I'll do."

Sandy was seated at his desk when Marie came in a moment later. She walked over to his chair and kissed him on the top of his head. He heard her sniffle; she was crying.

"What are you crying for?" he asked.

"Because," she answered in a voice filled with tears.

"Oh," he said with a smile. "No kidding, though, I'm really sorry, Marie."

"Oh, for God's sake," she cried, the tears really falling, "you're entitled!"

"No," he said in an almost stern but quiet voice, "no, I don't believe that. I don't believe anyone is entitled to treat anyone the way I was treating people around here yesterday. That's a belief I've only come to in the past few years, but . . . I really think that, Marie."

"I know you do," she said, "and you act it, too." She wanted to add, "That's why this place will continue to eat you up alive." But she didn't. She said instead, "I'll get you coffee," and left.

Sandy walked onto the floor. Walter Noble shrank when he saw his boss approach him. Sandy said, loud enough for all to hear, "Walt, I want to apologize for yesterday. I was bushed from my trip and in a lousy mood." Then he walked back toward the offices and over to Frank's door. "Jesus, Frank, I'm sorry about yesterday. I don't know if it was jet lag or what, but I had no right to blow up at you like that. I apologize."

Kozlow smiled.

"Shake?" Sandy asked, extending his hand.

"Shit, Sandy, of course. Forget it." They shook hands.

Sandy worked at his desk for an hour, then called Lisa. Flo put her on the line at once.

"Hi," Sandy said, "how was your meeting?"

"Fine," she answered. "But more important, how was London?"

"Very, very good," he said. "Can you have lunch?"

"Lunch? Today?"

"Yes."

"I don't see how," she said. "I mean, it's after eleven now; there isn't time to cancel my date."

"How about a drink this evening, then?" he asked. "I've got some interesting things to tell you."

"That I absolutely can't," she said. "I'm meeting my husband for dinner, and we're going to a concert. He's going out of town tomorrow and will be gone overnight . . ." She stopped.

"Lunch tomorrow?" he said. "See how persistent I am?"

Lisa laughed. That pretty laugh. "You are indeed," she said. "Yes. Lunch tomorrow."

"Good," he said. "I'll come uptown. I have to be there for afternoon meetings anyway. So you pick a place."

◇ ◇ ◇

She chose a Japanese restaurant on Fifty-second Street. They had to leave their shoes near the entrance and sit on the floor. Sandy was carrying a package.

"What's new?" he asked when they had finally managed to square away their legs under the table.

"Nothing much with me," she said, "but there's big news from 176."

"What news?" he said. He couldn't think of anything new.

"Your apologies of yesterday," she answered.

He cocked his head. "How did you hear about that?"

"The secretaries' network around here is pretty reliable."

"Well, then," he said, "I assume you also heard about my out-rageous yelling of the day before."

"I heard that the yelling was what passes for normal for many of us. The apologies — I think that's fairly rare. Anyway, I think it was a hell of a thing. Really . . . decent."

Sandy was perplexed but pleased. She had never compli-mented him before, never for something personal.

"I have something for you," he said, pulling a square tin out of his package.

"What is it?"

"Tea. Royal blend. From London."

Lisa smiled. A tin of tea was an almost impossible inconven-ience in her GlobeBank office. When she wanted tea in the af-ternoon, she had Flo pour out a cup of hot water from the pot on the Mr. Coffee machine, then added a teabag. For this tea, had he only known, she would need a teapot. And there were no tea-pots at GlobeBank.

Somehow, his mistake was endearing. The gift was touching.

"Thank you, Sandy. It's lovely. Thank you for thinking of me." She paused, staring at the tin. "And I love the tin," she said, turning it to show him. It depicted an elaborate cuckoo clock, the cuckoos posing as two liveried servants. One was hold-ing a candelabrum. The other held a tea tray. Between them, an ornate gilt clock struck the hour of four.

"Oh, look," he said, "there's another clock on top. Four o'clock."

She leaned closer to him. They were both still. She held the tin in one hand, and he held it with one of his. Their foreheads were nearly touching.

A waitress knelt by their table. "Do you care to order?" she asked in a thick accent. Sandy sat upright quickly. His right leg moved inadvertently away from the kimonoed waitress and against Lisa's crossed legs. His leg fit just under her knee. He stayed that way while they ordered, his leg supporting her. Through his trouser leg, he could sense that her skirt was hiked up above the knee. When the waitress left, he shifted again so that they were no longer touching.

They drank hot sake and laughed companionably over their inadequacies with the thin Japanese chopsticks. After the meal,

Sandy had trouble uncoiling his legs. Lisa took his arm and exaggeratedly hauled him to his feet. They were still laughing when they left the restaurant.

Sandy spent the afternoon meeting with LaRocca's people about the conversion for the International Services Division. At five o'clock, he found an empty office where he could catch up on paperwork. Some of his recent uneasiness had returned, and the fading March light filled him with melancholy. He was reluctant to go home alone; the thought of calling Pam or some other woman did not interest him.

He picked up the phone and dialed Shearson Hayden Stone to see if Bob was free for dinner. There was no answer at his office.

Through the open door, he could see a corner of the reception area for National Services West, Lisa's division. The sans-serif letters VICES EST were just visible. He was certain Lisa was still there.

Maybe she'd be free to have a burger, he speculated. After all, she did say her husband was going to be out of town. Can I ask her twice in one day? All this time we're spending together. Well, we are getting to be friends.

He dialed her extension. She answered in an abstracted voice: "Hello. Lisa Gould."

"You'll never believe it, but it's me again, asking you about yet another meal."

She laughed. "Where are you?"

"Right across the hall, actually. I'm looking into your area, and from what I can see, its name is VICES EST. I had no idea that's what you are producing."

She laughed again.

"Listen," he said, "it's six-thirty. I've just wrapped up an interim report for Kilgour on the LaRocca conversion. It's dark. It's cold. It's gloomy. It's March. I really hate like hell to eat by myself. How about if I take you out for a burger?"

"Give me fifteen minutes," Lisa said.

When they got to the restaurant, she ordered a spinach salad. Sandy screamed in mock disbelief. "I call that un-American," he said.

"Is LaRocca's conversion really completed?" Lisa asked as she broke off a piece of French bread. Sandy hailed the waiter and ordered another beer.

"Not completely complete," he said, "but well into parallel operation. It's going quite smoothly, very few bugs. I think another month, two at most, will do it. He'll be standing alone by June first."

They talked shop for a while. Lisa took up her favorite topic, Martin J. Camden's theory for Directional Control Management.

"Do you really go for that? I think it's bullshit," Sandy said.

They argued hotly, Lisa taking the position that it was important to have a structured frame of reference for effective management action, Sandy contending that you followed your feet and did the best you could.

"For God's sake, Sandy," she said in a fervent voice, "you don't just follow your feet in engineering, do you?"

"The hell I don't," he replied, "and anyway, I'm talking about people management here, not the management of technical variables. But in fact, both are susceptible to a little human passion." He remembered Myra Bennett's remark. "Anyway," he said, "even engineers have hearts. Didn't I lure you here by telling you I was melancholy tonight?"

"You don't seem to have much trouble luring me these days," she said softly.

"I'll get the check." Sandy motioned to the waiter.

The next day, both Lisa and Sandy were caught up in their separate tasks. Lisa's monthly managers' meeting, featuring a film on productivity, was a big success. Kilgour did come to the cocktail party and did chat with Camden. Lisa told Barry later, over their Bar-B-Q chicken, that Kilgour was thinking seriously about bringing Camden in for a seminar on DCM for all the sector's division heads. It would be a big win for her, she said.

Barry, preoccupied with preparations for his trip to Paris on Sunday, only murmured, "That's great, Lis'."

Kilgour even mentioned Camden at the Friday morning division head meeting. Lisa looked over at Sandy; he rolled his eyes upward meaningfully and pushed his hair off his forehead. That piece never stays put, does it? she thought.

Lisa and Barry had a very quiet weekend in Connecticut. Barry was busy reading briefs and checking precedents. The heating system was misbehaving, and they passed the time bundled up in layers of sweaters. She made the calls to Elliott's Home Service; they promised to have it fixed by the following Wednesday.

On Sunday, Lisa drove Barry to Kennedy and waited with him in the first-class lounge. "Please, sweetheart, try and be sensible this trip. Don't run yourself into the ground."

"I'll do my best," he said and kissed her.

She drove back to the apartment alone.

First thing Monday, Flo buzzed Lisa on the intercom. "Your mother," she said.

"Hello, Mom."

"Hi, dear. Barry get off all right?"

"Yes," said Lisa. "I miss him already."

"Listen, dear," Marge Gould said, "why don't you plan to come out here one evening? Have dinner with Daddy and me, stay over. You can take the train in in the morning."

Lisa groaned inwardly. "Actually, Mom," she began, "I have a lot of stuff to do at the office and around the house."

"Well, one evening won't hurt. Your father and I would like to see you, and I don't think it would hurt for you to come out here for an evening."

"You know, if I do that, I have to catch the commuter train. It's always mobbed. I probably won't even get a seat. It's a real pain in the neck. And it exhausts me."

"Well, you know, we don't see that much of you. And it happens to be very exhausting for us to come in. You know, your father doesn't like to drive very much anymore, and he won't let me drive in, so it's a very big deal for us, and we just aren't up to that sort of thing anymore."

Lisa sighed, defeated. "OK, I'll come tomorrow. But I can't stay over. Absolutely. You'll have to let me catch the late train after dinner."

"Well, we'll see how you feel when you get here. We don't have to decide that now."

235

She took the five thirty-six from Grand Central, which was, as she had predicted, mobbed. When she got off at New Rochelle, she could hardly pick out her parents' car from the line of Bonnevilles breathing exhaust. Finally she spotted the blue one with the MD plate.

Lisa got in on the passenger side. "Hi, Mom," she said. She leaned across to kiss her mother's cheek and was touched, as always, by the soft crepe of her skin and the faint odor of Norell.

"Your father's going to be late, he has to pay a condolence call."

"Oh? Who died?"

"Do you remember Sam Baron — Dr. Baron, the dermatologist?"

"The guy we went to when I was thirteen? With my acne?"

"Yes," said her mother. "Such a shame, he was still a young man."

"What did he die of?"

"Heart attack. Very fast. Still," she mused, "I wouldn't mind going that way myself." They pulled into the driveway. "I have lamb chops," she said.

They took off their coats, and Lisa collapsed into one of the familiar chairs.

"Want a drink," her mother asked, "while we wait for your father?"

"I'll fix it, Mom. What'll you have?"

"A little bit of Scotch, a lot of water, lots of ice."

Lisa fixed her mother's drink, then poured a Dubonnet for herself.

They sat in the living room.

"Heard from Barry?" Marge Gould asked.

"No. He's up to his ears in meetings. I really don't expect to hear from him until tomorrow or Thursday."

"He's away a lot, isn't he? You take it a lot better than I did when your father and I were young." She sipped her Scotch. "I remember once a year, he'd go to the AMA. In those days, we didn't have the money for me to go along. You and Jeff were still small; there was no such thing as a babysitter for a week."

"We must have kept you busy."

"Oh yes, you kept me busy, but I can't say I enjoyed being

without Daddy." She drank some more. "It really made me miserable when he was away."

Lisa remembered photographs of her father at that age. There was one of him standing beside the new car he had just bought. Harold Gould would have been in his mid-thirties then. He had dark, wavy hair; his mustache gave him a jaunty look. He looked tall, slim, and broad-shouldered in his double-breasted suit. Lisa had a vision of her father as an attractive man her own age.

She looked at her mother. "I bet Daddy hated to leave, too."

"Yes," Marge Gould said. "We were very close. We always hated to be separated overnight."

This is funny, Lisa thought. I'm a grown woman, and this is the first time I've ever thought of my parents as lovers. I bet they still hate to be separated overnight.

The back door opened. Her mother yelled, "We're in here, Harold!"

Dr. Gould walked into the living room, unwrapping his muffler. He looked worn out, gray. "How's the big-shot banker?" he said in a tired voice. He leaned over and kised his wife, then Lisa.

Lisa embraced her father. "Hi, Daddy. Let me fix you a drink. You look bushed."

"Did Mommy tell you about Sam Baron? Not even sixty. A real loss. He was a wonderful guy."

"I'll start the oven," Marge Gould said.

"So what's new at the bank?" Harold Gould asked Lisa. "Are they still stealing money from the poor?"

"Well, I'm still working like a maniac on this conversion," Lisa said, handing him a Jack Daniel's.

Dinner was surprisingly pleasant. Lisa realized it felt good to be a little girl in her parents' home for a few hours — not a division head, not a wife, not even a friend.

Her mother drove her to the late train. "This wasn't so difficult after all, was it? You should come out like this more often."

"We'll see," Lisa said.

The train rolled along slowly. The car had a dank smell. Lisa wondered what the half-dozen people in the nonsmoker were doing at this hour, going into New York. She leaned her elbow on the windowsill. It had begun to rain. Razor-sharp diagonal lines of water slashed the outside of the window, making any view impossible.

She thought about Sandy. We are friends, she decided. It's been growing since the off-site. Jessica likes him, too. I really respect him. He's one of the few people at the bank who really pulls his weight. He hasn't got a phony bone in his body.

The train rumbled to an unexplained halt. Oh, Jesus, Lisa thought, this is why I hate coming out here. The rain grew heavier, beating against the window.

She remembered the way Sandy looked running on the beach in Puerto Rico. How can he be so lanky and so graceful? she wondered. The picture of him was very clear. The train coughed, then started.

The hair in a triangle on his chest. His smooth, muscular arms. The faint suggestion of bristle on his chin. She remembered him swimming out to sea like a dolphin with the water rippling off his back. He had stood beside her after his swim, dripping water onto the sand. She remembered looking up his legs at the rise in his wet bathing suit.

My God, Lisa realized, I've fallen in love with him.

On Wednesday, she pushed hard all day, trying to burn off her uneasiness with work. Flo brought some lunch to her desk and tiptoed out.

She was still there at six-thirty, bent over her papers. Everyone had gone home. It was a fiercely cold, wet, and windy March night when people liked to be in their own houses. There had been no word yet from Barry; she supposed he would call tomorrow. She looked up. Sandy was standing in her doorway with his coat on.

"Still here?" he said.

"Well, my husband's in Paris all week and I thought I'd use the time to catch up." Lisa felt that her voice sounded strained.

"Can I persuade you to quit now and come out for a drink?" Sandy asked.

Lisa got up and went to get her coat. They walked out into the windy street, starting north on Park.

"Listen," Sandy said, "I have a better idea. I have a beautiful bottle of Burgundy — a Christmas gift from my broker — and some first-class steaks in my freezer. Why don't you come on over and we'll have dinner at my place?"

"Yes," Lisa said.

◇ ◇ ◇

I can't assume that he feels the same way about me, Lisa thought in the cab. We're colleagues. We're friends. He has a bottle of wine. We're having dinner together. She felt a little numb.

When they got to his apartment, Sandy started bustling around. He hung Lisa's coat up in his tiny closet, disappeared into the bedroom, and emerged a minute later without his jacket or tie. Then he rolled up his sleeves, took the steaks out of the freezer, and brought the wine and a corkscrew into the living room. "My sophisticated friends tell me that you're supposed to let the wine breathe," he said as he twisted the corkscrew, "so why don't you put on a record and I'll get glasses and plates and stuff."

Sandy had the complicated stereo system Lisa might have imagined. She picked out a Debussy record. "How do you work this?" she asked. The sound of her voice came from far away.

Sandy bent over, holding two wineglasses. "Hang onto these a second," he said. He set the record down very carefully on the turntable and adjusted the fine-tuning knobs and dials with easy precision. Lisa concentrated on his hands, his long fingers making the delicate adjustments. "OK," he said. Music filled the room.

"Enough breathing for the wine," Sandy declared. He poured two glasses and handed one to Lisa. They sat at opposite ends of the sofa.

Lisa felt that she should say something. "Nice wine."

"Is it? Yes, it is." Sandy was very cheerful. "Did I tell you it was from my broker? At Shearson. He's also my friend. We were at M.I.T. together. He knows a lot about wine, buys it by the case."

He stopped suddenly, realizing that he was rambling. They both sipped their wine.

"How long have you had this apartment?" Lisa asked.

"A couple of years. Since my separation. I was pretty lucky, actually. I found it right away, and it was a real bargain, especially when you consider what apartments in Manhattan are these days. I know people now who are trying to buy co-ops, and it's just crazy. Furnishing this place was something new for me. I picked it partly for the view. Did you look out?"

Lisa turned toward the window.

"You can see all the way down Manhattan," Sandy went on. "There's Head Office, there's Citicorp Center. From the right spot, you can sometimes see 176. There's the Chrysler Building. Empire State. The World Trade Center — see the twin towers?"

He was rambling again.

"I didn't even know I had this record," he said. "When I first moved in here, I went to Goody's and just bought a pile of records. I probably haven't even listened to all of them. I like this, though. What kind of music do you like? I remember you said you went to a concert last week."

Lisa turned from the view to face him. "Oh, I don't know," she said, "all kinds."

They were silent.

"I'd better check the steaks," Sandy said. He went into the kitchen.

"The steaks still have awhile," Sandy said as he returned. He sat down in one of the Breuer chairs opposite Lisa and started picking at something on the edge of the seat. He seemed to be utterly absorbed by the task.

Then he looked up. "Lisa," he said. He cleared his throat. "This is difficult for me." He looked down at the seat again for a minute, scraping at it with his fingernail.

"Lisa," he said again, "what I want to tell you is how happy it makes me — how glad I am, I mean — that you and I, that we seem to have become friends. I mean, it makes me glad that someone I've admired as a colleague — and I admire you very much — what I'm trying to say is . . ." He stopped.

Then he began again firmly: "Lisa, you know that I'm not close to very many people. I guess I'm a bit of a loner." It seemed to be getting a little easier for him to speak. "But ever since our time together in Puerto Rico — well, you know how much our talk meant to me, how it moved me, how attached to you I've

240

become." He stopped again and looked at Lisa directly. Then he continued. "Lisa, I hardly know what's gotten into me. I know I've been babbling like a maniac. What I've been wanting to say, Lisa, what I've been wanting to say to you for a long time now, is that I've become very attached to you." He stopped again and looked at her helplessly.

Lisa said nothing. She felt the blood rushing in and out of her ears. Her eyes felt hot, and she wasn't at all sure that her head wasn't wobbling on her neck.

Sandy started again: "Lisa, I trust you as a colleague and as a friend. I wanted you to know how I felt, and I hope that if it sounds silly to you, it won't interfere with our friendship." Again he stopped, and he seemed to be thinking of something. "Because I like you very, very much. But I thought that I wanted you also to know that I've become attached to you, Lisa. Lisa," he said, his face crumpling a little, "I've fallen in love with you. Isn't that strange?"

Lisa looked over at him. Sandy, the room, everything Sandy had said, the music coming from the sound system — all seemed dreamlike, the scene going on behind a scrim tinged pastel blue, a slow-motion movie filmed through gauze.

She got up and walked over to him, knelt in front of his chair wordlessly, and put her head on his lap. They were motionless for a long minute. Then Sandy reached over and tilted her chin up. Lisa could see the dark bristles on his lip and cheek and a few wiry hairs curling over the neck of his shirt. "I love you, Lisa," he said again. And he leaned over and kissed her. Then again. And again.

He tastes so sweet, she thought. Oh Sandy, she thought, oh. "Sandy," she said, "oh darling. Oh my darling, oh love, oh love." She kissed his chest through his shirt; she unbuttoned the buttons on his shirt and kissed his chest and the sweet flesh, his long, lean sides, his warm belly; she licked his neck and breathed in the smell, all the while thinking, the way he is, the way he smells, so sweet, so sweet in the hollow of his throat.

They moved together into the bedroom. She sank onto the bed; he lay beside her. He kept saying her name, brushing her face, her neck, her eyes with his lips. He kissed her mouth again. His hands shaking, he began to unbutton her blouse. Her eyes were riveted to his face. She couldn't speak.

He lifted her to remove the blouse and slipped her skirt down her legs. Her shoes had fallen to the floor. He pulled down her pantyhose and panties.

He reached around her back to unhook her bra.

"No," she said, unhooking it in front. He looked at her.

"Take off your clothes," she said in a hoarse voice.

It was all like a dream. She watched from the bed as he undressed, standing beside her. His body was as beautiful as she remembered; she had not imagined it.

She reached over and touched him, ran her hand across his stomach and between his legs. She began to kiss the inside of his thighs, then pulled him down beside her onto the bed.

They put their arms around each other. Their legs entwined. "I've wanted you for such a long time," Sandy said.

"Don't talk," she murmured, kissing him. She licked his eyelids, tasting each delicate lash. She was all over him, running her fingers through his hair. "God, your hair." She kissed his neck.

They rolled over. He kissed her mouth again, her chin, her neck, her breasts. He pressed kisses all over her stomach and in her soft pubic hair. Kissed the inside of each thigh, bit her slightly on each knee, kissed the arch of her foot and licked the spaces between her toes.

"Come here," she said.

He put his face against hers. She could feel the bristle of his beard scratching her cheek. His hand found her breast. She could feel him hard against her thigh; she reached down and ran her hand over his smooth skin.

"Now," she said in a voice she still could not recognize as her own. "Please."

She guided him, wrapping her legs around his waist. Inside her, he felt that he was flying, soaring high above the earth. "Lisa, my darling, my beautiful sweetheart," he cried.

She pressed against him.

They rose and fell in rhythm against each other, moving as one. They were locked together in a passion that seemed to have no bottom.

All at once, Sandy stopped moving. Lisa felt herself opening, petal by petal, bursting into bloom like a giant flower.

"God!" she cried. "Oh, my God!"

Sandy clenched his teeth. His eyes were shut tight. Lisa felt him pulsing inside her, again and again and again.

She looked up to see that he was weeping. "I love you," she said.

"Oh, God, Lisa, I love you too. I haven't loved anybody for such a long time."

Part Four

1

JESSICA SAT IN HER OFFICE, staring at a Steinberg cartoon on her wall and not seeing it.

My pulse is racing. Relax, she told herself, it'll be OK. You'll get to Lisa and it'll be OK. Jesus. This place.

She had met with Mark Krausner in his office. Lisa, giving notes to Jessica for the Manpower Monitor, had once called Krausner "one of the more effective of my group managers — and he has flair."

Krausner had called her in to say he was finally satisfied with the copy for a brochure he wanted.

"You already hired a design and production guy for this, right?" Krausner asked.

"Right. Jack Resnick? He did *The Hollow Floor*. And the Nat West brochure. Very talented guy."

"Does he have a firm or does he subcontract the various things?"

"The latter. He's a free lance." Jessica could never say the words without imagining a medieval knight, dressed for some reason all in black, with a black mask, mounted on a black charger, and carrying a black jousting lance.

"Because I have a photographer friend," Krausner went on, "who's very good. Outstanding. I'd like you to ask Resnick to use him for the photos."

Jessica was surprised. "Well," she said, "I think Jack's got his guy lined up, but I'll mention your friend to him. I mean, Jack has photographers he's used to working with, and I don't really like to interfere. I think that's more or less counterproductive. But what's your friend's name? I mean, I'll mention him to Jack. Maybe Jack knows his work."

Jessica realized she was droning on.

"David Winter," Krausner said. "Let me put it this way. If Resnick doesn't use Winter, I will cancel Resnick and give the entire design and production contract to Winter."

Jessica was stunned. She felt anger beginning to move inside her in whirls that threatened to rise to her throat and spit out words she couldn't control. *Easy.*

"Mark, that's unethical. Also ugly. And I don't think you can do it."

Krausner looked surprised. He hadn't expected to be thwarted. "Oh, I can do it. I'm paying for the brochure. It's mine."

Jessica deliberately lowered the pitch of her voice. She was afraid of growing shrill. "We all agreed to use Jack," she said. "He's done a lot of work on this project; he's lined people up."

Krausner cut in quickly. "You know, you didn't proceed on this whole thing precisely as you should have. You're supposed to ask for competitive bidding, and you didn't. You could be in trouble on that, Jessica."

"Maybe," Jessica agreed. She was talking fast. "But that doesn't excuse ... Mark, I'm not, under any circumstances, going to pressure Jack as you suggest. It's ugly and unethical. I think I said that." She hoped her smile was hard.

"I have a perfect right to review contracts I'm paying for," Krausner said, "as well as the process by which they were obtained."

Jessica stood up and gathered her papers. "Mark, that isn't what you're saying. We both know what you're saying. It stinks."

She had tried to see Lisa right away, but Flo said she was tied up.

"What about lunch?" Jessica asked.

Flo punched CLNDR on the Ardec. "Sandy Lippert for lunch."

That's not exactly going to be a thirty-minute sandwich, Jessica thought. She said aloud, "Look, Flo, tell her that I really want to talk to her — it's important. If she could give me some time, maybe before lunch, on her way."

"OK." Flo could see Jessica was serious. "You know she always tries to make time for you. She says you ask for so little."

I may be asking for a lot this time, Jessica thought.

How long had she been sitting here, staring at the wall? Great, she thought, now I'm staring at walls. What had Krausner tried?

Intimidation? Extortion? Blackmail? Would he take a cut if Winter got the job? "One of the more effective group managers," Lisa had said.

There was a knock on the open door — Lisa, dressed for outdoors. "Hi, Jess." Lisa put on one glove. "I hear you need to see me. Can it possibly wait till tomorrow? I'm meeting Sandy Lippert for lunch halfway downtown, and we both have a lot to go over. I think we're finally getting some resolution on these functionals, which I need for my review with Kilgour. The conversion adds so many layers; I really *am* immersed."

Too much, Jessica thought. Don't try so hard, Lisa. She remembered Barry Berman. They had met a few times; he had made her laugh. Poor Barry, she thought. She realized that Lisa's face showed something she had never seen there before, almost a desperate, pleading look. Maybe poor Lisa, she thought. How the hell do I know? Who should know better than I that you can never second-guess what goes on between a husband and wife?

"It'll keep," she said. "I'll catch you in the morning. Have a good lunch."

Lisa hurried off past Linda Glover in Jessica's doorway. "What's with Lisa?" Linda asked. "Where's she off to without her attaché case?"

God, Jessica thought, this woman doesn't miss a trick. And it *was* dumb of Lisa not to carry papers. People noticed things like that in this place.

"She has some lunch appointment, and I think she's running late."

"Oh." Linda turned her attention to Jessica. "Speaking of lunch, how about it? I'll even pay. I owe you one for helping out on that report."

Helping out on, Jessica noticed, not helping *me* on. Then she was annoyed with herself. Oh, come on. It's just a way of talking. "All right. Lunch. Why not?"

"Are you meeting with Lisa today?" Linda asked as they headed for the elevator. "I overheard you telling Flo you needed to see her. What's up? Big doings?"

Jessica swallowed. Who was paranoid here? She or Linda? For a moment she was sorry she had helped Linda with the report at all; she couldn't remember why she'd done it. Because Linda had asked, she reminded herself.

The elevator doors yawned open, and Rick Schmidt emerged. "Hi," he said more or less to Jessica.

"Hello, Rick," she said. "I see you're East again."

Jessica may have had mixed feelings about Linda Glover, but there was no doubt about her feeling for Rick Schmidt. She loathed him. He was, in her mind, precisely the kind of narrow-minded, narrow-souled man who typified what she called "the middle manager mentality that gave us Haldeman, Ehrlichman, Mitchell, Magruder, and Dean — not to mention Nixon." She had said to Lisa that "Rick Schmidt would have been a big hit in the Third Reich." Lisa had laughed, but to Jessica it was a serious remark and reason for dismay.

In all the sagas of love and strife and heroism she had read, what emerged for Jessica was the necessary order of the universe. The wrath of heroes — in *The Iliad*, in *Beowulf*, in the *Volsunga Saga* — had to be restrained off the field of battle or the world order would be shattered. Rick was no Achilles to Jessica, no hero, just an army captain who had loved the war in Vietnam and still talked about his weekly kill records in the same breath as his high-performance production records at GlobeBank. But he was, in her eyes, a man full of that same dangerous wrath. He "fit" the world of war, and perhaps, too, the warlike world of the corporation. But he did not "fit" her world, and the truth was that she feared his type.

And Linda Glover, as almost everyone knew, had been having an affair with Rick Schmidt for many months.

"I'm doing research for a major paper," Rick was saying. "By the way, I used your Autotran piece. Hope you don't mind."

"Of course," Jessica said. Then she remembered the last time Schmidt had been East, about a month before. It was on a day she had had lunch with Linda. Linda had come to her office to pick her up and had asked, casually, if she could have "another copy of the Autotran paper."

It was suddenly clear to Jessica that Linda had given that "another copy" to Rick. There was something else. Jessica was beginning to feel that these highly visible lunches Linda made a point of having with her when Rick was in town were a way of trying to belie the affair. Jessica gave Linda legitimacy.

"You know," Jessica said smoothly, "on second thought, Linda, I'm really not feeling good. I'm just going to go tell Flo I'm going home." She added, not without malice, "Maybe Rick will take you to lunch." She strode off down the hall without waiting for a reaction.

Everybody cheats, she thought. Rick Schmidt and Linda Glover. Mark Krausner. Lisa Gould. It's in the air, and we're all breathing it. Me, Abby, all of us.

She surprised Abby when school let out that afternoon. They wandered around the Lower East Side, pretending interest in various products so they could get warm in the stores. Then they had an early dinner in Chinatown.

◇ ◇ ◇

The next morning, Jessica was in the office by eight-thirty. She called Lisa, who told her to "come on over."

Lisa's reaction to the story of Jessica's exchange with Mark Krausner was eloquent. "Shit," Lisa said. "Christ! How could he do that?" They talked for a bit about the implications. Then Lisa said, "What do you want me to do, Jess?"

Jessica was taken aback. It seemed to her that Lisa ought to *know* what to do. She said, "I don't know what to ask you to do, Lisa, but I'll tell you what I'm going to do. Or rather, what I'm not going to do. I'm not going to do anything more than ask Jack if he's heard of this Winter guy, Mark's photographer friend. What I'd like is your backing, your assurance that the contract won't get canceled because I refuse to pressure Jack. What you do about Krausner is your business."

Lisa was silent, thinking, while Jessica went on. "That's the only way I'll do this job, Lisa. If you give me a job to do, then I need your support in doing it. Otherwise . . ."

Lisa smiled. "Otherwise what? You'll quit the bank? Come on. You know I back you, of course. I'm just trying to decide how to handle it." She considered the issue, wordlessly, for another minute. Then she sat up and quickly rapped out a directive, the executive decision-maker's final decision: "Write me a memo, copy to Krausner. Just recap what you've done on the

251

project thus far, what point you're up to, et cetera. And that Krausner has seen and approved the copy. And that you are going to discuss with Resnick the possible use of David Winter as photographer."

"I'll say I'm going to *mention* Winter to Jack."

"OK. Word it however you want. It's your memo."

Jessica got up to go. At the door, she turned and asked, "What are you going to do about Krausner?"

Lisa shrugged. "I don't know. I've been watching him closely, anyway. For other reasons. I don't know. What else, Jess?"

"What else?" was Lisa's signal that a conversation had ended. Jessica left the office. She had gotten what she wanted, but there was a residue of foreboding inside her, a bad taste in her mouth. She went into her own office, closed the door, and phoned Jack Resnick.

2

"WELL," SAID SANDY, "this is it."

Lisa waited, leaning against his arm, while he paid the cab driver. Rain pelted the window; it was a blustery day and it would be good to get inside. The entrance to the building was only barely noticeable between an elaborate sidewalk greengrocer and an outcropping of a newsstand. Oranges, grapefruits, plum tomatoes, and bunches of radishes on the right, and on the left the *News,* the *Post,* the *Village Voice,* and papers in Russian, Greek, German.

"Behold the urban love nest," Sandy said, leaning over Lisa to open the door.

They dashed into the entryway. "Wait here just a minute, sweetheart, will you?" Sandy said a little breathlessly. "I want to get a bottle of champagne. Special occasion." He kissed her cheek. "The liquor store is right at the corner. No use both of us getting soaked. Be a second," he called back over his shoulder.

Lisa stood, shivering. We've come such a long way in such a short time, Sandy and I, she thought. Our own place. She looked around. On one wall was a hand-lettered sign: BE SURE THIS

DOOR IS LOKT. THIS MEANS YOU (SINED) SUPER. On the other side was a vertical row of buttons and a horizontal row of mailboxes, some of them slightly bent. She glanced at the names: Anderson. Schultz-O'Toole. A blank. T. Putnam. Masako Kurasawa, Rodriguez. Super — Ring Two Times. Owanisian. Dance Studio. Must be the top floor. Or somebody is named dance studio. Ms. Studio. Sounds Italian. Lisa giggled. A blast of hot air came up from the vent on the floor, fluttering the hem of her Burberry.

The front door flew open and Sandy dashed in, his hair plastered to his head, the rain streaming down his forehead and dripping off the tip of his nose. In one hand was a wine bottle, its neck sticking out of a paper bag. In the other was a bag of sandwiches and a bunch of flowers. "Roses. For you. Come on." He took a key ring out of his pants pocket and opened the inner door.

They climbed up two flights of dimly lighted stairs and stopped in front of a door with three locks. "All this safety makes for a lot of keys," Sandy said.

Lisa noticed that the keys were attached to a large plastic 1 with "For haircutting we're #1. Sal and Nick" embossed in red letters. Sandy took a minute to fit the right keys to the locks, then pushed against the unlocked door, swinging it open. "Well, love," he said, "just a second." He wiggled the wine bottle and sandwiches into his coat pockets, then scooped Lisa up and carried her into the apartment, his hair making a little circle of drops on her coat. He set her down and kissed her, this time on the mouth, a long kiss. When Lisa opened her eyes, she felt momentarily dizzy. "I'd better get a towel before I drown us," Sandy said. He emerged a moment later without his coat, rubbing a Holiday Inn towel with its yellow center stripe back and forth over his hair.

"Oh, Sandy," Lisa said, melting. She peeled the florist's wrapping off the flowers. "They're so beautiful. Iş there something here I can use as a vase?"

"Are you kidding?" He pointed to shelves behind Lisa, crammed with bowls, plates, vases, urns — vessels of all sizes, all shapes — glazed in sea greens, dreamy blues, earthy browns. "This apartment belongs to a potter."

Lisa smiled. "I like it," she said.

"Come on, I'll show you around. The tour. This is the living room, dining room, workroom, and study. As you can guess by the presence of the studio couch, it's also the bedroom. I tested the springs, and they seem fine." He ran his hand over Lisa's cheek. "And that door there, with the towel hanging over the knob, is the bathroom. Now step along with me," he said grandly, steering her into the tiny galley kitchen. "Champagne on ice awaits your pleasure. Actually, darling," he said, leaning over to kiss her, "I'm going to put the champagne in the freezer to get cold." He put the bottle, still in its bag, in the freezer.

"Not bad, is it?" Sandy remarked. "Isn't this nice?"

It *was* nice, she thought. A place of their own.

After the first time in his apartment, they met whenever they could. They never discussed what they were doing or talked of a "relationship." Each was starved for the other. It felt unnatural to them only in the sense that everything seemed heightened, intensified.

Lisa had left Sandy's apartment that first night just before dawn, in a sudden panic that Barry might have been trying to reach her. She telephoned him the next day from the office, ready with an excuse. But no, he made no mention of having called; he was cheerful, he missed her. Everything's fine here too, she told him; she was working hard, she might go to the movies with Joyce and David tonight, she missed him too.

That night she was back in Sandy's apartment. She hardly knew herself. Everything was so ripe, so giddy. In Sandy's bathroom she found herself embracing his towel, inhaling his odor.

When Barry came back, it was harder to meet, and they had to resign themselves to quick lunch hours at Sandy's apartment. Lisa told Flo to try to keep her calendar free of lunch meetings, explaining that she was dieting and wanted to use the time for some extra walking. Flo never questioned Lisa's returning from lunch flushed and breathless two or three times a week.

Sandy's apartment seemed magical to her. She marveled at all his possessions — his shaving gear, his shoes and socks, his boxes of cereal — as though every familiar, homely object were touched with a special grace.

Sometimes in the middle of a morning she would close her eyes and stroke her own cheek, remembering his touch, needing him. When she could, she would phone him: "Meet me. Please hurry. I love you."

And then Doris Gelb appeared.

How could she have forgotten Doris Gelb, her mother's oldest friend, who had pinched her cheek when she was small until it was sore, who had been the first to comment on her teenage acne — "What happened to your fabulous complexion, darling?" Doris Gelb, the busybody of the world, lived in Sandy's building.

How on earth had she not remembered? She knew the address had sounded familiar. She could see herself that last time, taxiing to his building. Please hurry, I love you. And then Doris Gelb coming at her out of the elevator.

"Lisa! Darling! What are you doing here?" And the doorman listening for all he's worth.

"Doris!" She leaned over to be kissed. "What a surprise!"

"Well, I live here, darling, so it's not such a big surprise. And you? Visiting?"

"Well, no, not really. Just a quick stop. Someone from my office lives here," she said, thinking fast. "Who's away on a trip, but has some stuff I need. So I said I would pick it up." It sounded lame to Lisa, who felt she could hear her own pulse throbbing in her head.

Doris Gelb moved her head from side to side and clucked. "Such devotion. You going right back to the office?"

Lisa reached around for the OPEN DOOR button; Doris Gelb hovered on the elevator threshold. "Oh, yes. This is just a quick stop."

"Well, then, lovely to see you, darling. Don't work so hard, you look a little tired. Love to Barry!" Lisa could still hear her voice as the elevator doors closed.

After that, the apartment was impossible. What if her parents found out? What about Barry? No, it was too risky. Sandy understood and said he would take care of it. He'd get them someplace small, a place of their own.

◊ ◊ ◊

255

"Isn't this nice?" Sandy repeated, his arm around Lisa. "We can come here whenever we like. And no Mrs. Gertz to upset the applecart."

"Gelb," said Lisa. She sighed contentedly and leaned against Sandy's arm. "You're a genius."

"There's a radio," he said. "How about some music?"

They sat on the couch feeling very dreamy, listening to the music, eating sandwiches. The office seemed far away. There was nothing in the place that suggested anything but intimacy. Even the pottery on the shelves seemed to whisper of one person's hands, and nothing more.

"I wish I could stay here forever," Lisa said after a while, half meaning it. "But the trouble is that what I actually have to do is get myself back for a two o'clock with John."

"Oh? What's going on?"

"He wants me to go over the Customer Profile Report I gave him last month."

"For Pruitt?"

She nodded. "I suppose you'll be on his calendar next week. I hate this grilling we have to go through before every annual stockholders' meeting. It seems like such a waste of time, explaining your explanations. But then, I guess John has to go through the same thing with Pruitt, and he doesn't want to be caught unprepared."

"Well, anyway, I have to see the TopTec vendors at two-thirty. They seem to think they can interest us in a smaller CPU."

"What's the pricing like?"

"Can't tell," Sandy said. "They want to walk me through a whole package. If it's interesting, I'll arrange for a presentation for you and all the other guys." He looked at his watch. "We have another twenty or thirty minutes. I don't want to think about TopTec now. I just want to be near you." He stroked her hair and drew her closer.

When they were putting on their coats, Sandy said, "Close your eyes, Lisa. I have something for you."

She closed her eyes.

"Hold out your hand."

With her eyes shut, Lisa felt him kiss her palm, put something in it, and fold her fingers around the object.

"Now open."

She looked down. She was holding a bunch of keys attached to a big clear plastic heart.

"Your keys to this place," Sandy said, and squeezed her shoulder.

Lisa opened her handbag and zipped the keys inside her makeup kit. "Now we really have something of our own," she said.

◇ ◇ ◇

The Third Avenue studio became a haven for Lisa; she couldn't imagine what would happen when Sandy had to give it up. Maybe he wouldn't have to, at least not as soon as he expected. He told Lisa that he'd gotten a postcard from the landlady, saying that she was being considered for another quarter of teaching; was he interested in another three months of renting?

Whenever they found a free half hour or more, they would meet. Still, Lisa insisted on extreme caution — excessive caution, Sandy often thought. They developed a code of phrases so that even when they talked on the phone, no one would know that they were checking to see if the other was free or arranging a meeting. They got to the place once or twice a week at lunchtime. Sometimes they would barely shut and lock the door before falling onto the couch in a blizzard of discarded clothes. Other times they would sit quietly, as they did their first day there, and talk or listen to the radio. Sandy would often make one of his special herb omelettes; or Lisa would cook spaghetti sauce, which she would freeze in half a dozen small containers that just barely fit inside the tiny refrigerator. Sandy would watch her from the couch where he lay, stretched full length, his hands behind his head.

One day she showed up with a Bloomingdale's shopping bag, out of which she pulled a plaid flannel bathrobe. "I want to keep this here," she said, "and feel at home in it." Little by little, the place filled up with small possessions.

Lisa bought Sandy a soap-on-a-rope; he bought Lisa a silly pink shower hat with nylon lace trim. They bought two Baccarat wineglasses, feeling proud and self-conscious in the store. "They think we're newlyweds," Sandy whispered. They took showers together, squeezed uncomfortably inside the old-fashioned shower curtain ring. She washed his back; he washed hers.

Sometimes one of them would get caught at the office at the last minute and would arrive late and breathless. They decided to have their own phone put in so they wouldn't die from worry. Once, around seven at night, after Lisa had waited for an hour in her plaid bathrobe, the phone rang. Sandy couldn't come, something about a bug in the system, there was nothing he could do. Lisa sat down and wept bitterly, as though her heart would break. I must be getting my period, she told herself.

Another time, waiting for him, she prowled back and forth, to the bathroom, to the kitchen area, around the table, back to the bathroom. She cleaned the sink and the bathtub. She shook out the Indian throw and put it back on the couch — the cleaner side out. She went over to the shelves of pottery and tried to put the pieces in order: mugs with mugs, bowls with bowls; big, medium, little. Where can he be? she kept wondering. Sandy hadn't called yet, it was almost an hour. Inside one enormous brown bowl with an uneven glaze — awful, Lisa thought — was a stack of old mail, probably the landlady's. She looked it over idly. Crafts magazines. An old *Village Voice,* an old *SoHo News.* Bills. A letter with a British stamp addressed to Thos. Putnam. An ad from Bloomingdale's for Clinique. The model was extraordinary, unreal in her beauty and fragility. Obviously not a division head, Lisa joked to herself as at last, at last, she heard Sandy's key in the lock.

Once in a while, when Barry had a breakfast meeting, she would rush to the studio, not bothering to shower; they would do it there together. One time when Lisa got to work, rosy after their early morning lovemaking, she was embarrassed to have Flo compliment her on her coloring. "Maybe *I* should start walking to work," said Flo, who lived in the Bronx. "You look so healthy."

3

JOHN ROLAND KILGOUR STOOD at the huge window that formed one wall of his office. He was coatless, his hands in his pockets, his eyes fixed on a point on the glass just before him.

The scent of Elaine Green's perfume lingered in the large office, and Kilgour was helping it linger, remembering her presence beside him on the sofa only a few moments before.

She was wearing a lavender silk blouse and a gold choker. He looked down the length of her neck as she bent over the papers, just glimpsing the smooth white of her breast. His gaze moved down her body to the crossed legs, the curved thigh that emerged from under the dark gray skirt. His eyes narrowed as he looked at her, nodding at what she was saying.

Now, even with her gone, his head was spinning.

It was no good. Unhealthy. Bad for his blood pressure.

He was not used to this, not used to being thrown off kilter by a feeling, not at all accustomed to being diverted from his single-minded forward drive by sensations he could neither manage nor command. It would not do.

He had to have Elaine Green, and he had to have her soon. He stood by the window staring at the glass, waiting for his nerves to settle down, figuring out how he would get her.

The next morning, Kilgour announced that he needed solitude in order to work on his quarterly review for Hardesty and Pruitt, due the following week. He was going to get a suite at the Carlyle and work there. No calls. No disruptions.

He took home two attaché cases full of paperwork that night and left a memo for his division heads: "In my absence, Ray LaRocca will act as sector head. My secretary will know how to contact me in case of emergency only."

He covered himself the next morning by calling Faber and O'Connor and asking for some material to be sent to him by messenger.

He made one other call. "Elaine? John here. Yes, I'm working on the Human Resources section of the draft for my quarterly and I could use some input from you. Do you think you could possibly come to the Carlyle this evening and go over it?"

Elaine felt a chill go through her. She had been expecting this, certainly since Puerto Rico. Since the off-site, Kilgour's attitude toward her had changed. He had been less gushing, a bit harsher with her, yet even more bothersome.

She also knew that the promotion and salary forecast he

would be submitting in his Human Resources plan contained a recommendation that she be named a vice president. All that was needed was the signature of John R. Kilgour.

"Sure, John," Elaine said. "What time would be good?"

Kilgour smiled in triumph. "Say, seven? Does that suit you?"

"That's fine," Elaine said quickly. "I have no plans for this evening." She would have to call Alan Gersh and tell him she couldn't make dinner after all, but that was no problem. "I'll see you at seven."

"Right," said Kilgour.

◇ ◇ ◇

Elaine left a message for Alan at his Goldman Sachs office. She looked at her watch. Four-fifteen. She had a lot to do. She was supposed to see Lisa Gould at four-thirty. Lisa always ran late. It might be five by the time they met, five-thirty or later by the time she got out of the office. No good. She dialed Lisa's number.

"Hi, Flo. It's Elaine. Look, I've got a real problem with this four-thirty with Lisa. Kilgour just called and wants a deliverable from me. I'm really going to have to hustle to get it together. Can I cancel?"

Flo said sure, Lisa would understand. Having a deliverable for Kilgour took precedence over everything; it was the ultimate priority.

Elaine managed to find a taxi to take her to her one-bedroom apartment on East Sixty-third. She took a hot bath, laced with scented oils and bath beads. She sipped a glass of wine as she lay in the tub; it was a good way to relax. She decided to put her diaphragm in now, and just bring a small tube of stuff. That way she'd be ready, just in case, and there wouldn't be any of those silly "Excuse me, I just have to step into the bathroom for a moment" things that always broke the mood.

She dressed in the very expensive French lace panties and bra she had bought at that boutique on Madison. They were a wonderful color against her skin, a kind of burgundy brown.

She put on her Calvin Klein silk blouse, the dark brown one, and a camel Cacherel skirt, her brown Ferragamos with the gold clasp, two long gold chains around her neck, a slim gold chain around her wrist, and the gold shell earrings. In a thin brown leather purse, she put the tube of jelly, two tens and two fives, and a lipstick.

She did her makeup before the mirror. Six-thirty. She would have one more glass of wine, then brush her teeth and go.

Lisa was frankly glad when Flo told her Elaine had canceled their four-thirty. It meant she would have time to get some paperwork done before leaving the office. And she would have to be home by seven, absolutely. They were expecting guests at seven-thirty, an out-of-town client of Barry's — a lawyer from Tulsa, of all places — here with his wife and anxious for a gala evening.

Barry had arranged to give them one. After drinks at the apartment, they had an eight o'clock reservation at Le Cirque, then they'd go uptown to the Café Carlyle to hear Bobby Short. The Tulsan, Barry had learned, loved jazz piano.

Lisa was not looking forward to the evening. For her, it was a duty to be performed. Tonight she must be Barry's wife. Always herself, of course, and always the executive, but mostly Barry's wife. He had a way of boasting about her to people ahead of time so that they were already somewhat knowledgeable about her career. In voices thick with awed confidentiality, corporate lawyers from far-off places would discuss financial services with her. She had some speeches ready for these occasions, which she could pull out no matter how bored she was. Barry never tired of hearing them. He was so proud of her.

He had never fallen out of love with her, she reflected as she brought a final cup of coffee to the desk and shut the door behind her. He had never stopped being amazed at the fact that they had found one another, that they had married one another, that they were a happy couple. She graced his life, and he counted on her.

Lisa sighed. Barry's dependence on her had been so much on her mind these last weeks. The truth was that, though she felt she loved him, she found him a little dull, a little predictable. This made her feel restless, and her restlessness made him seem even duller. She wondered if he had noticed anything — anything at all. But he trusted her as much as he loved her, she argued back to herself, and he loved her very much.

Enough. She'd get this work done and go home to do her duty.

It was twenty after six when she left the building. She walked slowly, going over in her mind some of the issues she would need to take up the next day. There would be no time later to think straight about work; she would be too involved with Mr. and Mrs. Whatever-their-name-was.

At Sixty-fifth Street, she heard a familiar voice calling "Taxi!" It was Elaine Green.

"Elaine!" Lisa said. "Hi. Where are you headed?"

Elaine stared at Lisa. A panicky look crossed her face. She clutched some papers she was holding, extending them to show Lisa. "I've got this deliverable for John, you know. And I'm just off to give it to him."

"Hand delivered, is that it?" Lisa's tone was easy.

"Right."

"You look like you're going out after that. Got a date?"

Elaine's face brightened, as if it had all become clear. "Yes, I do. That's why I'm so frantic to just drop this and get going. But getting a taxi at this hour on Third Avenue is murder."

"Well, good luck."

"Thanks. See you tomorrow." Elaine kept signaling for a cab.

The Tulsans, Andrew and Trish Merriam, turned out to be rather pleasant people, warm and funny. Lisa reminded herself that that usually happened when she dreaded something in advance — it turned out to be nice. Seated in the pale red light of Le Cirque, amid the beautiful flowers and elegant settings, Lisa decided she was having a lovely time. Good food. Good talk about things other than the conversion at GlobeBank or the politics at Barry's law firm. She was looking forward to the Café Carlyle, feeling bright and cheery as she pondered a choice for dessert.

◊ ◊ ◊

Kilgour had given Elaine his room number over the phone, telling her to "come right up." She walked past the desk in the Carlyle lobby to the elevators, getting off nonchalantly at his floor.

Kilgour opened the door at her knock. He wore a blue shirt with a thin gray V-neck sweater, dark gray slacks, and loafers.

"Come in," he said. "Make yourself comfortable. Have you eaten? Because I ordered something for you from Room Service."

Elaine was taking off her raincoat. "No, I haven't, although I don't know that I could manage very much."

Kilgour smiled. "We'll see." Then he said, "I thought we'd work around the coffee table."

Elaine sat in the chair at one end of the rectangular table. Kilgour sat on the couch.

"Why don't you have a look at this draft I've done," he suggested. "I'd like to hear your comments."

It was a messy draft. John Kilgour was notorious for his handwriting, but Elaine had mastered it for the most part and could usually follow what he wrote. Right now she was wondering if she hadn't perhaps been mistaken about what he wanted tonight. He looked so serious, sitting there sipping a drink. He was, of course, known to be very disapproving of such things as divorce. Adultery, it was generally assumed, was something he hardly recognized. He prided himself on his chic wife, on his pretty daughters, on his role as a family man. Maybe, she thought, he really wanted to work.

"Would you like a drink?" he asked suddenly. "Wine?"

"Oh, sure. I'd love some." Elaine nodded.

"You drank wine in Puerto Rico," Kilgour went on, "and I think you'll like this."

"I'm sure I will," she said, realizing that her first instincts had been correct.

There was a knock on the door. Elaine hurriedly bent over the papers, looking intent. Kilgour opened the door to a waiter and a table full of rounded plate covers.

Kilgour ate heartily. Elaine picked at her food, eating a little of the salad. Kilgour kept filling her wineglass, and she kept emptying it. She talked about the Human Resources forecast that Kilgour would be presenting the next week. He listened while they ate, not saying much in reply.

He folded his napkin, finished with the meal. "Well, now let's talk about you," he said.

"About me?"

"About your forecast." He leaned forward. "There's a piece of paper over there that recommends that Elaine Green be named a vice president at an eleven percent increase." His voice was low and soft. His face was quite red. The wine, she thought.

"I know."

"There's a space on the paper for my signature." He had come even closer. His hand was on the table, halfway toward her. She put her hand on the table, within reach.

"I know that, too."

He took her hand. "Do you also know that I find you very, very attractive?"

She said nothing.

Kilgour ran his thumb across her fingertips. He seemed to be studying her hand. "I have never been unfaithful to my wife," he said. That was stupid. Shouldn't have said that.

"Not that my wife has anything to do with this," he went on. "This is something you'll come to understand when you're married — as I'm sure you will be. I'm sure there are many men who see, as I do, that you're a beautiful, intelligent, very desirable woman."

He brought her hand to his lips, then set it back on the table, under his. "I think you know I can do a lot for you, Elaine." Kilgour was almost whispering. She kept her eyes lowered. "And I'd like to, I'd like to. But frankly, I find that my interest in you is a great distraction to me. Having you near me, and yet untouchable . . ."

Elaine was quiet for a moment. Then she took her hand away and looked at him. Suddenly she stood up. Still staring at him, she began to unbutton her blouse. She watched his eyes move down her body as she slipped down her skirt. His eyes were glowing. His lips turned up in a slight smile.

She stood there in the lace panties and bra and kicked off her shoes. She lowered her panties and pantyhose and unhooked her bra. Her clothes formed a circle on the floor. She stepped over the rim of the circle and moved toward him. She could hear him breathing hard.

He put his arms around her waist and looked up at her. "You are lovely," he said. He began to nuzzle her breasts with his face. Then he stood up and led her into the bedroom.

The covers were turned down. That's what they do in hotels, she thought. Kilgour turned the light out, leaving the door to

264

the living room ajar so that a line of light fell softly in the bedroom. She got into the bed. Kilgour sat on the edge of it, his
back to her, and quickly undressed. He doesn't want me to see
him, she thought, smiling. He slipped in under the covers and
rolled over to her. He began to kiss her, hard. His breath was all
alcohol, stifling. He began to move his mouth down her body.
Elaine lay back and tried to relax.

Afterward, as he lay sleeping beside her, his heavy breathing
not quite a snore, she reflected that it hadn't gone too badly. He
had certainly been pleased, crying out with a hoot of pleasure
when he came. "Just as I'd hoped," he said afterward. "Better."
Then he rolled over, turning his back to her, to sleep.

There had been less of that kind of pleasure in it for her. He
had certainly been ardent, perhaps too much so, grunting with
each thrust. He had never really filled her up, she decided. She
had wrapped her legs around him and pushed at his buttocks,
but it had not been enough — for her.

The pleasure had been rather in the feeling of power she had
as she watched him, caught between her legs, and felt the sweat
dropping off his forehead and glimpsed the look in his eyes, his
lips pulled back to reveal teeth clenched with effort. She had
cooed to him, egging him on, "More, more, make me," and had
undulated beneath him convincingly.

Elaine reached up carefully and turned on the bedtable lamp.
Very stealthily, watching for any movement from the sleeping
form beside her, she pulled down the covers and peered over his
back to look at him. The hairs on his chest were gray, it was true,
but his body was fit. If his stomach was not absolutely flat and
smooth, neither were the stomachs of many younger men she
had been with. His shoulders were broad, and his neck was only
slightly creased.

She looked down between his legs. Kilgour lay in an almost
fetal position, and his limp penis dangled downward. It was
tiny. Well, not tiny perhaps, but very small.

Elaine suppressed a giggle and quickly turned out the light.
She lay back against the pillow. She would have to ask him to
shave from now on before they met. The stubble of his beard
had scratched her and had probably left a rash. But that would
be easy.

She looked at the glowing digital clock. Almost nine. She

would wake him in a while, do something with him, then leave. It was going to be fun, she decided, stretching slightly and arching her back. It was going to be fun to have him under her control. Wouldn't it be a stitch if people knew what she knew, that John Kilgour was small where it counted and rather a bore at fucking? She suppressed another giggle. It was going to be fun making him do what she wanted. She could, she realized, cop a quick feel in the office and watch him jump. She could ask for favors. She could take time off, lots of time off. Probably get some trips, too.

But first she had to remember to have him sign that promotion sheet before she left tonight. Maybe before they made love again tonight. Elaine Green crossed her arms over her chest and began to think of how to wake him up.

◇ ◇ ◇

Bobby Short's second set didn't start for another half an hour. Barry ordered a bottle of champagne and raised a toast to "expense accounts — long life and good health." Everyone laughed, and they all agreed that law firms were more lavish in their entertaining than banks. "GlobeBank's the best of them," Lisa said with defensive pride, "but it's true that banks have less style in these things."

GlobeBank. Sandy. He intruded into Lisa's thought like a quick flash of lightning. He had called at four forty-five, just as she was about to go to the Ladies' Room. "Call you back in five minutes," she had promised. And then she had forgotten. She had just forgotten. She remembered being preoccupied by the paperwork, relieved when Elaine canceled their meeting because it meant she could get to it. She remembered thinking guilty thoughts about Barry. Well, the last thing she needed now was guilty thoughts about Sandy. She must call him.

"Excuse me," she said quietly, and rose from the table. She made her way out of the club into the small entry hall, dashed up a short flight of steps into the lobby, and looked about for a pay phone.

It was odd, she reflected as she sauntered across the lobby, how he had slipped her mind. She spent so much of her life thinking about him, wanting to be with him, loving him. But here, this evening, with these people, it had all been another world. GlobeBank suddenly didn't belong. Sandy didn't belong, didn't fit. He was, after all, her secret.

He answered on the second ring.

"It's me," she said. "I'm sorry. I . . . I got crazy at the end of the day. Everything exploded at once. I couldn't call you back."

"Where are you?"

"At the Carlyle. With . . . these people from out of town. I thought I told you."

"Oh, yes." He sounded far away, drained. "I waited till seven for your call, then I tried your office."

Her heart turned over. "I'm sorry, Sandy. Darling. I'm sorry."

"It's OK."

"No, it isn't. It isn't OK." Her words sounded hollow to her.

"Will we meet tomorrow?"

"Yes. Oh yes."

"You'd better get back now. I'll . . . I'll see you tomorrow."

"Yes, dear. I'll be there. Call you in the morning."

Lisa hung up and turned back toward the lobby. On her right, the elevator doors opened. An older couple emerged, then Elaine Green. Lisa glanced at her watch. Eleven-twenty. Elaine's freshly made-up look of five and a half hours ago was gone. She still carried the papers she had said she was bringing to Kilgour. There was a look on her face of — what? — satisfaction? Her eyes seemed heavy, and her walk was a stroll.

Lisa watched Elaine walk across the lobby and out into the street. She stood very still near the phone booth. She knew, of course. She knew at once. John and Elaine Green were sleeping together. It was an open secret that he was "hot for her," as Danny Faber rather crudely put it. As for Elaine, who knew? She made no bones about her desire to get ahead. Lisa, who thought her stupid, had often wondered how she had gotten as far as she had. But then, there were all sorts of stupid people at Elaine's level, most of them men. They hadn't slept their way to the top, and there was no reason to assume Elaine had. There were lots of ways to get ahead, Lisa knew — kiss the right ass, get lucky, manage to be in the right place at the right time. Elaine could just as easily have done those things.

On the other hand, she could have done it in bed. Lisa hurriedly entered the Ladies' Room of the Café Carlyle. She tried to remember Elaine's career path to this point, whom she had worked for, whether she might have . . . Oh, hell. What did it matter? The point was, she was certainly sleeping with John Kilgour now. Tonight. In the Hotel Carlyle. Where he had gone to find "creative solitude" and work on his report for the president and chairman. Lisa snickered, sitting before the mirror combing her hair.

These things happened. They happened a lot. And it was just possible that Elaine Green loved John Kilgour. He was not, Lisa decided, an unattractive man. Those things happened, too. My God, she thought with a rush, it's happened to me.

She left the Ladies' Room and rejoined her husband and their guests.

4

"WE NEED ABOUT FIVE SHOTS at this location," Jack Resnick told Jessica. "It's for page twenty-one of the copy."

Jessica flipped through the pages of her draft of the booklet. Jack watched her, peering over the top of his clipboard. The location was the area outside Lisa's office. The photographer was setting up lights.

"Right," Jessica said, scanning the script. "So what shall we do first? The two guys poring over the report?"

"Good," Jack said.

Jessica turned to Flo. "Flo, can you please buzz Tom and Scotty? They said they'd model for this."

Flo made two quick calls, and the two men appeared. Jack sat them on a sofa that formed part of the reception area. Jessica grabbed an orange GlobeBank looseleaf binder from Tony Maresca's office. Jack began to direct the two men.

"You're just going over these figures here. Scotty, can you just tip the edge of the book up a little so that we can see the GlobeBank logo? Good. Now just open your mouth a bit, Tom, as if you're talking. And if you could both just freeze." The little shrieking noises of the camera's motor could be heard. "That's good," Jack went on smoothly. "Good! Super! OK! Thank you both."

The two men, joking with one another about Hollywood contracts, disappeared down the corridor.

"Now a shot of someone at the CRT," Jack said, moving away from the couches. He sidled up to Jessica. "Can we get somebody besides the woman who belongs there?" he whispered. "We've got an awful lot of blacks in this brochure."

At that moment, Linda Glover emerged from Tony Maresca's office. "Will she do?" Jessica asked.

Jack nodded.

"Hey, Linda," Jessica called out, "can you come here?"

Jessica put a hand on Linda's shoulder and propelled her toward the desk. "We're shooting a sequence showing an efficient, productive, snazzy office area filled with efficient, productive, snazzy workers for my new brochure," she said. "How about modeling? All you have to do is set your fingers lightly over the keyboard. Will you? Because we're desperate for a female Caucasian."

"You've got to be kidding," Linda said. "I'm not going to portray a secretary. I'm an officer. Upper level."

Jessica chuckled. She thought Linda was joking.

"Really, Jess," Linda repeated, "not the division's financial controller, for God's sake. I think this is terrible."

Jack was popping back and forth before Jessica's eyes, rethinking the shot. Jessica looked at Linda, who was reddening. My God, she thought with a sinking feeling, she's serious.

"Jack," she said quietly, "hold up." He caught her meaning and followed her down the hall.

"We can't use Linda," Jessica said in a whisper. "Apparently it rankles too much to portray a secretary, even for a brochure."

Jack grimaced. "Jess! You're kidding. Jessica, this is show biz! Make-believe! And the shot won't even show her face!"

"I know. But we can't use Linda."

Jack stood before her for a long minute. His gawky frame sagged at the middle, as it always did, Jessica thought, and his long arms drooped at his sides. He put a hand on Jessica's cheek. "It's got to be difficult to keep your sense of humor here, Jess."

"Sometimes impossible."

◇ ◇ ◇

"Any messages, Flo?" Linda walked over to Flo's desk shortly after leaving Jessica. It had been a bad morning altogether, starting with a hysterical phone call from Rick, an angry call from Charley, and a bad meeting with Tony. Linda could still hear his high-pitched voice talking on the phone from his office next to Lisa's. And now this absolutely off-the-wall behavior by Jessica. It was just too much.

"A few," Flo said, pulling the small green message sheets from the slot marked LG. "Anne Morrissey called a couple of times. She said it's really important that you get back to her."

Linda nodded.

In her office, Linda punched Anne's number on the phone. "Anne Morrissey."

"Anne, hi. It's Linda." Linda snapped open her attaché case, removed the folded *Wall Street Journal,* and closed the case.

"Linda! Thank God! Where are you?"

"Oh, I was in a meeting. What's up?"

"What's up is that I'm not asking you, I'm telling you: I've got to come up and see you. Can you have lunch?"

"Sure, Anne. I guess that's OK. Can you be here at twelve?"

"Twelve. I'll be there."

Anne Morrissey was a year younger than Linda Glover, an acquaintance from business school. She looked up to Linda, admired her, wanted to emulate her. It was a reaction Linda liked very much. She had always thought she would like to be a Girl Scout leader, when the time came to assume outside activities.

So she had kept in touch with Anne Morrissey, had helped her get a job at GlobeBank, had made a point of being seen with her to ease her way into acceptance.

Now, after only two months on the job, Anne was having trouble with her supervisor.

"I'm just not getting any real direction, Linda. I have no job description, no sense of my role in the department's goals. I mean, she gives me these little tasks. No real projects. And no kind of ongoing thing. I don't think there's a real job for me there."

Linda nodded gravely and concentrated on her plate.

"Plus," Anne went on, "there's a real personality problem between us. I mean, I can understand it in a way. She's five years older than me. I mean, she didn't do B-school or anything. So I come along, and I'm young and an M.B.A., and they tell her she's got to train me. She probably figures I'm going to outstrip her in no time. She's so resentful. I mean, I can understand that. But it's just an untenable situation for me."

Linda smiled silkily. "I bet you wish you'd come to work for me."

"I'll say." Anne didn't mean it. She had gone over this in her mind a thousand times when she was interviewing at Globe-Bank. She admired Linda, yes, and saw her as a role model, to be sure. But she knew she wouldn't want to take orders from her under any circumstances.

"Well," Linda said, "maybe we can work it out. I mean, I think the main thing is to get you out of there."

"Oh, right. I mean, the situation is untenable. It's just going to get more untenable, too."

Linda spoke slowly. "Well, I think I've got a slot for you." It could be a good move. She could get Anne for a low price; it would just be a lateral move, no promotion. She'd have a numbers cruncher who spoke her language from the start, the same language they had both learned at the same B-school. Anne already adored her; if she got her out of this munchkin job, Anne would really owe her.

"I don't know," Anne said, staring shrewdly past Linda at the dark-mustached waiter bearing a tray of Dos Equis and thick piña coladas to another table. "Don't you think it might look a little, I don't know, like a sort of conspiracy, a little bit contrived?"

Linda took another bite. "It doesn't have to. Those things only last a day or two, anyway. Tell you what. I'll nose around quietly and see where the open slots are. I'm pretty good buddies with our personnel person. If there are no slots — and if I were you, I wouldn't get too optimistic — or if we can't cut a deal, then there's still my slot, OK?"

"OK, Linda, that's great. I really appreciate it."

"But this could take time, Anne. I hope you know that."

"Oh, sure."

"I mean, officially, no one's supposed to even think of a transfer till they've been on board nine months. So we'd have to construct some very good reasons to cut this deal."

"Sure. Right."

"Meantime, the thing you've got to do is just put up with it," Linda advised in her best mentor's tone. With a break or two, she could get Anne Morrissey cheap — cheap and grateful, the best combination. "I mean, just go in there, and whenever she bares her ass, you kiss it. Yes her to death. And Anne," she concluded, surveying her charge's Blassport dress, "tone down the chic, will you? Your boss probably resents your looks, too. Try wearing something tacky a couple times a week."

"Sure, I can do that. No problem."

"What the hell? Right?"

"Oh, yeah."

"If you have to kiss ass, then that's what you have to do. It can't hurt."

"No. Sure. Thanks, Linda, really. I wish there were some way I could repay you."

"Well," Linda laughed, "there probably will be."

5

FOR THE SAN FRANCISCO flight, Sandy had been sure to ask for an aisle seat in the front row of a section. His legs extended past the partition, but for once he wasn't pushing around his carry-on luggage with his feet. He relaxed. Five hours. I'm coming, Lisa, he kept thinking. Wait for me. They would have what they had never had before — time. Uninterrupted time together. No cares, no obligations. He would see to that. This was their time — theirs alone.

He looked out the airplane window past the heads of the people sitting on his left, both of them asleep, attached to their armrests by headset wires. The sky was pale blue, the light thin and lemony. Another plane trip. Last week he had been on the Concorde from London. Concorde both ways, thank God! Well, Kilgour owed it to him. And only a short time in London. He had been eager to get back, eager to get to California and Lisa.

◊ ◊ ◊

Sitting in the Concorde's comfortable seat, Sandy went over his London agenda.

He would arrive in an hour — nine P.M. Good. He would go to a pub — the Rose, most likely — then have dinner sent up to his room and get a good night's sleep.

In the morning, first thing, he would head for the bank. His bank. Or, rather, Thomas Putnam's bank. He wanted to withdraw the cash early, have that behind him, the money in his pocket, when he went off to do business.

He had a ten-thirty review with Simon Fenton and Arthur Bennett, a working lunch with other members of the Autotran team, then a formal presentation and a tour of the operation. He would undoubtedly be taken to dinner.

"Good evening, ladies and gentlemen. We are now preparing for our landing at London's Heathrow Airport. Kindly fasten your seat belts and extinguish all smoking materials.

"It is currently nine-fifteen in London. Temperature is fifty-two degrees Fahrenheit, eleven degrees Celsius. A light rain is falling."

A very light rain, Sandy reflected as he approached the taxi stand. "Inter-Continental Hotel at Hyde Park, please," he told the cabbie.

He checked in quickly and went to his room to change. The phone rang. It was Myra Bennett. Sandy forced enthusiasm into his voice.

"How are you? Nice to hear from you," he said as he one-handedly got out of his shirt.

"You had a good journey, I trust."

"Yes, great. I came Concorde."

"I know. Arthur told me."

Sandy waited for her to speak. He reached for the light gray turtleneck in his bag.

"Arthur also tells me you plan a very short stay this time."

"Yeah. Really just in and out."

"Think you'll have some time for me? I so enjoyed our last meeting."

Sandy sighed. "I really don't see how, Myra. There's just tomorrow, and I've got meetings all day. I leave first thing Friday."

"What about tomorrow morning? Arthur says you're not due at the bank until about ten-thirty."

"Yes, well, that's because I have some chores to do. I wanted to get them done because I knew there wouldn't be any time once the meetings got going."

"I see." She didn't sound angry, thank God for that.

Then she said, "You haven't gone and got yourself a serious relationship with someone, have you? Not that it ought to have anything to do with you and me, but I know what a romantic you are."

Sandy smiled. How he would love to answer truthfully, to say, "Yes, Myra, I have gone and got myself a serious relationship, only it's with a division head at GlobeBank, the famous Lisa Gould, the famous *married* Lisa Gould. So it's a relationship that exists mostly in a cheap, third-floor walkup until I get to San Francisco, a relationship that has to be kept even more secret than the highly pleasurable afternoon you and I spent here — when was it? It seems like years ago."

Instead he replied, "No, no. Nothing like that. It's just the pressure of business. That's all."

"Well, in that case," she said, "I won't keep you. Try to make it a longer stay next time, Sandy. I think you won't regret it."

Thursday morning, Sandy left the hotel wearing a three-piece suit and carrying his attaché case. He walked to Knightsbridge, striding along like a man in a hurry, a man with a purpose.

He breakfasted on kippers in a small restaurant in the Brompton Road, bent over a London *Times,* waiting. He did not want to be the first customer in the bank.

He strolled into the Bedminster branch a little before ten, going directly to a window and presenting his check. It was for a very large amount, fifteen thousand pounds sterling. Sandy expected some questions from the teller and was ready with answers.

But after the teller checked the account, there were only two questions: "Did you want this in cash, sir? Large or small denominations?"

"Large denominations will be fine," Sandy answered. He slipped the wad of large, colorful notes into Thomas Putnam's billfold. Then he thanked the teller and left.

Back to the Brompton Road, where there was a Barclays Bank branch. Sandy immediately exchanged two thousand pounds sterling for dollars. He caught a taxi and headed for GlobeBank and his day of meetings. He would change the rest of the money later — at the airport, back in New York, in San Francisco, anywhere. It didn't matter. The money was in his pocket, without any questions asked, without any eyebrows raised. Autotran was paying him back.

◊ ◊ ◊

Lisa and Sandy had agreed on elaborate precautions for their meeting in San Francisco. Lisa's air passage was on TWA, her flight scheduled for Tuesday evening, her return scheduled for Friday night. Sandy would fly out on Wednesday on American, with a return flight for Sunday. They were attending separate meetings and were staying at different hotels. They would meet by chance.

Barry drove Lisa to the airport. "Try to have some fun out there, sweetie. It should be great this time of year — remember how we used to love this season when we were in Palo Alto? And congratulate ourselves on not being in New York? Really think again about staying through the weekend."

Lisa sighed. "I'll see. Maybe. I'm not sure." She still found it hard to lie to him directly.

The car pulled up outside the TWA terminal. They both got out. Barry hauled Lisa's suitcase from the trunk and handed it to a skycap with her ticket. "There, Lis'. You're all checked through." He always took care of her like this, handling the logistics of travel. As if they were beyond my capabilities, she thought defensively. She felt angry at being pampered, then guilty for her anger. She slipped her arm through Barry's. "What would you like from San Francisco?"

"Just you. Safe and sound."

She flattened herself against him. Oh, Barry, she thought, dear Barry. "Be good in Paris," she said. He was leaving Thursday. His last trip, he hoped. "Springtime in Paris. And don't overeat just because it's your last trip."

"Thank God," he said, hugging her, "last trip. No more separations."

The thought momentarily paralyzed her. "I'd better go," she said.

Her flight was uneventful, the taxi ride into San Francisco exciting by contrast as they rolled along the freeway ramp that skirted the city. She studied the elegant skyline.

The new Landmarker Hotel downtown was impressively beautiful. She felt a slight panic as she rode up to her room in the open-sided elevator that looked down on the vast internal court filled with late evening drinkers, most of them, she guessed, from the convention. In her room, she unpacked quickly and went right to sleep.

The convention, staged by a consortium of western banks, brought together the financial officers of large corporations and the executives of the banks they dealt with to discuss financial service operations. From GlobeBank came a dozen account managers from the National Banking Sector who would spend the next few days wining and dining their customers while Lisa attended the sessions and made and heard presentations. They were all to meet that morning for breakfast in the GlobeBank suite, large, high-priced rooms that would serve as a hospitality bar and general meeting area.

At the breakfast, they rehearsed again the breakdown of tasks, responsibilities, and contacts that they had gone over so many times in New York.

At nine o'clock, Lisa went off to her first session of the long day.

Fourteen hours later, Lisa, two GlobeBank account managers, and three chief financial officers from large Texas oil companies were having a nightcap in the Landmarker's lounge. Lisa had been on the go all day; she hadn't once gone back to her room to freshen up. There had been meetings all morning, then lunch with a major customer who was disgruntled over repeated errors in GlobeBank's dealings with his firm, a hotel and recreation conglomerate, then more meetings. Afterward, she had joined the two account managers and their customers for drinks at the Top of the Mark and a banquet dinner, prearranged, at the Empress of China on Grant Avenue. Now the evening was coming to an alcoholic close. Another few sips, she decided, and she could make her excuses.

One of the oilmen had just told a joke: ". . . and four to turn it," he was saying. Lisa joined in the laughter. She noticed how rumpled and sweaty everyone looked, their faces tinged pink with excess. She wondered if she looked the same.

"For heaven's sake!" one of the GlobeBankers cried. "Isn't that — ? What's his name, Lisa? He's in your sector, the funds transfer system guy."

Lisa turned to look. "It is," she said, sounding surprised. "It's Sandy Lippert."

The GlobeBank account manager waved at him. "Sandy!" he called. Then he leaned over the small round table. "I think you might want to meet this guy. He built our proprietary funds transfer system. You know, Autotran. The system we use to move your domestic and overseas stuff. Might interest you guys to talk with him."

Sandy, his tie off and his collar open, approached them with a smile on his face. Lisa, keeping an attitude of polite interest, felt the rush that seeing him always produced inside her.

"Hello!" Sandy was at his most buoyant.

"Hello, Sandy," Lisa said, shaking his hand. "I had no idea you were in San Francisco."

"Just got in today," he said, "a conference over at the St. Francis." He looked around at the gathering.

"Let me introduce you," Lisa said. She went through the names and identifications.

"Sandy, join us for a drink," one of the oilmen said.

"Oh, gee," he replied, "I don't know. A couple of the fellows from the conference and I have just been through Fisherman's Wharf. And I do mean *through.*"

Everyone laughed appreciatively. "Well, I'll have a nightcap, I guess," said Sandy as he pulled up a chair. "I actually just dropped off a couple of the guys here. They couldn't get rooms at the St. Francis. I think it's a step up," he said, assessing the height of the tower.

Lisa took her key out of her purse and set it on the table while she continued to rummage through the purse. Sandy was talking about his conference.

"It's computer professionals," he was saying, "but it's strictly financial services industry. I think there's going to be quite a bit of talk about Autotran."

She put a hand on his arm. "Excuse me, Sandy," she said. She watched him look down at her key; the room number was incised on it in large gold numbers. "If you gentlemen will excuse me, I'm really very tired." She stood up. The men stood with her. "And I've really heard a lot about Autotran already." She smiled, then turned and went up to her room.

He came to her secretly that night. And the night after. On Friday, they moved together into the little hotel on Jackson Street that Jessica had mentioned. It had glowing wooden floors covered with braided rugs and an iron bedstead painted gold. There were fresh flowers everywhere.

The room was a bower; California was, for them, a bower. For the second time in her life, Lisa felt that California was a miracle, a miracle of abundance. But this time she also had Sandy. It was spring, and the air was full of colors. Gold and blue that first afternoon, when Sandy took her across the Golden Gate Bridge into Marin and she looked east to the bay, holding her hand up to her eyes against the dazzle of light melting into the water. Sparkling colors in Muir Woods, where they wandered the marked trail hand in hand past the tall trees, the blue brooks, the cascades breaking the light into tiny leaping diamonds.

They pretended that they had time, that the bright gold days would stretch ahead forever. There was so much to do, so much to see. It was a profusion; it took their breath away. One night Sandy pulled the car off the main highway and drove down, under, then up. They were on a hill, with the bridge and the city spread before them. The sky was midnight blue, the bridge copper and gold, high, proud, arching its back. Lisa moved so she could see Sandy's profile against the bridge. She felt a surge of pure happiness at the back of her throat and leaned over to kiss him, again and again, to illumine him, make him shine with her kisses.

"This is *our* time," he said to her over and over again, "and it will be all *yes.*" They ate one glorious meal after another, rented a yellow Mercedes. He bought her everything she looked at, showering her with gifts. She loved them all and would — somehow — explain them to Barry. A silly gold cable car charm. A sea-green jade bracelet from Gump's. A pale gray cashmere sweater. A string of pearls. Coral earrings set in pink gold. And small things — a porcelain egg, a straw hat, a scarf.

He paid for everything in cash. Lisa had no questions about that. It answered her own sense of caution. There would be no record of this trip — no items on credit card statements, no stubs in checkbooks.

Sandy had never felt so free. It was as though he had started life again, a better life, in this place. Love made the things he saw, the things they did, at once clearer and softer. He felt kind, somehow, loving the world around him. Everything, as he had promised, was an affirmation. Nothing caused a moment's hesitation — not even money, of which there was a limitless amount. And certainly not time, which had expanded into bright days and long nights of intense, tireless lovemaking.

Sunday, their last day, they went to Fisherman's Wharf. Sandy wanted to see it again with Lisa.

The waterfront streamed with tourists. Lisa and Sandy drove along the Embarcadero, past real waterfront, warehouses, lots, piers. They found a restaurant on the water and ate crab sandwiches on the terrace. Across the bay, sailboats skimmed gracefully. The sun felt like a light blanket on Sandy's skin and seemed to outline Lisa in gold. Like a halo around her body, he thought.

In the afternoon they went to their room, to their bed. They made love slowly, deliberately.

Afterward, Sandy spoke softly. He had something to say. "I've lived so stupidly in a lot of ways. And not very happily.

"It's true," he went on. "I had a silly upbringing, I suppose. I see now that it was rather . . . narrow, I guess. I had funny ideas, funny values. I was probably wrong to marry Kathy, but I was certainly wrong to wreck the marriage. I invested myself in the wrong things, the wrong way."

He took Lisa's face in his hands and looked into her eyes. "But it doesn't matter, you know. Because if it hadn't all happened just that way, I might never have met you, Lisa. And then I'd never know *this*. That people could love like this, could feel like this. Do you think most people have this? Do you think most people have this in their lifetime?"

She shook her head. "No."

"Then I'm lucky," he said. "I'm really lucky."

He saw her eyes glisten before she pulled his head down to her breasts.

◇ ◇ ◇

They had agreed to take separate taxis from Kennedy into New York. Two listings on two expense accounts. They waited together at the baggage carousel. Neither of them spoke.

Lisa's bag spilled out onto the carousel. She grabbed it and set it down beside her. "I'd better get a taxi," she said, looking at Sandy. "I love you," she said quickly, then picked up the bag and headed out toward the street.

His eyes followed her out the automatic doors, the sudden burst of traffic noise from outside filling his ears for a moment. He saw her as she watched her bag being loaded into the trunk of a yellow Checker cab, saw her get into the taxi, saw her lean forward to tell the driver where she wanted to go.

Lisa sat back in the seat. Her hand came up against the window to wave once. She did not look at him.

Sandy lifted his suitcase and his folding suit-pack off the carousel and went out into the cool New York night.

6

IT WAS TWO-THIRTY ON Friday afternoon, and Frank Kozlow was considering going home. It had been an easy, lazy week. Sandy was in San Francisco, at the data processing conference, and had hardly even called in. In fact, Frank reasoned, Sandy had probably left the conference by now and was heading north. He had said he was going to "disappear for the weekend out there." So there was no real reason not just to close up shop and go home to enjoy the spring afternoon.

The phone rang.

"Utility. Frank Kozlow."

"Hey, Frank. Sammy Fried here. I'm in the data center. We got trouble. The system's down."

"Shit! When?"

"Just now."

"What is it? How bad?"

"We crashed a disk. It looks real bad."

"How much did we lose?"

"Hell, Frank, I don't know that yet. We'll have to get the recovery tapes. I just got here. I'm letting you know because Sandy's out of town and somebody's going to have to authorize overtime and extra workers."

"All right, hold on, I'm coming. Where's Mel? Did you get hold of Mel Luboff?"

"He's on his way."

"So am I."

Frank sighed and looked at his watch. Damn. Sandy was probably in a winery in Sonoma by now. He would have to handle this all alone.

A blast of cool air from the special air conditioners the computers required hit him as he entered the data center. He heard his heels ringing on the hollow floor. The humming din of the machines assaulted him. He could never understand how the data center guys stood it. Mel Luboff told him he never heard the noise, never felt the cold. "You get used to it," he said.

Over the top of a row of minicomputers, Frank could see Mel. He was holding a disk up to the light, examining it through the dark, translucent cover.

Sammy Fried stood next to him. He just about comes up to Mel's shoulders, Frank thought. Mutt and Jeff. Also the best technical talent around. Sammy Fried, short and barrel-shaped, with a face that always seemed sweaty, had worked with computers since their inception. There was nothing about them he didn't know or understand. Mel Luboff, tall, skinny, with hair that looked like a crew-cut even when long, was just a natural. He could build or fix anything — from a Parsons table to a workshop to a high-powered computer.

"Looks like somebody dragged a spoon across the surface," Mel was saying as he lowered the disk to the table.

"Hi, Mel," Frank said. "What's the damage? How many payments records did we lose?"

Sammy answered. "We're still waiting to run the recovery tape. It's going to be big. Somebody should inform Lisa Gould. This disk was almost all National Services West."

"I'll call her office," Frank said. Gould outranked him; maybe she would be willing to call out the cavalry. He would sure as hell rather have her name on an authorization for overtime than his own.

But Lisa Gould was out of town, seeing customers on the coast. She was out of reach and out of touch, like Sandy. He was on his own.

The phone on the other side of the data center rang. Mel scurried over to pick it up. The data center operators went about their business, oblivious to the cold, the noise, the disk crash.

Mel walked over to Sammy and Frank, his hands in his pockets, a smile on his face. "Hold on to your hats," he said, "this is a beaut. The recovery shows there's six billion worth of payments on that disk. No idea how many were in the machine when the thing crashed and never got on the recovery tape at all."

"Holy shit!" It was Frank.

"Jee-sus," Sammy said.

"What's it going to take?" Frank asked Mel after a moment. "What do you need for this recovery?"

"Give me an hour, Frank. I'll give you a complete shopping list in an hour."

Frank Kozlow went back to his office to wait. The train time-table was on his desk. He remembered he had been hoping to get home early. Forget that. He might not get home at all. He pulled a file to do some paperwork while he waited.

Mel's call was on time, but his news was bad. "We're going to have to do a manual reconcilement," he said, "otherwise we're never going to know what was in the buffers or whatever when the thing crashed. I mean, we've got to know what was inside that didn't get on the recovery tape, right?"

"Right." Frank groaned.

"So the only real way is by hand. Item by item. Dollar amount versus item count. It's going to be a bitch."

"What'll it take?"

"I figure a dozen people. We got eight in here now. I'd feel better with four more."

"How long will we need them?"

"I'll tell you, Frank, this is going to go all night and all tomorrow at least — if we're lucky. You can forget about posting this to the bank's books, by the way. You better make that call first.

Let 'em know they're out a mere six billion in availability to play with."

"They're going to love that."

"Oh, yeah. But the uptown Accounting boys already want to break our ass, so another six billion between friends can't do much more damage."

◇ ◇ ◇

They went through three different shifts that night and into Saturday. Special clerks, at triple time for night differential and double time for Saturday. Frank Kozlow and Mel Luboff took turns sleeping on the sofa in Sandy Lippert's office.

The data center smelled of hamburgers and Coke. Frank kept making coffee. He and Mel chipped in on the work every now and then, sitting at the table with the clerks, checking dollar amount against item entry down long lists on accordion-like print-outs. "This is a hell of a way for a nice Jewish boy to spend Shabbat," Mel said at about four A.M. But he stayed with it, joking with the clerks, helping out, solving problems, keeping spirits up. Frank realized later that Mel hadn't really been obligated to stay; he wondered why he had.

At ten on Saturday morning, Frank decided to call Lisa. He had gotten her home number from Flo the day before, as well as her number in Connecticut, just in case. Flo had said that Lisa's reservation was for a Friday evening return, but she didn't know if Lisa would go to the apartment or to Connecticut. Lisa hadn't called in.

Frank dialed the New York number. No answer. There was no answer in Connecticut, either.

7

JUST AFTER LUNCH, that quiet time in offices before the phones start again, before typewriters are back at full throttle, Jessica was reading over some copy she had written. She was waiting for Derek Sykes.

It was a favor for Sandy. "Listen, Jess," he had asked over the phone that morning, "would you mind giving this kid some time? He's from England, London School of Economics, and he's here doing a paper on how big organizations put in technology to improve productivity. And I thought, you've got all that written material about Autotran and stuff. To supplement the interviews Derek's been doing. Would you?"

Derek Sykes was punctual. Jessica began with small talk. London. Her cousin Louis who had gone to LSE. Derek's studies, his future plans, how he was liking New York.

She held out a sheaf of materials. "I've put together a package of things," she said. "Have a look."

Derek liked the newsletters. "Oh, these should be quite interesting, yes. And this booklet is about the false floor, is that it? Where they keep the power cables and so forth? Oh yes, the speech. I'm told this is *the* definitive statement."

He picked up the Autotran paper, flipped over the title page, and began to read.

"Now, this I have," he said. "This is Rick Schmidt's paper, the one he submitted for the Wolcott program, isn't it?" He set the Autotran paper back on the table. "Yes, I met with Rick yesterday, and he gave it to me then."

Jessica had a sense of foreboding. "Rick's paper for the M.B.A.?"

"Yes," Derek said, reaching into his briefcase, "for his course in systems computerization." He pulled out a gray folder and handed it to Jessica. "This."

The title read: "The Impact of Technology as a Change Factor on Organizational Perspective — GlobeBank: The Automated Funds Transfer System." In the lower right corner was the course name and that of the professor. In the lower left corner was: Richard H. Schmidt, Wolcott Fellow.

Jessica turned the page and began to read. The first paragraph was all Rick. "GlobeBank is an extremely big financial institution," it began.

The second paragraph was different. "The funds transfer is the basis of virtually all banking transactions. Whether the service being performed for the customer is a loan, a letter of credit, a collection, or a foreign exchange transaction, in the end, funds are transferred from one party or location to another."

Jessica's head was moving up and down, nodding. She recognized these words. They were hers.

"Interesting," she said to Derek Sykes as her eyes continued to scan Rick's paper. Anger was rising within her — and a kind of fear as well.

"Would you mind if I Xeroxed this, Derek? Rick never did actually give me a copy."

She excused herself and walked to the Xerox room. No one else was there. She began to feed the sheets of paper into the machine. Better make two copies at least, she thought, her hands shaking.

It was plagiarism, pure and simple. That personal pique fed her reaction she had no doubt, nor did this bother her. She was furious at Rick's arrogance, so unmindful of her work that he would steal it as casually as he pleased. There was no great art to what she had done in these pages. Still, it was her work. She had researched this system. She had organized the material. She had thought out how best to present it. She had written it — clearly, lucidly, effectively. Goddamnit!

Jessica realized with a start that she cared about her writing, that for all her railing against GlobeBank and the silliness of her job, she really did care about the craft of writing and about her own value as a writer. Rick Schmidt had damaged that, and she was angry.

There was more to it than that, however.

Although it was true that she had written the paper — everybody knew it, including Rick — it was also true that the paper belonged to GlobeBank. It had first been distributed around the bank when Autotran was new, then "reissued" six months later with a new cover. It had been circulated throughout the corporation — in New York, around the country, overseas. Every copy of it was marked: Distributed by Banking Operations Sector, Global Bank Corporation.

Rick Schmidt had submitted a BOS publication for academic credit in a university without giving any credit or attribution, without a single footnote of reference. This was plagiarism, and it was wrong.

Later that afternoon, after Derek had gone, after she had finished the few tasks she had for the day, she closed the door and read Rick Schmidt's paper carefully.

It was twenty-one pages long. The first ten pages, except for the opening paragraph, were word-for-word, sentence-for-sentence, copied from the GlobeBank paper she had written. To add insult to injury, Rick's transition from her writing to his own contained a scornful slur.

"This has just been an overview of this particular system. Given all the corporate flair to sell the concept, plus presuming the reader understands the basics of the corporate funds transfer process, I'd like to turn to some of the things we learned in developing it," he had written to lead into the few pages of his own paltry thinking. Jessica thought them the work of a functional illiterate.

She put one Xerox of the paper into an orange GlobeBank file folder and set it in a drawer of her desk, underneath a set of poems by Abby. She put the other copy into a large interoffice envelope and stuffed it into her WNET tote bag to take home. She was not going to think about this now; she would think about it later. Now she was going to go home and get Abby packed for a month away at camp. Tomorrow, she herself was going off for a weekend, to the summer rental near Rhinebeck taken every year by Sonia Kirschner, her college roommate, who was now a big editor in a big publishing firm. Frederica Levin, another close friend from college, would also be there. The three of them would slop around in old clothes and eat a lot of junk food. Sonia would read manuscripts, Freddie would play the piano, and she, Jessica, would just lie on the grass thinking about nothing. She was not going to let a man like Rick Schmidt trouble her life.

David, Abby's father, was going to see Abby off to camp at Port Authority that Friday afternoon. Jessica cried a little when she said good-bye to her daughter in the morning. She gave her a stamped and addressed postcard and told her, "You mail that the minute you arrive, OK? And I'll telephone on Wednesday. And I'll see you in four little weeks!" Then she went to the office.

Her resolve not to think about Rick Schmidt was hard to

keep. Linda Glover passed the open door of her office and waved. Flo called and said that Lisa needed ten copies of the new Autotran paper at once — a bunch of visiting Sun Belt bankers were in her office. LaRocca's office called and asked if she could ask Schmidt to speak about the Wolcott experience at LaRocca's monthly managers' meeting. "Ask him yourself," Jessica replied, though politely. The Wolcott experience, my ass. She imagined Rick speaking truthfully: As you all know, he might say, I have long cheated on my wife and family as well as on those who work for me and those I work for. I have cheated on my expense account and on petty cash vouchers here at Head Office, on trips abroad, and at the Wolcott Foundation program. However, while a student there, I was able to expand and diversify my cheating skills with an outright theft of a paper that belongs to GlobeBank. The methodology was simple: I just submitted the GlobeBank paper under my name without giving any credit or attribution. Applause from the assembled mob of eager young managers, keen to get ahead. Rick Schmidt could tell them how.

At least Jessica didn't have to deal with Rick himself. Although he was back from California and working for Lisa, he was usually holed up in his office on another floor, coordinating with the Utility consultants about the conversion. Occasionally he passed her door; perhaps Lisa had summoned him or he had manufactured an excuse to "have a meeting" with Linda. When he did see her, he was always friendly, and Jessica replied politely. She was not sure she would be able to sustain politeness the next time they met; she knew the sight of him would make her flesh crawl.

◇ ◇ ◇

Jessica could relax with Sonia and Frederica in a way that she couldn't with anyone else. These were her closest friends, friends since college, where, as a trio, they had made a point of disdaining intellectual achievement in favor of getting off a funny line.

They had been part of one another's lives ever since, nursing each other's careers, marriages, divorces, lovers, new apartments, new political views.

Sonia Kirschner had pursued a career, constantly and single-mindedly, and had risen high in her field. She loved her work and did it well — by doing it all the time.

Frederica Levin had gone to England directly from college, married an actor, divorced him, and had returned home to land a job in theater management — her specialty, concert pianists. She too was good at her work — aggressive, brassy, knowledgeable. The best part of it, she would say, was being able to go free to all New York's musical events. Freddie could claim truthfully that the baby grand piano in her large West Side duplex had been "stroked," as she put it, by Emanuel Ax and Lionel Hampton, "though not at the same time."

The three women had known one another so well for so long that they communicated in code, their own buzzwords, truncated phrases.

"What's the deal?" Jessica had asked Sonia when she phoned her from the office.

"Frederica's at four."

"Eating?"

"On the way."

The house was a converted barn, with a cathedral ceiling and a broad, screened porch. Jessica sat there in a wicker chair, nursing a beer, looking out at the still night in the astonishment she always felt that the sky outside of New York City was full of stars.

Sonia had gone right to work, curled up on the living room sofa with a manuscript that she managed to keep perfectly neat. Freddie was at the piano, playing Chopin.

Not a bad time or place to consider one's life, Jessica thought. She had not said a word about Rick Schmidt or plagiarism to her friends, and she began to wonder if it would mean anything to them. They always chided her for "never discussing her work." "There's nothing to discuss," she would answer. Unlike their work, she contended, hers was neither interesting nor exciting nor particularly worthwhile. "It's just a job," she would say, "a paycheck for rent and vacations and Abby's camp. Easy to do. Silly, but basically worth it."

Frederica had stopped playing. Jessica heard the refrigerator door open. "Anybody want anything?" Freddie shouted. "Jess? Beer?"

"Yeah, OK." She went into the living room.

"Unbelievable drivel," Sonia was saying. "This writer thinks she's Jane Austen. She's not." Sonia paused. "But then, which of us is?" It was a phrase she used often.

Freddie handed Jessica a bottle of beer. "Did you want a glass?"

"This really amazing thing just happened at my office," Jessica began. She told them about Rick Schmidt and the paper. She heard herself going on to tell about how Mark Krausner had tried to pressure her into using his friend on the brochure. She told them how common it was for people at GlobeBank to take credit for other people's work, how, if you thought about it, her own job was to be someone's ghostwriter — everyone's ghostwriter, in fact. She told about the expense account cheating, the extramarital affairs at the bank's expense, the incompetence, the striving for status and title.

It took a long time to tell it all. When she finished there was silence, except for the scratchy sounds of crickets outside.

"So that's what you do on your job," Sonia said. "Very nice."

"You've got to get out of there, Jess," said Freddie. "Just quit. Just get out of there. Get another job somewhere."

"Where? What the hell kind of job do you think I can get?" Jessica asked gloomily. "I'm only educated, you know, I'm not skilled. I don't have what they call 'marketable skills.' Anyway" — she leaned back — "what makes you think it's any different anywhere else? Doesn't everybody else cheat? And sleep around? And knife everybody else to get ahead? I'm probably being unbelievably naive to be shocked by all of this."

A slight breeze came from the porch. The stars shimmered, and one fell suddenly, quickly, as if weighted, off the middle of the sky. "This is the way the world works, isn't it?" she asked, looking at where the star had been. "On avarice, greed, and absolute indifference to moral values. Rick Schmidt and his ilk — and they're all over the place at GlobeBank — they're the winners. They run the goddamn world. I'm a loser, a cipher they can easily pay no attention to."

"Jess, come on," Freddie said, "don't you think you're making too much of this? Don't get so carried away. You always get so damn cosmic. It's all those years of reading Norse epics and finding parallels with other cultures. You were always a great one for defining the 'underlying pattern.' Remember how we used to kid you about it?"

She remembered, smiling.

"You always insisted you had to see how everything cohered," Freddie went on. "You always insisted things *had* to cohere. But they don't always cohere. Look. This guy — this Schmidt — is a snake. Maybe everyone at the damn bank is a snake, all driven by self-interest. So why not take a leaf from their book and pull a little self-interest yourself and just get the hell out of there. And stop being destroyed by it."

"It *is* destructive," Jessica allowed. "Losers like me lose twice. Because it *does* matter. It matters that this is the way things are, and I don't want to get so worn down that I think it *doesn't* matter." She shrugged with her next question. "But what can I do?" she asked. "Where can I go? I have to make a living."

"There are lots of ways." It was Sonia. "You could always start a business writing papers to get people through business school. I mean it. They have such things — check the classifieds in the *Village Voice*. All sorts of offers to write papers for people, take their exams. I mean it."

The three of them sat in appalled silence for a moment. We're all horrified, Jessica realized. Thank God for that.

Freddie said, "It's all a bit more corrupt than one really realized, don't you think?"

"Oh, absolutely!" Sonia agreed heartily. "But then, which of us isn't?"

8

ELAINE GREEN PICKED UP the phone.

"Human Resources, Elaine Green speaking."

It was Kilgour. "Can you step in here a minute?"

She picked up an orange file folder marked Confidential and walked across the reception area to Kilgour's office. She stopped in front of Barbara Finn's desk, making sure the secretary could see the label on the folder. "Is he on the phone again? He just called me."

"You can go right in," Barbara said.

Kilgour did not look at her when she walked in. "No," he said into the phone, "I'm not signing any increase for him unless he gets in gear and meets the schedule. He signed off on that schedule and he's got to meet it." There was a pause. "Right. Right," Kilgour said, then hung up.

He motioned to Elaine to close the door. "God," he said, "I sometimes wonder how I manage with the imbeciles who work for me." He slid his hand inside her shirt. "Mmmmm," he said, "silk. I like that."

"Who were you talking to?" Elaine asked.

"O'Connor." He grimaced.

He kissed her, then led her over to the couch. They both sat down. He thrust his hand into her shirt again, fingering her nipple.

"Listen," he said, "I've got to be in Chicago on Monday. I'm going to go out there Sunday night. I got you a plane reservation leaving La Guardia at three on Sunday. You'll come back Monday morning at seven A.M. We're staying at the airport Hilton."

Kilgour counted out eight hundred dollars. "This should cover it. You can pick up the tickets at the TWA office at the Waldorf. And while you're there, buy yourself something else that's silky." He leaned over and nuzzled her other breast with his mouth.

"John! Don't leave a mark on the blouse!"

He snickered, and they both rose. He slapped her rear and returned to his desk.

◊ ◊ ◊

At lunchtime, Elaine walked down Park Avenue to the Waldorf. The airline office was downstairs.

"Smoking or nonsmoking?" asked the bored clerk.

"Nonsmoking, please. Aisle, if you have one left."

"I think so." The clerk was straining to sound as friendly as the TWA employees' manual required.

"How are you paying for this?"

"Cash."

It was a coach ticket; she gave the clerk three hundred-dollar bills, put the change in the zippered compartment of her lizard handbag, and walked up the carpeted steps to the lobby.

She lingered by the shops. In the Mark Cross window, she noticed a canvas suitcase covered with the MC signature. She wanted it. She would figure out a way to get John to buy it for her.

Something silky for now, though, she recalled. I'll go over to Saks.

In the lingerie department, she found a mauve silk nightgown with spaghetti straps and a low V back. She tried it on and it skimmed her hips in a way that she calculated would be provocative. "I'll take it," she told the saleslady. She looked at the price tag: $230. She paid cash.

Elaine spent Friday night and all day Saturday in Amagansett with the Wards; they always had a lot of people out on weekends. She lay on the beach all day and was too sunburned to enjoy the dinner at Gordon's on Saturday night. Still, she resented having to come back into the city early on Sunday. "A big deadline at the office," she told Debbie, Jack, and their other guests.

The early jitney moved fast on the Long Island Expressway. What a drag, Elaine thought, I've got to turn right around and come back out this way to the airport. The jitney went uptown on Third and left her at Sixty-fifth Street.

She dropped off her bag, showered, and changed into her white duck skirt and the green Herman Geist shirt. In her attaché case she packed the new nightgown, her blue bra and bikini, hose, and a royal blue dress that didn't crush, for Monday. She caught a cab on Third Avenue.

"Triborough or Queensboro?" the cabbie asked.

"Might as well take the Triborough, since you're pointed uptown. Anyway, I'm not paying for it." She leaned forward and read the cabbie's name: Saul Goldman.

"You traveling on business?" he asked.

"Yes. Going to Chicago."

"Cooler there it's not going to be. So what airline are you flying?"

"TWA, please."

"So what kind of business are you in?"

They stopped for a red light at Eighty-sixth Street. She looked west, across the street. A group of girls — Puerto Ricans, she thought — were eating hot dogs, the sauerkraut hanging like Christmas tinsel out of their mouths. People were standing dreamily in front of the movie theater, looking at the stills. Far west, she could see the tops of the trees of Central Park, motionless and dusty in the summer heat.

"I'm in banking," Elaine answered. She didn't feel like talking; it was a long ride out to La Guardia. She leaned back.

Flight 339 left on time. Elaine read *Business Week* for most of the flight.

Even on a hot Sunday afternoon, O'Hare Airport was confused and bustling, full of conservatively dressed pro-nuclear demonstrators who tried to speak to her as she walked briskly across the enormous floor. Outside, it was only a matter of crossing the drive to the O'Hare Hilton.

In the room, she called Room Service and ordered a bottle of white wine. Kilgour would be there by seven. The wine arrived, a Styrofoam tray with a Styrofoam ice bucket. The green bottle sat inside the bucket, surrounded by ice. Elaine poured a glass and sat down to wait.

This isn't much fun, she thought, wishing she were back on the beach in Amagansett. John always expects me to be on call, and I'm always the one who has to sit around waiting. Maybe he buys me silk nightgowns, but I'm still his employee. Paid in silk nightgowns from Saks.

Well, you knew what you were getting into, she said to herself. And you've gotten what you wanted — the vice president title, some nice things.

This isn't one of them, she decided, looking around the room. At least the last time he kept me waiting like this, it was in the Santa Barbara Biltmore. She smiled, remembering how the beach looked from the terrace and the beautiful woodwork in the cocktail lounge on the main floor.

I can't make any plans, though, she reminded herself sullenly. He wants me when he wants me. Like last month, when I had to break that weekend date with Peter because his goddamn wife went to her mother's. And today the Wards. It's just typical.

I guess it's worth it. There are times when he has to do what I tell him. Anything to get that little thing up.

She heard his key in the door. "That's fine, I can manage," he was saying heartily to the bellhop. He took his Crouch & Fitzgerald bag and threw it on one of the beds.

"Jesus, it's hot. You look sunburned," he said. He sat down on the other bed, took off his jacket, and loosened his tie. Elaine went over and sat down next to him. "Tired?" she asked.

"Not too tired. I'm going to take a shower, though."

He stood up, took his clothes off, and went into the bathroom.

"When you come out, I'll show you what I bought," she said to his back.

◇ ◇ ◇

"Lovely," he remarked, looking at the nightgown. "Put it on."

She undressed and slipped the nightgown over her head. "Like it?"

He pulled the towel from around his waist and turned on the radio. He started twirling the dials. "I'm looking for some dance music." Finally, he found a station that satisfied him. Lush strings. Slow foxtrots. Elaine remembered that he was much older than she. He took her into his arms and they danced, Kilgour humming in her ear. He stopped every few seconds to rub his groin against the silkiness of her nightgown, his hands stroking her smooth thighs and buttocks through the cloth.

The music changed to a tango. Elaine suddenly felt giddy. The wine she had sipped steadily while waiting was getting to her, making her feel light-headed. She swirled off, dipping her hips in a disco style, clicking imaginary castanets in the air. Kilgour poured himself a Scotch from the bottle of Chivas he pulled out of his suitcase and sat down to watch. Elaine's dance was getting wilder. She was dancing in circles; she yanked the bedspread off one of the beds and twirled it around her like a toreador's cape. The silk nightgown rippled on her hips. She saw his eyes widen slightly. This turns him on, she realized.

Kilgour's hand was on his penis. The tango stopped and Elaine stopped. "Dance," said Kilgour. He started rubbing himself. She danced through a samba and a couple of show tunes. "I'm worn out," she said.

294

"I'm not," said Kilgour.

Elaine sat down, slightly out of breath. "Sit on me," Kilgour said. She eased herself down on his lap. "My new nightgown is getting all sweaty."

"Take it off," he ordered, his voice hoarse.

She raised herself up slightly, pulled the gown up over her head, and dropped it on the other chair.

"Look at me," Kilgour said.

She turned to look directly into his face. His eyes were glittering; she had never seen him look like that. "Look at me," he ordered again, "keep looking at me."

Very slowly, he raised his glass of Scotch — nearly full, she noticed, a water glass from the bathroom — and poured it down each breast, a little at a time. He watched it run down, dripping off her nipples onto her stomach and her pubic hair.

"Get on the bed," he commanded.

She lay on her back. Kilgour knelt beside her.

"I'm going to lick all that good Scotch off your tits," he said. He started licking her. "Oh, my cunt, oh, wet pussy, oh, fuck." He licked her up and down.

His mouth sucked hungrily between her legs. She giggled, seeing how hard he had gotten. His cock is in my face, she thought. Might as well ... She shifted slightly and took him in her mouth. He tasted of soap from his shower. She ran her tongue over the tip of his penis, lingering at the opening. He moaned with pleasure. "Suck me," he commanded. She moved her head, pumping, lubricating him with her saliva, feeling the blood beating against his skin. "Faster," he said. She moved her head faster, put her hand on his testicles, stroking them. "Now slower." He grabbed her hair, pulling her head back and forth the way he wanted.

The wine bottle was on the floor near the bed. He could just see it. He reached until he could pick it up, pulled the cork out with his teeth, and poured what was left of the wine onto the floor. He licked the neck of the bottle until it was wet. "Lift your leg," he said. He shoved the neck of the bottle inside Elaine, twisting it back and forth.

She had watched him with fascination, knowing that he was going to put that bottle into her. It felt smooth, cool, hard. She could feel her loins tightening around the glass. Up and down went her mouth on his penis. Flecks of saliva appeared at the corners of her mouth.

"I'm coming now," he cried out. She felt the spasms in her mouth — one, two, three, and then four, and that was all. Then her mouth was full, the warm, salty liquid slid down her throat, and she could feel drops trickling down her chin.

She squirmed on the bottle, tightening her thighs as Kilgour turned the neck around and around. He was watching her face, but she suddenly didn't care what she looked like. She hunched up on her elbows and stared at the bottle between her legs. "John," she said, "oh yes." He looked at her, smiling. She threw her head back. Her legs started to jerk. "Aaaooohh . . ." she sobbed. She felt herself exploding.

She slowly became aware of the radio again. It was playing a medley from *My Fair Lady*.

Kilgour had fallen asleep. Elaine looked at her watch. It was a quarter to ten. She would have to wake him up if she was going to get any dinner. Can't have Room Service in here, she thought. The room smelled of sex mixed with spilled Scotch and wine; clothes and bedding were all over the floor. I'll take a shower before I wake him, she said to herself, get his scum off me.

9

JESSICA HAD LOOKED FORWARD to the four weeks Abby would be away as a time when she could do exactly what she liked with her evenings. She wanted to see plays and go to concerts. She also wanted to spend time with Roger Bleiweiss, a TV producer she had met recently whom she found quite attractive.

She was able to do it all, but it was somehow poisoned for her by her nagging worries over GlobeBank. The Rick Schmidt incident, she realized, had opened a whole Pandora's box of feelings about GlobeBank and the people there. She was known for her irreverence, of course; what was startling to her was to realize that all her witty insults about the place were in fact deeply felt. It's all true, she decided; everything I've been saying about the place is true.

Rick had been the last straw. On the subway to and from work, during operas in the park, lying with Roger on a blanket under the stars, listening to huge voices coming out of tiny figures hundreds of yards away, in the office and out, she argued with herself over what to do about it. She talked about little else. On the Friday morning before Abby was due home, as she and Roger were getting dressed, she had come up with yet another reason that doing anything about it was futile. "The only one I can really talk to about this is my boss," she was saying, "but in fact, Rick didn't work for her when he did the deed. So I'm really stuck."

Roger zipped up his faded Levi's and pulled on a gray shirt. "He worked for GlobeBank, though, didn't he? And your boss is a big muckety-muck at GlobeBank. Doesn't she have a reason to protect the bank's good name?"

"That may be stretching things a bit, Roger."

He went over to her. She stood in the middle of the bedroom, wearing underwear and a slip. She was bent at the waist and was drying her hair furiously with a towel.

"Will you please get your head out from under that thing for a minute?" Roger asked.

Jessica stood up, and Roger laughed.

"You look like Medusa," he said, "but listen to me anyway."

"That's a terrific thing to say to somebody," Jessica said, smiling. "It's a little like saying, 'You remind me of Hitler.' "

"Just listen a minute," Roger said, putting his hands on her shoulders. "I think you should do something about this plagiarism thing. It is driving you crazy, and frankly, you are driving everyone around you crazy. I speak as one who has been around you — as well as in, on, and under you — a great deal lately." Jessica smiled. She lowered her cheek to brush it against Roger's hand. "I think that, for your sanity, you have to do something."

"Yeah, but do what, Roger? That's the thing."

"Talk to your boss. That's what you seem to get back to each time. You say she's a decent sort. Tell her about it. Why are you so hesitant?"

"Because," Jessica said very slowly, "because I'm afraid she might tell me I'm being silly."

"I thought you admired this woman!" Roger threw his hands up in mock despair.

Jessica was shaking her head. "It's not that simple, Roger. Oh, shit! People like you, you and Frederica and Sonia, all of you — you don't work in these corporate environments. You really don't know what it's like."

"OK, tell me. What's it like?"

Jessica's head was still moving back and forth. "Admire her? I don't know. She's the best of a bad lot. Like her? I suppose so. Christ! I've got to like somebody where I work; I spend most of my life there. But I don't know, I don't know. She is what she is. That's what I'm afraid of."

"And what is she?" Roger asked softly.

Jessica looked at him in exasperation. "She's a division head," she said.

◇ ◇ ◇

Jessica's first stop that morning was at Lisa's office. She was going to ask Flo to get her on Lisa's calendar, but instead she ran into Lisa herself.

"Hi," she said. "I'd like to get on your calendar today. It's a personal matter, very important."

Lisa looked at her with a steady gaze. She called over to Flo, "Have I got any free time today?"

Flo pressed CLNDR. "Not really. Do you need some?"

"Yes," Lisa answered. "For Jessica."

"You've got Tony and Taddeusz at three this afternoon. You could probably see them later, or Monday."

"Handle it, Flo, would you?" Lisa turned to Jessica. "Come at three. Is that OK?"

"Fine," Jessica said. "That's fine."

She spent the morning marshaling her arguments. She wrote them down on a piece of paper: The good of GlobeBank. Your role as a senior manager of the institution. Key to Rick Schmidt's character. The meaninglessness of his M.B.A. degree. What this does to other M.B.A. degrees. The Wolcott program's reaction. Damage to me.

At three she went to Lisa's office and sat in one of the chairs outside the door, which was open. Tony and Linda were there — going over numbers, no doubt, Jessica thought. In her hands were the two papers, the one she had written and Rick's.

At three-fifteen, Tony and Linda emerged, laughing. Jessica headed toward the open office door. Linda hovered near her. "Excuse me," Jessica said quietly to Linda as she closed the door.

Jessica sat opposite Lisa at the long, blond table. She placed the two papers in front of her and began.

Lisa didn't interrupt. She listened while Jessica told how she'd discovered the Schmidt paper, heard her call what Rick had done "plagiarism," heard her mention "academic integrity" and "the good of this corporation in the long run," heard her say that "at Bryn Mawr, you were almost automatically expelled for this."

When Jessica finished, Lisa looked down at the papers and flipped through them briskly. She leaned forward, her hands clasped in front of her on the table.

"First of all," she said, "I don't think this is as bad as you make it out to be. I mean really, Jessica, what exactly did Rick plagiarize, as you put it?"

Jessica swallowed. She put her hand on the paper. "He presented this, which I wrote, as his work. That is plagiarism, Lisa."

"The words are yours, Jessica, but the ideas are his. Be honest."

"What ideas? This is a goddamn description of an automated funds transfer system. There is no great thought here. He gave me information, yes, but so did Sammy Fried. So did Sandy Lippert. So did a lot of people. But that's not the point," Jessica went on. "The point is not who built Autotran. The point is who wrote this paper. You know the answer to that one."

"Hold it," Lisa said, "just a minute. OK? Just relax." She cast about in her mind for what to say next. "OK, I agree. He stole it from you, and perhaps you can call it academic plagiarism. Now that we agree on that, let's discuss the issue realistically."

Lisa stood and began to pace the room. "You know how these fellowship programs work? I'll tell you how they work. The guys who go to these programs have already been successful managers somewhere. When they have a paper to write, they dip into their own experience. You would do the same thing."

"I wouldn't cheat, though," Jessica said quietly.

"Why is it cheating for him to write about a project he worked on?"

"The cheating is not in the fact that he wrote about Autotran; the cheating is in the fact that he submitted as his work a paper that belongs to this corporation and that *he did not credit this corporation.*" Jessica felt herself growing angry. She had promised herself she would not get angry; she tried now to calm down.

"Oh, hell, Jess, they all do it! Everybody does it!"

"In the first place," Jessica said, her voice steady again, "that's bullshit. Everybody does it, so it's OK? That's in the first place. In the second place" — Jessica sighed. Why did this have to be so difficult? Why did she have to explain all this? — "in the second place, you're wrong. Not everybody does it. I don't do it. I don't cheat." She paused. "Do you?"

Lisa blanched. She said nothing.

Jessica spoke again quickly. "I don't believe you would plagiarize, Lisa. I don't believe it. But that's not the issue here. The issue here is that Rick Schmidt did."

Lisa had sat down again. "I just don't think I see it as all that terrible, Jessica."

"Look Lisa. You care about this corporation, don't you?"

"Yes, I do. I do care about it."

"Don't you see" — Jessica was growing hot again — "doesn't it seem to you that this sort of action undermines GlobeBank at some level? Some very important level? This man is a vice president of this bank. He acts in a highly unethical manner. Don't you think that's bad for GlobeBank in the long run? If you care about the bank, this has got to matter to you. It just *has* to."

Lisa surreptitiously looked at her watch. In a few hours, she and Barry would be heading for Connecticut. She dreaded the thought. She and Sandy hadn't been together for three days. It would be at least another three before they could meet.

"I don't know, Jess," she said quietly. "I guess I just don't see it that way." She regarded Jessica's costume. Dark curly hair and big hoop earrings. Another T-shirt that she undoubtedly bought at the dime store. A wide, flowery skirt.

"Really, Jessica," Lisa said, "I think I can understand your personal pique. Nobody likes to have their work used like this. I guess if I were you, I'd be upset too. Between us, I don't think Rick is the nicest guy in the world, either. But I'm not concerned with nice guys. I need good production managers. And Rick is a hell of a good production manager. I need him in my shop."

That, thought Jessica, is that.

Lisa sighed. "Well, here's what I can do. I can talk to Rick" — the thought was distasteful, but it *was* her job, it was why she was a senior manager — "and tell him he is not to deal with you directly on any assignment he may have; he has to come to me for approval, and I'll assign it if I see fit."

Nothing, Jessica thought, she has understood nothing. Am I so out of step with things here?

Lisa smiled. "Will that do it?" she asked, her manner cozy and friendly.

Jessica said quietly, "No. That won't do it at all."

"Well, what the hell do you want me to do?" Lisa was annoyed. "Why don't you just tell me what the hell you think I should do?"

"I don't know what you should do, Lisa. You should do what's best for the corporation. What that is, I leave to you to figure out. That's why you're a division head drawing down eighty thousand a year or whatever and I'm a staff flunky." Jessica stood up. "I can't tell you what to do, only to do what you think right." She paused. "Just as I will do what I think is right."

Jessica picked up the two papers. "You have a busy afternoon, I'm sure," she said as she went out the door quickly, almost running down Flo in the process.

"Everything OK with Jessica?" Flo said in a concerned tone.

"Yes," said Lisa, "I handled it."

◇ ◇ ◇

Jessica opened the blinds the next day to a sunny, warm Saturday. She had brought in the paper and was sipping a cup of coffee when the phone rang. An old friend, Gene Mandel, wanted her to come by that evening. He was having a few people over for a cookout on the large terrace that was the reason he had bought his small apartment.

"What shall I bring?" Jessica asked.

"Potables. You still drinking beer these days?"

She said she was and would bring some.

The phone rang again. It was Frederica. "Hi. If you're foot-loose, why don't we have a long lunch someplace?"

They met at Charlie's, in the theater district. It was crowded when they arrived, but by two, the actors and the theatergoers had all headed for their matinees. Jessica and Freddie lingered over salad, wine, and numerous coffees.

"Did anything ever happen about that plagiarism thing?" Freddie asked.

Jessica dismissed the topic with a wave of her hand. "Oh, I don't know, really. I don't feel like talking about it; I talked about it a lot for a while."

So they talked of other things: of Abby, of Jessica's excitement over Abby's return, of men, of summer, of work.

"You know, Jess, have you ever thought about writing ad copy? You're very clever at aphoristic kinds of things. I think you'd do very well at it. Maybe you should try doing some free-lance stuff."

It was, Jessica realized, a possibility she had never considered. She told Freddie she thought she'd like to try. As they left Char-lie's, she wondered what other possibilities there might be.

◊ ◊ ◊

There was a group of about twenty at Gene Mandel's. Jessica knew some of them quite well; others were new faces. Everyone had a rather lobsterish look, she thought. They've probably all been out sunbathing today.

The discussion got on to politics, to the race for the Demo-cratic senator from New York and who are you backing for mayor next time around. The sunset was violet and pink. Jessica had brought two six-packs of beer. There was a lot of wine.

People moved in and out between kitchen and terrace, bring-ing things, preparing salads, getting more ice. The terrace was wide and spacious, going around three sides of the roof. It held a picnic table with benches, two chaises, and several chairs. A stack of records on the stereo inside alternated Vivaldi with the Who, Waylon Jennings with Itzhak Perlman.

Jessica was getting mellow on beer and the view of the river, tinged by the reflected sunset.

Night came on. Everyone was high, happy. People began to tell funny stories about the office.

Jessica suddenly tried to picture some GlobeBank people here, at this party, on this terrace, tonight. It was a totally different world. They'd be lost here. They would fit in, she decided, about as well as she fit in at GlobeBank.

The realization was a cold one. She was in the wrong world. One third of her life was spent in a place in which she was an alien, if not a pariah. Jessica shivered.

"You cold?" asked Gene Mandel, sitting beside her at the picnic table.

"No." Jessica smiled, leaning against him. "I feel lovely."

She spent Sunday cleaning the apartment, shopping for Abby's favorite foods, buying fresh flowers for the homecoming. She read the paper and took a walk. Four-thirty came at last; she got on the subway and headed for the West Side and David's apartment.

Abby opened the door. Jessica's face registered an instant of amazement before she gathered her daughter into a ferocious hug. "Oh, excuse me, miss," she said, moving back to look at her again, "I thought you were my daughter, Abby, but you're at least eight hundred inches taller than Abby. Also, my Abby has the pale white skin of a kid who is constantly kept cooped up in the city by her unfeeling mother. And my Abby has dark hair, not this reddish stuff you've got."

Laughing, Abby protested, "Come on, Mom."

Jessica turned to David. "Who's the imposter? Do you know?"

"I have no idea. She's done a pretty good job, though. She really picked up a lot of inside information that only Abby could know."

Jessica looked at her daughter through narrowed eyes. "OK, kid, what did you do with Abby?"

"Mom! Come on!"

Jessica smiled and hugged Abby again. "I am so glad to see you. You look so beautiful! Did you really have a good time?"

"Oh, sure. *Really* good!"

"Well, you'll tell me all about it at dinner. Now go get your stuff together. I want to talk to Daddy for a few minutes."

"Anything up?" David asked with concern as Abby pranced down the hall, Jessica following her with her eyes.

"She looks terrific, doesn't she, Dave?"

"Yes, she does. So what's up, Jess? Will you please sit down?"

Jessica sat. "I want to tell you about something that happened at work." She told him about Rick Schmidt and the plagiarism and about Lisa and their talk.

"What are you going to do now?" David asked.

"What do you think I should do? What can I do?"

David leaned back. "How can I answer that, Jess?"

"Tell me my choices."

"Well, you can go over Lisa's head."

"No good. I can't talk to those guys at all."

"OK. You can deal directly with the Wolcott trustees. With the professor, maybe. You could probably sue Schmidt, you know." David leaned forward. "If you establish that you're a professional writer — and you can — and if you can prove that he plagiarized, which probably means presenting documentation — notes and stuff — then you could probably sue him for professional damages. But I wouldn't recommend it," he concluded. "It would be a colossal pain in the ass. Long, difficult. And if you hurt this guy, who knows what he might try to do to you? We already know that he's not exactly God's gift to decency."

Jessica stood up and walked to the window. Outside, people were strolling lazily along Seventy-ninth Street.

"David, if I quit my job, will I get unemployment?"

David seemed surprised. "No, I don't think so. There are certain situations . . . but no, I don't think in your case. Are you thinking of quitting, Jess?"

"The place . . . the place has become hateful to me. I'm losing my perspective, Dave, my sense of humor. I can't see straight anymore. I can't tell if I'm blowing this thing out of all proportion or what."

He shrugged. "They're *your* proportions, kid. I've always thought they were pretty good ones. And listen, if it's money you're worried about . . . Well, don't worry about money. Just do what you think you should do. Decide."

Jessica leaned over and kissed him. He understood. It helped her. "Thanks, Dave."

Abby came back into the room.

"OK," Jessica said, "what's it going to be? Chinese? Japanese? Italian? Mexican? Hungarian? You've probably eaten nothing but white bread for a month."

"Can we have a hamburger?"

"Very patriotic. We'll go to the Allstate. OK?"

"Yea!" said Abby.

In the narrow, brick-walled restaurant, over a hamburger and a glass of milk, Abby talked nonstop about camp. She had a new, absolutely, positively *best* best friend from Teaneck. They had promised faithfully to write and phone and visit.

"Can I, Mom? Can I go there? There's a bus."

"Listen, Ab, take a break and do some eating," Jessica said. "I want to ask you something."

"What?" Abby bit into her hamburger.

"Suppose," Jessica began, leaning over to wipe Abby's chin, "suppose you were involved in something you had to be involved in."

"Like what?"

"Don't talk with your mouth full. Well, like school. I mean, you have to go to school. It's the law, right?"

Abby nodded.

"And suppose you discovered something yecky going on there. Something bad, something wrong. What would you do?"

"Tell you," Abby said quickly.

Jessica shook her head. "Suppose I'm not around. Forget parents. What would *you* do?"

Abby considered. "Well," she said slowly, "I would tell the principal."

"OK. Good girl. And suppose the principal said to you that you were making too big a thing of it, that everybody did it, but you still really knew it was wrong. What would you do then?"

Abby put her milk glass to her mouth. Jessica heard loud laughter from the bar. At the next table, a woman hailed the waitress: "Sukie, can I have another Guinness, please?"

"Well," Abby said, "I would tell the *New York Times* about it."
Jessica smiled. "You would?"
"Um-hum. And I would quit school."
"Why?"
"Well, because if I told the principal, and he knew I thought it was yecky, how could I stay there? And if you stay around yecky stuff, then you get yecky too."

Jessica looked at the little girl with love. She knew she should tell her to stop kicking the table leg, but she didn't.

◊ ◊ ◊

Jessica wrote the letter that night. First thing in the morning, she gave it to Flo to give to Lisa. Then she went into her office to start cleaning out her stuff.

Lisa Gould, VP
National Services West Division, BOS
GlobeBank

Dear Lisa:

In accordance with GlobeBank policy and procedures, I hereby tender my resignation, effective two weeks from today.

An accumulation of events has convinced me that the Globe-Bank environment is unsympathetic to my goals and style. I believe I will be more productive, both professionally and personally, outside the GlobeBank structure.

I will also tell you that I intend to pursue the matter we discussed last week with the appropriate professor in the Wolcott Foundation's Senior Management Program.

I would not wish to leave the corporation without telling you how much I appreciate your many kindnesses to me. I wish you great success in your career.

Sincerely,
Jessica Moser

Jessica was poised on tiptoe, reaching for some looseleaf binders on an upper shelf, when she heard her office door slam shut behind her. It was Lisa.

Her face was white, splotched with red dots of anger. She shook Jessica's letter at her. "What is this? What's going on? What are you talking about?" Lisa's voice was cold and tight.

"I've quit, Lisa, just like it says in the letter. I'm leaving GlobeBank."

"You're not leaving GlobeBank!" Lisa said it with disdain, as if the idea were preposterous.

"Yes, I am. I really am."

"Jess, but why? Why?"

"I think the letter explains it."

Lisa sank down into the chair. "Oh, Jessica. This Schmidt thing has taken you over. You're making it into a crusade. Why is it such a big deal, such a goddamn serious thing with you?" Her voice became icy.

"Lisa," Jessica said after a moment, "if I had had any doubt about quitting, any scruple of an iota of a doubt, that dispels it. Did you honestly not know I was serious?"

"Oh, Jessica. Rick Schmidt is such a nonissue."

"It wasn't just Rick. That was the last straw, that's all." Jessica took a deep breath. "Now listen, Lisa," she said, "because I want to tell you this as straight as I know how." She spoke evenly. "So hear me out. Maybe it's true that Rick's plagiarism is a small thing. Maybe I've blown it up out of all proportion. But I try to see it the way you see it, and I just can't. I've been thinking a lot about this, Lisa. Believe me, it wasn't just a matter of striking poses. There have just been too many things."

"What do you mean, 'too many'?" Lisa asked.

"Do you remember the Eddie Phelps business, for instance?"

"Sure I do. What about it?"

"This is what about it. Kilgour holds absolute sway around here. Not since Louis the Fourteenth has such absolute power been held by one man."

"Stop it, Jessica," Lisa said. "That's a stupid, wise-ass thing to say."

"Maybe so," Jessica admitted, "but it's also true. As witness Eddie Phelps. One day Kilgour decides to automate the Municipal Tax area, right? And maybe knock a million more heads?"

"Yes. Right," Lisa said tentatively.

"So he gets Eddie to do a big study and come up with a plan. And by and by Eddie comes back with the answer that 'it won't fly' — or whatever the expression is. Am I getting it wrong?"

"Not exactly the way I'd put it, but no, you're not getting it wrong."

"It won't fly because the cities are not willing, are light-years away from cooperating with us on the input or the parameters and flows, or whatever it is. Still right?"

Lisa nodded.

"And what does Kilgour say to that? He says, 'Do it anyway.' As if by the force of his will he can make this thing succeed. And Eddie goes back and tries again."

"I don't know what you're getting at, Jessica," Lisa said hotly. "What's wrong with that? John Kilgour has done a lot of things around here by the force of his will, as you put it. That's why we are where we are."

"My point exactly," Jessica said. "But let me finish. I'm just getting to the good part. So Kilgour gets him to buy two million dollars' worth of equipment, right? Computers to 'make it fly.'" The disdain in her voice was audible to her, and she cleared her throat. "The project flops. Big surprise. Eddie — who's been with the bank for thirty years — Eddie, needless to say, is left holding the bag. Even though he predicted disaster. And now he sits in some small crummy office, working on 'special projects,' and for the last three years he hasn't gotten a raise because every time his papers come through, Kilgour nixes it. Kilgour doesn't want to see Eddie Phelps, doesn't want to hear his name."

"Well, after all — " Lisa started to say.

"No, let me finish, Lisa. Meanwhile, the credit on the two million for the totally unused equipment that we never picked up is coming due next month — Mel Luboff told me — and the bank is about to pour another two million into this flopperoo. But not as a consolation prize to Eddie. Nothing for Eddie."

"I still can't see exactly what you're getting at," Lisa insisted. "This is a business, not a social agency. A business takes risks. And where there are risks, there are also consequences. You know that, Jessica." She thought of Eddie Phelps in his small office and felt a twinge. "But don't make us out to be monsters. That's naive. And you're not naive, Jessica, you're smart, and you're good at what you do, and I came in here to ask you to reconsider."

"Monster? I'll tell you what's a monster, Lisa. This place is a monster. It gobbles people up."

"It hasn't gobbled *you* up," Lisa cried.

"No, it hasn't," Jessica said calmly. She felt better now. "And it won't. That's the point about Eddie Phelps, Lisa. Don't you see? It isn't just that they walked all over him, but that he took it. He just took it. Well, I'm not going to take it."

Lisa silently creased the letter in her hand into thirds, and into thirds again. Finally she said, "I'll see if I can get you some money, some termination pay." She stood by the door. "You could have had a real future here, Jessica. I intend to go very far, you know; I was counting on taking you with me."

"That's one journey I can't afford," Jessica said.

10

"SANDY, WE GOT trouble."

Sandy looked up from the memo he was writing. "What's up, Frank?"

"A potential blowup. Big. We have an electrical fail."

"Shit! Where?" Sandy was on his feet, the pen still in his hand.

"One whole line," Frank said. "A whole line of machines is out, all along this one cable. The machines aren't just down, they're dead. Head Office is screaming."

"Did you call Electrical?"

"They're on their way." Kozlow was nodding.

"What about BUG?" Sandy asked, referring to the Back-Up Generator GlobeBank had installed long ago, after the first New York blackout.

"It's up, but it isn't churning much juice."

"Shit!" Sandy said again. "What the hell good is a back-up generator if it doesn't goddamn generate?"

He threw the pen down on his desk. The memo would have to wait. Everything would have to wait. The power failure was big; the implications were big. No one knew that better than he.

All Autotran did all day was transfer funds. It was the backbone of virtually every transaction the bank processed. Input came from machines up at Head Office, or was phoned in, or was Faxed down, or was sent on special forms in special pouches brought every half-hour in special vans.

Other input — a lot of it — came across GlobeBank's Inter-Traxx, the international communications switching network. Europe's transactions went to London; transactions from the Far East went to Tokyo; transactions from the Middle East, thousands of them, constant shifts of petrodollars, were funneled through Riyadh and Cairo. And they all came to Autotran via InterTraxx.

The international traffic was already a burden on the system. It was why Sandy had spent almost half his time on planning the London Autotran, was about to spend another week in London, in fact, so that transactions could be processed there and not sent to New York. It was why plans for a Tokyo Autotran facility and a Cairo Autotran facility were on the drawing boards.

With eight machines down, the others would be excessively burdened. Maybe enough to blow up the entire Autotran system. The back-up computers were only for emergencies; they couldn't handle all the traffic. If Autotran blew, the bank would be back to manual processing. The backlog would be enormous. The bank would miss deadlines, lose float, be liable for stiff penalties. Service would be disrupted, customers would be angry, money would be lost.

Well, disaster was one of the eventualities he had taken into account in designing Autotran.

"Frank, get on the phone to all the division heads. Break into meetings if you have to. Tell them what's up; tell them we're moving to an automatic queue mode. Tell them to alert their people." Sandy's hand was on his own phone. "I'll call Kilgour. And Frank," he called out to Frank's back, "tell them we'll stay in touch. Marie!"

His secretary was in the doorway as Sandy finished punching Kilgour's number. "We've got a potential blowup, Marie. Get me Sammy Fried. He may be uptown with LaRocca. Tell him to . . . Barbara? Sandy. Is John available? It's an emergency."

"Keep me informed," Kilgour said gloomily when Sandy had told him the news. "That's some generator we put in. Works all the time except when you need it." He snorted. "Call me once an hour."

Marie rushed in. "Sammy's on his way. I told him what I heard Frank tell you. Is that OK?"

"That's good."

"There's more. The people on the floor are getting calls from the machine operators uptown. The uptown machines are flickering, they say. Some are slowing down. The people up there don't know what's going on."

"They will soon enough," Sandy said. He ripped a piece of paper off his pad and ran down the hall.

Pushing open the glass doors to the floor, Sandy stopped suddenly. It was the quiet. Reduced keyboard clacking. The floor *looked* different, strange. There was an entire line of machines with solid black faces where Sandy expected, at this time of day, to see flashing words and figures. The people who worked those machines were all near the coffeepot, some standing, some sitting and chatting quietly. The machines stood blank. The guts have been ripped out of the place, Sandy thought.

He strode forward. "Vince? You want to give me a hand?" he said to one of the men, Vince Palumbo, an old-timer and a reliable Autotran operator. His machine was one of the eight that were down.

"Did Electrical get here yet?" Vince asked, falling into step with Sandy.

"Not yet." Sandy pushed open the heavy glass door into the control booth. "Hold this, will you, Vince?" He handed him the sheet of paper. "I just want to bring up the system."

Sandy deftly worked all the buttons on the console, activating an emergency break-in to all Autotran communications. The break-in notified every machine that an all-screen message was coming down the switching system.

Sandy sighed and looked at his watch. "I'll give them a minute to come to attention," he said. In his mind, he pictured people in GlobeBank offices all over the world waiting now for his message. He knew how it would be uptown at Head Office, in National Services West, in O'Connor's shop, in Doug North's world. Got to hang up, dear, my machine's going wild. Something big must be happening.

He had built this in: the Contingency Alert Mechanism, CAM. It had been considered, in theory, one of the best control and security features of Autotran. Now it would be tested.

He looked at his watch again. Eleven forty-two. In London, where machine operators waited for his message, it was four forty-two in the afternoon. Late for London. That was bad. In Tokyo it was tomorrow, but early enough in the day. In Tokyo they were also waiting for his message. In Cairo, in Sydney. InterTraxx hovered in suspension, waiting for Sandy Lippert's message. It was, he realized, a unique power.

"Vince, just read what I've written, and I'll key it."

Vince Palumbo read slowly and carefully: ALERT BULLETIN STOP ALERT BULLETIN STOP ELECTRICAL FAILURE NEW YORK STOP AUTOMATIC QUEUE MODE IN EFFECT NOON NEW YORK TIME STOP SECURE ALL TRANSACTIONS VIA HARD COPY STOP REPEAT: SECURE ALL TRANSACTIONS VIA HARD COPY STOP STAY ON LINE FOR REGULAR BULLETINS STOP.

Sandy swiveled to a small keyboard and quickly programmed a timing mechanism that would activate the message every five minutes for the next half-hour. Sammy should be here by then, he reasoned, as well as the electricians.

"Thanks, Vince. Where the hell are the electricians, for Chrissake?"

He walked over to the coffeepot.

"How's it going?" Edna Repke asked.

"Under control," said Sandy. "Listen, did we have any absences today?"

"Howard Shlinsky took a personal day. And Rosalie's out."

"And Don," added Sal Ferrara.

"Oh yes," said Edna. "Don Osterman's out."

"Were they on the line that's down, any of them?" asked Sandy.

"Don's machine is on that line," Edna answered.

"So that makes two machines live and unmanned. Edna, Sal, could you please bring them up. And stand by. We may have to put you on duty there full-time today. It'll be a hassle, but I'm sure you know what's going on here."

"Sure, Sandy," said Edna, rising from the small brown sofa.

Sandy turned around. "OK, everybody. Can I have your attention?" His voice was artificially big. The workers turned to look at him.

"I guess you all know we've got a minor blackout along one cable here. I don't know yet how bad it is or how long it will last. The first concern is to control it and not overload the rest of you. As you know, I've just sent a bulletin out from the controller to all points, and we're going into an automatic queue mode in a few minutes. So just keep working steadily and handle what comes in as it happens. If any of you" — Sandy's voice grew louder, deeper, somber — "see any flickering of light on your screen, or if you notice any slowing at all, just let me know, will you? Just finish the transaction on the screen and let me know at once. OK? Thanks."

He went back to his office.

"Frank, did you reach everyone?" Frank was on the phone; he nodded.

"Marie" — Sandy was still moving — "can you get Luis on the phone?"

"He just called, by the way." She was punching the number.

Luis Sierra was the daytime operator in the InterTraxx room. Over the phone, Sandy confirmed what Luis had already learned from the Alert Bulletin.

"I think we're OK, Luis," Sandy said. "Just hold tight. Let me know if anything irregular happens. I really can't give you much more news until the electricians get here."

Frank came in. "I reached all the division heads. Everybody's OK. North made some nasty comment, but everyone else was pretty nice."

"Fuck North. Listen, Frank, we've got to set up a process for the next twenty-four hours. Just in case." He sat down. Frank sat down opposite his boss and grabbed the lined pad from the desk. Sandy wondered briefly where he had put the messy draft memo he had started. Had he thrown it out?

"First, start putting together a list of names for a nighttime work force. You better plan to stay here yourself. I'll stay. We'll assume Sammy will be here. And the group heads.

"I want a process for impounding copies of all the transactions put on hard copy. Only Head Office stuff, obviously, not the overseas. *If* we blow up, we're going to have a hell of a record-keeping and reconstruction job ahead of us. Officially, it's the responsibility of Head Office, but I want us to cover our ass. *Their* ass, actually.

"Phones. I want both my lines free for incoming calls. We'll use your phone for any outgoing.

"Food. Order up lunch for the whole floor. No breaks from now on. Call the catering service and tell them we may need a whole shitload of dinners. And we may need them through the night.

"What else? Can you think of anything?"

Frank was still writing. He shook his head.

"OK. Give me that list of people by two o'clock, will you? We'll see how things are then. We may need an additional back-up for a third shift. Where the hell are the goddamn electricians?"

"Sandy." It was Marie. "The electricians are here."

The two electricians hung back, behind Marie, like children seeking protection at their mother's skirts, or perhaps, Sandy suddenly thought, out of some notion of respect for his position, the spacious office, the title. He felt an instant's amused irony at that possibility, for here he was, here they all were — bank chairmen and sector heads and vice presidents — all dependent on the skill of the two men now hovering outside the well-appointed office.

"Come in, please," Sandy said.

"You got a cable out?" the older man asked, waving the crumpled work order toward Sandy.

"Right," Sandy answered. "Eight machines along one line."

"We'll need to see the line and check out the closet before we can locate the trouble."

"Right," Sandy said, moving out from behind his desk to lead them to the floor.

"It's these machines here," Sandy said as he, Frank, and the electricians arrived on the floor.

"Um-hmm," said the older man. Sandy noted the plastic nametag pinned to his shirt pocket, K. Newton.

Newton motioned the younger man to the far end of the floor, then moved to the line of dead machines and began lifting the floor tiles that revealed the power connections underneath. Sandy and Frank moved down the line and began the same routine. The four men met in the middle of the floor. Stepping back, it seemed to Sandy that there was an irregular trench with upright covers from wall to wall.

"We'll take it from here," Newton said. "Jerry, let's go through these together."

Sandy and Frank watched as the two men moved from hole to hole, probing with their hands, seeming to pull plugs.

"We're going to check the closet now," Newton said as he and Jerry pushed back through the glass doors. Sandy followed them down the hall to the closet, sending Frank back to the office to cover the phones.

Jerry — J. Pyle, according to his nametag — unlocked the sealed closet and flipped the light switch. Sandy peered over Newton's broad shoulders to the wall of the shallow closet.

It was covered with a thick carpet of tiny wires — blue, green, red, yellow. Narrow and pliable, they were sometimes bunched together by color, sometimes jumbled together like a rainbow. Sandy could imagine it as the textured back of a large and fantastic animal.

"Looks OK to me, Ken," Jerry said, "but let's go over it." He reached for an instrument from his tool belt and squatted down, surveying the lower portion, while Newton worked above, pulling wires and touching them to one another, reconfiguring them, trying different combinations.

"Can I get you gentlemen some coffee?" Sandy offered.

"That'd be great," Newton said without stopping his exploration. "Black, please."

"Black for me, too," said Jerry from somewhere around Newton's knees.

Sandy ambled back to the office area.

"Marie," he said as he pushed his way in through the door, "have you got coffee? The electricians would like some. Two black. Hey, Frank! Anything happening?"

"I'll get it," said Marie.

"Lisa Gould called," said Frank. "Wanted to know if we knew anything more. Should she keep her people late?"

Sandy shook his head. "We don't know yet. They're still looking around. I can't rush these guys; they know what they're doing. I'll give Lisa a call."

Lisa was "in a meeting," Flo said. Sandy gave her the message,

315

reassuring her that Utility would keep the division heads informed. He checked his watch and thought, Better call Killer once more.

Kilgour took the call at once.

"The electricians are here, John, looking around. You know we got an Alert Bulletin out across the switch to all points."

Kilgour said he knew. He had informed Hardesty and Pruitt, he said, "and I told them it was under control. I'll be feeding them input as soon as I get it. You should keep that in mind, Sandy."

"Right. Soon as I have word."

Sandy took the two Styrofoam cups of coffee from Marie and went back down the hall. Ken Newton and Jerry Pyle were leaning against the wall, talking. They took the coffee gratefully.

"Well, Mr. Lippert," Newton began. "We're going to have to dig up more of your floor. The points along the line of outage are OK, and the closet checks out clean. I can't be sure, but my guess is that there's a break along the connector cable. So" — Newton slurped some of the hot coffee — "we're going to have to trace it."

Sandy nodded. "What can I do to help?"

"Actually, the best thing you can do is try to sit tight, maybe check your other machines and make sure they're not overloaded. What happens with this system is if there's an outage in one of the connectors, some of the juice gets thrown into other feeder lines. I don't know how busy you are in there, but you might want to lessen a bit of the traffic."

"Right. I will."

The three men moved through the glass doors onto the floor. "Sandy!"

He turned. Sammy Fried was coming down the hall.

The electricians set down their coffee and went to work, pulling up covers, gathering the steel-wrapped cable that was spread, snakelike, within the hollow floor.

"I hear you used CAM," Sammy said, "sent out an Alert."

"Yes. We're in an automatic queuing mode. Have been since noon. Jesus, I'm glad you're here."

Sandy and Sammy moved to the control booth. Sammy checked some counters, peered at the blinking lights on the console. "It's moving," he said. "The queuing is up."

"Stick in here, will you, Sammy? I'm going to shift some of the operators. The electricians think we ought to lessen the load a bit. We may be here all night, you know."

Sammy was getting out of his suit jacket. "I know," he said.

The doors to the floor pushed open again. Frank and Marie walked in carrying large cartons. "Lunch," said Frank. "And more coming." He went back into the hall and got two more cartons.

Sandy tapped the shoulder of every third operator. "Take a lunch break," he said. The relieved operators stood, stretched, and moved toward the coffeepot.

Marie and Frank stood over the table with the cartons. It was like a grab bag. "Ham and Swiss on rye," Marie called out. "I'll take it," one of the operators offered. "Chicken salad?" Frank asked. "Tuna. Liverwurst. Plain ham. We got milk, Coke, Fresca, and Tab. Potato chips. Cookies. Dig in, everybody."

Frank picked up a full carton and began moving down the floor, passing out lunches to the operators still at work.

"How about some lunch?" Frank asked Newton and Pyle.

"Not just yet," Newton said, looking up briefly to smile. He was hunkered down on his ankles, pulling gently at the cable being fed to him by Jerry. The younger man, stretched out on his stomach, was reaching his long arm down into the hollow floor, gathering up cable.

Frank went back to the coffeepot. "Are we going to be here all night?" one of the operators was asking Sandy.

Sandy shrugged. "I just don't know yet, Arnie." He jerked his head toward the electricians. "It depends. Anyway, *you* won't be here all night. We're working on bringing in another shift if we need it."

"Well, because I'd be willing to stick around, you know. I think a lot of us would." The others nodded. "Those who can, you know. We could sleep an hour and work some more, whatever."

"That's great," Sandy said. "It would definitely be great to have experienced and knowledgeable people like you sticking around. Why don't we wait and see? I really appreciate it, Arnie. All of you."

He looked at his crew while they ate. Dried-out meat on bread that tastes like Kleenex. No plates. Cans of soda. And now they're offering to stay here all night. He wondered about it, but only for a second. He knew they were feeling what he was feeling right now. A special camaraderie. People pulling together in a crisis. Because they're really proud of their work, of Autotran. It's the unique thing in their lives. It's different from being at home. This — he savored the tension of the floor — this is fun, he realized. And it's ours.

"Mr. Lippert." It was Ken Newton.

Sandy sprang to his feet and went over to where Newton, now standing, was holding a circle of cable in his hand.

"We've got it," he said. He pointed to Jerry, kneeling on the floor, who held up a severed piece of cable.

"Chewed through," Newton said. "Maybe mice. Probably rats. Take a look at those teeth marks." Sandy moved closer to look. "It happens a lot," Newton went on, "particularly down in this part of town, right on the water. The rats get in through various ducts, and frankly, these hollow floors are a natural for them."

"That's it?" Sandy asked. "That's the problem?"

Newton nodded. "It'll take us maybe half an hour to resplice this good and tight. Then maybe we'll talk about how to avoid its happening again."

"Half an hour?" Sandy asked. "You mean we can be running at full power in half an hour?"

Newton grinned. "Maybe sooner," he said.

"That's great," said Sandy. "Thanks a lot, Ken, Jerry."

It *was* great news. No blowup after all. No losses. No real disruption in service. Disaster had loomed and had been averted. The system had worked. His control process had worked. CAM had worked.

Kilgour would be relieved. Hardesty and Pruitt, too. The division heads would ask for action to ensure it wouldn't happen again. Frank, good old Frank, who always expected the worst, would be delighted.

Sandy walked back to the floor to tell his workers that they wouldn't have to stay all night, maybe just an hour or two of overtime to clean up the backlog on the queue. He realized that they, like himself, were going to be disappointed.

11

THE SINGING STARTED the minute they turned onto the
F.D.R. Drive — all the songs from *Oklahoma!*, *My Fair Lady*, "If I
Only Had a Brain" from *The Wizard of Oz*, which Barry claimed
to have watched seventeen times on television, and "Bess, You Is
My Woman Now" from *Porgy and Bess*, repeated twice in a
swooping baritone.

Lisa clenched her teeth and looked out the window. Pearl-
Wick Hampers. Gracie Mansion. The old Municipal Asphalt
Plant that looked like an antique radio.

"I have often waaa-aalked down this street before," sang
Barry, passing another blue Mercedes just like theirs. The driver,
a black man in a big white hat, smiled at Lisa.

They passed the Cross County Shopping Center. Lisa closed
her eyes, remembering her father sitting next to her in the Ford
on Sunday mornings, reassuring and patient, as she practiced
driving in the big empty parking lot. "Now, easy does it, sweetheart, a little more on the gas pedal," Harold Gould had urged
as they drove around and around. Lisa opened her eyes. The
trees looked weary, oppressed by the length of the summer. Two
weeks without Sandy, she thought.

"Hungry?" Barry asked. "Want some coffee? Shall I stop
soon?"

"Let's not," Lisa answered. "Let's just get there."

"Right. Tell me if you need to rest, though."

"Rest?"

"Yes. Go to a restroom. That's a joke," he added.

Lisa looked out the window. The trip seemed longer than
usual.

The house smelled musty; Lisa went around opening all the
windows while Barry brought the bags in from the car. "The
screen in the upstairs bathroom *still* isn't fixed." She was annoyed. "I thought the Home Service was going to take care of
it."

"I'll call them as soon as we get settled."

"Damnit. You just can't depend on *anyone*. Make sure they come right over. I'll be damned if I want to spend the night being eaten alive by mosquitoes just because they can't manage to deliver on their promises."

"Relax, sweetheart." Barry tried to be soothing. "This isn't BOS, you know. They don't think in terms of *deliverables*. You're in the boondocks — that's supposed to be the idea."

Lisa was still testy. "Well, I'll tell you one thing, at GlobeBank I never get eaten alive by mosquitoes." This seemed funny to her, and she finally laughed. "I'm sorry, love," she said, "I guess I really need to unwind."

◇ ◇ ◇

They ate meals on the back porch unless it was raining. In the morning Lisa would sleep until eight-thirty, finally coming down in her caftan for coffee and one of the wonderful bran muffins from Okun's, in town. As usual, Barry had been up for hours, had gone into town for the *Times* that he couldn't bear to live without and for a little breakfast treat for Lisa. He never failed her. Sometimes she wished he would. They would sit over breakfast, reading the paper, Barry starting with what he called the "entertaining section" and Lisa with the business section. Barry was usually in his beloved LETHAL LEGALS T-shirt, a relic of the time his firm had played the softball team from Cosgrove, Enfield, Whitman and Branch. The shirt, once bright blue, was now a mottled lavender. Lisa hated looking at it, but avoided hurting Barry's feelings.

After breakfast she would go out to work in her garden, pulling up weeds that protested against being uprooted by a week-end farmer. Her tomato plants had yielded three tomatoes, all pulpy and tasteless, which Barry ate with a great show of gusto. The zinnias and dahlias are doing pretty well, she thought as she turned the hose on the garden.

They had each brought books. Lisa read *Princess Daisy* and hated herself for adoring every page. She also brought *Trinity* and, again this year, *Moby Dick*, which she had been trying to read during every vacation since college, without success. Barry, who loved history, was engrossed in *Royal Charles*, after which he

320

planned to read the Weinstein book on Alger Hiss. The lawyer in him couldn't resist seeing the building of a case. "This guy really seems to have some points, Lis'," he said one day, riffling through the pages.

Most afternoons they would walk the half-mile to the lake for a swim. The water had grown tepid and full of weeds, as it always did by August. The swimming was not at all refreshing; Lisa said she felt like she had been thrown into a bowl of chicken egg drop soup. But they went anyway. It was the thing to do in the country. Sometimes in the evenings they would go to McDonald's for dinner and to the drive-in for a movie. Barry would hold Lisa's hand, running his thumb around and around, between, over, and under her fingers. She wished he wouldn't do that, and when she couldn't stand it anymore, she would pull her hand away, only to feel guilty when she saw a bewildered look cross Barry's face.

Lisa had always found the long empty days in the country restful. She loved the mindlessness, the floating golden afternoons of naps and walks. The country usually acted as soothing syrup. But this time she was edgy and restless. The need to see Sandy was a lump in her throat, chronic, painful, not to be spoken of.

"Let's go somewhere," she begged Barry.

"Sure," he said, "what's your pleasure?"

"Can't we drive around this afternoon and just sort of poke through some of the antique places?"

"Of course, love. Anything special you want?"

"No, nothing special. I just feel like moving around somewhere. I don't know, maybe we can use a new chair near the fireplace. And I would really like a brass tray to put under the candlesticks your grandmother gave us, if I can find one that isn't too fancy."

They set off one afternoon, returning at twilight with a caned rocker tied to the top of the car. Barry was driving, Lisa beside him with her head turned to the right, looking out the window. A flock of birds rose suddenly out of a field, wheeled, and flew off, dark against the mauve sky. Lisa's eyes filled with tears. She pressed her fist against her cheek and swallowed hard to keep from crying.

". . . so the personnel guy told me that I would have to start a documentation procedure on her. Well, you can imagine how that sat with me. I told him that I absolutely refused to document someone just because she's not terribly intelligent. Her intelligence is between her and God."

There was a problem with one of the secretaries in Barry's office. I've heard this already, Lisa thought dully. I won't tell him. The countryside rolled past; kitchen windows were transformed into lighted squares. It was dinnertime. Lisa thought of the silly, cramped kitchen in the place on Third Avenue and of the plastic containers of spaghetti sauce in the tiny refrigerator.

"What do you want for dinner?" she asked Barry.

"How about one of those steaks in the freezer? I'll take it out to defrost as soon as we get back. It shouldn't take too long." Lisa felt as if she had been struck. Sandy's apartment. That first time.

"What's the matter, darling?" Barry asked, alarmed. Lisa was crying without making any sound, the tears streaming down her face.

"Nothing, it's nothing," she said. She looked in her handbag for a Kleenex. "I'm just tired, I'm still unwinding. It's OK." She patted Barry's arm. "Don't worry, sweetheart." She tried to smile. "A steak would be lovely. Let's cook it outside."

The time dragged on. The last day, Saturday, was unbearably hot, even in the country. Lisa spread a blanket on the back lawn and set herself up with a Thermos of iced tea, a book, and a big bag of salted almonds. Her country bathing suits were looking a little tired, she had noticed, pulling on the more faded one. Barry had brought out a director's chair and was sitting beside her, wearing his running shorts and a white painter's hat he'd picked up somewhere, PUR-ALL PAINT PRODUCTS. CARLSTADT NEW JERSEY.

"Hot," he said. "Can I get you anything, Lis'?"

"No, thanks." She kept her eyes on the page of her book, thinking, He's all sweaty. I hope he stays in the chair. She glanced at him furtively. Oh, Barry. Dear, sweet, lovely Barry. Why am I so angry with you? Why do I pick fights with you for things you can't help? He was rubbing the side of his nose as he read *Perjury*. You're the same sweet man you've been since I met you, and suddenly I find fault with the way you breathe, with everything.

She brushed some hair back off her forehead. "Want some tea?"

"Mmmm. Sure," Barry said.

She poured some into the red Thermos cup and handed it to him, watching intently to see if he drank out of her side. *What the hell is the matter with me?* She peered at the cup, looking for the smudge her mouth would have left. *Sandy, she thought, where are you at this very moment?*

"More tea?" she asked Barry. "More, love?"

12

LINDA GLOVER STRODE WITH the wave of commuters across the floor of Grand Central. It was her first day back on the job in two weeks, and she was looking forward to it.

She had a lot to look forward to, she decided, and she was anxious to get to it. Not that she hadn't enjoyed the vacation. To her surprise, the vaguely planned trip through New England with Charley had been great fun. She had been sure she was going to hate the trip. The thought of hot days in the hot car, of Charley's relentless searches for the cheapest motel around, motels where summer insects would lie dead in the rusty shower drains — the anticipation had not been pleasant.

Yet it hadn't gone that way at all. True, there was a lot of driving, but they had followed cool back roads through small towns, deciding by the day, sometimes by the hour, where they would head next. Poring over maps, side by side in the front seat, they had grown closer. They had enjoyed the sights they saw and the things they did — Fort Ticonderoga, the ferry ride across Lake Champlain, the sudden decision to head for Canada, their big splurge night in Montreal, a lobster lunch in Portland, body-surfing off Cape Cod.

Charley had seemed relaxed; he cracked jokes and was eager to make love. He was opening up to her again, expressing his need for her in many ways. She did not deny him.

Charley had first talked about buying a house. Now was the time, he said. Interest rates were going to keep on going up.

They had always saved money on a planned basis. Now they should double their effort, take out more each month to put into a special account for the down payment, watch every penny. Once he started talking about the house, he seemed calmer about his job, seeing it as a necessary means to a desirable end, a paycheck he could pour into the purchase of the house.

Then he began to talk about a baby — very carefully at first, very tentatively. After the house, he would say, after we've got the house, maybe we ought to start a family.

Linda had not reacted to either of these plans at first. But slowly, she too began to want what he wanted. A house, maybe a family. There was a right time for these things. They made a certain impression, rounded out an image. House. Baby.

And a new job. Linda was tired of being staff. She wanted to get away from the constant numbers-crunching of the controller slot and on to the line, managing people, controlling a budget, planning and implementing. Three days before she and Charley were due to go on vacation, she was scheduled for a deuce with Lisa; she meant to bring up the subject then.

A deuce was BOS slang for what everyone found an irritating GlobeBank policy: all sector heads and all division heads were required to meet twice a year, on an individual basis, with all of the people who worked two levels down from them. Because it was for two levels down and twice a year, the meeting had been dubbed a deuce. Linda reported to Tony who reported to Lisa; the division head met with the group head. It was Lisa's policy to make one deuce a meeting and one a lunch.

The lunch was salad platters in Lisa's office. Trust her to skimp wherever possible, Linda thought wryly, remembering the tales she had heard of LaRocca's deuces at Clos Normand, of O'Connor's deuces at Charley O's that lasted all afternoon. Still, Lisa was pleasant enough, and the news was good.

Linda was, Lisa said stiffly, an excellent performer. She deserved new responsibility, and she would get it. "You're going on vacation, aren't you?" Lisa had asked as the lunch came to an end. "There will be some changes here shortly after you get back; we'll be reorganizing around the Autotran setup. You'll be in on that, Linda, and I'm sure you'll do well for us."

The lunch had preceded by a couple of hours the appointment Linda had with Rick. Maybe, she reflected, what Lisa had told her had confirmed her newly made decision, the decision to break it off with Rick.

The truth was, she was tired of him. Since his return to Globe-Bank from California, their meetings had been more frequent and less exciting. They had the regular use of Tom Fratellini's apartment two afternoons a week. Fratellini just stayed at the office until six. The routine was predictable. Sneak out of the office, claiming "a meeting down at 176," taxi over to Brooklyn, get to Tom's place by about four, get undressed, get into bed. Even the sex was predictable. Rick always acted crazed when she got into bed beside him, pushing roughly at her breasts with his hands and mouth, shoving into her harshly, tiring quickly. He had no imagination, she decided, and she was tired of giving him detailed instructions when she wanted something a little bit different. She was tired, too, of their talks afterward. His inside information about GlobeBank was not very "inside." She realized, as he evidently did not, that his moment at GlobeBank had come and gone. There was not much more room for him there; his year away had cost him his place in the club. He could be of little use to her anymore.

And with things going so well at home, with Charley once again sort of interesting, almost loving . . . I always come back to Charley, she thought as she ducked into a cab for the ride to Brooklyn. After each of these little affairs, I come back to him. I suppose I always will. Charley, after all, had helped her most of all. With a smile, she remembered their first months together, with Charley helping her lose her Rhode Island accent, teaching her how to put on makeup, drawing up lists for her self-improvement.

It's time to come back to Charley now, she determined, to reinvest in him now, in time for this vacation.

She wondered, as she paid the cabbie and made a mental note of the amount — Rick would give it back to her from petty cash — whether to tell Rick before or after they made love. She decided to tell him afterward. Knowing it was to be their last time might make it a bit more exciting for her, anyway.

Rick was there when she arrived, clad only in his Jockey shorts, pacing.

He led her hurriedly into the bedroom.

It was as she knew it would be — quick, frenetic, unsatisfying.

Rick rolled off her and reached for a cigarette. She picked her panties and bra off the floor and put them on, then went into the kitchen.

"You want a beer?" she called out. "There's some here."

"OK."

She returned with two cans of beer, no glasses. She handed one to Rick, set hers on Tom Fratellini's night table, and began to dress.

"What's the hurry?" he asked. "It's only five now."

"I've got a lot to do," she said. "Packing. We leave Friday for vacation."

"Hey, don't remind me. Two weeks. It's going to be a dry time."

"Rick," she said, slipping her dress over her head, "we have to talk."

"What's up?"

"Put something on, why don't you, and let's sit down."

He did as she asked. She was seated in the brown velvet chair, bent over, putting on her shoes. "I don't know quite how to say this," she began, "but I can't see you anymore. This, today, this was the last time."

Rick's face grew red with anger. "What the hell are you talking about?"

Linda shook her head. "It's just no good anymore. It's too dangerous, for one thing. There are rumors, I know there are. And that's no good for either of us."

Rick said nothing.

"Besides, things are a lot better between me and Charley."

Rick spoke very slowly. "You mean," he said, "you don't want to keep fucking me."

Linda glared at him. "Have it your way," she said. "It's over. I won't come here anymore. I won't sleep with you anymore."

"Goddamnit, Linda!" Rick's voice was high, squeaky. "My home life's a joke; my job sucks. The only reason I stay at Globe-Bank is because of this, because of you. I've had offers, you know, a lot of offers. I could leave tomorrow, at a better salary and a better deal. I stay for you."

326

"That's your problem," she said with a shrug. "Better take the next offer."

"Fuck you!" Rick stood and stepped toward her. His face was bright red. "I've made some sacrifices for you — a hell of a lot of sacrifices, in fact. I think you fucking owe me something."

Linda rose slowly. "I don't owe you a goddamn thing," she said. "We've both gotten something out of this affair. Right now, my return isn't worth it. So don't tell me I owe you, because I don't."

She took her shoulder bag and started for the door. "If you calm down, call me tomorrow and we can talk. I'm leaving."

He grabbed her arm. Hard. "You fucking whore! You can't do this. Oh, please, Linda, you can't do this."

"Come on, let go," she said as calmly as possible. It made him angrier.

"I could hurt you right now if I wanted to, you know." Rick tightened his grip on Linda's arm and clenched his teeth. "I could fucking rape you!"

She stared at him. Her lips curled downward. "Rape me?" she mocked. "It'll be *hours* before you can get it up again."

◇ ◇ ◇

Rick did phone the next day. He was quite calm. It was as if he had rehearsed his speech and the tone of voice in which he would deliver it. "I'm sorry about yesterday, but this isn't something you can spring on me. We'll talk about it when you get back."

He expected me to have a lousy vacation, she thought, and come running back to him. Linda smiled as she sauntered up Park Avenue. But it didn't work out that way. Not at all. She would play it very cool, she decided, when she saw Rick. She could afford to; she had the upper hand.

Out of habit, she peeked into Jessica's office as she headed down the hall to her own. With a start, she remembered that Jessica had quit the bank the previous month. God, I *have* been away a long time, haven't I?

Head Office was buzzing with rumors when she returned. Tony had seen a copy of the new org chart but wasn't allowed to talk about it. Sammy Fried claimed to know nothing. Flo, not surprisingly, said the memo was due out the following week; it was still being drafted. Linda wondered briefly if Rick knew what the new setup would be.

She saw him as she was coming back from lunch. He was standing in front of Head Office talking to Art Homer. Hands in his pocket, a smile on his face, he looked very self-satisfied. "Hello, Rick," she said.

"Oh, hi," Rick answered, and continued talking to Art.

Nancy Beal, with whom Linda had lunched, waited till they were alone in the elevator. "Did you hear about Rick and Lorraine Amato?"

"Who?"

"Lorraine. You know, Art Homer's secretary. The one who wears the pink lipstick."

"What about her?"

"Well, at the party for Art's promotion, she and Rick were really going at it."

Linda felt herself redden. "What do you mean, 'going at it'?"

"Really bumping and grinding out on the dance floor. Then they disappeared. And later, a bunch of people were getting a ride back to Brooklyn with Don Franklin, and when they got to Tom Fratellini's house, Tom asked them to wait: 'Let me see if my apartment's free.' So he went upstairs and came right back down. He told them he couldn't get into his apartment because it was 'being used.' Evidently Rick and Lorraine were up there."

Linda said nothing.

"Anyway," Nancy went on as the elevator arrived at the twentieth floor, "it sort of got all over the bank. Everyone says they've been carrying on ever since. And there's also a rumor that Rick is being interviewed by Marine Midland and may have a job there. I guess he's sitting pretty."

Linda remained silent. So Rick was sitting pretty. A new girl, maybe a new job. Lots to look forward to. Well, so what? So did she have lots to look forward to. The house, maybe a baby, a bigger job in a couple of weeks. But the high-spirited feeling of that morning had a hole in it when she thought about Rick.

13

LISA WOULD ALWAYS REMEMBER what a crisp and beautiful day it was — the air clear and sparkling, the colors bright, the buildings and streets clean and scrubbed. She had walked with a quickness that mirrored the vibrancy around her.

Autumn in New York. It made her think of Jessica, who loved this city and this season. Jessica had been fun, Lisa thought with a smile of affection, and she had been a friend. I miss her. I do. It had been a long time since she had left. When was that, July? And this is October. Not so long ago at that. But it certainly seems that way.

Lisa pushed through the glass doors. The raised lettering on them never failed to thrill her: Banking Operations Sector, National Services Division — West, Lisa Gould, Vice President.

Flo came in carefully with Lisa's huge mug, steaming with coffee. "Did you ever see such a gorgeous day? Real autumn, isn't it?"

"Mmm, great." Lisa cupped the mug in her hands. "Know who I was thinking about this morning on my way in?"

"Who?" Flo was standing before the table, her arms crossed over her chest.

"Jessica."

"Awww," Flo groaned.

"What do you mean, 'awww'?" Lisa was half laughing. "She's not dead, you know."

"I know. I just mean I miss her."

"Me, too. And I decided I really ought to get in touch. Do we have her address and phone number and stuff?"

"Sure. It's still on the Rolodex."

◇ ◇ ◇

At noon, Lisa threw on her coat and hurried out of the building. She found a taxi on Park Avenue and took it to 1473 Third.

Sandy wasn't there yet. She undressed, wrapping herself in

her flannel robe. She heard him coming up the stairs; his two-steps-at-a-time gait was unmistakable.

He let himself in. "Sorry I'm late." He kissed her and took off his clothes.

They made love happily, gratefully. Afterward, he lay on his back and she on her stomach.

"I'll tell you," Sandy said, "what's really becoming clear to me. I mean, Danny is a very good manager. Very disciplined, very sound, really a hands-on guy and on top of all the issues." He rolled over on his side toward her.

"But after working with you, I have to say that a guy like Danny just doesn't have the brightness, you know, the kind of quick intelligence you've got."

"Danny's a bright guy," Lisa said.

Sandy shook his head. "No, not bright. Not really *bright*. He's intelligent, he understands things, he *absorbs* well, but he's not bright in the real sense."

"He's awfully nice, though."

"Yes, he is. I like Danny."

"Sandy, it's twenty to two."

"Yeah. We should split. Who first?"

"You go, dear. I don't have anything until two-thirty."

He got up and began to dress. "God, I'm starved. I'll grab a hot dog on the way. I sure as hell am losing weight from this love affair."

Lisa laughed.

She was nearly dressed when he kissed her and left. She heard him running down the stairs, heard the outside door slam. Sandy simply could not close a door gently.

She took a taxi down Lexington as far as Sixtieth Street, where street construction plus the midday crowds for Blooming-dale's and Alexander's made the going unbearably slow. Lisa decided to pay the cabbie and walk.

"Ted Wilford has been calling you," Flo said as she returned to her office.

"Who?"

"Ted Wilford. You know him?"

"Never heard of him. Who's he with?"

Flo shrugged. "I don't know. I thought you knew him. Anyway, he's calling back just before your two-thirty meeting." She looked at her watch. "Any time now."

Lisa nodded and went into her office.

The phone rang and she heard Flo pick it up. "Just a moment, Mr. Wilford, she *is* expecting your call." The buzzer sounded.

Lisa picked up the receiver. "It's Wilford," Flo said.

Lisa punched the lighted button on her phone. "Lisa Gould speaking," she said.

"Mrs. Gould, this is Ted Wilford, I'm in the treasurer's office at Ensold Corporation."

Lisa always disliked being called Mrs. Gould. "Yes, Mr. Wilford," she said, "what can I do for you?" After all, Ensold was one of the bank's biggest customers.

"I'd like to ask you this, Mrs. Gould — "

Lisa cut in. "It's *Ms.* Gould, Mr. Wilford." The hell with what a great customer he is.

"Oh, I do apologize. I believed you were married."

What a jerk. "I am," Lisa said coolly in a practiced voice. "My husband is Barry Berman; I am Lisa Gould. Why don't you call me Lisa?" She tried to sound pleasant.

Ted Wilford was easygoing. "Fine, Lisa. I'd like to ask if this is a completely private call."

Lisa wrinkled her forehead. What the hell *was* this? "Will you hold on a minute?" She moved to the door and closed it. "OK," she told him when she had returned to the phone, "this is a completely private call. Now what can I do for you, Mr. Wilford?"

"Ted."

"Ted." Jesus. Who the hell was this guy? she wondered. I don't have all day to kid around.

"Lisa, there's a matter of some urgency that I wish to speak to you about. It's a very grave matter, and I think it would be best for both our companies if our talk were absolutely confidential, if no one even knew we were talking."

"What's it about?" Lisa felt the hair on the back of her neck begin to stand on end.

Wilford acted as though he hadn't heard the question. "What I propose to do," he said, "is fly in to New York tonight. Ensold keeps an apartment in a building over on Seventy-third Street, and I'll stay there. I wonder if you would meet me there tomorrow morning for breakfast."

"Mr. Wilford — I mean, Ted — this is all very strange. Could you tell me a little bit more?"

"I really don't want to talk about it on the phone. I will just repeat that I am part of the treasurer's office here, and the matter concerns our account with you. Frankly, Lisa, my other choice is to go to Toby Pruitt, and I would rather talk with you first."

Lisa felt annoyed at the high drama. "Well — and I don't mean to be impertinent — but is all this cloak-and-dagger business necessary?"

"I think it is."

Lisa sighed. "I *will* need to change some plans. Can I get back to you?"

"Good. I'd appreciate it." He gave her his number. "I would also appreciate it, Lisa," Wilford added, "if you could alert your secretary to the need for discretion."

With an assurance that Flo could be trusted, Lisa hung up.

"Flo! Come in and shut the door," Lisa said. "Listen. I don't know who this guy is, but he has some very big deal on his mind and he's hysterical about anyone knowing he's in touch with me. Do I have your word to keep his name quiet?"

"Of course. What's up?"

"I don't know, but it's Ensold, and that could be big trouble. Do me a favor, will you? See if you can find out who this guy is. Wilford. Try the library upstairs — one of those reference books, *Who's Who in Business* or something. If that doesn't work, try an Ensold Annual Report. Or just call the damn company and ask them. Title, position, reputation if you can get it. I wish I knew what the hell was going on."

Lisa went to her two-thirty meeting. At three o'clock, Flo peered through the glass into the conference room. Her face was serious.

"Will you guys excuse me a second?" Lisa said. She and Flo went back to her office.

Flo consulted her notes: "Theodore Brownell Wilford is an executive vice president of the Ensold Corporation with the position of chief treasurer."

"Jesus. He said he was 'with the treasurer's office.' I'll say."

"Wait a minute. He's Yale '56, Harvard Law '59, M.B.A. from Stanford in '61. Reputed to be a financial wizard, has one of the fastest track records ever at the corporation, is generally considered to be the heir apparent for the presidency."

Lisa considered for a moment. Finally, she said, "Flo, is his call on the daily log yet?" It was GlobeBank policy to keep a daily record of all calls received by senior managers.

"Not officially yet, no. I mean, it's not stored on the disk yet."

"Can you keep it off?"

"Here's what I can do. I can key in that call number, whatever-it-was — twenty-six, I think — that it happened at one forty-five or whatever, but leave the name blank. Then I'll just know. Is that OK?"

Lisa nodded. "That's good. And let's really keep this to ourselves. I don't know what it's about, but it's clearly big." She drummed her fingers on the desk. "Why would he come to me, though? Must be something to do with National Services West."

"What do you think it *could* be?"

Lisa answered slowly, "I don't know." She saw the look of concern, almost fear, on Flo's face. "Well, there's no sense speculating. We'll know tomorrow morning. I'm meeting him for breakfast. If I'm late getting in, by the way, make some excuse." Lisa looked at her watch. "I'd better get back to the conference room."

A sense of foreboding persisted throughout the afternoon. It hung over her as she walked home, as she and Barry broiled the chicken they had taken out of the freezer that morning, as they watched a Great Performances concert on Channel 13.

The feeling was like a tickle in the back of your throat when you're getting a cold, she thought — not bad enough to cough, but a consistently present irritation.

It was there when she went to bed and when she awoke and dressed for breakfast in her pinstriped three-piece Evan Picone suit.

She had told Barry nothing. They parted as usual in front of the building, then she wandered slowly uptown to Seventy-third Street.

The building in which Ensold kept the apartment for visiting executives was an older one by the standards of the neighborhood, at least twenty-five years old, Lisa decided. A uniformed doorman asked for her name as he lifted the house phone and buzzed the apartment. "Lisa Gould from GlobeBank," she told him. He ushered her to the elevator.

As she emerged, she saw a burst of sunlight down the hall. At the end of it was a tall form, the features indistinguishable because the light was behind him, pouring through an enormous picture window. Another gorgeous day, Lisa thought as she moved smilingly toward the open door.

"Lisa, I'm Ted Wilford," the man said, extending his hand. Handsome, Lisa registered at first glance. Wavy black hair and bright blue eyes. There was a cleft in his chin. Wilford wore a wide-lapelled gray suit over a royal blue shirt that made his eyes seem even brighter. No tie. Very California, Lisa thought.

She extended her hand. "How do you do? Nice to meet you."

"Come in, please," Wilford said, his smile revealing straight white teeth. He showed her to a table heaped with fresh fruit and hot croissants. "I'll get coffee," he said.

They made small talk as they ate. How was the weather in California? she wanted to know. Lovely, Wilford happily replied. And where actually did he live? In Belvedere, in Marin County. Did she know it? She had been to Marin, she said, through Sausalito and Tiburon and for a walk in Muir Woods. Her heart opened as she remembered that walk with Sandy. Belvedere, she knew, was one of the wealthiest towns in the country, though she didn't say as much to Wilford.

Wilford pulled a file folder from his open leather attaché case and set it down before them.

"We have an extremely effective financial control system at Ensold," he began. "Some analysts have called it brilliant, and I'm inclined to agree. That shows very little modesty on my part because I'm the fellow who designed and developed the system."

He poured himself another cup of coffee and offered her the pot.

"The system is designed with some very basic goals. Completeness, for one. Flexibility. I can ask for all sorts of custom-tailored reports, and the system will spit out just about anything I want. Finally, control."

Wilford sipped some coffee.

"To me, control means not just an ongoing assurance that things are OK, but really a built-in alarm system, a flag that automatically gets raised if there's even an undefined kind of trouble."

Why is he telling me all this? Lisa wondered uncomfortably. She reached for another croissant.

"I have various kinds of flags," Wilford went on. "A lot of them are very technical or very proprietary, inside information that we're not really prepared to divulge." He smiled. "Even to our lead bank.

"But in the end — and I think you'll be sympathetic to this — in the end, the most important flag I have is my own instinct. You're a key decision-maker, Lisa. I think you can appreciate that a kind of sixth sense has contributed to your success, a kind of instinct that alerts you to things others don't notice, or alerts you to them in a way that is different."

Lisa nodded. Wilford clearly expected a response.

"Yes," she said, "I think that's valid."

"Some months ago — in April, actually — our GlobeBank activity sheet showed an eleven-thousand-dollar gap. Now, one of the beauties of our financial system at Ensold, one of the things I'm very insistent about, is that we do not accept such gaps in reconcilement. You know — I'm sure you know — that most companies the size of Ensold just don't pay attention to a discrepancy of eleven thousand — or even twenty thousand. They figure that's loose change that just falls through the cracks. A little human error here, a faulty tape there, a machine down somewhere — it doesn't matter. They think those losses are to be expected, and they figure them in their write-offs."

Lisa could hear the wind outside. It rushed musically, softly.

"We don't do that at Ensold at all. We reconcile daily, to the penny, and we don't take kindly to discrepancies. So when this one came up, I ordered an item-by-item check of our activity through GlobeBank. The check came up clean; all the transactions were legitimate. And of course, despite the genius of my system, this sort of unexplained gap *has* happened before. Rarely, but it's happened. I try to leave room in this world for the inexplicable" — Wilford smiled again; God, he was good-looking, Lisa thought — "but I don't really like it," he said.

335

"Anyway," Wilford continued, "that unexplained gap was a big red flag in my eyes, and I didn't forget it. By the way, I've got another pot of coffee going. Shall I get it?"

"Oh. Well, sure, yes, I could do with another cup." How many had she had today already? Three? She was going to be awfully jittery.

Wilford returned with a Melitta pot this time and poured some rich-smelling coffee into her cup. "This is Jamaica Blue Mountain," he said, "very hard to come by. You can sometimes get it in New York, at a place called Porto Rico Importing in the Village, and at a place we have back home. I love the stuff.

"It happened again the next month." His words brought her back abruptly.

"Only it was for nine thousand that time. In June, we were off by sixteen thousand. Then in July, nothing. We were in proof to the penny with you. August showed a sixteen-thousand gap again. And then eight thousand last month.

"So as of today, we're about sixty thousand dollars off, plus the costs of tracking this issue. Now that's not a hell of a lot of money for a big company — except, of course, it mounts up." Wilford smiled. Lisa smiled in return.

"But even more than that, I think, was that the damn thing just bugged me. It's odd how one feels about a system one has built. The system becomes your child, in a sense, and you fret over it and feel a proprietary interest, just as you do with a child."

Just like Sandy, Lisa thought.

"And I just felt a real need to find out what was going on — as a matter of personal curiosity, you might say. I was also quite intrigued; something was getting the better of me. It was a challenge, like a chess game. Do you play chess, Lisa?"

She shook her head. "No. My husband plays. He . . ." She didn't finish. It was beside the point.

"Not that it was purely personal, of course. Our policy is to reconcile to the penny, to keep airtight control, to track precisely our transactional activity. So it was still a business issue, as far as I was concerned, to investigate the discrepancy."

Wilford picked up a spoon and began to beat it lightly against his hand, like a drummer.

"I decided to run some checks. One of the first tests we ran was to pull out all the transactions during the period in question that were within a target range of five to seventeen. We allowed for a thousand above and below what we saw. But the numbers had been so consistent, you see.

"On the first run, we hit pay dirt."

Wilford sat back in his chair, resting his arms on the wooden chair arms, like a prince on his throne.

"For the period April through September, the period in question, there were in fact numerous transactions in our target range. All of them stopped at the decimal point. A lot of them were for even thousands." Wilford leaned forward. "That raised a flag. That's unusual. Money doesn't usually work that way. Business isn't that neat."

Lisa heard a car screech to a halt outside the window, a wail of sirens in the distance.

"The next thing I did was something I did alone, in the privacy of my office, by myself. I pulled the transaction detail for each of those transactions." Wilford paused. "That's one of the services GlobeBank gives us that we find particularly useful — the ability to call up all the details of a transaction on-line and in real-time.

"You know what? *They were all the same.*"

Wilford let his words sink in. He cocked his handsome head. Lisa thought, He knows he's gorgeous, and he uses it for effect. She waited.

Wilford was ready now. "Each of the transactions had the same details. A transfer from our disbursement account through GlobeBank, via the Clearing House, to a beneficiary holding a current account at Bedminster Bank in London, one Thomas Putnam."

Despite herself, Lisa felt a small shiver. The details of the transaction rang inside her head for a moment.

"Philip Surtees is the chief cashier of the Bedminster Bank. That's equivalent to chief financial officer. I've known Surtees for years. We served on a couple of international commissions together, that sort of thing."

Lisa could imagine it. Specially fitted out conference rooms in drafty European palaces. Once they had been ballrooms, their marble walls and floors ringing to the strains of waltzes, the glitter of candlelight in glass chandeliers. Where bored monarchs once partied, the new royalty — the leaders of world business — now met to ensure their continued tribute.

"I called Phil. Asked him to do me a favor, something that, if not illegal, was nonetheless not quite appropriate. Phil agreed that a greater good would be served by doing it, and he also agreed to do it personally. So he did a check on the customer and gave me a rundown on the account of Thomas Putnam for the past several months. Putnam had opened the account in March. All the deposits had been in that target range — between five and seventeen thousand. All had come in from the States as third-party transfers. All the payments had been made by major U.S. corporations through their accounts at Globe-Bank."

Lisa felt another shiver. Thomas Putnam. Thomas Putnam.

"Phil was kind enough to give me the names of the other U.S. corporations involved, about a dozen and a half. I'm acquainted with the treasurers at four of them. I called and asked if they could check to see if they had been having any reconcilement problems since April. All four said yes, in varying amounts. I then asked them to check for any activity, payment activity, to a beneficiary named Thomas Putnam. Mind you: I asked these questions at first as if they were private investigations. None of the people I called knew I was calling any of the others.

"Do I have to tell you that all four confirmed that there had been payments, legitimate ones in every way, to one Thomas Putnam — payments of from five to seventeen thousand dollars — since last March?"

Wilford, Lisa realized, had her spellbound. He was telling her a wonderful suspense yarn. It hardly seemed real — the elegant breakfast, the beautiful man, the step-by-step discovery.

"The dollar total that this fellow Putnam has accumulated, at least among the five of us, is about two hundred thousand dollars. What he got from other companies, I can't say.

"Lisa, neither Ensold nor any of the other four companies — nor, I am sure, any of the others that Surtees named to me — has any knowledge of a customer or beneficiary named Thomas Putnam. I have checked our records very thoroughly. I have checked our customer lists, our employee lists, our lists of former

338

employees and customers, consultants, vendors, employees of our customers with signature authority. The closest I came was a Hilda Putnam, who used to be a collections clerk at one of our subsidiaries. There is no Thomas Putnam."

Wilford leaned forward.

"My investigation is over, Lisa. I can come to only one conclusion from all that I have learned: Thomas Putnam, whoever he is, has managed to gain access to GlobeBank — to Autotran itself." Wilford brought his fist down hard on the table. "Someone in your shop, Lisa, is stealing. It's a serious matter, a serious crime — obviously. But also a serious matter for Globe-Bank."

Lisa's face was impassive, but her mind was churning. Thomas Putnam. She had heard that name. Stealing. In her shop. Found out by the treasurer at Ensold. A man who paid attention to nickels and dimes. Stealing. At GlobeBank. Bad security. Stealing by someone in her shop.

"It certainly is a serious matter," she said. "Why, may I ask, have you brought it to me? Why not go to Hardesty or Pruitt? Or to John Kilgour?"

Wilford smiled. "Our relationship with GlobeBank has been a long one — and a good one, I think. You are our lead bank, and you have been extremely helpful to us. I think we have been good to you. We've gone along with all the changes you've made in the back office. I will tell you that I was your major advocate within Ensold. I have always believed that the technological revolution you people have effected in the processing is right on. I've kept a careful eye on it all — and on you, Lisa.

"You *are* my customer contact, you know. You carry the ball in the western region. Besides, I know John Kilgour. And I know Toby Pruitt well. When an EVP at Ensold talks to an EVP at GlobeBank — or to its president — that's practically public. Somebody always knows. Pruitt's on the Ensold board, Lisa. He's a pretty powerful and outspoken guy there. I think it's best for both you *and* me if he hears that we've done him a good turn. It seems to me that you're the person best suited to find the source of the trouble — and besides, we're both Stanford alumni."

Wilford opened both palms to Lisa. "Look, Lisa, this could be a big scandal. And terrible for GlobeBank. Cheating at the heart of the new Autotran environment? Disaster for the bank — for Autotran, for Kilgour, for everyone."

"I can see that," Lisa said at last. "But, given the size of this, its potential impact, do you really think it's up to me? I mean, me alone?"

Wilford shrugged. "It *is* your jurisdiction."

"You think."

"Lisa, it has to be."

"Ensold isn't exactly an obscure little firm, you know. Yes, you're my customer, but there are CRT terminals all over the bank, all hooked into Autotran. Anyone could have done this. I've never even heard of Thomas Putnam." The name echoed in her mind again. *Thomas Putnam. Thomas Putnam.*

"Nevertheless, he exists. Somewhere," Wilford reminded her. "And you said it yourself: We're your customer. That makes it your jurisdiction. Besides, if this scandal blows up, who do you think the scapegoat will be? No matter how valuable you are to them, these people are not about to drop John Kilgour. Anyone below you is too small; anyone above you is too big. You'll be the fall guy, if it comes to that. But it doesn't have to."

Lisa clasped her hands together under her chin. "It's a lot to absorb," she said. "A lot."

"I know," Wilford said. "I've been building this up for a while, and you're getting it all at once." He tapped the file folder. "I've documented the entire investigation for you here: names, dates, numbers, et cetera. Naturally, I ask you to keep it absolutely confidential."

Lisa snorted. "God, you don't have to worry about that." She sighed. "I think I'll have another cup of coffee."

He poured it for her.

"I wish I knew how, where, to begin," she said, thinking aloud. "Employee lists, yes. Consultants. I mean, if Putnam *is* an outsider, maybe he's been walking in and out pretty regularly. Or maybe he's got the goods on somebody in my shop — an extortion racket."

She bent her head back, tired — tired at the thought of it, tired already from what lay ahead. And still the foreboding, the shiver she had felt earlier, the ringing echo in her head.

"Oh boy," she said quietly.

Wilford smiled sympathetically. "I know," he said. "You've got your work cut out for you. And it isn't going to be pleasant. Listen, Lisa. If there's anything I can do, call me."

She nodded and stood up.

"Ted, I appreciate this. The entire way you've handled it. You're a good friend of GlobeBank, I can see that. I'm sure if others knew, they would be as grateful as I am. I hope you will consider that I speak for GlobeBank when I thank you."

Wilford, holding her Burberry, looked surprised. "But Lisa, you *do* speak for GlobeBank. Don't you know that?"

◇ ◇ ◇

The wind caught her as she emerged from the building. A great gust rushed through her hair and blew open the flap of her coat and made her clench her teeth in a kind of grin and squint her eyes. Oh, but the day was beautiful.

Above her, the wind was freer. It caught the tops of the spindly trees dotting the side streets of the East Side. It swirled papers above her head, out of reach.

Lisa turned downtown.

Wilford was smooth — that was her main conclusion. Very suave, very bright. Mostly, however, he paid attention to detail. He had that kind of analytical mind, a mind like Sandy's but probably, she admitted ruefully, with more brilliance. He was more hard-edged than Sandy. Not as sweet. It was easy to see how Wilford had gone so far.

In this matter — and its gravity could not be minimized — he had behaved perfectly. He had protected himself, his system, and his firm. Now he was extending to GlobeBank the chance to save itself. It was a kind of gentleman's agreement, only in this case, one of the gentlemen was a lady.

Nor could Wilford be faulted morally, she admitted, stepping off the curb. Only a real stickler might say that he should have gone to the police. Most people would agree that he was being ... *compassionate* by allowing GlobeBank this breathing space. Lisa chuckled to herself. A multinational would show compassion only to another multinational.

Of course, it wasn't funny. A serious crime had been committed in her shop by one of her employees. Stealing.

341

There was no other word for it. Lisa shuddered in revulsion. That the act was criminal was bad enough; that was the public evil. But in her mind, such an act of stealing was a violation of the most sacred trust, a trust reposed in every employee by the bank, the board of directors, the shareholders.

Lisa knew that she was sometimes the butt of jokes because she was tight-fisted. She would not sign vouchers submitted by her staff when they had lunch together on business matters. She personally checked every expense report to the penny. She remembered Jessica's accusation about Rick Schmidt acting unethically "on GlobeBank money." Well, LaRocca had signed those overblown vouchers, not Lisa Gould. Ray was very easy about such things. So was Danny. So was Brian O'Connor, God knows; it was said he hadn't paid for his own lunch in the ten years he'd been at the bank. But Lisa Gould was different. Certainly there were gray areas, boondoggles, like the Wolcott program. But still, she believed strongly that the money in her budget was not "her" money. It belonged to the corporation, to the corporation's shareholders, to be used for the corporation's growth. Every penny squandered was a penny taken from GlobeBank itself.

She stopped for a light. For the first time, she took her bearings. Across the street, Citicorp Center gleamed. The light changed, and Lisa crossed Fifty-fourth Street toward the slant-roofed building. Jessica had called it the "one new building that had changed the skyline of Manhattan for the better." She was right, Lisa decided.

An alert passerby would at that moment have seen the chic and attractive young woman stumble slightly as she failed for just a second to negotiate the curb on the southeast corner of Fifty-fourth and Lexington. The young woman recovered quickly, the passerby would note with relief.

Lisa had felt the stumble as more of a lurch. She had felt pushed from behind, right in the back of her knees. She had remembered, all at once, where she had seen the name Thomas Putnam.

14

"SWEETIE?"

"Yes, dear. What is it?" Lisa looked up from the sink. She had spent ten minutes scrubbing the broiler pan.

"Do you have a minute?"

Lisa turned off the hot water, took off her rubber gloves, and put the Brillo pad down. "Of course, love." Barry had half a cup of coffee that he was nursing along in place of dessert. "What is it?" she repeated. She brushed damp wisps of hair back from her forehead and blew upward along her face. "Can I get you something? No? Sure? OK."

Barry turned the handle of his cup back and forth for a few seconds, thinking.

"Lisa," he said finally, "you're my wife and I love you. I think I know you pretty well by now. I think you know that I respect your privacy and try not to pry or ask embarrassing questions. I also know that your lofty position at the bank" — he smiled fleetingly — "does not come without exacting a certain price from you, maybe even from me. All this I accept. But now that I have stated the case for the defense, so to speak" — he reached across to poke a strand of hair behind her ear — "let me state the case for the plaintiff."

Lisa said nothing. Of course, she thought, how could I possibly have expected him not to notice? She tried to look at him directly, but her gaze kept sliding down to the sink, to his cup, to his smallish hands.

◇ ◇ ◇

She had called Sandy, of course. She had to. He would be expecting to see her, and she couldn't. Not yet.

"Sandy?" He was at his desk. It was late. She tried to hold the telephone steady, but her hand was shaking badly.

"Lisa. Hello, sweetheart."

"Sandy, I . . ." Her voice caught. She started to cry.

343

"Lisa!" He was alarmed. "What is it, darling? What's the matter?"

It was a few minutes before she could speak. "Sandy, listen, I've just had some very bad news, something shocking — "

He interrupted her. "Darling? What is it? What's the matter?"

"Let me finish. It's something, something . . ." Her voice broke again. "I can't talk about it."

"What can I do? Can I help? Lisa, darling. I can't bear to hear you cry like that. What is it? *Tell me.*" His voice was commanding.

"Sandy, listen. I won't be able to see you for a couple of weeks."

"Lisa! What's the matter? Is it Barry? Does Barry know?"

"No, it's not that. Something else. Sandy, please. Don't press me. I need some time to think. Let me call you in a week or so. I just need some time to think."

"If that's the way you want it." He sounded hurt for a minute, but then the love flooded back into his voice. "Will you be all right? Is there anything I can do? *Really,*" he insisted.

"No. Nothing."

There was silence for a full minute.

"Lisa, I love you."

She paused for a second.

"I love you too."

"Sweetie," Barry continued, "it's hardly a big detective feat on my part to say that I know that something has been bugging you for a while. Maybe you think that when you can't sleep and you spend half of every night turning yourself and your pillow from side to side that I won't notice. But I do, believe me, I do. Lisa, you look terrible, you have rings under your eyes. I'm worried about you."

"Oh, Barry, I . . ." She didn't know what to say.

"Is it something with Kilgour?" he asked, trying to help. "Are you in trouble? Or, Lisa" — he looked at her hard — "is it something *I've* done?"

"Barry, no, it's something at the bank." She tried to control her voice, which shook slightly. It was the same scene with both of them. "Something has come up." She cleared her throat. "I just can't seem to get a handle on it."

"Easy, sweetheart. Can you tell me about it? Can I help?"

"No, you can't. This is something I'm going to have to work out myself. I just have to think things through before I can decide what to do. Don't worry about me, love." She tried to smile. "I'll be OK. Yes, really, darling," she added, looking at his anxious face, "I'll really be OK."

"Of course," he said. "But is there anything at all I can do?"

"No. Yes." She went around the table and put her hand on his shoulder. "Be patient with me."

◇ ◇ ◇

The days were mostly a blur, but she lived through them. Routine took over.

Meetings, memos, decisions. Sometimes she would look at the faces around her, peer at them to see if they were looking at her any differently. Am I acting strangely? Or do I just seem strange to myself? She felt singled out by grief, as though she were branded. Sometimes it was impossible that the crowds on Park, on Lexington, all the people coming and going and eating lunch and meeting one another, could be proceeding with their lives as if everything were normal. But as far as she could tell, everyone seemed to think that *she* was acting normally. She may have seemed tired, maybe, but that was perfectly understandable.

More meetings, memos, decisions. Sign your name; we need your initials on this; turn this around by tomorrow, will you, Tony? But all along, the same themes running through her head: Oh, God, what should I do? What should I do? All the time we were . . . A long time, Wilford said. Since April. She remembered odd moments, tiny unexplained actions. What should I do?

Presentations in the conference room. Executive summaries. Recommended action. Learn the numbers, rehearse, know the facts, make the decisions. *Make the decisions.*

One morning she ran into Toby Pruitt on the elevator and honestly couldn't remember who he was until he had gotten off. "Good morning, Lisa," he had said. She had smiled and said, "Good morning. Aah, nice day." "Isn't it?" he said, getting off.

345

I've lost control, she realized. That thought, at least, was clear. She was not accustomed to a lack of clarity. Miss Fix-It Lisa Gould slices through unruly mess, goes to the heart of the issue, uncovers it in all its shining clarity, then devises the neat, clean, carefully planned solution. All beautifully packaged. The Lisa Gould formula.

At the Friday morning division head meeting, Lisa was on the agenda. Sandy would be there, of course. She had a moment of faintness before she went into the room, and she detoured into the Ladies' Room to catch her breath. Standing at the mirror, she prayed that seeing him would somehow push her over the brink into resentment — hatred, even — and would make it easy for her to act. But when she saw him, his face was gray and sad. Help me, he seemed to say. She felt a rush of love and protectiveness. She delivered her report by rote. It seemed to fight past a lump in her throat.

After the meeting, Danny asked her to have lunch.

"Can't today," she answered. "I've just got a whole bunch of little things that have been piling up."

She closed the door to her office and sat down at the table. She would do this the way she did everything: Think it through carefully, gather the facts objectively, analyze coldly. The solution would reveal itself. That's how it always worked.

Lisa pulled a fresh lined pad to her. On the left of the page, she wrote: Possible Solutions. And next to it: Primary Impacts. Good. It was neat, organized. A matrix. List the solutions in the left-hand vertical column. Then, for each one, describe the impacts and the people affected. Then weigh the impacts relatively. Then calculate the values, and there would be the answer.

Lisa stared at the page and waited for thoughts to run from her head down her arm into her hand and out her felt-tipped pen. Nothing came. After a while, she tore up the piece of paper and started fresh.

Make it simpler. Back to basics. Like Kilgour — hone it, pare it down. Linearization. Fragmentation. Don't even call them solutions. She wrote: Possibilities. That page, too, remained blank.

Walking home that evening, she remembered a lunch she had had with Jessica. She had been eloquent over the genius of Directional Control Management, DCM, and its guru, Martin Camden. Jessica was skeptical of most things.

346

"I'm not saying it isn't gimmicky," Lisa had argued, "but so what? The fact remains that as an approach, as a construct for decision-making, it has wide applicability. It's a framework for reasoning, Jess, reasoning that will result in effective action. There isn't anything it doesn't apply to."

"I have a sneaking suspicion, Cookie" — Jessica at her most cynical called people "Cookie" — "that there are some things in this world not susceptible to neatly boxed solutions by DCM."

"Oh, Jessica. Come off it."

She had been right. Jessica had been right. Dear Jessica.

15

JESSICA SHOPPED LIKE a European — the neighborhood inspired it. Carrying two string bags, she went to the Korean produce shop for some fruits and vegetables, to the kosher butcher for a chicken she would roast and keep around to nibble on, to the cheese store for some Muenster and Brie, and to the Italian bakery for a round loaf of semolina bread and one small cannoli.

At home, she put away the groceries to the strains of *The Merry Widow*, the old Schwarzkopf version she loved. It was a precious recording, and she whistled and sang to the familiar numbers.

With the waltzes still pouring forth, she sat down at the kitchen table to work. The music was appropriate, she decided, since the client wanted the script to be "upbeat."

She wasn't sure how long she had been typing when the door buzzer sounded. She looked quickly at her watch as she rose. Nearly one o'clock. Who the hell could that be? she wondered. She wasn't expecting anyone.

"Yes?" said Jessica into the intercom.

"Jessica, it's Lisa Gould."

"Lisa! Come up!" Jessica buzzed her in and went to stand in the open doorway.

This was certainly a surprise. Lisa coming here? Lisa in Chelsea was enough of a shock. Lisa in New York on a weekend was distinctly odd.

The object of Jessica's speculation stepped out of the narrow elevator.

"Lisa! This is terrific."

"Hi!" she said, smiling.

"It's so nice to see you. Come in, come in."

"I really apologize, Jess. It's absolutely against my principles to barge in on somebody without calling, but — "

"Give me your jacket," Jessica said.

"I'm really surprised to find you in. I've been composing the note I was going to leave for you all the way down the street." Lisa handed Jessica the jacket. "Barry's playing handball."

"I'm delighted you're here," Jessica said. "Come and sit." She nudged Lisa gently toward the puffy brown sofa. The two women curled up on opposite ends.

Lisa had long been curious about Jessica's apartment. In addition to the brown sofa, there were two mismatched chairs — one a contemporary design with a footrest, the other, white wicker with a shabby flowered cushion. The low coffee table was wood, massive, hewn from a tree trunk, it seemed. Prints and posters cluttered whatever piece of wall wasn't obscured by the high bookshelves: the Steinberg *New Yorker* cover depicting a New Yorker's view of the world, some engravings that, Lisa guessed, illustrated old Norse myths, some delicate ink drawings, a bright poster of Haiti. The bookshelves themselves were messy, with books stuck in every which way, giving the appearance that any one of them was just about ready to fall out or that if you loosed the wrong one, the whole set of shelves would topple.

Lisa noticed that the record player was turning and the power was on, though no sound came out. "I think you left your record player on, Jess," she said.

"Oh God," said Jessica, leaping up. "I always do that! The automatic thing is broken. Abby is very smug about reminding me to turn it off."

"Where is Abby?"

"She's with her father this weekend. Listen, I'm just about to make myself a grilled cheese sandwich. How about it?"

"Oh no, Jess, I don't want you to go to any trouble."

"No trouble. Come on, you can sit at the table and watch. And tell me all about everything."

Lisa followed her into the kitchen. She noticed the papers and books on the table, the typewriter, the neat pile of typed manuscript. "I see you're working. How is it going?"

Jessica, slicing the Muenster, smiled. "The truth is, Lisa, I'm actually making more money now than when I was on salary. I'll just stick these under the broiler. When I started, I was pretty terrified, I don't mind telling you, but it's really worked out well."

"What is it you're doing?"

"Oh, free-lance stuff. This is a script for a sales meeting for a publishing house. An audiovisual presentation." Jessica sat down at the table opposite Lisa. "And I do speeches and booklets and some editing and some proofreading. Everything! Anything."

"How did you get started?"

"The usual. Connections. A friend got me some work writing the blurbs on book jackets. And that led to other publishing houses. And one friend led me to another. And sometimes friends led me to strangers. Oh, I don't say I've got a secure future for the rest of my life, but for now, it's good."

"I'm glad, Jessica. I really am. And I'm glad to see you. We still miss you, you know."

Jessica smiled, pleased. "That's nice to hear, strangely enough. So how is everyone? How is dear old GlobeBank?"

Lisa lowered her eyes. "The same, I guess. I don't know. Things are kind of funny right now."

"Funny? How? Is it the conversion?"

Lisa shook her head. "No. That's all done, by the way. National Services West achieved full implementation ahead of schedule."

"Can't say I'm surprised."

"Can't really say you care much, though, can you? Come on, Jessica, the truth."

"The truth?" Jessica leaned toward Lisa. "The truth is, I never did care."

Lisa laughed, just a small laugh, but it felt wonderful. It was, she realized, the first laugh she had had in days. "I'm so glad to see you, Jessica!"

Jessica was on her feet. "What would you like to drink?"

"What are you going to have?"

"Coffee, I think."

"Fine. Me too."

"But how are all the folks?" A counter separated the kitchen from the dining area. Jessica pulled plates and utensils out of cupboards and drawers as she talked. "How's Flo?"

"Flo's great. Her eyes tend to mist over when she talks about you. And she hasn't taken kindly to your replacement. Nobody has. That poor woman. You're a hell of an act to follow."

"Who is she?" Jessica set out the plates and flatware.

"Her name is April Mathis. Nice enough, I suppose. Very posh background."

"Is she good?" Jessica was measuring out coffee for the Melitta.

"She's OK. You have to explain everything to her, though. She's no you."

Jessica smiled. "And how's Tony? Linda?"

"They're fine. Tony's still my chief controller. Linda's moved up. Surprise, surprise. I've made her a full group manager, running a set of clusters, and she's charged with moving along the product management process. She's doing a good job, but I watch my back. As I told Barry, she's terribly capable — capable of anything, that is."

"How's Rick Schmidt?"

"Funny you should ask. He left GlobeBank. And not on the best terms."

"Oh? Surely you didn't fire him?"

"No. But we were all pretty pissed off that he went off to another bank after we sent him to school and poured all that money into him. Ray gets apoplectic at the mention of his name."

Jessica brought over the sandwiches and a bowl of potato chips. "How's Sandy?"

Lisa was glad she was chewing when the question was asked. It gave her time. "Sandy? He's fine, I guess."

"Well, I guess there's only one other person I need to ask about." She paused. "How is Lisa? How are you, Lisa?"

Oh, God, thought Lisa. Oh, the hell with it. She pushed her plate away.

350

"For one thing, I'm afraid I'm not very hungry."

Jessica was nodding. "How about for another thing?"

Lisa ran her hand through her hair. "I couldn't be much worse, Jessica."

Jessica nodded again. Quietly, she said, "You look like hell. You look like you haven't slept for weeks."

"Days, merely days."

"Everything OK with Barry?"

"Barry? He's fine. He's dear."

"Everything OK between you?"

"That's not the problem," Lisa said after a moment.

"OK, I'll get us the coffee, you describe the problem."

Now that she could talk about it, now that there was a sympathetic, trusting, and trustworthy person to tell it to, Lisa didn't know how to begin.

"I don't know how to tell this story. Jessica, a crime has been committed. At GlobeBank. In BOS."

"What kind of a crime?"

"A swindle. On Autotran."

"Oh." Jessica brought in two mugs and the coffee. "Holy cow."

"The treasurer at a very, very big corporation that is also one of our best customers discovered it. Ens — his company was one of a bunch of companies being ripped off by this person. He kept it quiet until he could get to me. He put it to me that I should investigate and find out who the thief was. If I couldn't, obviously we'd have to go to the police. We still may have to go to the police."

Lisa warmed to the plot. "The guy created a phony beneficiary. He keyed in transactions: transfer thousands from company A via Autotran to the beneficiary — thousands here, thousands there. Over a period of seven months. Multiply that by twelve, eighteen companies. It comes to a very big number."

Lisa smiled ruefully. "It was rather cleverly done, in a way. This creation of an identity to be the beneficiary — it must have taken some doing. The bank had to have seen an I.D., license, references. I don't know exactly. But a person was created with a real address. And then he, the swindler, just wrote checks against the account."

Lisa had forgotten about her coffee. Now she sipped some. It was black and strong.

"He knew about big corporations too. How they hardly ever pay attention to discrepancies of small amounts — small to them, anyway. He might have gone on forever if this company hadn't had this particular treasurer. A real stickler, Jessica. A man who sees a million dollars as a lot of pennies. If it hadn't been for that — "

"So he came to you," Jessica interrupted.

"Yes."

"Did you locate the culprit, Lisa?"

Lisa nodded, miserable.

"Don't tell me who it is, Lisa. You don't have to. And I don't want to know."

Lisa's eyes brimmed with tears. "You have to know, Jessica. I can't . . . I can't carry this alone anymore. You have to know." She paused. "It's Sandy," she said quietly.

Jessica stared. She lowered her coffee mug to the table. Lisa's face seemed to hang. The tears had spilled over and were coursing down her face. Her mouth was a ragged line. She said nothing.

Jessica rose and walked around the table. She pulled out the chair next to Lisa and sat down. Putting an arm around Lisa's shoulders, she drew Lisa's head down to rest on her own shoulders.

"My God," Jessica whispered. "Oh, my God. Poor Sandy."

Lisa sobbed.

"That's it," Jessica said encouragingly, "let it go. You don't have to hold up here. Let it go, Lisa."

Lisa felt herself sag against her friend. Poor Sandy, Jessica had said. Oh, Sandy, I loved you so much.

Jessica gently wiped Lisa's cheeks with a paper napkin. "You knew I had guessed about you and Sandy, didn't you, Lisa? Long ago. After the off-site, I think. I am so sorry, Lisa, I am so sorry."

Lisa cried harder. Cried now for the end of the affair, wondering if that had been what she grieved for all along.

"I don't know how to describe it — it's as though I've become a character in somebody else's dream," Lisa was saying as Jessica put on another pot of coffee. Outside, the shadows were lengthening, and the Saturday shoppers hurried home. "I try to think ahead and I see a whole bunch of scenarios, and they're all impossible. They all cause misery, somewhere, to someone. Or I think back and try to figure out how . . ."

Lisa's words were muffled in a new sob. She swallowed it and righted herself.

"I think back, Jessica, and all I can see is Sandy. We were so close. I don't know how to describe how close we were. And then I think, all the time we were like that, there was this whole side of him that was something else, that I never knew about or suspected. And I begin to wonder if that wasn't why, why I was attracted to him, you know."

"Don't start trying to analyze that sort of thing, Lisa. That way lies madness. Anyway, I don't think you ever really know."

"He seemed so vulnerable, you know. And I think he did seem kind of mysterious to me. Unknown. Unpredictable. Barry . . . Barry was so familiar." She added quickly, "I love Barry, Jessica. Do you believe that?"

"Of course."

"But I just fell in love with Sandy. There's no other way to put it. I just fell in love with him. Oh God, it was wonderful. We made love together — it was like nothing I've ever had." She pulled another napkin out of the wooden holder, an obvious purchase from one of Jessica's trips. "I cannot bear to think of him suffering."

"Lisa, don't. Don't eat yourself up."

"What way is there?" Lisa's fist hit the table. "Damnit, Jessica, if you know a way, tell me!" She was crying again.

"Let's think. Let's think." Jessica set her elbow on the table and rested her chin in her hand. "How did you find out it was Sandy?"

"The identity he created, Thomas Putnam. I saw mail lying around addressed to Thomas Putnam. At our place. Sandy sublet a little studio on Third Avenue."

Jessica was still thinking. "How much did he steal — all told?"

"We still don't know exactly. A lot. Several hundred thousand."

353

"And you know whom he stole from?"

Lisa nodded.

"That's a lot of money, but is it so much for a GlobeBank to pay back?"

"No, not really."

"Couldn't you do that? Couldn't you just pay back the money to satisfy the companies that got ripped off? And then quietly, well, fire Sandy?"

Lisa shook her head. "I thought of that. It won't work. Too many people know there's been a swindle."

"I thought you said the treasurer had told only you."

"At GlobeBank. But the treasurers of these corporations know. The head of the bank in London where he opened the account knows. I think Flo knows. She knows something's up, anyway."

"Flo you don't worry about. Jesus, Lisa. Flo's on your side."

Lisa looked up. "That's it, isn't it?" she said quietly. "How well you put it. It's a matter of taking sides. What is my side, Jessica? And what makes a thing best for my side? Saving my marriage? Or saving my lover? Or saving my job?"

Jessica shrugged. "How about saving all three? And Globe-Bank in the bargain?"

Lisa smiled wanly. Her eyes were still swollen. "Sure, Jess. Just tell me how to do it."

Jessica paused. Then she said softly, " 'If I am not for myself, who is for me? And being only for my own self, what am I? And if not now, when?' Hillel."

"What? What does that mean?"

"Hillel," Jessica repeated. "A famous rabbi. I guess it means, Preserve yourself, cultivate yourself, but don't be selfish and don't procrastinate." She smiled. "You must act, Lisa. You hold the cards here. It's in your power to act, and you really must."

Lisa put her head back and closed her eyes. "I want it to go away. I want it to be two weeks ago, when all I had to worry about was whether my meeting would end in time for me to get to the place, to meet Sandy." She stumbled over his name and began to cry again. "Goddamnit!"

Jessica was silent, letting Lisa cry. Finally she said, "It won't, you know. I mean, it won't go away. It never does."

Lisa sat up, eyes wide. "Tell me what to do! Jessica, please tell me what to do."

354

"Lisa, listen." Jessica jerked open the refrigerator and retrieved a beer. "You're a decisive executive. So decide. Execute. You know how to control hundreds of people, millions of dollars. Control this. Cut a deal, for Chrissake. I've watched you, I've watched you carefully. You follow your own compass. You're above the rules. You make the rules for others, and you do it easily because you know you'll always be an exception. You make use of whatever and whomever you need. Don't tell me you don't."

Lisa said nothing.

"You assessed John Kilgour years ago, and you decided to hitch your wagon to his star — but not too closely. When you worked for LaRocca, you walked a fine line between him and Kilgour. You could afford to. It was your line; you knew exactly where it was going to take you. Me. You used me. You gave me a long leash, and sometimes you ran with me on it. But you very rarely forgot my purpose — which was to make you a star."

Jessica drank some of her beer. "I don't think you're evil because of this; I don't think this makes you a son of a bitch. Everybody uses everybody. I used you as much as you used me, you know. Everybody uses everybody." Jessica took another sip. "But you're better at it than most of us."

Lisa noticed that Jessica's face was reddening. Was it excitement or the beer?

"To stop a crime, and pay back a theft, and keep a poor, sweet man from — God knows what — and save your marriage — that's kind of heroic, isn't it, Lisa?"

Lisa looked down. "Yes." Then she said, "It's true about Sandy, isn't it? You've said it twice now. 'Poor Sandy.' What do you think it was? Why do you think he did it?" She thought for a moment and shook her head. "This sounds silly, but I really believe he did it because it was something to do. I suppose the bottom kind of fell out of his life, you know? And there wasn't anything anymore, nothing to be excited about. But there was the system, the damn system. And what he could do on it."

"What about you?"

"I came along after he had already got this in his head. Everything compartmentalized. I think he had developed a lot of separate connections but couldn't put them all together. That, at least, is the only way I can figure it."

355

"What about you and him, Lisa? Will you . . . will you get over him?"

Lisa smiled through her tears. "What choice do I have? But first, I have to handle it. I have to act." She stood up. "I should go. I'll walk back. Maybe a walk will help me think better. This has been helpful, Jessica. You've been helpful. Thank you."

Jessica handed Lisa her jacket. "Listen to me," she said. "If you ever feel you need me, I mean *ever*, I'm here."

"I guess I knew that," Lisa said quietly. "I guess that's why I came."

The two women walked to the door. Lisa turned and quickly hugged Jessica. " 'Bye," she said. "Wish me luck."

" 'Bye," said Jessica. "Good luck." As Lisa entered the elevator she added softly, "You're going to need it."

◇ ◇ ◇

Lisa walked slowly up Sixth Avenue, calmer than she had been in days. It was important to feel that strength again, the power she was accustomed to feeling. It was the way she had felt when she first met John Kilgour and saw, clearly and simply, that he was a man whose closest aides were people with the skills he lacked. Find something he lacks, she had told herself. As LaRocca had, as Sandy had, as Elaine Green had. And what had *she* brought to Kilgour? A touch of the modern technocrat, a bit of the best and the brightest, that was all. But it was enough.

It was the way she felt when she reorganized her division, playing with organization charts, filling in boxes with functions and names. She was in control — these jobs, these responsibilities, these people. It was like dressing paper dolls; you changed the costume whenever you wanted to.

She needed to feel that way about this situation. To see it clearly, to analyze it coldly. What were the variables? That was the first question. Her lover, a crime, her marriage, her career, saving face. What levers could she pull to move those variables? Where did her power lie? What — and whom — could she manipulate?

She had come to Thirty-fourth Street. There was a noticeable thickening of the crowds. She didn't know much about Thirty-fourth Street, she realized, or about the kinds of people who

356

shopped here. She heard a lot of Spanish being spoken, and there were a lot of blacks. Families with large numbers of children hauled filled shopping bags. It was the end of the day; the children were whiny, the parents running out of patience. People were streaming west to Penn Station, east to the subway or the PATH train. They were lined up at the fast-food stands, wolfing down hot dogs and fish fried hard in thick batter.

I'm hungry, she thought. She hadn't been hungry for days, either.

It was possible to find a solution after all, as she had always done. She was a wily shark in a business with barracudas. What had Jessica called her? A "decisive executive." "Decide," she had said. "Execute."

Lisa realized with a start that she was about to make the most important decision of her career.

Or the last.

16

BARRY WAS HOME when she returned. "Hi, darling," she called out, her key still in the lock. "How was the game?"

"I was slaughtered," he said, emerging from the kitchen. "Want a beer?"

"No thanks. But I'm starving." She took off her coat and headed toward the refrigerator.

"How was your walk?" Barry asked. "Did you get very far?"

"You know what I did? I walked down to Chelsea and rang Jessica's bell." Lisa made a sandwich while she talked. She found a cold chicken leg, pulled a leaf of romaine off a head in the vegetable bin, and took the jar of mayonnaise from the refrigerator door.

"Jessica? No kidding? I'm surprised she was home. How is she? It's a long time since she left the bank, isn't it?"

"She's fine, great. Doing very well free-lancing. She's just the same — funny, cynical, tender, and wise." She closed her eyes for a minute. "I really miss her, you know, Barry?"

357

"A friend, as they say, is a friend, Lis'. You look better. Your visit seems to have done you good."

"I feel better," she admitted, taking a bite of her sandwich. "Can I change my mind about the beer?"

Barry got a glass from the shelf, filled it halfway, and set it down on the table.

"Sweetheart," Lisa said, "would it be OK with you if I went up to the country for a couple of days? I just feel that, well, that I finally have a chance to figure out this situation, this mess. But I just need a couple of days there alone. Because you know, Barry, for the first time since this whole business started, I have a small feeling that I might be able to sort things out."

"Darling, of course." They sat for a minute.

"Barr'? Will you call Flo on Monday and tell her I have the flu and that I'll be back on Wednesday?"

"Sure, sweetie, of course. When do you think you'll go?"

"Tonight," said Lisa. "I think I'll go tonight."

For a few minutes when she woke up she sensed that something was wrong, missing. Then she realized that she was in the house alone, that there was no Barry bustling around downstairs with fresh bran muffins and the paper. Today, she thought. She pulled on her quilted bathrobe and went downstairs. Kilgour. I have to think of a way to cut his choices, make him help. She filled the kettle and spooned coffee into the Melitta filter. There's no way Sandy can stay at the bank, is there? Pay back the money? No, no way at all. He committed a crime. News gets around so goddamn fast. She found some bagels in the freezer, wrapped one in aluminum foil, and put it in the oven to defrost. Decide. Execute, Jessica said. God, all the decisions I've made at the bank. How easy everything seems when the people are heads, heads to knock or resources to deploy. How easy to move them around. Maybe some of them suffered too and . . . She was unable to complete the thought. The sky outside was bright, the air crisp. Nice day, she thought.

What are the givens? She was standing in the shower, welcoming the relaxing stream of hot water that flowed over her. A crime. He might be arrested. Oh, my God. She was choked by sudden sobs, crying for the first time since her visit to Jessica. Damn him. Damn him. She sat down in the bathtub, the shower pouring down on her head. Why did he have to do this to me? She turned around in the tub, pulling her knees up to her chest. Why does it have to be me? That son of a bitch. She realized that she was going to be sick and got out of the bathtub just in time to throw up. For several minutes afterward, she lay on the bathroom floor, wet, her hair dripping, the shower still running. Her crying subsided slowly. The spasms in her stomach became fainter. Lisa felt calmer; she turned off the shower and stood up and dried herself. Sandy, darling. Forgive me. You didn't do it to me — but you might as well have, since it's going to cost me something to fix this. A lot.

At least I know where I stand now. The Current Situation. And I know what I want to happen, at least I think so. The Ideal Future. Some ideal future. I wish I could tell that one to Barry. Or Jessica. It has a certain . . . She leaned over, brushing her teeth, trying to get the sour taste out of her mouth. Sandy has to leave the bank, go away, far. But that's it. No more than that. No jail. She closed her eyes for a minute. No police. No publicity. No harm to Sandy. She started to feel sick again, shook a little, then straightened up. What I need now is how to get there. Do it the GlobeBank way. A plan. Current Situation. Ideal Future. Path of Motion Plan. Path of *Emotion* Plan, she said to herself, rubbing the last moisture out of her hair with a towel.

She sat at the kitchen table, a mug of coffee beside her, looking down at her lined pad, then let her gaze drift out the window to the yard. She could see a rabbit nibbling at some long stalks of grass, his jaw moving rapidly, his nostrils twitching.

Winter soon. What's going to happen to the poor thing?

Think, she said to herself. Now think. She wrote PATH OF MOTION PLAN in large block letters across the top of the page and stared at it for a minute. Nothing. Maybe I'd better start with before and after. A little easier.

She tore off another sheet of paper from the pad and wrote CURRENT SITUATION. Under that she wrote:

1. A crime has been committed.

2. The identity of the thief is known to Lisa Gould, a division head at GlobeBank.

3. The crime and many of the details are known to the treasurer of one of GlobeBank's major customers.

4. The thief could go to jail.

5. There is bound to be suffering.

Suffering. Oh yes. Yes, indeed. That part I know about. She wandered to the front door and stepped outside. The air seemed palpable, the way it always did the first day or two in the country. She took a deep breath and turned her face up toward the sun for a minute. Oh God, she thought, how am I going to get through this?

Back at the table she continued her list.

6. The criminal and the division head have been lovers for more than six months.

7. They are lovers at this time.

8. The division head is not going to let her lover be put on trial.

9. The division head is not going to let her lover go to jail — "Whatever the cost to me," she said out loud, her voice strange in the silence — whatever the cost to the divison head, she wrote on the pad.

I suppose that's it, she thought. Her eyes burned, but she felt better for having done even this much. Jessica was right. How well she knows me. Decide. Execute. Untie knots. That's what I do well. But that's also what does well for me, she said to herself, getting up for more coffee. I'm unplugged unless I'm planning something. Even something like this.

IDEAL SITUATION, she wrote on the pad, underlining it twice. Ideal it isn't, but it will be the best I can do. The very best. For you, Sandy, my darling. She wrote:

1. Everyone has to get something.

2. The criminal keeps his reputation intact, no trial, no imprisonment.

3. The bank gets rid of the criminal without adverse publicity.

4. The bank's customers get repaid.

5. Ensold's treasurer gets—what? she thought. What does Wilford get out of this? — promoted, she wrote, to whatever office he desires. We can take care of that. Or Kilgour can. He'll have to work through Pruitt. Hardesty too, maybe. That's going to have to be up to him.

"But it's Kilgour. Of course," she said aloud. She went to the sink, rinsed out her cup, and set it upside down on the drainboard. The day was growing warmer and the kitchen was suffused with bright yellow autumn sunlight. Lisa went back to her pad. PATH OF MOTION PLAN, she wrote, underlining it three times.

She thought, Kilgour will have to identify the Ideal Future goals with his own self-interest. But how am I going to do that? Appeal to his business sense? Better for customers to keep it quiet? For the bank? He'll have to know everything, of course. About me and Sandy? Yes, everything. There's no other way. She wrote:

1. Division head will acquaint Kilgour fully with all the details.

He'll wrinkle his oh-so-controlled nose at the idea of Sandy and me. How is he going to take the real bombshell, though? Lisa sat still for a few minutes, rubbing her thumb against her forefinger. This was the critical place, and her mind was trying to slip away from the page, away from the task, back out into the crisp and sunny air. And how am I going to make him do what I want? Especially in this case, when all his instincts will be to move in for the jugular? She went to the sink and splashed some water on her face. The rabbit had gone off somewhere, but a large bird was on the grass, standing still, cocking its head back and forth. Lisa looked at its round eyes. The bird seemed inquisitive. She watched it until it flew off, called by an unknown errand. He won't be brought around by any appeal to his business sense, she acknowledged. That's out of the question. It wouldn't even make sense to me. If it weren't Sandy, I'd advise Kilgour to prosecute. Hard and fast. If the newspapers got hold of it, we'd have to make sure they saw that we were tough and swift about getting rid of our bad apple. "No," she said aloud. "What I have to do is threaten him."

2. The division head will blackmail the sector head to ensure his cooperation, she wrote.

She smiled. Blackmail Kilgour. Funny. Lisa threw her pencil down on the table.

17

LATE TUESDAY EVENING, LISA TELEPHONED Kilgour at home, closing the bedroom door against Barry's possible curiosity. His wife answered with a ringing, musical hello.

"Sally? It's Lisa Gould. Awfully sorry to bother you."

"Lisa! How are you, dear? Nothing wrong, I hope."

"No, no. And it's not even an emergency. But I'm out of town, and my schedule is hopelessly tied up. And since I know John is so hard to reach during the day, and I really do need to get to him . . ."

"It's all right, dear. We were just winding up dinner."

Lisa heard Sally Kilgour pass the phone to her husband. "It's Lisa Gould. Long distance."

"Hello, Lisa." It was Kilgour.

"John, I apologize. I told Sally there was no emergency, and I think it would be best if you tried to sound like that's what I'm telling you right now."

"Oh?" Kilgour's voice was tentative.

"I'm not out of town, either; that was just part of the excuse."

"I see."

"It's essential that we meet, John, and it's equally essential that absolutely no one know it. No one at all."

"Oh. Well, what is the precise issue?" Kilgour was being very cautious. He was good at this.

"Not over the phone. But it's serious. We could be in trouble, a whole new kind of trouble. When I say 'we,' I mean you and me. Our jobs. Our futures."

Kilgour's answer was swift. "We'll handle it as you think best, Lisa. You know I trust you."

"Good. I've thought about it, and I think the best thing would be for us to meet at my place in Connecticut. We'd have privacy. Barry has to go to Boston tomorrow on some family business and won't be back till late."

"All right. It sounds important."

"You'll have to work up some story for Sally, I realize, but that shouldn't be too difficult."

"No, no problem."

She gave him directions. "I'll be leaving the city just before five. Why don't we say around seven-thirty, a quarter of eight. For dinner?"

"Well, we'll see what we can do. Right. I'll tell Sally you said so. OK, Lisa, good-bye."

◇ ◇ ◇

Kilgour was punctual, despite a heavy storm that showed no signs of letting up. Rain pelted the driveway as he drove up, slashing vertical lines in the BMW's headlights. From the front window, Lisa watched Kilgour get out of his car, umbrella first. She was struck anew by how small he seemed, how unprepossessing. Her corporate mentor. Supermanager, one of the articles about GlobeBank had called him. The man who had changed forever the face of banking and its guts. After Kilgour's renaissance of the back office, the entire financial industry had changed irrevocably.

He had done it, this slight man, now handing her his raincoat, his umbrella, running a hand through his sandy-gray hair. He had made it happen, using to the fullest the power he held over thousands of people and billions of dollars.

To Lisa he had never been a source of fear, as he had been to so many others. He had always been a source of learning, a source of support, and she had always looked up to him.

But tonight she needed to hold the upper hand over John Roland Kilgour.

"Come on in, John," she said. "You must be drenched. Can I get you a drink?"

"From your tone when we talked on the telephone, it sounds as though I may need one. I'll have some Scotch, please. A little soda."

"Please make yourself comfortable," she urged, leading him into the living room. "I'll be right back."

She fixed his drink in the kitchen and poured herself a glass of Chablis from the dark brown Grolsch beer bottle she and Barry used as a decanter in the country. Through the kitchen window, she saw jagged lightning tear through the sky. The lights flick-ered for a moment.

"Must be getting closer," Lisa said, handing Kilgour his drink. "I hope we're not going to have the electricity go out on us."

Kilgour sat in the easy chair beside the sofa, leaning back slightly. Lisa sat down in the middle of the sofa, crossed her legs, and stretched one arm along the back. Start, she commanded herself.

"I've been thinking all day how to say what I have to say," she began. "I think the best way is just to plunge in." She sipped her wine, then set the glass down on the coffee table. She could hear the rain beating on the roof.

"John, there's a thief in BOS."

Kilgour's face registered dark surprise. "What?"

"Someone in BOS has been tapping a number of our corpo-rate customers. For a total in the several-hundred-thousand-dol-lar range. And he's been doing it on Autotran."

Kilgour leaned forward. "Oh?" he said quietly. She noticed that his free hand was gripping the arm of the chair tightly.

She nodded. "Ted Wilford came to see me recently. The treasurer at Ensold."

"Wilford? Came to see you?"

"Ensold was one of the companies being ripped off. The only one to notice it at the beginning, by the way. Did you know that Wilford's financial control system requires daily account recon-cilements to the penny? On every account? For every item?"

"He's a bright boy," said Kilgour, a tone of admiration in his voice.

"Wilford came to me because Ensold's in my shop. He as-sumed that the swindle was happening via Autotran and that it was being done by one of my people. He had already done a fairly thorough investigation. As he put it, 'Right up to the walls of GlobeBank.' "

Lisa reached for her wine. Kilgour waited, still gripping the chair.

"Wilford had tracked the reconcilement discrepancies and ran a check on them. It turned out that the specific transactions had all been paid out of Ensold's disbursement account, via Auto-tran, through the Clearing House, to an individual account at

364

Bedminster Bank in London. Wilford knows a guy there — I guess Wilford knows guys everywhere — and the guy found the beneficiary for him and gave Ted a complete rundown on the account's activity. That's how Wilford found out about the other corporations, and he checked with them. They were also having reconcilement gaps, though they would never have noticed or cared if Ted hadn't brought the matter to their attention."

"Ted's a thorough young man," Kilgour said. His voice stayed very low and quiet.

"All of the transactions had been done the same way. The corporation was the remitter; the flow was via Autotran at GlobeBank through the Clearing House; the beneficiary was this individual account in London. The amounts were always between five and seventeen thousand."

She paused. Kilgour was still. A coiled spring, thought Lisa.

"Ted assumed that the thief was one of the CRT operators. I had the notion that maybe somebody was being pressured. You know, somebody outside the bank was doing a kind of extortion number on one of our people." She lifted her glass again and emptied it. "We were both wrong."

The room blazed with another lightning flash. Thunder followed instantly, starting as a rolling drumbeat, exploding into a violence that rattled the doors and windowpanes.

"My God, that was close," Lisa said. "I can never get used to these country storms. Can I get you another drink?"

Kilgour looked at the glass in his hand. Then he drained it. "Please," he said.

"And, oh listen, I'm being a rotten hostess. I'd better get our dinner started. I have steak. Will that suit you?"

"Yes, steak is fine."

"Rare?"

Kilgour nodded. He seemed preoccupied; his mind was elsewhere, searching for control.

"Why did Wilford come to you?" he asked when she returned to the living room with their drinks.

"I thought about that," Lisa said. "I gather he didn't want to be the messenger of bad tidings to you, or to Hardesty or Pruitt. I gather he has good reasons for that. He's ambitious."

Kilgour nodded slowly.

"His coming to me was perfectly appropriate. I would even say it was compassionate. He could have gone right to the criminal authorities. He had enough evidence to just turn it over to the cops — the Feds, I guess — and keep his name out of it altogether. I think Ted thinks he's done GlobeBank a favor. And I think he's right."

Kilgour sipped his Scotch. "And what did you do when Ted came to you like that? Clearly, you didn't share it with me."

"I'm sharing it with you now, John."

"But you've already done some investigating."

She nodded.

"You've found out who the guy is."

She nodded again.

"Are you going to tell me?"

Lisa smiled. "Right now, I'm going to serve us some dinner."

Lisa rose and entered the kitchen. Kilgour followed, standing in the doorway. He was watching Lisa take plates from the cupboard when the lights flickered again and went out. The house was lit only by the flashing of the sky.

"I was afraid of that," Lisa said. "It happens here all the time. One second — I've got candles." She pulled something down from a shelf, rummaged in a drawer. Kilgour heard a match being scraped across a matchbox, then saw Lisa's face glowing in the light of a utility candle. "We keep a whole bunch of these around," she said, lighting another one. She set the second candle on the kitchen counter. "The trouble is these all-electric kitchens." She pulled the door of the broiler open and peered in, holding a candle in front of her. "Looks like we're in luck. I think the steaks are done."

"Dinner by candlelight," she called over her shoulder as she set plates and food on the table.

"You know," Kilgour said, clinking the ice in his glass, "this doesn't have to be so bad, in a way. I mean, if you've really got the thief. And assuming he's not about to run." Kilgour paused. "Is he, Lisa? Is this guy really caught?"

"Please sit down, John," she said, motioning with the candle to indicate Barry's chair. "And how about some wine? I have a nice California Cabernet Sauvignon."

"What I mean is," Kilgour continued, "this really doesn't

366

have to be so bad for us — or for the bank. We could even conceivably get some mileage out of all of this, Lisa. I can see a scenario that says we could all come out looking quite good."

"Oh?" She looked at his face, the shadows cast by the candle flickering across it. The windows shook in protest against the storm; the candle flame blew into a thin line, blazing upright again. Kilgour was still thinking out loud.

"It'll depend a lot on Wilford. He's got to let us blow the whistle on this, let us take the credit for uncovering the crime. That may be possible. Wilford wants to be president of Ensold, and Toby Pruitt sits on the Ensold board. In fact, he controls a couple of votes there. Ted owes me a favor as well. I let him see some of Ray's early control systems years ago; they were the basis for his own financial control system — though, obviously, Ted's goes well beyond ours." Kilgour set his fork down. "By now, I wish I could get a line on what's put into *that* system."

Was this crime real to Kilgour? Lisa wondered. Did it bother him as anything more than a public relations problem? It had to. She would remind him of that when he was finished with his scenario.

"Anyway, if we can announce that we found the swindle, that Autotran itself discovered it, that would be OK. You know, we could get Lippert up there talking about the self-monitoring security systems built into Autotran. In the meantime, he better get in gear and figure out where the security went haywire. But if we can make that announcement at the same time that we turn the guy over for prosecution, I think we could even gain by it." Kilgour paused, chewing again.

"There's a way of doing this" — Kilgour was gesturing with his steak knife in much the same way, Lisa fleetingly realized, that he gestured with his pen in meetings — "a way of doing this where you sort of hint — or 'imply,' I guess, is the word — that it's probably going on in a lot of banks. You sort of let fall that it's a real possibility everywhere. And much as we screen our clerks, we know that isn't enough. So while we continue to push for complete automation, where you eliminate the possibility of human theft altogether" — Kilgour's knife sliced the air — "nevertheless, at least at GlobeBank, we keep doing these checks."

A small smile crossed Kilgour's face, which in the near darkness was as eerie and ominous as a war mask.

"It *is* a possible scenario, Lisa, you have to admit. And it will make you and me — and Wilford, of course — look good to Charlie and Toby. I think it'll work."

"It's certainly preferable to the truth, isn't it, John? Of course, you can point fingers and fix the system. No one can do that better than you. But the whole affair might slow you down a bit, don't you think? Might even stop you in your tracks."

Kilgour had stopped chewing. Lisa felt a rush of excitement, a heady feeling.

Kilgour's voice was almost a whisper. "What are you saying, Lisa?"

"I'm just bringing to your attention a reality that may have escaped you. After all, there are a bunch of us whose wagons are hitched to your star. Obviously, we want you to keep on shining."

Slowly, Kilgour said, "Obviously, I know that. But let's not talk about pointing fingers."

Lisa shook her head. "No, John," she said. "Neither way — not the truth and not your scenario — can be how this thing works out."

"No?"

"Listen to me, John." Her voice became urgent as she leaned forward. "I know how it has to be. Believe me, I *know*."

"Well, this is interesting," he said mockingly. "You suddenly seem to know all the answers. So suppose you tell me what they are."

She hated him at that moment.

"It's quite simple, really." She was speaking fast. "The money will be paid back. You will arrange with Ted Wilford to keep the whole matter away from the authorities. The thief, as you rightly call him, will be quietly released from GlobeBank. Maybe some severance pay. You will agree to job security for me, and I will have to ask you to sign that agreement. And that will be the end of it."

In the candlelight, she could see that Kilgour was smiling. "Lisa, Lisa, it won't fly. A crime has been committed, and the criminal has to be prosecuted, not given severance pay." He was avuncular now. "And just how do you expect me to pay back hundreds of thousands of dollars and not have it show up somewhere? And how am I supposed to convince Ted to keep his mouth shut?"

"I don't know. You're a resourceful man. I'm sure you'll find ways."

Kilgour snorted. "You know what you've told me, Lisa? You've told me that for some reason, the thief is someone you're very anxious to protect. I'd like to know why. Don't you think it's time you told me? Or do I have to run my own investigation?"

She shook her head. "It wouldn't work, John. Oh, I'm sure you'd find out, but it would take months, and by then the rumor mill would have taken all the decisions out of your hands. There were special reasons that I was able to find out so quickly." Now, she told herself. Don't flinch. She took a breath.

He waited for her to finish. Damn him, she thought. He's not going to put me on the defensive.

"The thief is Sandy Lippert. And Sandy and I have been lovers for over six months. The telltale clue was something that he left lying around the apartment we . . . met in."

Kilgour was staring, for a moment truly speechless. "You? Sandy?" His face twitched slightly, but no one who didn't know him very well would have seen even a minute loss of control. "So that's it. Well, that's a shame," he said. "One of our own. Sandy should have known better than to do something like this to me when I gave him a second chance."

Oh, God, he's so calm, Lisa thought. But always *him*. What Sandy did to him. He really thinks he and the bank are the same thing.

"Well, that's the end of his career. Too bad. He had a lot to offer. A lot to offer." Kilgour shook his head, as if to banish Sandy from it forever. "We'll have to think through a strategy so that the trial won't make us look too bad. The press could make mincemeat of us on this one. They love white-collar crime, they love bank robberies. A twentieth-century Bonnie and Clyde." He smiled thinly.

"John, there isn't going to be any trial. And there aren't going to be any reporters." Lisa's voice was icy, and she could feel the old sense of control flooding through her. "That's the point of all this. I am willing to go to great lengths to see that Sandy is not hurt."

"Don't be an idiot, Lisa. You know better than to allow your . . . indiscretion" — his mouth twitched a little with distaste — "to affect your judgment about something so fundamental. Lippert stole and he's got to go to jail. That's the simple part."

"I understand that you are probably shocked and angry, John. This is a messy situation." How cool I sound, she realized. Good girl, Lisa, keep it up. She suddenly saw Joe Barclay, long ago at the Stanford Faculty Club, and blinked to get rid of the ghost. "But if you think about it, a trial, Sandy going to jail, doesn't help anything. It doesn't get you out of the bind — or me, either. It doesn't do anything for the bank."

"I don't see it that way, Lisa. How can it possibly not get me out of the bind? We find a crime, we purge ourselves — that's it."

"No so, John. It could get us in deeper. Look, you trusted Sandy. Raised him to division head. Won't that suggest something about your judgment? And let's suppose that the thing goes to trial, that it becomes public. I would have to testify. I would have to admit that we were . . . lovers. That would be awful for me. You will have to imagine how awful. I'm married, John. Happily married." He grimaced slightly. "But let's put all that aside for a moment. Try to think of how our customers would view continuing a relationship with a bank where two of the top officers are — how can we put this? — thieves, accessories to crime, involved in a 'love triangle,' I believe is the expression? How will it affect our bottom line? My customers are not East Coast sophisticates. They may run global businesses, but there's an awful lot of Mom and apple pie out there. No, John" — she shook her head again — "purging ourselves, as you call it, is not the way to go."

"I can't say that I see it your way," he answered quietly. "I think we would be respected for having the guts to cut off our own rotten flesh with a knife. Lippert has to go — hard, fast, and clean. But you're right in one sense, Lisa. I'm certainly not going to let you go down with this.

"Let me speak frankly. The bank has invested a lot in you. I think the investment is paying off, and that it will continue to pay off for a long time to come. But to be blunt, Lisa, that wouldn't be enough right now. I could probably go out to the street right now and find a dozen M.B.A.'s, bright, young people who are ready to gobble up the world." His eyes narrowed. "There are very few people who can't be replaced, Lisa. As a manager, you know that as well as I do. I'll tell you what would make me want to keep you out of this." He looked at her slim body in her slacks, her sweater. His eyes rested for a moment on her breasts. Lisa felt intensely uncomfortable but didn't allow herself to move a muscle. He had never looked at her that way before. "You're a woman," he continued. "You're a woman and my protégée. Everyone knows that. And I'll be goddamned if I'm going to let anyone say that John Kilgour pushed a protégée — especially one who's also a woman — to the top only to find her not made of the right stuff. No, Lisa, we're going to find a way to keep your . . . *involvement* with Sandy out of the trial."

"And what about Sandy? Wasn't he a protégé?"

Kilgour shook his head. "Not mine. LaRocca's, maybe, or Schmidt's. I'm the guy who had Lippert handed to him and found him not good enough. And I'll see him in hell before I let him be known as 'my' man."

Time for card one, Lisa decided.

"Let me tell you something, John," she said, keeping her voice low. "Getting Sandy off means a great deal to me. A *very* great deal. If this business goes to trial, John, I will insist on testifying. You can appreciate what that will cost me. My marriage, very likely. My job, of course. My career. But you have an analytic mind. Try to imagine also what it would cost you. You say you can't let me go down because you'll look bad for having picked me. Surely you will also want to consider how GlobeBank will feel about all this seamy stuff in your sector. Remember, you were the one who told me that the bank didn't even like to promote high-level people who were divorced. You were the one who filled me in on how 'old school' Hardesty and Pruitt are. How do you think they're going to feel about a sector head who doesn't have enough control of his top managers to know what's going on — or if he knows, condones behavior that is not . . . gentlemanly, if I may use the word." Her smile was bright, as if

371

she were discussing her weekend plans. "Please don't think that I'm being flip or that I mean less than what I'm saying. *I mean this, John.* Oh, I do mean it! What I'm telling you is that if anything — anything at all — leaks out about Sandy, I am prepared to make the biggest possible mess over it. We would all sink in that storm, John. Think about it."

"You'd go that far?" He still seemed very cool, she thought, but the corner of his mouth twitched again. He's not taking kindly to being threatened. Nobody does that to Killer Kilgour. "I see this means a lot to you. You have a lot of guts, Lisa. I admire that. Maybe you underestimate me. You may not realize it, but I may be able to *persuade* Charlie and Toby a little. I've been around for a long time, you know. We understand one another. All it takes is drinks at the Century, lunch, and I can have everything smoothed over. *My* way, Lisa. My way!" Spearing a tomato on his plate, he held it up in the air. "I'm afraid that Sandy will have to go. If you insist on throwing yourself on the funeral pyre, so to speak — well, despite what I said before about not wanting to lose you, I'm afraid I might have to pay that price. Lisa, I've been around a long time. I know you can't win them all. Not even John Kilgour can win them all." He seemed no longer to be talking to her directly, Lisa thought. It was as if his mind had turned slightly and he were looking out some unseen window.

OK. Now. Card two.

"You're so right, John," she said. "Nobody can expect to win them all. But you and I — we're both scrappers, aren't we? If we lose one, it's not from giving up too early in the game. Listen, John," she said. Her voice became urgent. "Please listen to this and listen hard. I had hoped it would not come up, but it has. What you do on your own time is not anybody's business. Not my business, anyway. Any more than what I do on my own time is yours. Not until something makes it my business, and something has. So let me tell you plainly that if you don't agree to protect Sandy exactly as I outlined, I am going to see that information about your personal life reaches your wife, your daughters, Hardesty and Pruitt, and your colleagues and subordinates at the bank. Everybody."

"Come on, Lisa." He smiled and shook his head at her. "This

is silly. You're being childish, attacking me with empty threats. I'm disappointed. I expected better of you."

"Of course you did, John. That's why it would be a mistake to underestimate *me*. When I say 'personal life' I mean Elaine Green. What's going on between you and Elaine Green."

Even in the candlelight she could see him whiten. Oh, my God, she thought, don't let go now — you have him hooked.

"What in hell are you talking about?" he asked defiantly.

"Now *you're* the one who's being childish, John."

His fork clattered to the table. "How many people know about this?" he whispered at last.

"Just me. And I found out entirely by accident. You don't have to worry that Elaine was indiscreet. It was a matter of chance. I happened to be at the Carlyle with friends the night you were staying in town to work on your review. I saw her on her way up there. I saw her hours later as she was leaving the hotel. You know how it is, your antennae start to wave a little. And then her promotion. Her business trips and personal days, days off that just happened to coincide with your trips out of town. I'm not stupid, John."

He said nothing. "And I kept notes," she lied. "Weren't you the one who taught us all to notice everything, collect every piece of information, even if it seemed irrelevant at the time? I don't care about your private life. I just thought that the information might be useful someday."

He smiled at her brilliantly, but his eyes were cold and hard. "Protégée," he said. "My protégée."

"Another drink?" Lisa offered. She disappeared into the darkness that encircled them and brought back the bottle of Scotch. She set it down in the middle of the table.

"Look," she said. "I'm suggesting that we get everybody off the hook. Let's be rational — it's the only way to go. The customers get paid back, the system gets fixed, nobody spreads any alarms that Autotran is less than fabulous. Wilford gets an IOU. And Lippert . . . Lippert leaves. He's out of sight. Forever. Things go on just as before. For you and Elaine too, John. Once the information is no longer useful, I go back to square one about your private life."

Kilgour had poured himself a stiff drink and his glass was now half empty. "Very well, I agree," he said quietly.

"One more thing," Lisa reminded him. "I mentioned it before. Protection for me."

"Protection for you!" He laughed loudly, the sound echoing through the empty house.

"Yes, exactly. I want a written agreement to put away in my personal files that my progress at the bank will not be impeded by this conversation. I expect you to keep the promises you made to me in the past about salary and about more responsibility. I want to feel quite sure that our discussion tonight will have no effect on your decisions in those areas. Because I'm good, John, and you know it. Maybe I'm better than either one of us thought."

"My dear Lisa," he said, "you have the killer instinct."

"I take that as a compliment, John. But I can return it. Just look at who my teacher was."

◇ ◇ ◇

The storm had let up by the time he left; the road home to Pound Ridge would be less treacherous for John Kilgour's return than it had been for his arrival.

Did we really have a meal here, in this dark room? Lisa asked herself, drained of energy, staring at the dining room table. Mindlessly, she took the dirty dishes to the sink, rinsed them, and put them in the dishwasher. Did it really happen? Kilgour across the table? The sink smelled of Scotch and she turned on the hot water. The deal we made — is it real? She walked into the living room, carrying a candle. There was her attaché case on the chair. Inside it was Kilgour's handwritten statement that he would continue to look after her career and ensure that she would be rewarded appropriately for her contributions. What does that mean anyway? He's not making any sacrifice. Except revenge at being bested. She looked at the tightly snapped, anonymous face of the attaché case, glowing in the dim light. But he'll find a way to use me, my power, someday. No, he's not giving up so much.

They had agreed, calmly, that she would deal with Wilford. She would explain the situation to him, would make certain

374

commitments. Some would concern financial services. Others, Toby Pruitt's role on the Ensold board. Kilgour would actually handle Pruitt, mild Pruitt. Meetings would be set up, occasions where Wilford and Pruitt could meet quietly, over elegant dinners, with no one else listening to what they might say.

And it would be up to her to handle Sandy. "Handle" Sandy, she thought sadly. She had insisted on that. His fate was in her hands. I never wanted to control him; it was the place where I didn't have to control. Not even myself. But no more.

She heard a car in the driveway. Barry. He came in, loosening his tie, and pitched his raincoat onto the hall coatrack. Lisa came up to him with a candle and held it far out to one side as she kissed him.

"Sweetie, what happened?" he asked. "The storm?"

"I'm afraid so. The lights went out a couple of hours ago. It's OK, though; I managed. So how did it go? Was the drive back terrible?"

"Not too bad. The rain let up around Springfield. I was glad to be on the road, though."

"How was Aunt Lil?"

"Weepy. What else? Disposing of your husband's medical practice can't be too much fun, even if it makes you a wealthy widow. She and Morty had been married for over forty-three years, I just found out. She really felt that his practice belonged to her a little bit. Anyway, it brought up all those memories. It was just hard to see it go, I guess."

They sat down on the couch, the candle sputtering on the coffee table in front of them. "And you? How was your meeting?"

"OK."

"OK? Does that mean it's been resolved? It's all over?" He took her hand.

"Yes. Mostly," she said quietly.

Lisa could hear water dripping off the edges of the roof and trickling down the rain gutters.

"Does that mean you can tell me about it now?"

She shook her head. "I don't think so. It's one of those things you just can't ever really talk about. Other people are involved. People are in trouble, hurt."

"And you?"

"Me? What about me?"

"Are you out of trouble?"

"I wasn't . . . I'm not in any trouble, Barry."

"But were you hurt?"

She looked at him. Familiar, predictable, kind. Her husband. "It's OK, Barry. I'm OK. Really."

Barry squeezed her hand in reply. The next moment, she heard a faint hum. The lights flickered, went dark again, and came back on. Lisa could hear the refrigerator whirring back into life, making up for lost time.

"Looks like the crisis is over," she said. "How about if I fix you some eggs? You must be starved."

18

SHE CALLED SANDY THE NEXT DAY the minute she arrived at work, a little after eight. He picked up the phone on the first ring.

"Lippert."

"It's me."

"Lisa!" He sounded surprised. "Are we back in touch?" There was an edge of sarcasm, but it disappeared immediately. "Are you — is it all right?"

"I'm fine, yes."

"It's been awhile, a long while. I didn't know if — "

She interrupted him. "Sandy," she said, "we have to meet today."

Silence. I've hurt him, Lisa thought. And I'll hurt him much more. Oh, Sandy darling . . . Her eyes filled with familiar tears.

"About four?" he said. "At the place?"

"Four is fine."

◇ ◇ ◇

Lisa was there fifteen minutes early. Walking up the stairs, her hand on the wobbly railing, she felt the deep sadness of an ending.

On the landing, she held the key to the lock, letting the big plastic heart dangle, remembering their first time here, when Sandy had kissed her palm and given her the key ring.

Along Third Avenue, young mothers pushed children in strollers with brightly colored seats. Groups of teenagers in private school uniforms — navy blazers, gray flannel trousers or skirts — nudged each other and licked at ice cream cones. It all looks so normal, Lisa thought.

She heard his key in the lock.

Sandy was out of breath, having taken the stairs two at a time, as usual.

"Sorry," he said, "a last-minute phone call. LaRocca himself. Wanted to know about the new printer IBM announced." Then he stopped talking and looked at her inquiringly. He made no move toward her. She realized that he was not going to kiss her, that he was waiting for her to do something. *We're becoming strangers already. I wish it were six months ago and Sandy could kiss everything away.*

"Sandy, we have to talk." Lisa's voice was steady.

He looked at her. "Sure. What gives?"

"Let's sit." Her body felt heavy. She walked to the kitchen table and sat on one of the chairs. He sat down facing her.

"What gives?" he asked again.

She had rehearsed the opening, but she was a little wobbly as she began. "Sandy, a little while ago I had a meeting with Ted Wilford, the treasurer of Ensold?" She paused to see if his face registered any recognition. There was none. "He flew in from California especially to see me," she continued. "It was a highly confidential meeting; Wilford made a big point about confidentiality. He has an amazing MIS system out there. It reconciles their monthly books to the penny. The slightest discrepancy gets flagged."

She took a breath and studied the red plastic tablecloth, unable to look again at Sandy's face. Go on, she urged herself.

"Anyway, Wilford told me that a series of discrepancies had come to his attention — eleven thousand here, sixteen thousand there. But they were happening month after month on a regular basis. Wilford is a very methodical guy. He started tracking the discrepancies, adding up separate transactions. They were all

377

third-party transfers through us, through my division, through Autotran."

She looked at him now. He was waiting, expressionless.

"Wilford followed up, made calls. He knows everyone. It turned out the same thing had been going on with some other big companies, most of them also in my division. Same thing, same pattern. Everybody told the same story: transfers. All in a certain dollar range. All through Autotran. All payable to Thomas Putnam, an account at Bedminster Bank, London. The people at Bedminster say the account has shown activity of several hundred thousand dollars. At least."

She stood up, too nervous to sit still anymore.

"Wilford thought Thomas Putnam was maybe somebody working in my division. I didn't know what to think. I thought maybe Putnam was a guy blackmailing someone in my shop. I really didn't know what to think.

"It was all very upsetting, as you can imagine." She looked at him directly. "But something about the name stuck in my mind. I knew I had seen it or heard it somewhere. Not that it's an unusual name. But it just rang a bell in me."

Lisa took a deep breath. "Sandy, then I remembered where I had seen the name Thomas Putnam. It was here, Sandy. The mailbox. And on envelopes here. Envelopes in one of the bowls on the shelf. I was waiting for you. You were late. I noticed the British stamp, the queen. Sandy, it's you." She came around to the front of her chair and sat down. Sandy put his head in his hands.

"Sandy, what happened?" Her voice was low, hoarse. "Why *did* you?"

He shook his head. "I don't know, I don't know." He looked at her. "How long have you known?"

"A while. Two weeks. Sandy, I just don't understand how you could have done it, kept on doing it." Lisa rubbed her forehead. "It's stealing. That's what it is. It's a crime."

"Maybe. I guess so."

"Why, Sandy? How could you do it?" she repeated. "How could you do it to me?"

"Lisa, don't say that. Don't say it. It had nothing to do with you. Nothing."

"But it did. Of course it did. Can't you see that?" she pleaded. "It's my bank. *Our* bank. It happened in my division. Sandy, I love you," she insisted. "How could you do it?"

"I don't know," he said again. "It seemed to make sense. It felt right. I just don't know."

"I've tried to understand, Sandy," she told him. "I thought I knew you. I tried to imagine what might have been going on in your mind. You built Autotran. You designed it. Is it that you felt . . . I don't know . . . that you could play games with it or something? Is that it? That you could just make it move money around any way you told it to? Because it's your system?"

"If you say so." He looked at her helplessly.

"Because that's all I can think of. That it was a game."

He shrugged his shoulders in reply. "Who else knows, Lisa?"

"Well, Wilford" — she took a breath — "and Kilgour. I told John."

"John knows? I guess I'm going to have to decide what to do."

"No, you won't, Sandy. You won't have to decide a damn thing. It's all decided. I've taken care of it."

"What do you mean, you've taken care of it? What does *that* mean?"

"It means that I got John to agree not to prosecute. Never mind how, but I did. And it means that he will get Wilford to cooperate also. And it means — " she was becoming agitated again — "it means, Sandy, that John is going to have to find a way to budget the dollars to pay back our customers without having it pop up in uncomfortable places."

"And that's it? You've *managed* the whole thing?" The smallest sneer had crept into his voice.

"Sandy, Kilgour will save your skin. It wasn't easy. He wasn't happy. But he'll do it. The price is that you'll have to go away, far away. Disappear. A new life. Not a bank. Nothing like a bank. Not near any of our customers. It means . . ." She stopped. "It means I love you, Sandy, and I saved you and I have to let you go." Then she put her hands over her face and cried.

He moved to her, held her very tight. Her face was pushed hard against his neck. In his neck, where he couldn't see, she closed her eyes tight with pain and let the tears come. Her hands made fists behind his back.

379

Then he was holding her face in his hands. His eyes were roaming over her face. As if he's memorizing me, she thought.

She led him over to the pulled-out couch, the familiar cover, the pillow. They undressed silently. She tried not to hear the drumming in her ears. She lay on her back and lifted her arms toward him. As he came into her arms, she thought again how beautiful he was. How will I ever stop wanting him? Every day. All the time. How will I ever get over having known this?

She knew she must remember this very well, must experience it very intensely, must store up the memory of every moment so that it would always be there when she needed it.

He was kneeling over her, his hands outlining her breasts. She ran her fingers through his hair. She reached down his long body and took him in her hands. He lifted his head and looked at her, kissed her face, shoulder, neck. I must remember this, she told herself.

Her hands caressing him. His hands enfolding hers. Together, they led him inside her. Must remember, she thought.

Then she stopped thinking. Wrapped tightly around him, with him inside her, she didn't think at all.

They lay on the couch quietly together for a while, holding hands. Sandy kissed the top of her head over and over. She could hear him breathing in the still room. Finally, he brushed his lips lightly along her ear, murmured "I'm sorry," gathered up his things, and left.

Lisa looked out at the room through half-closed eyes, her eyelashes making a veil between her and all the familiar objects. She thought she felt nothing — not happy, not unhappy. Then she thought of Sandy's lean body lying on her, his clean, sharp smell, the taste of his tongue. That was wonderful. It always was.

19

LISA STOPPED FOR THE LIGHT at Fifty-ninth Street. A long, angry stream of cars was heading west off the Queensborough Bridge, jockeying for position, ready to turn onto Park.

Spring had surprised New York again. Lisa was amazed, as

she was every year, by the miracle of it all. She had decided to head down Park Avenue this morning to admire the tulips. Tall and quirky, they ran in a spectrum down the island between north- and southbound traffic.

A horn honked. A gravelly voice yelled at her from the front seat of a taxi, through the open window: "You wanna get killed? You want your foot run over? Get up on the curb, lady! Do me a favor. Get your head out of the clouds!"

Sheepishly, she stepped up onto the sidewalk just as the light changed.

What was on the calendar today? An eight-thirty with Tony to go over manpower requirements. At ten, Linda's presentation on the product management process. I don't know what else Flo has plugged in for me until three. Then Kilgour. Kilgour at three o'clock.

Their meetings now were formal, businesslike. The old ease and aura of favoritism were gone. Whatever she had now was more than ever earned.

But he had kept his part of the bargain. And so had she. He had handled Pruitt and done it well. Lisa never found out precisely what had passed between the two men. All she knew was that Pruitt was now a great partisan of Ted Wilford at Ensold.

And Wilford was grateful. He had accepted her assurances that the matter had been taken care of with no further questions. Together, they had worked out a special relationship between GlobeBank and Ensold for the conglomerate's financial transaction processing needs. A discrete Ensold processing cluster was carved out of National Services West. Taddeusz had installed the unit in its own partitioned-off area, painted in sun-drenched yellows and oranges, with posters of Big Sur and the Golden Gate lining the plasterboard walls. The area was jokingly referred to as "Lisa's laid-back cluster."

Wilford called once a month. A tentative friendship had grown up between them.

"How's the weather there?" he would ask. "How was the off-site?"

"Well, I always enjoy Hilton Head," she answered. "The sessions were quite useful. How are things out your way?"

"Good, fine. By the way, your people did a real good job

working down that glitch in the commercial loan system last week."

For a few minutes they would discuss business. Then she would ask about his children; he would send his regards to Barry. Thomas Putnam had been blotted out of existence.

She didn't see Sandy for a while after their last time together. If he was in the bank at all, she decided, he was at 176 or was moving quietly, out of her view. He didn't come to the division head meeting on Friday, when Kilgour announced that Sandy Lippert would be leaving GlobeBank. "Going out on his own," Kilgour said. "Going into consulting." That was all he said.

Lisa was surprised at how little gossip or speculation the announcement caused. She had lunch with Danny after the meeting; he claimed not to be surprised. "I never really thought Sandy was cut out of the corporate mold. I think it's great he's going on his own. Really. I mean, look: He's divorced, he's more or less footloose. He'll do great. He's really a hell of a systems guy. And with the Autotran background, banks all over the place will be hot for him. Killer seems pretty pissed off, don't you think? He always takes these things so personally. Like he's been betrayed. I guess if there's a farewell party for Sandy, we're going to have to do it on our own. Why don't you arrange it, Lisa?"

She smiled feebly at Danny's suggestion, wondering how many such ironies she would have to suffer.

That afternoon, she remembered, she and Barry had driven to the country with friends, guests she had not known how to put off. She wondered how she would bear the weekend, how she would get through it. But, to her surprise, it had been a good time. Barry was in top form and made them all laugh — through breakfasts and lunches and dinners, through a snowman-building session and a snowfight, through the usual tour for guests of Bull's Bridge, the old covered bridge near the power station, and the Quaker Meeting House near Pawling, and through the whole ride that left them giggling as they entered the Old Drover's Inn at Dover Plains, their laughter shattering the air. How good it had been to laugh. A healing balm.

But then Sandy. Saying good-bye. Right in her office.

382

It had been a Tuesday and very cold. Very dark and gray outside. She was working alone at the long table when she heard his voice. "Hi, Florence. Is she in? I just wanted to say good-bye."

"Hello, Sandy," Lisa said through the open door, not moving from her chair, unable to move.

"Hi," he said. His voice was pushing to be cheerful. "Thought I'd come and say good-bye. Today's my last day."

He closed the door behind him, came and stood across the table from her.

"I have to do this fast," he said. His face was a mask. "God, I want you. Listen, I'm going away. It's all done. Everything's packed. Everything's set."

He seemed to sigh.

"I promised myself I wouldn't tell you where I was going. That's the least I can do. Anyway, who knows how long I'll stay?"

The phone rang. The button lit up, stayed lit. Through the door, Lisa heard Flo saying something about "tied up right now." Then the light went off.

"This is the worst thing for me," Sandy said. "Nothing's ever been as bad as right now. Not the divorce or the failure or even the moment you told me you knew. Nothing comes close to saying good-bye, knowing I'm never going to see you again."

She felt herself cave in then. As if some sharp, hard punch had been delivered to her stomach and all the wind had been knocked out of her.

"It's tearing me up," Sandy went on. "It's like a piece of me is being cut off."

Quietly, she said, "I know. Me too."

"Lisa, you are the best thing that ever happened to me. I don't really know how I will live without you. I love you very much. I just wanted to tell you that once more."

"Sandy," she said, "Sandy, I love you too. I'll never get over you." She paused. They looked at one another. My tousled Sandy, my green-eyed Sandy, went through her head.

"Now go very quickly," she whispered.

He stared at her for another instant, nodded, then turned and walked out of the office. He closed the door behind him.

◇ ◇ ◇

383

That door. This office. On that cold, gray day. Months ago. Today the sun shone golden, and there were bright colors everywhere. The sun poured through the wide windows, bathing the soft blond wood of the furniture.

Flo came in, a coffee mug in one hand and under her arm the day's fresh flowers.

"Some gorgeous day, huh?" Flo set the mug before Lisa and put the flowers in the silver vase. She fluffed out the arrangement. "You should see the dogwood in the Botanical Gardens," Flo said. "We took a walk there last evening. Gorgeous. And the lilacs — really something. You must have dogwood up in Connecticut, yes?"

"Oh yes," said Lisa. "Pink and white. I'll bring you some next weekend. You cut off the ends and stick them in hot water and they last quite a while."

"Hot?"

"Yes, to make sure they'll take up the water."

"No kidding? Hot?"

"Right."

"Imagine!"

There was a knock on the open door. "Are we on?" Tony asked.

"Yes, let's get started. A lot to do today."

Throughout the morning, she felt, as always, the steady thrill of power. It rested beneath the surface, just beneath, and its manifestations were so familiar that she hardly paid attention to them anymore. Power was a well-known passion by now, but a passion nevertheless.

Tony's staff work on the manpower requirement issue was good. Tony's staff work was always good. But she was impatient to make decisions.

"No," she said to his final recommendation. "I don't want to hire any junior people this year. Only group head level. I want to move the organization to a completely professional level, a high professional level. I want to be very topheavy on M.B.A.'s by year's end, Tony."

He nodded. "OK," he said, "I'll adjust for that."

"Good. Just give me a two-pager on it. By tomorrow?"

"Sure. By tomorrow."

Linda was next, Linda with her staff. Lisa took a wry pleasure in watching Linda manage her own advancement.

"You want to do this here or in the conference room?" Lisa asked.

"I think the conference room would be better," said Linda.

Lisa stood up. "Putting on a real show, is that it?"

"Sort of," Linda answered, unfazed.

Linda was in her element delivering the presentation. She became completely self-assured as she stood next to the flip-chart easel, painstaking in the detail she presented, issue-oriented in her approach. Lisa couldn't help admiring Linda's absolute confidence. She was on her way.

"Super job, Linda," Lisa said when the presentation was finished. Linda nodded coolly. "By the way, I saw Jessica the other day. She says hello."

Linda nodded again. "How is she?" she asked.

"She's fine. Great. Looks great, sounds great. She's doing very well, too. Could you just go back to the flow chart showing what happens between the technical sales manager and the product manager? There were just a couple of issues there."

◇ ◇ ◇

Lisa and Danny had lunch at Wolf's Deli on Sixth. Lisa watched Danny munch pickles out of the bowl.

"She feels lousy most mornings," Danny was saying about Harriet, who was pregnant, "but otherwise everything's fine. The doctor says the morning sickness can't last forever. Meanwhile, she's living on saltines."

"Tell her hello." Lisa smiled.

"You seeing Killer today?"

Lisa nodded. "I've got a three o'clock with him. Monthly review."

"I was there yesterday," Danny said. "He was in a really foul mood. Really chewed me out on my numbers."

Lisa looked at Danny with affection. Only he, among all the division heads, myself included, she admitted to herself, would reveal such a thing. The rest of us are all so paranoid we'd never tell a soul, much less a colleague, that we'd been chewed out by the boss. We're all competitors, all the time.

"I'll keep it in mind," she said.

"You? Don't you worry. You're Johnny's baby."

Their sandwiches arrived: overstuffed pastrami for Danny, corned beef for Lisa.

◇ ◇ ◇

Fifty-seventh Street was like a Mediterranean promenade. Men with jackets flung over one shoulder and women in pastel dresses, their arms bared to the sun, moved slowly, their hips swinging, their faces turned up to the clear blue sky.

"I've got to pop into Hammacher's," Danny said at the corner of Park. "Got to get a Cuisinart accessory for Harriet. Want to come?"

Lisa shook her head. "I really can't, Danny. I ought to review the Book before I see John. I'll talk to you later." She turned down Park.

"Didn't you go out?" she asked Flo when she got back to the office. "It's gorgeous!"

Flo, spooning yogurt into her mouth, lifted her eyes heavenward in despair. "Certainly, I was out. I just strolled. And then I brought this back for sustenance. I thought you might want me here, what with the Book due today."

Lisa smiled. "You're an angel. And you're right. I'm going to go behind closed doors with it right now. Get me to the church on time, will you, Flo?" Lisa went into her office, closing the door behind her.

At the blond table, she opened the looseleaf binder and started to go through it again. She had been over it the night before and had studied it in draft form since the weekend. Now more than ever, though, where Kilgour was concerned, she wanted to know her facts cold. Facts were all there could be between them.

"Quarter of," Flo said, "in case you want to freshen up."

She did. She washed her face and hands, brushed her hair, touched up her lipstick. She was aware of butterflies in her stomach and wondered why.

"Here's your copy," Flo said, carefully handing Lisa the marked-up looseleaf, "and here's Mr. Kilgour's" — it had his name on it, on a stick-on label on the front — "and here's the drop-off one for Donovan. All set?"

"All set," said Lisa. With the three notebooks under her arm, she walked down the hall.

"Hi, Barbara," she said from across the room. She noticed that Kilgour's door was closed. "Is Al joining us, do you know? I brought his book, anyway."

Barbara Finn smiled oddly. "Oh, no," she said, "it's just you and John and . . . just you and John today."

Lisa set Donovan's book on Barbara's desk. "OK. Well, I wonder if you'd see to it that he gets that."

"No problem."

"Is he tied up?" Lisa cocked her head toward Kilgour's office door.

"No." Barbara smiled again. "You're to go right in."

Lisa knocked twice and turned the knob. The first face she saw was that of Toby Pruitt. He was seated in one of the dark leather chairs at right angles to the long sofa on which Kilgour also sat.

Pruitt rose. He turned to Kilgour. "John, may I do the honors?"

"By all means, Toby."

Pruitt walked toward Lisa, his arms extended, a smile on his face. He placed his hands on her shoulders and beamed at her. "Lisa, allow me to be the first to congratulate you. And if I may, I've always wanted to kiss a senior vice president."

GlobeBank's president leaned over and kissed Lisa's cheek.

"Lisa," Pruitt went on, still holding her by the shoulders, "you are the first woman in GlobeBank history to achieve this rank. I want to say, the honor could not have fallen on more deserving shoulders."

The little speech sounded rehearsed. Lisa was very aware of the two notebooks held in the crook of her left arm. She remembered being a student, carrying notebooks like that, going from class to class. First at Mount Holyoke, where she had decided to "go into business," and then again at Stanford, where she had shone. And before that, long before, in high school, when she had had fantasies of herself as a famous doctor, or once or twice as an actress accepting her Oscar, and once, during an election year, as the first woman President, taking the oath on the steps of the Capitol, then hearing the Marine Corps Band play "Hail to the Chief."

This was what she had always wanted, after all. Even before she had known exactly how she would do it, what she had always wanted was to shine, to stand out, to be the first, or the best, or the only. She stood in John Kilgour's office now, with notebooks under her arm and one of the world's most powerful men holding her shoulders, realizing that she had just gotten exactly what she wanted.

Lisa smiled. "Thank you, thank you. I'm thrilled."

Kilgour rose, came around the coffee table, and extended his hand. "Lisa, congratulations. It's a richly deserved title." He leaned over; his dry lips pecked briefly at her cheek.

"Thank you, John. I want to say . . . I owe you a great deal. I owe a lot of this to you." The words stuck in her throat, and yet, she reflected, they were true.

"Well, for heaven's sake, let's everybody sit down!" Pruitt suddenly bellowed. He was still beaming.

Lisa set her notebooks on the coffee table. "What about the review, John?"

Pruitt laughed and looked at Kilgour. "That's why she's come so far so fast. She keeps her mind on business."

Kilgour smiled, then turned to Lisa. "Any issues?" he asked. Lisa shook her head.

"I think we'll forgo the review — just this once. You've actually got a lot of other things to attend to."

"I do?"

It was Pruitt who answered. "Indeed, you do. I think Barbara's got a whole package for you out there, doesn't she, John?"

Kilgour nodded.

"But the thrust of it is," Pruitt went on, "there's a small cocktail reception this evening for the new SVPs over at Laurent. There are three new SVPs, Lisa, and I think you'll be pleased to know that the other two are also from BOS: Danny Faber and Doug North."

"Danny? Oh, I *am* pleased!" Lisa smiled widely. "Doug, too. That's great!" She tried to sound sincere. She *was* glad for Danny, of course, and yet . . . it would have been so nice to shine all by herself.

"Then, Charlie Hardesty and I would like to take you to lunch at Lutèce next Tuesday. That's a little practice we have." Pruitt leaned toward her. "That is, of course, if you're free."

Lisa smiled and decided to go along with Pruitt's tone. "Well, I'll check my calendar. But I think I can fit you gentlemen in."

Pruitt laughed delightedly.

Kilgour got up suddenly, went to his desk, and pushed a button on the telephone console. "Babs," he said into the box, "you can let the word out now." He came back and sat down again on the sofa.

"There's a lot of press stuff the Public Relations people want to do with you," Pruitt was saying. "The schedule should be in your package, but I know there's an appointment for pictures, and there's a press release you need to approve, and they'll want a list of papers to send it to — you know, hometown and alumnae stuff — in addition to the *Times* and the *Journal* and the *American Banker* and *Business Week,* et cetera. PR will handle those. Then, next Thursday, you and Dan and Doug will be presented officially at the senior officers' meeting." Pruitt paused suddenly. "How does it sound, Lisa? How does it feel to be a senior officer of a corporation like GlobeBank?"

"It feels good," Lisa said.

They kept her there for another twenty minutes. Pruitt gave a little peroration about the responsibility that goes along with honor and title. Lisa thought that also sounded rehearsed and reminded herself to compare notes with Danny.

"Well, you'll probably be wanting to phone Barry," Kilgour said at last. He rose, extending his hand. "Congratulations again, Lisa."

"Thank you, John. Thank you, Toby."

She walked out of the office.

"Congratulations!" Barbara Finn shook her hand and gave her a folder. "There's all sorts of stuff in here, Lisa. You've got time, though. Enjoy."

"Thank you, Barbara." Her voice seemed hoarse. "May I use your phone?"

"Of course." Barbara rose quietly, walked away.

Lisa called Barry at his office. His secretary answered.

"Hi, Laurie. It's Lisa. Is he there?"

Then Barry was on the line. "Lisa! What's up, sweetie?"

"Oh, nothing much. Listen, dear, what are you doing at about five?"

"Why? What's up?"

"Well, there's this little cocktail party."

"Oh. Is it a 'must'?"

"Well, I feel I *should* go." She paused. "It's sort of in my honor."

"In your — Lisa! The title? SVP?"

"Yes, dear, I just found out."

"Hooray!" Barry was shouting. Then, more calmly: "Congratulations, love. Congratulations. Wow! I'm going to sleep with a senior vice president!"

"Barry!" But she was laughing. God, this was fun. This felt so good. "Where are you talking from? I hope nobody's in your office with you."

She laughed again. "Listen," she said, "I think I should call my mother, let her get an early start on bragging to all the relatives. But be sure to be at Laurent as close to five as possible, OK?"

She hung up.